A STANDALONE

WESTBROOK ELITE

WILDCARD

CAMBRIA
HEBERT

Published by Cambria Hebert
http://www.cambriahebert.com

Interior design and typesetting by Classic Interior Design
Cover design by Cover Me Darling
Edited by Cassie McCown
Copyright 2023 by Cambria Hebert

WELCOME TO WESTBROOK UNIVERSITY...

Where the only thing more elite than the Ivy League
academics and exclusive enrollment for the monied is the
swimmers.
Some colleges might revere football, baseball,
or even hockey, but not Westbrook.
At Westbrook, it's all about the water.
Or rather, who's in it.
More than one Elite swimmer has gone on to become a
decorated Olympian and nationwide sensation,
so it's all eyes on the hot men who spend more time in
Speedos than jeans.
Eventually, though, these guys have to get out of the pool.
And when they do...
Love, drama, and jealousy await.

*Westbrook Elite is a college sports romance series
of stand-alone novels
with sexy swimmers, suspense, and page-turning plots.
The only promise the author makes is that each book
will have a happy ending...
But who knows what it will take to get there?*

a Westbrook Elite novel

Pretty sure I was a serial killer in my past life.

Because karma is kicking my ass in this one.

Everything was copasetic. I was coasting on the wave of life… until a gnarly swell pulled me under, and I washed ashore to a nightmare. A nightmare there was no waking from.

So I packed my shit and moved all the way to the other side of the country—to the only place someone was willing to give me a second chance.

I came to swim, and though I'm on the team, I don't want to be Elite. These bros are exactly like the ones I left behind, and I'm not stupid enough to get betrayed again.

But then karma shows up and laughs right in my face.

I slept with my coach's daughter.

Because of course I fucking did.

And though she calls to me like a siren, that night was just a distraction. A one-time thing.

Until she shows up at Daddy's pool as the assistant coach. Now the very girl I can't get off my mind is the one just declared off-limits.

Naturally, my heart decides it can't beat without her jade stare, sassy mouth, and car that cruises so slow it uses a calendar as a speedometer.

Now I'm at the top of Coach's shit list, and everything I left in Cali comes knocking at my door. With Landry's safety on the line, I won't just roll over and take it. This time, I'll put up a fight.

There's no telling what I'll do or how far I'll go to make sure Landry isn't punished for standing by my side. When things get dangerous, I know this wildcard can't play this game alone.

Because even if trusting people doesn't come easy… loving her does.

A STANDALONE
WESTBROOK ELITE

C A M B R I A
H E B E R T

PROLOGUE

LAST YEAR...

RUSH

WHITE-CAPPED WAVES CRASHED AGAINST THE SHORE, GLIDING up the sand but not quite reaching where we sat around a flickering bonfire. The music was loud but was still background noise against the beach, crackling flames, and the laughter being carried by the breeze.

It was a warm Cali night, but down here in the sand with the surf so close, there was a definite chill, which caused goose bumps to prickle over my legs when the wind blew just right.

The longneck between my fingers was slick with condensation, and when I lifted it to my lips, sand rained from the bottom onto my boardshorts and hoodie.

"Bottoms up!" Blair cackled, smashing his fingers against the bottle to force it back to my lips when I started to lower it.

I gave him some side-eye but parted my lips, letting him dump some more of the brew down my throat. After swal-

CAMBRIA HEBERT

lowing, I swiped the back of my hand over my wet lips and
slapped him on the back of his head.

"By the time you finish that beer, it's going to be piss
warm. You need to catch up! I'm already three ahead of you,"
Blair said, not even acknowledging the hit. He was so drunk
he probably hadn't even felt it.

"Maybe you should slow down."

"*Pfffft.*" Blair exaggerated. "Why would I wanna do that?
Coach rode my ass so hard all week that I got a permanent
wedgie. And we finally have a day off tomorrow. I'm not
wasting it!"

A few Nobles cheered and chugged their drinks. I tipped
the longneck to my lips, pacing myself more than these fools.
I could understand their enthusiasm, though. It was rare
Coach gave our swim team a day off. I just wasn't sure I
wanted to spend it hungover.

"Skinny dipping!" Blair roared, leaping up from the sand
and nearly pitching into the fire.

"Whoa," I said, grabbing him before he became crispy.

He slung his arm around my neck. "Let's get nekkid!"

Shoving him off, I bent to set my beer in the sand. When I
straightened, he already had his shirt off and tossed it in the
sand.

"Swim, swim, swim!" the guys around the fire chanted,
and they were loud enough that it drew in some of the others
standing farther away from the fire.

Blair grabbed his shorts, and a few whistles cut through
the night.

Smacking his hand away from his waistband, I said,
"Leave your pants on."

"I'll give you two hundred bucks right now to run your
naked ass into the ocean and swim a few laps!" Cobalt called
from across the fire.

Forgetting Blair, I swung toward him. "He can't even

stand straight, and you think he can swim without drowning?"

"He's a Noble," Cobalt answered, glittering eyes not leaving mine. He did, however, lift his drink to try and cover the asshole smirk on his mouth.

Cheers erupted, as they usually did when someone brought up our team. The best college swim team on this side of the country. Maybe we were arrogant too. Why shouldn't we be? We were the best of the best because we worked for it.

"Sold for two hundred!" Blair pointed at Cobalt.

"No," I said, pushing him back. "Sit down."

"What are you, his mom?" Cobalt challenged, rising on the other side of the bonfire. The flames flickered and danced, casting shadows over his face as he came around to where I stood.

"Mommy!" Blair parroted.

I rolled my eyes. "No. I just don't want him to do something stupid. Which I would think you would also be against."

Cobalt was the unofficial captain of the Pembrook Nobles. Technically, our team didn't have a captain. Swimming was a solo sport. However, everyone looked to this guy with some sense of worship.

Except me. I thought Cobalt was an asshole. He knew it. Everyone knew it. Just like we all knew he hated me just as much.

Cobalt stepped into my personal space, beer wafting from his breath and mixing with the scent of burning wood and smoke.

"How about you give the hazing a rest tonight, Cobalt?" I said quietly.

His eyes narrowed. "Hazing?" His voice boomed over everything. "Rush thinks my little dare is hazing," he called.

"What say you?"

A couple guys booed.

His lips twisted with satisfaction like a wolf who'd just eaten a fox. "Sucks your sidekick isn't here to back you up tonight."

I didn't need a sidekick, and he knew it. Stepping up, my toes hit his. "We both know if he goes in the ocean, someone is gonna have to pull him out."

"Then maybe he's not a strong enough swimmer to be a Noble."

My jaw ticked.

"Maybe we should all just chill," Bannerman suggested. "And by chill, I don't mean going for a swim in the frigid Pacific."

I flicked a gaze toward the butterfly stroke swimmer, giving him a quiet gesture with my chin.

"Whose side are you on, Bannerman?" Cobalt bitched, a muscle jumping in his jaw.

"The side that doesn't have to give Blair's naked ass CPR."

A few guys cackled.

"Hey! My ass is nice!" Blair declared, then jumped to his feet. "I gotta piss."

Fucking drunkard.

I turned my back on Cobalt, cuffing Blair on the shoulder and directing him away from the fire. "There's some bushes over there, dude," I said, pointing him away from the surf. "Go water 'em."

He ran off, and I grabbed my beer from the sand to chug what was left. I felt like a damn babysitter. Noticing Cobalt was no longer glaring, I let my eyes roam the sand, teeth clenching when I found him.

About ten feet from the bonfire, he was standing with a group of girls, one of whom should not have been there.

Tossing the empty bottle into the sand, I stalked over. She

4

pretended not to see me, but she did. I knew from the way her body language shifted just slightly in my direction. Her laugh was too loud, too high, and entirely fake. I watched in annoyance as she laid a palm against Cobalt's chest. He smiled, laying his over hers.

Grabbing her arm, I yanked her away from him.

"Hey!" she protested as though she didn't know this was coming.

"Brynne."

"What the hell is your problem tonight, Rush?" Cobalt demanded.

Brynne's friends watched like it was the finale of some kind of reality show.

"Stay the hell away from her."

"You aren't the boss of me!" Brynne yelled, yanking her wrist free.

My eyes whipped to hers, which widened slightly when she saw I was not playing. "I am when your brother isn't here to do it."

"He's not the boss of me either," she quipped.

"C'mon, let's go." I gestured toward the lot where I'd parked my Corvette.

"I just got here."

"Well, you shouldn't have come at all." A wave of dizziness made my vision blur for a second. I shook it off and refocused on her.

"She has every right to be here just as much as anyone." Cobalt defended. "How about that drink, Brynne?"

I swung around, planting myself in front of my best friend's little sister to regard the swimmer I hated. "She's off-limits to you."

Cobalt stepped up. "Says who?"

"Says me."

Cobalt smirked. He did it so much it was basically frozen

on his dick face. "Oh, my B, brother." He spoke as if we were indeed brothers and not rivals on the same damn team. "I didn't realize you two were together. I'd never creep in on another Noble's girl."

Behind me, Brynne made a sound.

My gut tightened.

Hand shooting out, I grabbed a fistful of Cobalt's Noble hoodie and dragged him in. "You know damn well she's not my girl. She's my sister."

"I am not!" Brynne yelled, slamming her hand into my back.

Cobalt's amused stare bounced between my eyes. "Not your girl. Not your sister," he mused. "Seems you've got no claim."

A rumble built low in my chest, rising into my throat. But then Brynne was there, pushing herself between me and this asshole, dislodging my hold on his shirt.

She turned to face me, tilting her chin up as her long, tawny-colored hair whipped around behind her in the night air. "You have no right, Rush."

Her cheeks were flushed. Clearly, she'd been pregaming it up on her way here. She knew better than this. She was drunk and hurt and…

"You know that's not true," I told her.

That very hurt I'd just been thinking about flickered in her eyes. I thought I saw her lower lip wobble before her chin jutted out and resolve filled her stare.

"Just because you don't want me doesn't mean someone else won't," she declared, spinning so hard sand hit my shins.

Cobalt's arm slid around her waist, and he led her toward the fire.

"Brynne!"

She ignored me, leaning up to whisper something in his ear.

WILDCARD

I endured them flirting, his arm around her, the way they leaned close to talk. I endured watching her flirt with the guy I hated just to piss me off.

Until she straddled his lap and his tongue jammed in her mouth.

"Oh, hell no!" I roared, stalking over and hauling her right out of his lap.

She yelled and kicked, slapping my arms where I held her. I started toward the parking lot, but Cobalt's heavy hand fell on my shoulder.

I put her down in the sand and turned, swinging as I went. My knuckles smashed into his jaw, and he fell back on his ass. He didn't stay down, instead jumping up to rush me. I hit him again, sand scattering around the spot he'd fallen.

"Stay the fuck away from her, Cobalt," I warned. My vision dimmed, and I shook my head. I was so pissed it was making me lightheaded.

Get it together, Rush. You need to get her away from him.

Spinning, I took Brynne's hand and started ahead. She dug her heels into the sand until I was practically dragging her away.

"Ow!" she wailed.

I let go immediately, turning to face her. "Did I hurt you?" I frowned, glancing down at her wrist.

She rolled her eyes. "Like you care."

"Of course I care."

She made another sound. "But not the way I want you to."

I heaved a sigh. "Brynne."

Why couldn't she understand? She would never be anything to me other than my little sister.

"I'm not coming with you."

"Yes, you are. If you stay here, you'll do something you'll regret."

7

"Who cares?" she yelled, arms flinging wide. "That's my choice!"

Maybe she was right. But I still couldn't let her stay here. I couldn't look at Bodhi tomorrow when his sister did the walk of shame into their house.

"You're drunk and pissed off. We're leaving," I insisted.

Both her hands hit my chest and shoved, making me rock back on my heels. "No!"

I grabbed her around the waist and swung her over my shoulder. She yelled the entire way to the Corvette and even as I buckled her in.

"Look at me," I said when my ears were ringing from her protests.

Her lips snapped shut, and her eyes moved to mine.

"I'm sorry I hurt you," I told her sincerely.

Tears filled her eyes.

"*I'm sorry*," I whispered again.

She tried to look away.

I caught her chin, forcing her gaze back. "You're too good for him."

She said nothing else, and I shut her in the car, jogging around to the driver's side.

The smooth purr of my Vette was music to my ears. Before pulling out of the lot, I glanced through the darkened interior toward Brynne who had her face turned away.

I opened my lips to tell her that she'd thank me later for this but decided it was better to say nothing at all. Instead, I peeled out onto the empty beach road, the coast disappearing behind the dune.

The dizziness I felt before hit me again, and I gripped the wheel tighter, trying to steady myself. No matter how much I fought for clarity, an odd haze dropped over me like some kind of veil I had to peer through. Two streets over from the beach, my thoughts turned jumbled, slightly unclear, and I shook my head as if I could knock them all back into making sense.

"Watch out!" Brynne screamed.

The wheel jerked in my hand. Tires squealed, and a horn blared.

As my heart thudded against my ribs, the car smoothed back out on the road. Keeping a tight grip on the wheel, I asked, "You okay?"

"What the hell was that?" Her tone was tight with alarm.

"Sorry. Guess I just got distracted."

"Are you drunk?" she bickered. "This is rich! You accused me of being drunk and making bad choices!"

"I only had two beers," I said irritably. The inside of my mouth felt stuffed with cotton.

She said something I didn't hear.

All the lights on the street blended together. It felt like I'd never driven before.

This is dangerous, my brain whispered.

Downshifting, the Corvette slowed as I turned onto a side street, gliding to a stop at the end of an empty cul-de-sac.

The engine stuttered out when I took my foot off the clutch. The headlights seemed bright, so bright that everything in front of us was obscured.

"Rush?" Brynne asked.

"I should have eaten," I said, reaching into the back. "I'll drink a bottle of water, dilute some of the beer. Just give me a few."

Those few minutes never came. They dropped into an endless void... and took my entire life with them.

1

A COUPLE MONTHS AGO...

Rush

I DIDN'T WANT TO BE HERE.

Yet here I was on the opposite side of the country, touring a university during winter break when I could be surfing like I was actually considering the place when, in fact, my parents had already decided. Frankly, it was insulting. As if they thought I was too stupid to know this was all for show. As if I had a choice.

I wasn't stupid, and my enrollment here at Westbrook for the spring was already set in stone. Or should I say bought and paid for?

Trading one brook for another. Pembrook to Westbrook. Both universities were nearly identical. Prestigious as fuck, monied out the ass, and well-known for their swim teams. Yep, the parentals clearly thought the lights were on but nobody was home and I wouldn't notice I was literally on the opposite side of the country.

They're trying to help you.

No. They're embarrassed and hope once you're gone, people will forget.

I wished I were as dumb as they assumed. Maybe then my head would be blissfully empty instead of constantly squabbling like I had multiple personalities.

Maybe they think you did it.

Did I mention literally *all* my personalities were dicks? Guess what that made me.

So here I was, simmering in resentment while my parents acted all copasetic. (Did I also mention I'm from California?) I was trudging across campus in the fucking frigid air because, frankly, I'd rather risk frostbite on my balls than stay squished in that room with my parents for another second. Not only was I being exiled, but it was so cold here that if I milked a cow, I'd probably get ice cream.

Ignoring the way my teeth chattered, I walked until the pool building came into view. I hadn't planned on coming here, but it was no surprise. Swimming was my escape. A way to not only silence all the dark thoughts in my head but to exhaust them so they stayed quiet long after I was dry.

Swimming was also all I had left.

Which probably explained why I was here at Westbrook even though I didn't want to be. Not because the parentals threatened to take away my trust fund and all financial support. Fuck money. Not because I was persona non grata back in Cali. Fuck all those backstabbing fuckers.

It was because I'd lost everything already. Everyone. There was nothing left.

Coming here was my last attempt at holding on to something that was mine.

And yeah, I realized the thing I wanted to hold on to most was water. A substance that literally slipped through my fingers on the daily.

Even the water thinks you're undeserving.

Yeah, it didn't matter my body temperature probably matched those at the morgue. It didn't matter that this wasn't my school (not until the new semester started) or that I didn't have permission to be here at this hour.

When I grabbed the door and it opened, I considered it an all-access invitation. I mean, what were they gonna do if they caught me? Expel me?

Then they'd have to return the fat check my parents wrote to support their only son's new alma mater. AKA they bribed my way in.

Because no university would take you otherwise.

Rule number one of the rich: Never say no to money.

Rule number two: Money solves all problems.

Yeah, earlier, I was all, *Fuck money!* and you were all, *Hell yeah!*

Don't lie. I know.

But here's the thing. I'm not rich. My parents are. And honestly, I'd throw all that green in their face if it was for something I valued as much. Except my Corvette. She's my baby. Refusing to come here wasn't that. I already told you I wanted to swim.

No. I *needed* to swim. I also needed to think. To remember.

Maybe if I remembered, I wouldn't even need to be here.

Maybe you would.

I wasn't even sure which of those thoughts was worse.

Wasting no time, I toed off my shoes at the edge of the pool and shed my clothes. The water was undisturbed, the surface like glass. That tranquility stung like betrayal, and without hesitation, I dove in, shattering the stillness to create chaos. My body plunged through the waves, skin numb to its icy temperature as I dropped like a rock to the very bottom of the ten-foot depth.

Using the floor as momentum, I somersaulted before

settling into a cross-legged position. Remaining seated at the bottom of the pool was sort of impossible as my lungs still held air, so I used my arms to hover over the tile and sink into the impenetrable silence only water seemed to provide.

Down here, the atmosphere was mesmerizing, lulling me with the way its density absorbed some of my chaos, offering a slight reprieve. Ripples of dim light from the surface filtered through and danced in the moving waves.

Closing my eyes, I drifted to the night that had cost me everything but lived rent-free in my head. *Just let me remember something. Anything.*

FEELING JUMBLED, I REACHED FOR A BOTTLE OF WATER, MY HAND meeting air. Fuck. *Shoving open the door, I started to get out.*

"Where are you going?" Brynne called.

My head swam when I leaned in and hit a button. "Getting a water from my duffle."

At the front of the Corvette, I lifted the hood and reached into the deep "trunk" space where I kept my swim bag. There wasn't much room on the inside of my car, but it had two trunks for storage, one at the back and one up front near the engine.

Yanking out the bag, I downed an entire bottle of water in a couple swallows. The plastic crushed under my grip when I closed my fist around it and tossed it back into the bag. There were a few protein bars there, but just looking at them made me slightly queasy.

Snagging one anyway, I jammed it into the pocket of my board shorts and then dropped the gym bag back into place. I wrapped my hand around the top of the hood, pulling it down to push closed.

One does not slam a Corvette hood. One closes it with respect.

"Shit!" I swore, jolting back, the hood slipping out of my grip when Brynne basically materialized right there behind it.

The slam of metal made me wince, and I gazed down at the top of the flawless blue paint to make sure nothing was chipped or dented. The edges of my vision were blurred, so I leaned down for a closer look and glided my palm over the seam where the hood met the body.

"You look all right," I told her.

"Did you mean it?"

My head snapped up, attention going from my car to Brynne who was still standing there staring at me. The long strands of her bronze hair waved with the breeze that carried the scent of the ocean.

It took me a minute to understand what she said, and even when I remembered the words, I was still confused. "Mean what?"

"That I'm too good for him."

I made a rude sound. "He's angel hair, and you're elbow macaroni." Everyone knows elbow macaroni is superior.

She cracked a smile. The first one I'd gotten out of her in what felt like forever.

My brain was sluggish, the water doing nothing to dilute the beer. That was also probably why my attention was diverted to the silver bracelet fastened around her wrist. I didn't wonder why it was suddenly in front of my face because I was too busy being entranced by its sparkle.

"You're wearing it tonight," I said, reaching to touch it.

"Of course I am," she uttered evading my hand to pull my head down and press her lips to mine.

My delayed mind caught up, and all of me reacted at once. Eyes flying wide, I grabbed her by the shoulders and yanked her back.

"What the hell are you doing?" I half-yelled, holding her at arm's length.

"You said—"

"No." I cut her off. "I didn't say I wanted you to kiss me."

"Then why are you jealous?" she challenged. "Why pull me out of there? Why tell me I'm too good for him?"

15

"I'm not jealous. I pulled you out of there because you were acting stupid, and I told you that because it's true! No sister of mine is going to be shacking up—" Stinging pain cut off my words and sharpened the world around me. "Ow!" I roared. "Shit!"

I glanced down to where three claw-like scratches angrily stretched over my forearm, already welting red.

"Jesus, Brynne! I'm bleeding."

Her chest heaved, eyes shimmering with the tears that began streaking her cheeks. "I am not your sister."

But she was. That bracelet on her wrist proved it. And I would never see her as anything else.

She spun, hair fanning out like a curtain as she took off, bolting past the open passenger door of my car.

Swearing beneath my breath, I took off after her, the world spinning and then tilting a bit as I did. My feet scuffed with my stumble, but I recovered in time to catch up and wrap my palm around her upper arm.

"Brynne," I intoned, pulling her around and blinking rapidly to clear my wavy vision. "Where are you going?"

The scratches on my arm helped my head stay clear, the burning sensation a weird sort of anchor for my mind that wanted to slip away.

"Back to the party."

"You can't."

"Who's going to stop me? You're so drunk you can barely even stand!"

Anger cut through me, and I wrenched her closer. She made a little sound, her nails digging into the damage she'd already inflicted on my skin.

Swearing, I let her go, tugging my arm free of her talons.

She took off, her body fading into the night like it had never been there at all.

"Brynne!" I yelled in the direction she disappeared.

Or had she gone the other way?

I went to the Corvette, shutting the passenger door, then half fell into the driver's seat. The back of my head hit the headrest, suddenly too heavy for my neck to hold up.

I'd just rest a minute. Then I'd go after her...

HANDS GRABBED MY SHOULDERS, SHAKING ME LIKE A RAG DOLL. My body went taut.

She came back.

Relieved as fuck, my eyes popped wide to stare at the face hovering just inches from mine.

"Brynne." I spoke, but the word was nothing but a burst of bubbles, obscuring the face so close to mine.

Bubbles?

I blinked, my lashes fighting the water pushing against my face.

Wait. I wasn't in my Corvette. I was underwater.

Westbrook.

Hands grabbed my cheeks, fingers forcing my face up. There was no time to react as lips covered mine and oxygen flooded my system. My body seized almost as if it were rebelling against the air it was given.

The person gripping me fought back, wrapping their legs around my torso, and clutched my ears to force another puff of air into me.

I stilled, eyes flying wide to collide with a pair that was incredibly close. *Vibrant green in this blue underwater world.*

When she pulled away, I tried to snatch her back. Denying the attempt, she pointed to the surface and grabbed my hand.

Pushing off the bottom, we swam toward the surface together with me staring down at her fingers that were still entwined with mine. Craving another look at those eyes, I

17

sought her gaze, but her face was upturned, her attention focused above.

I want it all on me. Just me.

We burst through the surface at the same time, both gasping for air. My lungs shuddered and burned as I swam to the edge, tossing a muscled arm over the side.

"What the hell was that?" I demanded, swiping the water off my brow.

Smack! Her hand slapped the edge, and I couldn't help but notice how small it appeared.

How can such slight hands have enough strength to pull me from a memory?

That thought was a cold slap right to my face. *I remembered!*

"That was me saving your life!" the girl in front of me exclaimed, effectively pulling me out of the memory a second time.

"Woman, the day I need saving is the day Bigfoot is discovered."

She gasped, the water around her rippling. "Bigfoot is too real!"

I started to laugh, but it was met with aghast silence. *Wait. Is she for real?*

One glance at her round, meadow-green eyes and yeah. Yeah, she was being real.

Water splashed her face when I pulled my hand from below, quickly pressing the back to her forehead. "Did you waste all your air on me? You oxygen-deprived? I think you're hallucinating."

She snorted indelicately, shoving my hand off her and back into the pool.

She's beautiful. No one is ever beautiful with a swim cap stretched over their head.

"He could really be out there." Her tone was entirely emphatic.

"And my dick is small." I mocked.

"Must be why it was so easy to tow you up from the bottom of the pool," she retorted.

Oh, she has some sass, does she? Scowling, I reminded her. "It was easy because I swam up on my own because I *wasn't* drowning."

"Then what the hell were you doing down there? Having tea with the queen?"

My lips twitched. "Be more likely than seeing Bigfoot."

Her light gasp was cute as fuck. "I should have let you drown."

"I wasn't drowning."

"Who are you anyway? Do you go here?"

Delusional *and* nosy. The beautiful ones always were.

Am I right?

"I was trying to have some peace and quiet." Remnants of the lost memories I'd managed to find were like wisps of smoke in my head. I tried to clutch at them, but doing so only made them that much harder to grasp.

They're going to slip away again if I don't focus.

"You go here?" she pressed.

"No."

Her brows drew down, tugging down the swim cap plastered over her head too. "Then how did you get in?"

"The door was open."

She grimaced. "I forgot to lock it."

"Probably too busy daydreaming about Bigfoot," I muttered.

"You should leave." She decided.

"Me?" I asked, incredulous. "I was in the pool first."

"You don't even go here."

"You do?"

She blinked. Her facial expressions were so animated. I could have an entire conversation with her without words.

"Oh, this is rich." The chuckle I let out was deep. "You don't go here either."

"Well, I have a key." She defended.

"So?"

"So possession is nine-tenths of the law."

Maybe my brain was jumbled from before. Maybe I really had been borderline hypoxia down there. Or maybe she cast some kind of spell on me like a siren of the sea.

Whatever it was had my arm shooting out and curling around her short waist to drag her through the water until her body was flush against mine.

Her low gasp only enhanced the hex she held over me, and I squeezed her even closer against my chest.

"What are you doing?" Her voice was breathless, her chest rising and falling rapidly against mine.

Her bathing suit had cutouts at the waist. I knew because when my fingers flexed, they brushed against her bare skin, which was warmer than the water.

Leaning even closer, I spoke low against her ear. "If possession is nine-tenths of the law, then right now, you're all mine."

The force of her swallow was loud to my ears. The hand resting against my bicep tightened just a bit. Tilting her chin back, she gazed up with that killer green stare. The second our eyes connected, a jolt of awareness zapped through me, instant desire draping over me like a wet blanket, heavy and molded to my every inch.

Despite the temperature of the water, the blood in my veins heated. Chemistry cracked between us like someone dropped a live wire right into the pool.

I was no stranger to sex or lust. But this? Instantaneous combustion. It was unlike anything I'd ever met.

She felt it too. It was written all over that expressive face, practically polluting the water around us.

Captivated by her unfiltered reactions, drawn in by the life in her vivid round eyes, I was towed closer and closer, stare dropping to her lips as unbridled hunger forced out all thought.

I got so close we were once more sharing air. I never was much of a sharer, but damn, I'd share with her.

Just as I could nearly taste the sass on her mouth, her cool, wet palms slapped against my pecs and shoved. I let go, and she dropped into the water, entire body dipping beneath the surface before popping back up.

Her hand smacked against the pool ledge again, and water dripped off her bottom lip. "I came here to swim," she said, her voice weaker than before.

"So did I."

Her cheekbones were high and the widest part of her face, which only seemed to further accentuate what I could only describe as an earth-toned stare. Her chin was small, as was her forehead, giving her face a diamond-shaped appearance.

Her lashes were so dark they looked like velvet, and I found myself wondering if it was because they were wet or just that luscious.

Her throat cleared. "Well, I guess there's enough room for us both."

I felt my lips curl up at the corners. "You gonna share your pool with me tonight, little siren?"

Awareness flashed in the depths of her irises. I didn't have to look at her to see it. I could feel it. The water practically hummed with tension.

"You swim on that side," she commanded, pointing to the opposite end of the pool. "This is mine."

"I'll go over there," I told her, pushing off the side. As I

21

swam away, I spun to face her. "But you'll still know I'm here."

"Try not to drown this time," she called, and I couldn't help but laugh.

She slipped beneath the surface, disappearing from sight, and the familiar chaos I was so prone to reminded me it was still there. Reminded me why I was here.

Turning my back on the sassy siren behind me, I started to swim.

2

LANDRY

IF POSSESSION IS NINE-TENTHS OF THE LAW, THEN RIGHT NOW,
you're all mine.

Wasn't that man just drowning? Where did he find all the hot air he was blowing around this pool?

And why were my insides burning up?

The last thing I expected when I came here for a solo swim was to find some muscled hunk at the bottom of the pool. What were the odds? Slim to none. So obviously, if I could come across him, then Bigfoot did exist.

It was even more shocking because I was so accustomed to seeing muscled men in Speedos that I was practically immune at this point.

Except he wasn't in a pair of Speedos. He was in his boxers. Cotton boxers that were drenched and plastered against his thighs, which somehow left even *less* to the imagination than tiny spandex banana hammocks.

Fine. Maybe it was also because I had been plastered against his massive frame when he hauled me close.

God, he was big. Warm despite the cold water. His arm wrapped all the way around my back to circle my waist, holding me so tight I felt the defined ridges of his abdominals and the thickness of his thighs. How easily he could manhandle me. How intriguing that I wanted him to.

As I glided through the water, I watched him covertly. I told myself not to look, but my eyes drifted his way anyway.

He used a punishing pace, arms cutting through the water like it had no resistance at all. Seeing his obvious power and ability made me doubt what I'd seen. *There's no way he could drown.*

But. He'd been sort of listless at the bottom of the pool. Floating just above the tile, eyes shut as midnight hair danced wildly around his head. Thinking back, I supposed he was very calm, not at all panicked like someone in trouble. But still, something about seeing him panicked me. Like he was lost down there in that watery world and might not find his way back.

After one conversation, it seemed even more strange. There was no way the man above the surface was the same as the one I'd discovered below.

Arrogant. Unthankful. Narrow-minded. Loud.

I snorted at the thought, which is something I cannot recommend you do when you are swimming. Water rushed up my nose, going as far as to fill the sinuses at the back of my throat. It burned horribly and I started to cough. Wheezing, I stopped swimming to tread water as I continued to hack.

Why does this always burn so much?

A trickle of chlorinated water slid from behind my nose into my throat, making me gag.

"Easy now." His voice wrapped around me at the same time as his arm, tugging my back up against his chest.

The instinctual urge to surrender against him made me stiffen and hack more.

"You need mouth-to-mouth?" he asked against my ear.

My breath caught, all coughing ceased, and I sagged against him as my eyes watered. He accepted the weight like it was no bother at all and held me with one arm while swimming with the other, carrying me to the side of the pool.

What is he so wide for? I thought grumpily. *Why do I fit against him with room to spare?*

My throat was tight like all the chlorinated water I'd inhaled scalded the delicate flesh.

"Up you go," he said, palming my ass and pushing me out of the water.

"Hey," I half-gasped, half-demanded as he launched me over the side. The second my palms were on the deck, I pulled my legs up and spun to sit on the edge and glare. "I was swimming."

"I hate to break it to you, but you aren't very good."

I sneezed, then sneezed again.

His deep, quiet laugh had me pulling my palm from my face to scowl. "I got water in my nose."

His hand was so large it covered my entire knee when he reached up to pat it. "Why don't you just sit there and take a break?"

Of all the condescending... I glanced to my right, noting a pile of clothing. Considering I was in the locker room when he let himself in, these had to be his. "Oh. Are these yours?" I asked innocently.

His midnight eyes narrowed into half-moon shapes, and a little glee shot through me.

Snatching a gray hoodie off the top, I brought it to my nose and mouth just as... *Achooo!*

Silence reigned for long seconds after I used his hoodie as a tissue. The horrified look on his face was so amusing that I held the fabric against my face even longer as I watched him from behind the cotton.

I definitely, *definitely* was not smelling the fabric. I definitely, *definitely* did not like his scent.

A rumbly sort of growl floated up from the water, making my stomach clench with anticipation. His voice was dark, just this side of ominous, when he spoke. "Most people know better than to do something like that to someone like me."

Oh, why is he so delicious?

I let those words swirl around as I inhaled his shirt for the last time before tugging it away from my face. "Really?" I asked, swiping at my nose with the sleeve. "Why's that?"

He launched himself out of the pool with so much agility that I gasped in surprise. His body pushed mine down until I was under him, face up, with my feet dangling over the edge. He was a solid wall above me, hands planted on either side of my head. The muscles in his arms bulged as he held himself over me, and water rained from his skin to slide over mine.

His stare was impossibly dark, an inkiness so opaque you just knew it concealed a thousand secrets. His equally dark wet hair was plastered against his forehead, and water beaded on the tip of his strong nose. Even if I found the willpower to look away from his midnight features, the width of his shoulders literally blocked out everything else.

Everything about this man screamed danger.

But no part of me was scared.

Instead, I buzzed with excitement like a live wire had been cut loose beneath my skin. It was the first time in my life I wanted to play with fire. The first time I anticipated being burned.

Glittering eyes bore into me, and unabashedly, I stared back.

I expected harsh words. Perhaps a threat of some kind.

I did not expect his kiss.

I gasped on contact, shocked not only by the cool temperature of his lips but by the way he bulldozed into me without any hesitation at all. His confidence was an aphrodisiac, making my head spin.

Pool water dripped from him onto me, the droplets sliding from my lips and over my jaw. His tongue followed one of the wayward drops, lapping it up before it could get far, then came back to swipe over the seam of my mouth.

I opened immediately, and he sank in, tongue flicking against mine in a rough caress. I groaned, pushing my fingers into the wet hair at the back of his head to tug him closer. Our chests bumped as our lips mashed together, the air around us growing balmy.

I'd never experienced such overwhelming desire. Instant attraction was something I wasn't sure was real. But it was. *Oh*, it was. It didn't matter I didn't know his name. I didn't need it to know he had the ability to make me burn.

More of his weight pressed into me when his hand anchored around my throat. The touch was possessive and dominant and, because I didn't know him, borderline dangerous as hell.

My lashes fluttered open, finding his stare waiting for mine. The second our eyes collided, his hand tightened at my neck almost like a challenge. Heat shot between my legs, and it made me ache. Holding his gaze, I swallowed, letting him feel the way my throat worked beneath his grip.

He grunted in approval, the sound vibrating my very bones. Keeping my neck caged, he lowered his head once more to drop a succession of rough kisses—*one, two, three*—to my slack mouth before settling deep and plundering me once more with his skilled tongue.

He tasted of chlorine, but layered beneath it was something else. Something he tried to hold back, but it was so potent it flavored my tongue.

His mouth ripped away, and all I heard was our heavy breathing. All I saw was his kiss-swollen lips.

His irises were so dark I couldn't tell if his pupils were blown, but judging from my hazy vision, I knew mine were. The grip on my throat disappeared, and my skin tingled where he'd held. His body shifted, and the cold air brushed against my damp skin.

"Was that supposed to be a punishment?" I rasped, voice sounding like it was resting over hot coals.

His stare dropped back to my mouth, then dragged rather salaciously down to the column of my throat. Feeling bold, I tipped my chin, arching my neck to give him a better view.

He sucked in a sharp breath, then shoved away from me almost like he was mad. "I came here to swim."

He dropped back into the pool, and I lay there staring up at the rafters, trying to catch my breath. Goose bumps prickled my skin, and I realized I was freezing.

My toes slipped back into the water when I pushed into a sitting position. His hoodie, which was crushed between us, fell into my lap. I scooped it up before it could tumble into the pool, an unhappy sound ripping from my lips.

"What now?" he practically barked.

I thought he was going to swim. "It's wet," I said, brushing at the cotton as if I could wipe away the water.

"So?"

"So now it will smell like chlorine instead of you."

Silence so poignant fell over the entire space. Not even the constant moving water dared to disturb it. His stare practically drilled a hole through me, but I refused to look up. Heat rushed to my cheeks as I stared down at the damp shirt.

Way to admit you were literally just sniffing him.

"Just keep it," he said, water swishing as he spoke.

I glanced up in time to see him start to swim away.

"I don't want it," I called after him.

"Well, I'm not wearing it again. It's covered in your snot," he said, not even bothering to turn around.

"It was a little sneeze," I muttered, rolling my eyes.

He started swimming, pushing through the water as though he hadn't already done so many laps. And wait, wasn't he swimming freestyle before? Now he was swimming butterfly.

Another shiver racked my exposed skin, and my nipples ached from being so hard. It was totally because I was cold. Not because he'd just kissed the crap out of me.

Why do the jerks always have to kiss so good?

Seeking heat, my hands slid deeper into the soft fabric piled in my lap. Warmth caressed my chilled fingers, and I sighed with delight. It might be damp, but the hoodie still held our body heat.

I tugged it over my head, pushing my arms through the excessive fabric, and let it fall over the rest of me. It was so big the hem brushed against the tile. The inside was worn and soft, offering a buffer against the cold. Freeing my hands from the sleeves, I reached up to peel the swim cap off my head.

It landed with a slap beside me, and I breathed yet another sigh as my head was free from its prison. Seriously, peeling off a swim cap was almost as good as taking off your bra after a long day.

Pushing my hands into my thick, chin-length hair, I scratched lightly at my scalp, massaging out some of the tension and fluffing up the strands. I was happy to feel it wasn't wet so I wouldn't have to spend any time drying it. After another moment of finger-combing it, I flipped the left front over to the right and tucked a few wayward strands behind my ear.

The second I was done, the too-long sleeves of the hoodie fell back in place, concealing my hands. It was then I realized I couldn't hear him swimming.

I looked up. He was treading water in the center of the pool. Not swimming. Staring.

No. Hollowing me out with his obsidian gaze.

A low buzzing sound filled my head, almost as if all thought had turned to static. My lungs faltered at the way my stomach fluttered relentlessly, then stopped working completely when his long, muscled arms cut inaudibly through the water.

Ensnared by his fiery stare, I didn't move even though he made me restless. I stayed rooted in place, toes curled under the surface of the water, hands clenched in the protection of his hoodie.

"How dare you?" His voice was quiet and calm, the way it made me feel anything but. His strong, unhurried stroke carried him closer like a predator sure he'd catch his prey.

"W-what?" The question fell from my trembling lip.

"I came here to swim. To escape. To remember."

Soon, he would be close enough to touch.

"You interrupted me. Distracted me. Made it impossible to think."

Anticipation turned me jittery. His veiled anger made the blood in my veins zing.

"You're a fucking siren. Luring me with that vibrant green stare, running your mouth like you want me to shut you up. *Tsk-tsk.*" His tongue clicked with disappointment. "I gave you a chance, little siren."

I felt myself nod, happy I'd disappointed him. Hoping he'd punish me for it.

"I gave you a chance to get away." His hand encircled my ankle. A threat. A promise there was no getting away now.

I said nothing. I was pretty sure my voice wouldn't even work.

"And what did you do?" he mused. "Buried yourself in my hoodie and let loose that wild mane of hair. I'd call it a halo, but we both know you're no angel."

I felt my nose wrinkle. *My hair is not wild.*

He let loose a deep sound, his hand sliding from my ankle to squeeze my calf. All my attention snapped back to him, and I watched satisfaction burn like coal in his onyx eyes.

"I'm in a mood, little siren. I'm in a mood, and you lured me in."

Water rained off him when he pulled himself out of the pool. Cold droplets splattered everywhere, but I didn't notice because he towered over me in nothing but those flimsy wet boxers that had no chance of concealing the impressive bulge beneath them.

After just a moment of allowing me to stare, he offered his hand. "Can you withstand my storm?"

Probably not, a voice inside me whispered.

But I slipped my hand into his.

3

RUSH

MAYBE BIGFOOT DID EXIST. BECAUSE UP UNTIL AN HOUR AGO, I would have argued sirens didn't exist either.

Until a green-eyed, golden-haired mermaid robbed my ability to think. For months, I existed on chaos, anger, and hate. I wanted one thing and only one thing. To remember.

It didn't even matter that remembering would change nothing at all.

It was an obsession. A heartbeat. A need.

Swimming was my only reprieve.

She'd obliterated it all.

Riling me up with lust and making me *burn*. Making me not even care I'd finally gotten what I wanted. Because right now? I wanted her more.

How compelling she was to make me disregard the very thing that had collapsed my entire life.

It made me angry. Hostile even. Yet there was no denying

how she brutally awoke my hunger. And for that, she would pay.

The cost?

Her absolute submission.

My hand closed around hers in a crushing grip, her consent only riling me up more. After grabbing my discarded clothes with my free hand, I towed her toward the locker room, her feet practically running to keep up with my long stride.

The heavy door swung closed behind us, and I dropped everything onto the floor, pulled the hoodie—*my hoodie*—off her tempting little body, and shoved her up against it. Her breath whooshed out, and I didn't let her inhale another, instead dragging her into an ardent kiss. That first taste of her had been nothing but a tease, but now I was going to take my fill. She stretched up on tiptoes, and I reached around to grab her ass and lift. Her legs locked around my waist, body arching against mine.

Using my chest to pin her against the door, I shoved both hands into the thick, wavy hair that fell just past her chin. It was soft and silky, so I roughed it up, trying to anchor my hands in place. She made a throaty sound, and I pulled back, tugging her lower lip with me, then releasing so I could drag my lips over her jaw and toward her throat. Using the grip I had on her hair, I tilted her the way I wanted and scraped my teeth down the tendon in the side of her neck.

She groaned, hands gripping my biceps as I sucked across her collarbone. Her nails pricked my skin, sending a zing down to my dick, and my hips thrust up, the tip of my swollen head nudging the underside of her ass.

Another little sound vibrated her throat as she tried to wiggle down to feel it again.

Yanking her head back, I skewered her with a hot demand. "Look at me."

Her vibrant green stare obeyed, and I met it, letting the full weight of my starvation show, letting her see what she was in for.

"You're mine tonight. To fuck. To own. To do all the depraved things you suddenly make me want."

Her breathing was heavy, pushing her hardened nipples against my chest.

"And you're going to like it."

She made a little needy sound that went right to my dick.

Fuck me, those sounds were going to drive me insane.

"Say yes, little siren. My patience grows thin."

"Yes."

Pleasure made me growl. "Good girl," I praised, then attacked her upturned lips. When they were good and swollen from the assault, I yanked down the strap of her bathing suit.

A curse dropped from my lips as I stared at her perky, round breast. Her rosy nipple proudly puckered in the center, so tight it almost looked painful.

I latched on immediately, covering her with the wet heat of my mouth and beginning to feast with a drawn-out moan. Taking her in hand, I kneaded the flesh as my lips tugged at the center. Whimpering, she arched into the attention, hands gliding into my hair.

Taking that as an invitation, I sucked deeper, then closed my teeth around her nipple. She gasped, hands pulling my hair hard enough to sting. I did it again. And again.

"Oh my God," she groaned, her thighs tightening around my waist.

I pulled back instantly and lifted my head. "If you want to moan someone's name, it better be mine."

"Then tell me what it is."

"Jason," I answered, pinching her nipple and making her head fall back. "Say it. Let me hear it on your tongue."

"*Jason.*" She panted, squirming in my arms.

I rewarded her obedience by ripping down the other side of her suit and lavishing attention on her other breast. By the time I was done, both nipples were swollen and her skin was glistening with my saliva.

"You said someone else's name when I had you in my mouth," I intoned, feeling her shiver in my grip.

She's fucking perfect.

Letting her slide down my body, I set her on wobbly legs. "Make it up to me," I told her. "On your knees."

She dropped to the floor, and a powerful wave of possessiveness coursed through my veins when she tilted up her chin, waiting for my direction.

Hooking my thumbs in the waistband of my boxers, I peeled down the wet material, presenting my throbbing, needy dick.

Without any hesitation, she wrapped her hand around it and suctioned her warm mouth around the tip. I almost fucking nutted right there.

"Did you ask permission?" I rumbled.

As she pulled off, her eyes slid up my chest. "I assumed I had permission when you told me to get on my knees."

I arched an eyebrow. "Are you sassing me?"

"Yes. What are you going to do about it?"

I jammed my cock back in her mouth, this time more than the tip. She started to gag when it was halfway in.

Full disclosure: I have a big dick.

Pushing my hand into the hair on the back of her head, I held her still and retreated gently. It was one thing to be dominating but another to be an asshole.

A sound of protest vibrated my rod, and her hands went to my hips, pulling me back in. Silky, warm heat enveloped me, her cheeks hollowing out as she began to suck. The hand in her hair moved up the wall, and I braced my weight on it, watching her head bob. Slurping sounds echoed from below as she licked from the base all the way to the tip.

Groaning, I hunched my upper body closer as if having her all over my dick wasn't enough. Reaching down, I caught her chin. She lifted her face instantly, staring into me with those fucking green gems while her plump lips remained wrapped around my rigid cock. It was completely obscene and sent a shiver of pure pleasure down my spine.

"Look at you," I rasped, brushing my knuckles over her flushed cheek. "You're doing so good, baby."

Her lashes fluttered like butterfly wings, sweeping down against her cheeks as she slid forward, taking me in until my head hit the back of her throat.

My curse dropped between us, and I slid my hands under her arms and pulled her from her knees so I could taste myself on her tongue.

Her entire body melted against mine, her tits pressing against my chest, the skin-on-skin contact making my dick jerk. Impatient, I bent, fishing around in my jeans to grab the condom out of my wallet and rip it open with my teeth. The second I was sheathed, I grabbed her ass and lifted, invading her soft heat with a single thrust.

Her surprised gasp mingled with my groan, her forehead dropping to rest on my shoulder. She was fucking tight. The tightest grip I'd ever felt.

So tight it infuriated me.

Pulling her body almost completely off mine, I pierced her with a hot stare. "Are you a virgin?" I demanded, pissed off and turned on all at once.

She jolted, the movement making her clench around my head. She whimpered, and I groaned.

She squeezes me so good.

"Are you?" I demanded again.

"N-no."

I felt my eyes narrow. "You lying to me?"

"No! You're just huge."

I grunted. She wasn't lying.

With her eyes downcast, her next words were a little shy. "I-it's been a while."

Her vulnerability surprisingly called to mine, further proof she was nothing but a little siren. Even still, I had to match it. I had to answer her call.

"For me too," I said, gruff.

Her eyes zipped to mine, surprise clear in the hazy depths. I guess I couldn't blame her for thinking I did this often.

"Can I move?" I gritted out, my body screaming for release.

She wiggled her fine ass a little farther onto me, and a hiss escaped my lips.

"Go," she whispered.

I didn't have to be told twice.

I started thrusting up into her, our skin slapping together at the pace I set. Everything in my world condensed to the wet heat she dripped over me and the way it felt to invade something so soft with my stiff length.

She cried out, gasping and moaning, her body going slack as I pounded into her again and again. Sweat dampened my back, and my grip slipped, fingers sliding into her ass crack, one nudging the ring of muscle around her hole.

She made a shocked sound, but then her body melted into mine.

"You like that?" I rumbled, pushing her back into the wall. I laid my finger over the tight spot. "You want me to fill you up in more than one place?"

"*Jason.*"

I'd been hot before, but now I burned with fever. The urge to climb inside this woman and take over was so strong. I strained up on tiptoes, thrusting as deep as our bodies would allow.

The muffled sound of a door slamming cut into our erotic soundtrack, making my movements still. Her body stiffened. Alarmed eyes sought mine.

Echoing footsteps drew closer, and the unmistakable sound of someone grabbing the door handle ricocheted through the room.

Pulling her off the wall, I moved quickly and carried her deeper into the locker room. Just as I stepped around the corner where the sinks and stalls were, the door pushed open, and someone walked in.

My arms were shaking, so I stood her on her feet but kept my hands on her naked skin. Grasping my hand, she tugged me into the corner of the wall that separated us from whoever had interrupted.

My dick was still rigid, the blood coursing through my body still pulsing with need. I meant it when I said she distracted me from everything. Not even the notion of being caught screwing in the locker room was enough to dampen how much I wanted her.

The footsteps grew louder. Whoever was out there was moving farther into the room.

"There's clothes everywhere," a low voice bitched. "Slobs."

Her eyes shot to mine in panic, and she pressed a finger to her lips. *Shh.*

How erotic she looked backed into a corner with my wide body towering close. Her short, wavy hair was mussed from my hands, skin flushed, lips swollen, and there was a mark on her shoulder from my teeth.

I moved fast, grabbing her by the hips and spinning her

so her face was in the wall. Nudging my thigh between her legs, I pushed hers wide. I slapped a hand over her mouth when I took her from behind, her gasp muffled behind my palm.

My free arm snaked around her waist, pulling her back against my chest as I thrust so deep her toes left the floor. I held her like that, prisoner on my dick, to speak low against her ear, "You better be real quiet if you don't want him to see."

Her head started to shake, and I bit at her lobe. "I'm not done with you, little siren. Be a good girl and take my cock."

I thrust up, and her head fell back against my shoulder.

A door on the other side of the wall opened, and a light flickered on. Pulling my hand from her mouth, I palmed her breasts, massaging the flesh as I quietly fucked into her.

Her breathing was labored. My thighs burned. Her body clenched around mine, and I swear I grew bigger inside her. She huffed out a breathless sound when I rolled her nipples between my fingers and rotated my pelvis against her ass.

Muffled sounds of papers ruffling, a drawer opening and closing, and a chair creaking came through the wall. I kept driving into her, knowing we could be caught at any moment. Knowing I was balls deep in a woman while someone was just feet away.

The base of my spine started to tingle, and my balls drew up so tight it was almost painful.

The ringing of a phone stuttered my hips. Both of us stilled.

"Yeah," a muffled voice answered. "Be there in five."

The light flicked off. A door shut.

I palmed her hips and started fucking into her anew.

"What the fuck is this?"

The girl in my arms went rigid, and my hips faltered.

Holding her in place, I glanced over my shoulder, sure we'd been caught. But he wasn't there.

"A condom wrapper." The man fumed. Pretty sure it was my soon-to-be coach.

Oops. Forgot to pick that up.

"I do not get paid enough for this shit," he spat, then stormed out, the door slamming behind him.

Her body sagged with relief, forearms resting on the wall. Placing my palm in the center of her back, I pushed, bending her body at the waist and making her gasp. My body blanketed hers from behind as my hand curved around her hip to glide over her swollen clit.

"I thought he'd never leave," I growled in her ear, plucking her like an instrument.

Her body went tight, a whimper falling from her lips.

"Give it to me, little siren. Say my name when you fall apart on my cock."

With one last push into her core, she fell over the edge, a hoarse cry releasing from her lips as her body shattered around mine. A rush of warm wetness coated my dick, and for a heart-stopping moment, I was pissed that the condom kept it from making a mess of me.

She called my name, body slipping off the wall, and I caught her in my arms and held her while pleasure was all she knew.

The second she slumped, I started pounding into her, chasing after my own release, grinding my hips against her until they stuttered and my knees nearly buckled as the intense orgasm ripped me in two.

For long moments, I was stunned. I saw nothing. Heard nothing. Knew nothing except the ecstasy overtaking it all.

When at last I turned coherent, I slid out of her body and slumped against the wall, pulling her with me. With her cheek pillowed on my chest, her hot breaths puffed across my skin, which was still so sensitive from what we'd done that goose bumps raced along my arms.

She pressed a little closer against me, and I noted her body was quivering, likely overwhelmed. Widening my stance, I took more of her weight and began rubbing along her back.

"You did good, little siren." I praised. "So good for me."

She said nothing, but I knew the words pleased her. I felt her pleasure in the air.

After another quiet moment, she reached around and patted my ass. "You did good too."

I laughed. The kind of laugh that reached my belly. The kind I shouldn't even have energy for.

When my breathing returned to normal, I moved off to take care of the condom. When I turned back, she was staring.

The urge to kiss her slammed into me as though I hadn't just been buried in her body.

"So I guess since neither of us go here, we won't run into each other again," she said.

"Probably not." I agreed. It was on the tip of my tongue to ask for her number. Her name. I stopped myself. She'd been a hella good distraction, but that was all she was.

She turned to go, but her footsteps hesitated, and she turned back.

"I'm taking your hoodie."

I shrugged. "I already told you to."

Her head bobbed, the messy blond waves toppling around her face. She stepped around the corner, a split second out of my sight.

I found myself rushing after her, grasping her wrist, and pulling her around. She said nothing. Her eyes said it all.

"You made me all sweaty," I said. "You have to wash my back before you go."

Her eyes strayed in the direction of the giant shower, then back to me. "Okay."

I dragged her into the shower, turning on the spray. I knew I'd never see her again. It was what I wanted. But a few more minutes would be okay.

4

PRESENT DAY...

LANDRY

THE SHRILL PITCH OF A WHISTLE BATTLED BACK ALL OTHERS, SO loud it could be heard through the door as I approached. It wasn't just a quick blast either but a drawn-out screech that demanded to be heard.

As if anyone could miss that bone-rattling noise.

"Team meeting! Get your wet asses over here!" Coach's bellow cut right through the slim opening of the door the second I started to pull it open.

Splashing, grumbling, and wet feet slapping the pool deck filled the air as I hovered behind the barely open locker room door. Some might call it eavesdropping.

I called it recon.

A girl had to know what she was getting herself into.

"Listen up," Coach announced.

"Kinda hard to do after you made our ears bleed with that whistle," someone muttered.

"Bro, we're all going to be hearing impaired," another voice quipped, and I smiled, recognizing it immediately.

"Owens!" Coach snapped. "I don't have time for your shit today."

"What was that? I can't hear you."

I pressed a hand to my mouth, muffling the giggle.

Coach sighed loudly, and I pictured him pinching the bridge of his nose, calling on all his patience. Maybe assisting wouldn't be as bad as I thought. At the very least, it would be entertaining.

"As I was saying..." Coach went on. "Elite is bringing on a new coach."

There was a ripple of shocked silence followed by a hum of hushed whispers.

"You can't just leave in the middle of the season," someone declared.

"How could you do it to us?" Someone else worried. "It's only a couple weeks into the new semester."

"Is this because we hate your whistle?" Owens spoke up again. "'Cause you don't have to leave. We can compromise. Maybe get you a harmonica instead."

A few people snickered.

"Ryan, you better do something, bro."

"I'm not leaving." Coach interrupted. "A harmonica, Owens, really?"

"Might be nice," he muttered.

"I'm still head coach. I'm still in charge around here." Coach railroaded right over all the ridiculousness to get back to business. "But I've taken on an assistant coach."

A few murmurs went around, and Coach blasted his whistle to silence everyone. "I expect every single one of you to respect her. When I'm not around, she's the one in charge."

"You're always around, Coach. Sometimes I wonder if

you sleep in your office," a voice I didn't recognize commented.

Right on the heels of that, another guy called, "Wait, did you say *her*? Is our new coach a girl?"

Taking that as my cue, I stepped out of the locker room and onto the pool deck. The collective attention of a large group of men dressed in Speedos shifted to me. I wasn't a timid person, and swimmers didn't intimidate me. Still, it was a little unnerving to be the focus of so many eyes at once.

Refusing to show any kind of weakness, I walked forward, my sneakers splashing a bit in the random puddles lying about. Despite being dressed in a pair of high-waisted black leggings and a cropped windbreaker in Westbrook's ivy green, I felt a little exposed.

"This is our new assistant coach. Her name is Landry." Coach introduced me as I resisted the urge to run my fingers through my short bob.

"Whoa," one of the swimmers standing near the front mused. "She's our age."

I glanced toward Jamie Owens and Ryan Walsh, and they both smiled. Jamie started forward, but Coach held up his hand, stopping him. "Landry transferred here from Oberlin College in Oberlin, Ohio."

"Were you a swimmer?" asked the same guy who'd pointed out my age.

"Kruger! Who said that was your business?" Coach snapped.

"Well, I mean, she's the new assistant coach. Seems legit I would ask her if she swims," Kruger replied.

Coach picked up the whistle, but I caught his hand halfway to his lips and pushed it back down. "We really might all go deaf," I told him emphatically.

The guys laughed.

While he glowered, I turned back to the team. "I did swim at Oberlin, but I tore my rotator cuff not too long ago, and I can't compete. I transferred here to finish out my exercise science degree and to assist Coach."

As I spoke, a bizarre sense of awareness prickled across my skin, just an inkling of something at first, but it continued to grow until I was thankful for the long-sleeved jacket and leggings to hide the goose bumps racing over my skin. I shifted, thinking maybe I was standing in an area where there was a draft, thinking maybe I was just cold.

"You sure you want to assist him? He yells. A lot," someone asked, but I barely paid attention because of the way my stomach suddenly dipped.

The familiar timbre of Coach's voice answered, but I was too distracted to hear his reply.

Instead, my eyes seemed to follow some invisible trail, beckoned by something I couldn't even see. Until my eyes landed on their destination.

My breath stuttered. Lungs froze. Déjà vu flickered inside me, flipping my stomach inside out.

His obsidian stare wasn't that familiar, but it was unforgettable, a one-time experience that left a permanent mark inside me. I thought I'd never see him again.

He was here.

A single face among an entire group, a presence able to mute them all.

He was just as imposing as before, the intensity around him making my insides quiver, making my fingers curl into my palms. If I'd thought my reaction to him that night had been a fluke, I was just proven wrong.

"Seriously, Coach. You can't yell at a girl," someone nearby argued, but my eyes stayed glued on him.

Jason.

The whistle squealed. It didn't matter. I was hostage to the flicker of recognition in his stare.

"I'm not going to yell at her," Coach told the room before anyone recovered from the high-pitch sound. "She's my daughter!"

Jason's eyes jerked from me, and I swayed, suddenly unbalanced. Righting myself, I blinked, realizing chaos reigned.

"That's your daughter?"

"Brooo, you never told us you have a daughter!"

"No way, she's way too hot to be Coach's daughter."

"Guess there was at least one night he wasn't sleeping in his office."

The whistle erupted again. My ears rang. Reaching over, I snatched it away. "Enough already, Dad!"

Everyone went quiet.

"Definitely his daughter," the swimmer named Kruger whispered. "If anyone else did that, they'd be missing a limb by now."

I laughed.

"For the love of God," Dad muttered.

"This is Landry Resch. Coach Landry to you." He cleared his throat. "And yes, she's my daughter."

That attention-stealing, heart-thumping, stomach-flipping feeling from before? It came back. I didn't have to look around for it this time. I knew exactly where it came from.

Rolling my lips in, I turned slightly, peeking around my hair. He was staring again.

No. Glowering.

A touch on my arm made me jolt. And out of the corner of my eye, I saw him stiffen.

"Landry." Dad's voice was gruff. "You okay?"

I smiled at my father. "Of course."

He grunted, which I'd come to think of as his way of showing affection, then turned back to the Speedo gang.

"Just so we're clear, she's off-limits to you pervs."

"Dad!" I hissed. *Oh my God, I am going to die.*

"So keep your hands to yourselves."

No one said anything. I felt like crawling under the bleachers.

"I can't hear you!" he yelled, obviously not done mortifying me for the day.

I shouldn't have come here.

The thought had me glancing around to where Jason stood. The second I turned, his eyes snapped to mine. The silver-framed goggles on his head seemed so sparkly against his midnight hair and eyes.

Varying degrees of, "Yes, Coach," burst from the swimmers, promising to keep their "pervy" hands to themselves.

But my dark and broody one-night stand?

His lips stayed sealed.

5

RUSH

CLEARLY, I WAS A SERIAL KILLER IN MY PAST LIFE.

Because seriously. What in the fucked-up karma shit was this?

I screwed my coach's daughter.

Because of course I fucking did.

I liked it too. Actually, I more than liked it.

I thought I'd never see her again. Hell, I was halfway convinced it had been some sort of fever dream I'd slipped into because reality sucked so damn much.

But there she was.

Standing there in a pair of black leggings that molded to her body so fantastically.

I was hit with a vivid memory of what it felt like to have her molded around me. It'd been the hottest sex I'd ever had, and if I'd thought perhaps it was a fluke, the second our eyes collided, I learned that was a total lie.

Honest to God, she was a siren, instantaneously igniting

some insatiable craving inside me with her messy hair, wide cheekbones, and green eyes. The second she stepped out of the locker room, the rest of the room turned dim. It was uncanny really, the way nothing else existed when she appeared.

What were the odds the one girl I wanted a repeat with was the one coach just declared off-limits?

His fucking daughter.

Yep, I bet my kill list in my previous life was hella impressive.

My attention stayed on her as Coach blathered on about whatever, and when he dismissed Elite to the locker room, I didn't join in the mad rush to the showers, choosing instead to linger.

She was aware of me. That much was clear.

The flare of recognition when our eyes first met was unmistakable. Even after she turned back to the introductions, she stayed at least partly focused on me. I knew because whenever I would shift, she would too. The magnetic force between us was impossible to deny.

"Bro!" Owens's annoyingly enthusiastic voice was like nails on a chalkboard. He bounded into my line of sight, heading straight for the object of my current fixation.

The muscles in my jaw locked painfully when he lifted Landry off her feet into a bear hug.

I waited for her to tell him to put her down, for Coach to appear and blast him for touching his daughter. None of these things happened.

She laughed, hugging him back. "Jamie Owens."

I considered contacting a medium to get in touch with my former serial killer persona so I could get some tips for murder.

What? You know I got away with it. Just look at all the ways karma was kicking my ass in this life to make up for it.

"Bro, how long's it been?" he said, pulling back to stand right beside his best friend, Walsh. The pair was so far up each other's asses all the time they could probably taste each other's tonsils.

Smiling, Landry squinted, and the action made the tiny diamond stud in her nose glint.

That was not there before.

"Middle school?" she said, interrupting my thought.

"Ryan had a mouth full of metal," Jamie cracked, slapping his bro on the shoulder.

Ryan rolled his eyes. "So did you."

Owens slung his arm around Walsh's neck. "We had a glow-up, bro." Turning to Landry, he said, "Pretty sure you're still the same size, though."

She laughed, and the sound made me equal parts jealous and turned on. "I am not."

"Yeah," Walsh mused. "You are." Then he moved forward to pull her into a hug. "It's good to see you. You look good."

Did I mention they were both still in nothing but Speedos?

"Didn't you hear Coach not even five minutes ago telling you to keep your hands to yourself?" I snapped.

Walsh stiffened and pulled back from what was mine.

That's right. I said *mine.*

Walsh and Owens turned to me, but I ignored them.

Did I mention I thought they were Tweedledum and Tweedledee personified?

Instead, I focused on the blonde in front of me, folding my arms across my chest. "What's with the piercing?"

Her eyes widened a bit but then narrowed. "It's new," she said, reaching up to touch the tiny stud.

Hell, I might not even have noticed it if the light hadn't caught it.

"I like it."

"You don't need any more glitter on your face," I told her. *You're already sparkly enough.*

Her brows drew down. "You don't like it?"

Oh hell.

Why did that seem to bother her? And why did she reach up to it again like she was going to take it out?

"Do you two know each other?" Walsh interrupted.

I ignored him, but Landry didn't.

"No!" she said a little too fast.

So that's how this is gonna go.

"But apparently, whoever this is doesn't care for face piercings."

"My boyfriend has an eyebrow ring," someone said, drawing all our stares.

My God, he was here too?

Wes Sinclair. The third wheel to Ryan and Jamie. He wasn't as bad as the other two, but he was guilty by association.

Landry swung to look at the curly-haired swimmer.

Wes blushed, noticing all eyes had turned to him. He cleared his throat. "I, ah, like it," he said.

"Bro. You'd like Max even if he was a girl," Jamie cracked. "You'd turn straight for him." Turning thoughtful, he cocked his head. "Or would it be her?"

"Not your best joke, bro," Ryan told him.

Jamie turned to Wes. "Maybe don't tell Max about that one. I think he's still mad about my last bad joke."

Wes laughed.

"You have a boyfriend?" Landry asked.

The air around the group shifted, turning a lot less friendly and a bit colder. Walsh and Owens stepped a little closer to Sinclair, closing ranks around him. They were always like this with him. Honestly, it was probably their best quality. That and the fact they treated their girlfriends right.

"You got an issue with our bro being gay?" Walsh asked, his voice calm.

At that moment, the locker room door swung open, and a platinum head appeared. Lars saw us all standing there and smiled, starting over. Jamie and Ryan shared a brief look, and I made a noise, drawing their eyes and returning the stare, silently letting them know I had Lars.

A war waged inside me, part of me wanting to shield this girl from the shitstorm coming and the other part wanting to shield my friend.

Wes wasn't the only gay swimmer on Elite. Lars was too. He was also the only guy here that I considered a friend. His boyfriend, Win, was decent, but I wouldn't go as far as to call him bro.

PS: Apparently, excessive use of the word bro is required at this place.

I hadn't actually meant to like Lars, but we both transferred to Westbrook at the same time. Both of us arrived to Elite together, both far from home, both running from shit we didn't want to talk about. Lars was my assigned roommate, and sharing a tiny dorm room made it impossible to keep my distance. The more I was around him, the more I recognized something inherently lonely about him. It got under my skin.

"*Hej*," he called, the Swedish greeting sounding like hey in English.

"Bro," I called, shifting toward him automatically. The movement tugged at the center of my chest, trying to move me back so Landry was still in my orbit. I resisted, though. She might be a little siren, but homophobia was gnarly.

Instantly, Lars picked up on the vibe and glanced at Wes nervously, then to me. I gestured with my chin, letting him know everything was cool.

"Oh my gosh, no!" Landry said, bursting the tense

atmosphere. She rushed forward and flung her arms around Wes, going as far as to push up on her tiptoes so she could hug him. "I'm so sorry if it came off that way." She pulled back to smile at him. "I was just thinking how lucky your boyfriend must be because you're hot."

I nearly choked on my spit.

"Don't let Max hear you say that," Jamie quipped. "He's jealous AF."

"Jealous *and* pierced," Landry mused. "Does he have a tattoo too?" she asked.

Wes smiled, and Walsh and Owens visibly relaxed. "A whole sleeve of them."

Landry made a sound. "So when do I get to meet him?"

"How about we introduce you two first?" Ryan mused. "Landry, this is Wes."

"Nice to meet you, Wes." She smiled, and my body automatically shifted back as if realigning the magnetic pull between us.

"This is Lars." Jamie picked up where Ryan left off and slung his arm around Lars. "The only nuts he can have are Win's."

"Win is my brother," Wes told her.

Lars's pale skin turned pink, and his icy-blue eyes slid to the side before turning back. "What he means is I have an allergy to nuts. And yeah, I'm dating Wes's brother."

"I love your hair," Landry said, eyes going right to the platinum strands on his head.

"Better not comment on it when Win is around," Jamie mused.

I laughed under my breath. Lars gave me a look, and I shrugged. "He's right. Win doesn't like people staring at your *halo.*"

Lars muttered some stuff in his native tongue that was probably sarcastic as hell, and Wes laughed.

"You speak Swedish?" Landry asked.

"I'm from Sweden. I transferred here at the beginning of the semester."

"That explains the hair and eyes." She nodded. "I wish I could get my hair that blond. My stylist will never do it. Something about me going bald." Landry rolled her eyes dramatically.

"Your hair is fine the way it is," I grumped.

Everyone looked at me.

Little siren cleared her throat. "And who are you?"

I opened my mouth to tell her she didn't seem to have a problem using my name the night I made her scream it, but that asshat Walsh interrupted.

"This is Elite's self-proclaimed wildcard, Rush."

Landry divided her stare between me and Ryan, and frankly, I wanted to push his freestyle swimming ass in the pool so she would stop. "What makes you a wildcard?" she asked, her stare finally settling on just me.

Much better.

"I'm a wildcard 'cause I don't have just one value, one stroke, one talent," I told her, leaning in just a little and quieting my voice. "I'm unpredictable in and out of the pool."

She didn't back away. Her eyes stayed locked on mine. Unbridled chemistry crackled between us and kicked up my heart rate.

Then she was pulling back, tempting me to follow, before I blinked to break the spell. "Nice to meet you, Rush."

My tongue slid over my teeth. How dare she call me that?

"So you guys know each other?" Wes questioned, reminding me there a bunch of jocks in Speedos standing around.

"Bro, sure, we've known her since like second grade," Ryan answered. "We took swim lessons together."

"You mean you knew this whole time Coach had a daughter, and you never told us?" Kruger accused as he jogged over to join us.

Prism was following close behind, and they were both already dressed, Prism's ears jammed with his AirPods. He wore them so much it was odd to see him without them.

Ryan quickly introduced Landry to them and then said, "The three of us went to school together until she moved to Ohio with her mom in middle school."

Landry nodded. "But now I'm back."

"Don't worry. We won't hold it against you that the whistle tyrant is your dad," Kruger said, reaching out to presumably pat her shoulder.

I knocked his hand away before he could make contact. "No."

"Bro. Who pissed in your Cheerios?" Kruger asked me.

"You know he's always like this," Jamie whispered extra loud.

"We're going for breakfast at Shirley's," Ryan told Landry. "You should come. Meet our girls. You'll like them."

Landry's eyebrows shot up. "You two have girlfriends?"

"Does Yao Ming eat Chinese?" Jamie asked.

"Who is Yao Ming?" Lars wondered.

I shrugged.

"A bro that eats Chinese," Jamie said like it was obvious.

"Oh, I'm definitely coming," Landry mused. "I have to meet the girls that deal with you two on a daily basis."

Jamie opened his mouth to no doubt say something idiotic, but Ryan cut him off. "C'mon, let's change. I'm starving."

They went to change along with Wes, but I stayed rooted in place.

Just as Landry's alluring stare shifted to me, Ryan spoke up. "C'mon, Rush. Your sack's gonna look like a pair of shriveled raisins."

You see why I hate him, right? You see.

A laugh bubbled out of Landry, and my eyes narrowed. She slapped a hand over her mouth instantly, but that only muffled her giggles.

Sirens aren't supposed to be cute too.

"You told me I couldn't say that anymore, and now listen to you," Jamie complained.

Ryan ignored his bro's whining. "Rush."

My shoulder blades snapped together, the underlying warning in Walsh's tone pissing me off. I looked over my shoulder, nailing him with one eye.

He didn't back down. The asshole never did. "You changing or what?"

"So tell me about Sweden," Landry said, stepping up to Lars's side. "Are the people very different?"

Lars made a sound. "The people here are like cartoon characters compared to there. Win is the worst of all."

Notice he didn't say back home. He said there.

"Win is your boyfriend?"

Lars nodded, shy.

She went on. "Does he have tattoos like Wes's boyfriend?"

"What the hell are you so interested in tattoos for?" I demanded.

She and Lars looked up. I glowered.

"Rush!"

I gave Ryan the finger and then glanced back at my friend and my girl.

Just get used to it. I'm going to keep calling her that.

I guess there were worse people I could leave her with.

My eyes went solely to Lars's icy ones, and it was like he knew. I didn't want him to know.

Still, when I saw his barely there nod, something in me relaxed, and I turned to go change.

6

LANDRY

SHIRLEY'S WAS A DINER LOCATED RIGHT OFF CAMPUS, SO CLOSE
it basically was part of the university. I knew of it, of course.
I'd grown up here in Westbrook until moving away with
Mom, but it wasn't really a place we went much because it
was more of a college thing.

But this was my campus now. Westbrook was my university. Seemed a little surreal honestly. I always assumed I'd go
here. I mean, this was my dad's alma mater, and he'd been
coaching here for years.

But then my mom took me to Ohio. I ended up at Oberlin, and Westbrook seemed so far away.

I stepped into the diner with ivy-green booths lining the
walls and giant windows looking out on the street and trees.
There was a long counter running along the back, and it was
lined with dark-green padded stools with pendant lights
hanging over it. Tables filled the center of the room, and all
the servers wore uniforms with a name badge that read

Shirley.

I'd ridden here with Ryan, riding shotgun in his black Jeep Rubicon with Jamie taking up the back seat. Jamie drove a Jeep that looked just like Ryan's except it was cherry red. It didn't surprise me at all they drove matching cars. What was a little surprising was to see Wes getting behind the wheel of yet another Rubicon, this one bright yellow.

Jamie saw me looking and declared they were "Jeep bros."

It was ridiculous. But also kinda endearing.

"I'm so hungry I'd eat that old pair of gym shoes we found in the lockers at the beginning of the semester," Jamie announced as he and Ryan came inside behind me.

I wrinkled my nose, looking at him over my shoulder. "That's disgusting."

"Get the waffles on. The boys are here!" a woman working behind the counter called into the kitchen.

"That's why we love you, Shirley," Ryan professed, stepping around me to grin. Then he pointed to a few booths across the room and glanced at me. "That's our spot."

"You have a spot?" I mused.

A rush of cold morning air whooshed inside when the door opened behind us.

"There's my girl," Jamie said, affection dripping from the words.

I turned in time to see him scoop up a girl with long dark hair and smack a kiss on her lips right there in the middle of the diner. I could barely see her because his wide frame blocked her from sight, but I heard her laugh.

A girl with ginger hair dressed in a pair of wide-leg faded jeans and long-sleeved crop top stepped around them, her wide gray eyes glancing around and stopping on Ryan.

"Carrot," he rumbled, brushing past me to slide his hands under her arms and pick up her and her giant messenger bag so her sneaker-clad feet dangled over the floor. "Give me some sugar."

"I haven't had any coffee yet, Ry," she said, trying to scowl, but her glittering eyes betrayed her.

"Who needs coffee when you have me?"

Sighing, she leaned forward and kissed him.

"Ugh, enough with the PDA," Kruger complained, filing inside along with Prism, Wes, and Lars.

"Maybe you should join a dating app, Kruger. Get you some," Jamie cracked.

Kruger flipped him off and kept going over to the booth.

On his way past, Prism gave me a small smile from beneath a gray beanie that had white AirPods sticking out from beneath the edges.

I'd barely just met them, and I was already getting a feel for all their personalities. Ryan was the leader, Jamie was the charming joker, Prism the quiet one, Wes the cute one they all babied, and Kruger was... Well, he was a moron. I mean that in the best way possible. I wasn't quite sure about Lars yet. He seemed a little shy.

What about Rush? my subconscious whispered.

I don't know much about Rush. I only know Jason. It seemed very appropriate that he called himself a wildcard. He also didn't seem to get along with everyone else that well, and I couldn't help but wonder what was up with that.

With him on my mind, my eyes scanned the diner, wondering if he was there, anticipation building in my limbs at the idea of seeing him. When he didn't walk in and the door banged closed, I couldn't help the sharp stab of disappointment.

"Landry," Ryan called, drawing me around to where he stood with the petite redhead. "This is my girlfriend, Rory. Carrot, this is Landry. She's Coach Resch's daughter, Elite's new assistant coach, and me and Jamie went to school with her years ago."

I raised my brows, dividing my smile between them. "Carrot?"

Rory made a sound and rolled her eyes. "He says my hair is orange."

"Of course he does," I mused.

"It's so good to meet you." Rory smiled. "Ryan mentioned once that he knew Coach's daughter, but I had no idea you went here."

"Seriously, Walsh? You told her and not us?" Kruger called from inside the booth. "You betray us."

"Have an extra waffle on me, bro," Ryan called.

"You trying to bribe me with food?"

"If you don't want it, I'll eat it," Jamie declared. Beside him, his girlfriend groaned.

"Now I didn't say that," Kruger hurried to say.

"Too late. I'm eating it," Jamie deadpanned.

"Jamie, let him have the waffle," the dark-haired beauty stated, whacking him in his middle.

Jamie grunted like it hurt, but I knew it didn't. I'd seen his abs that morning.

He smirked and leaned down to her ear. "Guess I'll have to eat something else, then."

Her dark eyes narrowed, but he stuck his fingers in her ribs, making her giggle.

Eluding his tickling, she stepped forward, brushing the bangs out of her eyes, and held out her hand to me. "Hi, I'm Madison. Were these two like this when they were little?"

I smiled, giving her hand a shake. "Oh yeah. Menaces since birth."

"Disrespectful," Jamie commented.

"Well, it's nice to have another girl around here," Rory

said, hooking her arm through mine to lead me to the booth. "Tell us something embarrassing about them."

Madison gasped dramatically, stepping up to my other side. "Give us the dirt!"

The two guys behind us groaned, but I wasn't about to be deterred. "When we all took swim lessons together, someone kept peeing in the pool, so the teacher secretly put something in the water that would turn it bright green when someone did it again, and—"

"Whoa, bro!" Jamie burst between us, tucking his arm around Madison and giving me a light nudge toward the booth. "What happens at swim class stays in swim class."

Madison turned on him, fisting her hands on her hips while trying not to laugh. "Jamie Michael Owens, did you pee in the pool during swim class?"

Rory giggled uncontrollably.

He glanced at her. "Bad sister," he scolded.

She laughed more.

"Ry, you better get your girl," Jamie complained. Then to the table, "Talking about pee is not appropriate breakfast conversation."

"Says the man who just said he was going to eat a rotten old gym shoe," I countered.

Madison wrinkled her nose.

Ryan laughed as he pulled Rory into his lap inside the booth. "Now, baby, don't embarrass Jamie about his pee problems."

Jamie gasped. "I did not have pee problems!"

"Order's up!" A waitress approached, carrying a massive round tray piled high with plates.

"You're my hero, Shirley," Jamie said, sliding into the booth beside Ryan and Rory and pulling Madison with him.

"We didn't even order yet," I mused, stepping back in awe

at the plate-sized waffles dripping in butter that were being passed around. There were so many of them.

"This is just to hold us over while they make the rest," Jamie said, already stabbing the golden treat to take a massive bite.

I shook my head. Obviously, swimmers required a lot of calories, but the girls' team never ate like this.

Shirley stepped back, the tray in her hand now empty. "You'll get used to it, hon." Then she asked, "What can I get ya to drink?"

"A latte?" I asked. "Mocha?"

Shirley nodded and looked at Rory and Madison. "The usual, girls?"

They nodded, and she went off to get the coffee.

There was no room left at their table. The five men took up so much space they all looked squished. I glanced at the booth behind theirs, which was also filled with Elite, and debated what to do.

Lars slid out from his seat on the end and gestured for me. "You can sit here," he offered, his accent a little charming.

"Oh, no…" I started to protest, but he walked off to get a chair to pull up to the end where he sat down.

"Go ahead," he said, gesturing again.

"You aren't eating?" I worried, taking the seat he'd vacated for me.

"He can't," Wes said around a mouthful. He started to say something else, but the door jingled, and we all looked up.

A muscular guy with a scowl, black leather jacket, boots, and eyebrow ring came forward. He was accompanied by another guy who was just as muscular but seemed to be his polar opposite with chestnut hair, hazel eyes, and a dimple popping out beside his big smile.

The smiling one was carrying a white Styrofoam container and a paper cup with a black lid.

Because I was sitting right beside him, I heard the little sound Lars made in his throat, and I glanced over to see his eyes locked on the approaching pair.

"The bros are all here!" Jamie declared.

The smiley one what-upped the entire table with his chin before stepping up behind Lars's chair and reaching around to put the container on the table in front of him, flipping the lid. "Hi, angel," he said against his ear.

Lars tilted his head back so he could look up at the man who was caging him in with his hands resting on each side of him. "You brought me breakfast?"

"Coffee too," he said, setting down the paper cup beside the plate.

Ah, the nut allergy.

"*Min hund,*" Lars whispered, and his tone was so sweet I wondered what he'd said.

Dimples chuckled and cupped Lars's upturned chin, leaning in to press an upside-down kiss to his lips.

Clearly, this was Win.

And clearly, these two were adorable together.

"Who are you?" demanded a gruff voice beside me.

I nearly jolted from the shock of it compared to the syrupy-sweet scene in front of me.

"Max," Wes scolded from the other side of Prism and Kruger.

Max's dark gaze shifted to him immediately, and it was like watching a glacier melt. "Nemo, what are you doing all the way over there? Come over here and kiss me."

Kruger leaned into my ear. "The PDA around here is unbearable."

My lips twitched, and I glanced at him to whisper, "You seem jealous."

"Damn right, I am."

I laughed.

Shirley came back with a tray full of coffee and OJ. "Looks like the booth finally ran out of room," she mused. "There's an empty one there," she said, pointing to the one on the other side of the full one behind us.

"Give me a hand," Win said to Max, and the two picked up an empty table nearby and carried it over. Lars got up and pulled his chair back so the guys could butt the table up against the open end of our booth.

"That works too," Shirley said, handing me my coffee.

"Thank you," I told her, wrapping my hands around the warm cup.

"Nemo," Max intoned, impatience making him broodier than before.

He was hot. Clearly, I had a thing for assholes. And he called Wes Nemo? As in a little fish? *Swoon*.

Kruger and Prism slid out of the booth so Wes could get out, and the second he was, Max pulled him right up against his body and kissed him while shoving his ring-covered fingers into Wes's curls.

"Brothers really don't need to see that," Win complained.

Max ignored him.

Prism and Kruger slid back into the booth and motioned for me, so I did the same. We handed Wes's plates down, and he sat on the other side of me but in a chair pulled up to the added table with Max on his other side.

Lars and Win sat on the other side of the adjoining table beside Jamie and Madison.

"Landry, this is Max and Win," Wes introduced, then told the guys I was the new assistant coach.

"Bros, she's Resch's daughter," Kruger mused.

"Apologies," Max deadpanned.

I laughed.

The bell on the door jingled, but it was just an

afterthought because Shirley came back to take our orders, and everyone was talking over each other.

"You came!" Win called, and I looked over immediately, my heart leaping into my throat at record speed.

Jason—*no*. Rush was standing there at the end of the table with his dark brows drawn down over his equally dark stare. He looked pissed off to be here but was standing there nonetheless.

"Finally decided to hit up an Elite breakfast, huh?" Ryan mused, but he didn't exactly sound friendly.

Jason's eyes cracked to where Ryan sat deep in the booth. "Not sure I'm staying. Looking at you while I eat might give me indigestion."

In Ryan's lap, Rory gasped. "Shirley, you better get him double waffles and all the extras. I think he's hangry."

The waitress laughed under her breath. "You got it, hon." Then she turned to me. "What's your order?"

I was too busy watching to see how Jason would react to Rory. Clearly, he and Ryan had some kind of rivalry going on, and I wondered if it would extend to her out of association. Considering the way Ryan looked at his girlfriend, it seemed like something that would *not* go over well.

Jason scoffed, everything about his face softening. "Hi, shrimp. Thanks for ordering for me."

Surprise coursed through me. And when Rory's light giggle floated down the table, jealousy did too.

What is wrong with me? It wasn't like I wanted him to be a dick to her.

You want him to be sweet to just you.

"She has a name," Ryan rumbled, but Rory merely smiled and kissed his cheek.

"Pull up a chair, Rush," Lars invited, waving his hand.

"Miss." Shirley poked my shoulder.

Oh! I quickly ordered some scrambled eggs and toast, and she went off to put in the orders.

The second she was gone, I glanced across the table to Jason who'd sat down beside Win. I was having a hard time thinking of him as Rush. Rush was a stranger to me, but Jason was not. He basically looked like sex in sweatpants the way his body was sprawled back in the chair as though he didn't have a care in the world. But I knew better. I could feel the tension swirling around him. He might appear downright lickable and at ease, but really, he was on alert. On alert for what was yet to be determined.

Sensing my attention, he swung his eyes to meet mine, the action making my stomach somersault below my ribs. What was it about him that made me feel like I was being swallowed by a black hole? That when he was around, it was him and nothing else?

He was polarizing. An enigma. The notion to crawl under the table and up into his lap was so vivid I pushed against the seat back, preparing to slide down.

He shifted, swiveling just enough so his reclined body angled toward me instead of away. Almost as if my intrusive thought had been so vivid he saw it too. He silently widened his thighs in invitation.

Come cuddle in my lap, little siren. Surrender all your weight to me.

I bit down, teeth piercing my lip. The sting thankfully knocked me back to reality enough that I could get a grip.

My hand was unsteady when I lifted my mug, so I brought my other one up. My throat was tight when I swallowed, my pulse so uneven I could barely function, so I forced my eyes away from him.

It didn't help. His presence was just too intense.

"How did you know I was coming here for breakfast?"

Lars asked Win, thankfully giving me something else to focus on. His pale eyes narrowed. "Did you check the app?"

Win made a choked sound, and Max laughed under his breath. "Angel, I don't stare at that tracker every minute."

Lars whipped out an obviously snarky reply in Swedish, and Win laughed like it made his day, then said, "Rush texted me."

Lars leaned around his boyfriend to look at Rush. It was the perfect excuse for me to look back at him too.

"You texted Win?" Lars asked, surprise underlying his tone.

Rush's reply was gruff. "You gotta eat."

"I could have grabbed something after," Lars muttered.

"Well, now you don't have to."

Win smiled, slapping Rush on the shoulder. "Good looking out, bro."

Rush rolled his eyes, lifting his coffee to his lips. It was almost as if he were uncomfortable with the thanks. Our eyes connected over the rim of his mug, and for a single heartbeat, the moment hung suspended. *Oh, the effect he has.* But then he went and ruined it by smirking like he could read my thoughts.

Clearing my throat, I leaned toward Wes. "Tracker?"

Wes sighed insufferably. "These two," he said, pointing at Win and Max with his fork, "are annoyingly overprotective and have tracker apps on our phones so they always know where we are."

I felt my mouth drop. "For real?"

"I told him it was okay," Lars hurried to put in. "He asked before he installed it. He didn't make me."

It seemed very important that Lars made it clear Win hadn't done it without his consent, so I nodded encouragingly. "As long as you're okay with it."

Max grunted. "I don't care if he's okay with it or not. I only care about his safety."

"You should know," Kruger said, nudging my side and drawing my attention, "dry land ain't always that great for Elite."

"What do you mean?" I asked.

"I mean everyone around here got drama. Except me and P. We're unproblematic." Kruger smacked Prism in the arm. "Right, P?"

"Just call me nontoxic," he said, finishing off a waffle.

"Please, you're more drama than Maddie, and she's a theater major," Jamie told Kruger, who looked offended. "Probably why you can't ever get a date."

"Who says I can't get a date?" Kruger erupted.

"You," literally everyone at the table said at the same time.

I laughed, and Shirley appeared to deliver more plates of food. The second my eggs were in front of me, my stomach rumbled, so I grabbed my fork and dug in.

"I have standards is all," Kruger muttered, shoving a massive bite of eggs in his mouth and smacking his lips around them. "Hey, you single?"

Feeling the weight of several stares, I paused in chewing and glanced up. "Me?"

Kruger nodded. "Considering you're the only girl at this table not sitting in someone's lap, yeah."

Ryan paused, bacon midway to his lips. "Oh, someone finally up to your standards?"

Bang!

The extra table trembled, causing the silverware to rattle and the juice in the glasses to slosh, under the heavy weight of Rush's fist thumping down on the top. "How the hell do you assbags eat with all the mouth-running you do?"

Madison leaned in toward Jamie and whispered, "What's an assbag?"

Jamie snickered, and Rory giggled.

"It was just a question," Kruger muttered.

I said nothing, too captivated by his flashing, ireful onyx eyes.

I'm in a mood, little siren. Those deliciously ominous words from the night we shared echoed through my very bones. Like that mood of his didn't just leave an impression but imprinted on my very soul.

What was it about him that was so alluring? It went beyond his dark hair and opaque eyes. Beyond the permanent pout of his full lower lip. His hot-headed demeanor should have been off-putting, intimidating at the least.

But it wasn't. *He* wasn't.

Some girls would see him as a challenge. Someone they could try to tame. I had no such compunction. Some men were better left wild.

"It doesn't matter if she's single or not." Rush's voice was gruff and unfriendly. "Because she's too good for you."

I couldn't tell you anyone's reaction to that declaration.

I was too busy experiencing my own.

Ribbons of desire unfurled inside me, almost as though they'd been lying in wait. I set down my fork, no longer interested in food, as their velvety lengths expanded, teasing every exposed nerve as they slowly spiraled upward to tie themselves around my heart.

The heart that most definitely already bore his inscription. An inscription I hadn't even read because I had no idea it was there.

"Yeah?" Ryan's taunt seemed so distant to my ears. "So who's good enough, then? You?"

The ear-piercing screech of chair legs across the floor brought reality crashing back.

Rush towered over the table, a pinched look across his

stormy features. "I never said I wanted her," he spat and turned away.

The ribbon around my heart double-knotted itself as he stormed around the corner.

It doesn't matter. I'm already yours.

7

Rush

I DIDN'T REALIZE WHAT THE HELL I WAS DOING UNTIL A BELL jingled, snapping me out of whatever haze I was walking around in.

By then, it was too late.

Too late to turn and walk out, leaving the scent of frying bacon, waffles, and coffee in my wake.

This was her fault. My little siren.

Casting a spell, luring me to this godforsaken diner like I wanted to be here. Like I was welcome. I wasn't welcome anywhere. But I wouldn't tuck my tail and retreat. Welcome or not, I was still Elite.

And I refused to leave her here with all of them.

What did that get me? Me fuming in the bathroom, trying to curb the urge to pound Kruger's face into the pavement outside.

He can't have her.
Neither can you.

72

My laugh echoed around the empty room, the sound chilling even to my ears. I pushed my thoughts to a warm California sunset, the sound of waves crashing over the shore. I thought about the high of a righteous wave and the tang of saltwater clinging to my lips.

It didn't work. What once chilled me to the max now left me unsettled and angrier than before. I wasn't who I used to be. I wouldn't be again.

I was displaced, grappling with who I once was, and finding handfuls of what I was now.

I was nowhere near good enough. I wanted her so much it robbed me of air.

The bathroom door pushed open, and I spun, ready to tell whoever it was to get the hell out. Her lithe frame slipped through a slim opening and leaned against the door.

What the hell was she doing in here? Didn't she hear what I said? *I don't want you.*

"You told me you didn't go here," I spat, angry at everything.

Her voice was calm. "You told me the same."

"I transferred."

"So did I."

Her dad is your coach.

A frustrated sound ripped from my throat. "You are not allowed to date him. Any of them," I declared, jealousy eating me alive.

You know better than trying to tell a girl what to do. Think about last time.

"Okay."

My spiraling thoughts faltered, not expecting that reply. I expected a fight. A refusal. Hell, I didn't expect her at all.

Those things only enhanced my want, and I surged across the room, snatching her away from the door and into me. Our chests collided when I folded myself around her, holding so tight I could feel the erratic pounding of her heart through our clothes.

I claimed her lips, groaning on first contact and then again at her instant submission. My tongue plunged deeper into her wet heat until the volatile way I was feeling went blind, leaving only her.

I took like a greedy bastard, and she gave like she would never go empty. When I reached up to grab her face and hold it so she couldn't get away, she reached up and held my hands. I was the aggressor and she the victim, but I was the one brought to my knees.

My black mood turned dusky as we kissed, her lips a forgiving landing for every hard edge I possessed. What started out as demanding morphed into something softer, and I found myself nibbling on her lips, licking across their fullness like a starving man in need of food.

Her grip turned into a caress as her fingertips whispered over the backs of my hands, dragging to the inside of my wrists before pulling back to lay her palms against the sides of my neck.

I wondered if she could feel how my pulse hammered, just how hard she made my heart beat. The need for air disconnected our lips, but I stayed close, pressing my nose against her cheek as my uneven breaths puffed across her smooth skin. The rapid rise and fall of our chests were in tandem, and it made me feel like I wasn't alone anymore, that suddenly there was a connection.

The realization scared the shit out of me.

When a man hits rock bottom, fear becomes futile. He learns rather painfully that he can exist on nothing. She was challenging that, showing me perhaps where I thought there was nothing, something remained. *No.* Something could be found.

I started to push her away but instead tugged her closer.

Her legs wrapped around my waist when I lifted, my forearms sliding under her ass. Her lips were plump from kissing, coated with the sheen I'd left behind.

God, just looking at her made me crazy. Crazy with lust. With the urge to claim. "If you ever call me Rush again, I'll tell your dad I fucked his princess in his locker room."

Her green eyes turned to slits. "You wouldn't dare."

"Try me."

"He'd throw you off the team."

I shrugged. "I'd go back to California."

Her head tilted, a lock of blond hair sliding across her cheek. "Are you threatening me with your absence?"

My absence was hardly a threat. It was more of a reminder of what would be best. Still, I said, "Is it working?" *Of course it's not going to work.*

Her light scoff tightened my chest, and I palmed her waist to set her away. Her hands gripped my biceps, but it wasn't the hold that stilled my movements but rather her soft voice.

"Jason."

Nostrils flaring, I glared at her, wondering if I was imagining things.

She said it again.

My heart turned inside out. *She wants my presence.*

Growling, I dove at her, the force of my need pushing us against the door where I trapped her body with mine. Latching on to her lower lip, I sucked passionately, then did the same to the upper. Her little whimpers coupled with her hands gliding through my hair made my scalp tingle wickedly as the urge to get inside her roared through my veins.

A noise from out in the diner brought my head up, reminding me where I was and to fight against the drunk way she made me feel.

"What are we doing right now?" I said the words out loud, but I was speaking to myself.

"Kissing in the bathroom?" she mused, then giggled.

The sound pierced my heart, sending sparks of pain throughout my chest. Palming her waist, I pulled her off my body to stand her on her feet.

The top of her head barely rose to my shoulder. She was small. Smaller than I realized... *Because she takes up so much space inside you.*

My hands hovered at her hips until I was sure she was steady before backing off to move farther into the room.

"Jason?"

My eyes fell closed. It wasn't just a name but a possibility. A chance to be someone no one else knew, a person no one bothered looking for but she found.

"I'm no good for you." The words were like sandpaper against my throat, roughing me up on their way out.

"What?"

I kept my back turned, a coward's act, I knew. But I couldn't look at her and say this. I'd fold faster than a house of cards. She incited so much want in me that it overruled all rational thought.

"Go," I whispered. "Leave."

Her feet scuffled against the floor. I swallowed past the hard knot in my throat and listened for the door to open and close.

A light touch whispered across my side. My world went still. Forcing my eyes open, I glanced at where her hand brushed against my waist.

"Ja—"

I wrenched away before she could finish saying my name, before her touch could make me cave.

I had to be strong. I couldn't give in. I had to deny myself this thing I desperately wanted—not because it could destroy me but because it would destroy her.

Head bowed, I grabbed the sink, knuckles aching with the force I used to grip the white porcelain edge. Her taste still lingered on my tongue, and I washed it away with the ugly truth and a harsh tone.

"Get out of here, little siren. I break beautiful things."

8

LANDRY

TRANSFERRING TO A NEW COLLEGE A FEW WEEKS INTO THE spring semester could be the worst idea in the history of ideas.

Why is that, you ask? Let me pull out my list.

1. I lost all the credit hours I'd earned at the beginning of the semester at Oberlin.
2. My parents lost all the money they'd paid for the semester. Yes, my tuition here was free because of my dad, but it was still money down the drain.
3. I was behind on all my courses because I started late.
4. I had a shit ton of homework. Shit ton isn't an actual metric, you say? It is now.
5. My mom was pissed. We were barely speaking. This bothered me a lot less than it should have.
6. I moved in with my dad who was like the most bachelor-y

bachelor ever. Please, someone tell him a cardboard box is *not* a coffee table.

7. I was dealing with all that plus still recovering from a torn rotator cuff plus transitioning from competitive swimmer to assistant coach.

And finally,

8. Jason.

Care to guess which one of these things bothered me the most? Yep, it was the guy.

Polarizing, I tell you. He was absolutely polarizing.

First, he threw attitude at the diner, which I shouldn't even think was hot but totally did. Then I followed him into the men's bathroom, which probably broke a law somewhere, and he demanded—*like a caveman*—I was not allowed to date anyone. Cavemen must be my ultimate type because, bro, he kissed me so good that when he pulled away, I felt homesick.

Yeah, one breakfast with Jamie and "bro" was a permanent part of my vocabulary. I should add this to the list above.

Get out of here, little siren. I break beautiful things.

What did that even mean?

It meant a week of swim practice without him even looking at me. I tried too. Occasionally throwing a challenge at him at practice or telling him to swim an extra lap.

He did it all without complaint, silently taking the bossing without so much as an evil side-eye. I really wanted some evil side-eye.

It was utterly ridiculous. Every interaction I'd had with him up until this was such a far cry from the way he was behaving now. I was beginning to think I'd made the entire thing up.

I wanted something. Anything. Proof that I was under his skin like he was mine. All I got was polite indifference from a man I basically wanted to yell at me and make me submit.

This called for desperate measures. The desperate measures? I was a little short on ideas.

"Class dismissed," Professor Gladden announced from the front of the room, and people started grabbing their bags to escape.

"I thought this class would never end," the girl beside me muttered.

I laughed. "Longest hour ever."

I closed my laptop to stuff it into my bag along with my pen and notebook. Hefting it onto my shoulder, I stepped out of my row and headed up the steps toward the exit. Human Anatomy and Physiology was a big class because it supported several majors, so it was held in an auditorium-style room where the rows of seats rose from the front where the professor taught.

I sat in the middle, a compromise of not wanting to sit in the front but recognizing if I sat in the very back, the professor might think I wasn't taking the class seriously. I already stated in my lengthy list above that I was at a disadvantage from starting late, so every little bit helped.

It would also help if I could finish the paper everyone else had already turned in and complete a few labs I'd missed at the beginning of the semester. Oh, and keep current on all the assignments for this week while prepping for the upcoming three-hour lab.

Yeah, this class was a barrel of fun with its three-day-per-week lectures *plus* a three-hour once-weekly lab. I probably should have just not enrolled in this course and taken it later, but it was only offered in the spring, and I needed to take it so I could take A&P II in the fall.

Why did I choose to transfer colleges a few weeks into the new semester?

Because it was better than staying in Ohio.

With my mind completely preoccupied, my foot misjudged the step and missed. Flinging my arms out, I tried to catch myself but only managed to pitch backward, the weight of my bag not helping me stay upright.

I braced myself for the impact, already worrying about hitting my still-healing shoulder.

Arms caught me around the waist from behind and pushed, the person using their body to keep mine upright. Gasping, I looked over my shoulder as I stumbled a bit, trying to find both feet.

"Whoa," he cautioned. I caught a glimpse of platinum hair and pale eyes as he practically lifted me back onto the step.

"Lars." I gasped, reaching out to grab his forearm for balance. My voice was breathless, heart pounding as my body reacted to me almost busting my butt.

"You okay?" he asked, hands still at my waist like he was afraid if he let go, I'd roll away.

I mean, stranger things have happened.

"Yeah." I assured him, straightening and turning to face him. The strap of my bag slid over my shoulder and down my arm. The bag itself nearly smacked the stairs, but Lars caught it and deftly swung it up over his shoulder.

"You don't have to do that," I said, reaching for it.

"Don't you have a shoulder injury?" he asked, not giving up the bag.

"It's this one," I explained, pointing to the shoulder I was not using. It was also the reason I was using a shoulder bag and not a backpack like him.

He nodded, briefly glancing at the people we were holding up behind us. "Let's go."

"Sorry," I said to the girl who'd been dying to get out of here just moments before and then went up the rest of the stairs and out the double doors leading into the hallway.

A few doors down, another class was letting out, and the hallway was filling up fast as people milled about, some stopping to chat and others rushing away like they were late.

Lars fell into step beside me, and I glanced at him.

"Thanks for that," I said, a little sheepish. "I guess I wasn't paying attention."

He shrugged. "There's no cow on the ice."

I paused. "Um, what?"

He laughed. "It's a Swedish saying. It means no worries."

I laughed. "'Cause cows are heavy?"

"Finally, someone who gets it," he said, offering me a small smile.

"Well, at least I get something," I mused as we headed farther down the hall. "I didn't even realize you were in this class."

"I'm easy to miss."

Lars was the complete opposite of easy to miss with his white-blond hair, sharp jawline, and light-blue eyes. And he had an accent.

"Where do you sit?" I asked.

"In the front row."

I groaned. "At this point, I wouldn't even notice aliens beaming me up to Mars."

"Transferring schools is a lot. I'm sure it's even harder when the semester has already started."

I nodded. "It's been a little harder to catch up than I expected," I said. *It would be easier if you could stop thinking about Jason.*

Lars bobbed his head as we reached the stairs that led

down to the main floor and onto campus. Before I stepped down, he wrapped his palm around my elbow. I glanced down at where he held and then back up.

"You know, in case aliens try and beam you up."

"Was that a joke?" I teased. Lars was a little less ridiculous than the rest of Elite, quieter and a bit more serious.

To my surprise, his pale complexion turned pink.

"I can see why Jason likes you," I said, fondness overcoming my tone as he held on to me the whole way down the stairs.

His eyes flashed up. "Jason."

"Rush," I clarified.

He nodded. "No one else uses his first name."

"I saw it on the roster," I explained. It wasn't a lie.

Lars nodded and went ahead to push open the door leading outside. It had snowed a few days ago, and snow still covered everything but the sidewalks. All the trees lining the campus grounds were bare. The sun was bright in the sky, but the air was so cold it canceled out its warmth.

Curious, I asked, "Did he tell everyone to call him Rush?"

"Yeah."

But he told me to call him something else. Why?

"Coffee?" Lars asked, pointing down the sidewalk to a small cart with a dark-green awning overhead. After one week of Elite practices, I already knew coffee was basically his life's blood.

"Sure," I said. "I'll buy. A thank-you for keeping me from falling and taking down everyone behind me too."

"So, uh…" Lars began as we stepped up to the line. "I can help you catch up in class." He quickly added, "If you want."

"You would do that?" I asked, a little surprised.

He nodded. "But if you already—"

"I don't!" I said, quickly cutting off his shyness. "I would actually really appreciate that. It would help so much."

He smiled. "Okay. We can work together on the labs too if you want."

"You don't have a lab partner?"

He shook his head. "I don't. I usually prefer to work by myself."

"Oh, well, I don't want to impose."

"You're Elite," he said as if that explained it all.

I guess it kind of did.

"Plus, Rush likes you."

My stomach dropped. Such a casual statement, but it made my adrenaline spike. Despite the acrobatics my insides were suddenly partaking in, I tried to play it cool. "Well, considering he alternates between insults and the silent treatment, I might have to disagree."

Lars made a sound while waving away my words. "He's a little rough around the edges, but I can tell."

"How?"

"He's my friend."

The underlying pride in Lars's voice pinched my heart a little. And honestly, in any other situation, that answer would have meant nothing to me. But it seemed to mean so much to Lars. Like maybe he didn't give out his friendship so easily, and the fact he did with Jason spoke volumes.

In that moment, I was a little jealous.

"Here, put your number in," Lars said, holding out his phone.

I took it and typed my number and handed it back.

His fingers flew over the screen, and inside my bag, my phone dinged.

"Just text me whenever you want to meet up."

"Next," the barista behind the cart called, and we stepped up.

Lars ordered a double-shot espresso, and I ordered a latte.

"You're just going to drink it plain?" I asked when we had our orders in hand and were stepping away from the cart.

In response, he lifted the cup to his lips and took a sip. If I hadn't already seen him in a Speedo, I'd wonder if his chest was hairy.

The phone clutched in his hand started ringing, and he glanced down, his entire face brightening. "It's Win."

"Go. Answer it," I said, shooing him off.

He accepted the call, and before it was even fully up to his ear, I could hear Win's boisterous voice on the other end. Lars listened a minute and smiled. "*Min hund,*" he said, turning to go.

"Oh! My bag!" I called.

Lars turned back, his face sheepish. "Maybe the aliens would beam me up too," he said, tugging the strap off his shoulder.

I laughed.

"Aliens!" Win yelled through the phone. "They can't have you, angel! You're mine!"

Lars rolled his eyes. "He's an idiot."

Win gasped. "How dare you tell the aliens your boyfriend is an idiot!"

Still laughing, I motioned for the phone, and Lars held it out. "Hi, Win. It's Landry."

"Landry? Does Coach know you're an alien?" He made a sound. "Is Coach an alien too?"

"Bye, Win," I sang, taking my bag and hiking it over my shoulder.

"Thanks for the coffee," Lars said and then walked off, all his attention on Win and his phone.

Lifting the coffee to my lips, I started away, but a voice close by called out. "Hey."

I glanced back, not really expecting whoever it was to be

talking to me and surprised to see the girl who'd been sitting beside me in class coming toward me.

"I see you need some caffeine after that too," I said, gesturing toward the coffee she'd obviously just gotten from the cart.

"If I ever start snoring in class, please kick me," she mused. "It's so boring."

I laughed.

"So not to sound like a total stalker, but I was behind you in line, and I overheard that you're behind on some of the assignments."

I groaned. "I transferred in a few weeks late," I explained. "Some of the assignments were waived and the professor just told me to study the material for future exams, but other stuff, like the paper and some labs I missed, have to be made up."

"That really sucks."

I nodded. "I'm going this way. You?" I asked, motioning in the direction I was heading. I didn't mind talking, but it was cold, and I had another class.

"Yeah," she said and fell into step beside me. "I'm Brittney, by the way."

"Landry."

"The new assistant coach for Elite, right?"

I glanced at her from the corner of my eye, and she laughed, holding up her hands. "Again, not a stalker." She laughed. "Elite is a big deal here, so of course word got around that Coach's daughter transferred here."

It still surprised me how big of a deal Elite was at Westbrook. The swimmers were by far the most popular people on campus, so it made total sense that word about a new coach had gotten around.

"That's me," I said.

Her brown eyes sparkled, amusement shining in their depths. "What's it like being the only girl on Elite?"

I laughed. "It's like trying to corral a bunch of giant, dripping five-year-olds."

"But the Speedos, though," she mused, wagging her eyebrows.

I grinned. "Well, there is that," I allowed. "But the last thing I want to do is check them out when my dad's walking around."

Except for Jason. Not even my father's presence can keep my eyes away.

That was an understatement considering we'd continued having sex while my father was on the other side of the wall! You'd think my va-jay-jay would have shriveled up and gotten drier than the Sahara the second I realized it was my dad who'd walked into the locker room that night. Not only that, but he found the condom wrapper for the condom that was literally inside me *at that very moment.*

But did I shrivel up? No. Jason told me to be quiet and take his cock, and I got wetter.

"Landry?"

My attention snapped back to the girl looking at me like she'd said something and I was expected to reply. "Sorry," I said, sheepish. "I think I spaced out at the mention of my dad and Speedos in the same sentence," I told her, grimacing for effect.

She laughed. "Understandable."

I took a sip of my coffee, then pointed to a large building in the distance. "That's my building up ahead."

"Well, I just wanted to tell you if you ever need to borrow my notes from class or anything, I'd be happy to share them."

"That's really nice of you," I said.

"I mean, I know Lars offered, but it wouldn't hurt to have a backup."

I glanced at her. "You know Lars?"

She shook her head. "Just of him."

Elite. Right.

"I really appreciate the offer. If I need help, I'll let you know."

Brittney waved. "See you in class!"

I waved and headed to my next lecture, all the while wondering how to get the attention of a certain onyx-eyed swimmer.

9

Rush

You know all those lame jokes about swimmers not being able to run?

They suck. And they aren't true.

Well, maybe they are. But not for me. You know why? I'm a wildcard.

I'm not gonna let anyone think they know me. People think swimmers can't run? Surprise, bitches. Being good at one thing shouldn't negate being good at other stuff too. I wasn't some one-trick pony. I was a stallion.

That was why I dragged my ass out of bed early—actually, earlier than early—three days a week to go for a run before practice.

Four a.m. run, anyone? No?

That's why I'm the stallion and you're just a pony.

I'm kidding. Maybe.

This morning when my alarm went off, then went off again five minutes later, I had a serious case of *fuck my life* and considered skipping the run. Maybe being a pony wouldn't be so bad after all. It seems to work for you.

Look, it's just after four a.m., and I have to go for a run. Give a grumpy guy a break.

Truthfully, I hated getting up to go, but the running itself I didn't mind. It was good cardio and made my swimming game stronger. Plus, it was just one more way to shed excess energy and quiet the chaos in my head.

Even so, I was blurry-eyed and sorely tempted to crawl back under the covers when the frosty morning air hit me as I snagged a pair of joggers off the end of my bed. *A whole week.* I'd managed to keep myself away from Landry the entire week.

After my declaration in the bathroom at Shirley's, I didn't wait for her to leave. I left. If I had to stand there one more second, I would have had myself buried in her right then and there.

I couldn't. For so many reasons, the least of which was Coach. Though, I had no doubt if he found out about my filthy thoughts about his daughter, he'd probably make my life a living hell.

Joke was on him. I was already up to my ears in fire and brimstone.

That didn't mean she had to be.

So I stayed away despite the way she tested my patience. Another reason I was going to pound the pavement this morning.

After throwing on a compression shirt and zip-up hoodie, I tugged on a beanie and grabbed my room key. The hall was silent, everyone still asleep. Not even Elite was stirring yet.

I could have run in the evenings, but after one practice, sometimes two, plus classes and some weight training, I was usually too tired. Getting it out of the way early seemed like the best option. Plus, I liked the quiet on campus this early. It was still dark out, but the campus was well-lit, so there was enough light to see but still enough darkness to offer privacy.

It was a good time to think, to push my body as well as my mind.

I still couldn't remember more, though. Nothing new since that day in the pool a couple months ago. If only I could remember the rest of that night. *If only...*

Sweat dampened the shirt beneath my hoodie, the beanie on my head keeping it from dripping into my eyes. It was cold out, something that took a lot of getting used to when it came to running. I was accustomed to sand underfoot, not snow drifts piled along the salted and shoveled sidewalks.

Even though I hit my three-mile goal, I kept running, feeling like I still had excess energy to burn. I knew I shouldn't push myself too much farther. I had practice in less than an hour. If I was too exhausted, Coach would probably ride my ass.

I'd rather the assistant coach ride my dick.

I slowed my pace to a jog, letting my lungs relax, and used my sleeve to swipe a bead of sweat off my nose. Just as I was about to turn and head back to my room, I realized I was just across the parking lot from the pool.

I debated just heading over and hitting the showers there. I had extra Speedos and goggles in my locker, and I could just use those for practice. Before the rest of the team got there, I could stretch out my muscles.

A car turned into the lot, driving close to the entrance, and pulled into a parking spot under one of the big street-lamps. It was a silver four-door that was *not* a Corvette, so it didn't much interest me. Until I saw the blond head get out.

Even though I was a decent distance away, I knew who it was instantly. My body practically vibrated just looking at her. She was literally the only person I'd ever met who could turn me inside out like this. I watched her shut the driver's door, then reach into the back to grab her Elite duffle.

My feet started moving, carrying me closer without any input at all from my brain. It was as though I went on autopilot when I saw her, and the setting was to get as close as I could.

She stopped at the door, pausing to unlock it, and I dug my runners into the pavement, telling myself to turn around and go back to the dorm.

The last time I was alone with her at the pool... The thought had all the blood draining from my head to my dick so fast it made me dizzy.

Inside, the lights flicked on and spilled out onto the sidewalk.

Go home, Rush.

Go get your girl, Jason.

I fucking wanted her. Even with all the distance between us, she still tempted me like the Siren she was.

My feet shuffled. I'd take a step forward, then force myself back.

"Fuck," I muttered, completely disgusted with myself. This was ludicrous, letting a girl—a small one at that—make me so crazy.

I was going back to the dorm. I was done letting her have so much power over me. Bits of gravel scattered when I spun to head back the way I'd come.

Then a piercing scream ruptured the quiet dawn.

It ruptured any resolve I had to stay away.

And though I'd just run three miles, I took off in her direction as though I hadn't run at all.

10

LANDRY

YOU KNOW WHEN I SAID DESPERATE TIMES CALL FOR DESPERATE measures?

This was *not* what I meant.

11

Rush

"LANDRY!" I ROARED, WRENCHING OPEN THE HEAVY GLASS door. Urgent panic pumped my body so full of adrenaline that I was nearly shaking.

Her body bounced off mine when I barged into the building, the force with which I moved sending her flying back.

"Shit," I swore, lunging forward to grab her arm and keep her from busting her ass.

"Jason."

It was just my name. A fucking word. Why did it cut me to my very core every time it fucking slipped from her lips?

She made a sound, and my adrenaline spiked again.

Tightening my grip on her arm, I pulled her closer. "What's the matter? What happened?"

Her body collapsed, face burying into my chest. She was shaking violently, and her breathing was ragged. My arms locked like vises around her, a silent promise I wouldn't let anything hurt her.

Cradling the back of her head, I leaned closer. "Baby, was that you that screamed?"

Her cheek rubbed my chest with her nod, and she lifted her trembling hand to point at the pool behind her.

I looked up, my eyes going right to it. A dead body floating in the pool.

They were facedown, upper torso bobbing on the surface with their arms and legs hanging beneath them. The hair was long, floating out around the head like the water was trying to steal it. The fabric of their clothing was deep pink and dotted with flowers.

So familiar.

A violent visceral reaction exploded inside me. So fucking vicious that everything inside me shut down for a few heartbeats. The image was so overwhelming—*so sick*— my body and mind literally refused to function.

And then just as fast as it shut down, it all rushed back at once, a roaring tidal wave that brought with it a flash of nausea and drowned me in the past.

"Look at these photos!" a harsh voice demanded.

The sound of picture after picture slapping the table in front of me was like a succession of gunshots. Every one of the bullets hit its target. I didn't want to look, but I couldn't not see.

"Look at what you've done!"

"No!" The guttural refusal ripped so deeply out of me that it brought vomit up the back of my throat. Like a severe wildfire, it burned so much my eyes watered. Forcing it back down, I took Landry by the shoulders, coercing her away from my chest.

"Call an ambulance," I demanded, hastily shoving my cell into her hand and immediately diving into the pool.

The cold water should have been a shock to my sweaty, flushed skin, but I didn't feel it. Just as I didn't notice the way

95

my shoes and clothes soaked up water, their heavy weight attempting to suck me under.

The body bobbed against the waves I created, lifeless and at the water's mercy, and I squeezed my eyes shut against the horrible image.

Not again. Please, not fucking again.

"Brynne," I rasped, making it to the body and flipping it over onto her back.

Clumps of wet, matted hair clung to her face, obscuring her features. Lost in trauma, mind alternating between present and past, I wrapped an arm around her while trying to swipe it away.

Just open your eyes.

"Breathe," I pleaded. "Please fucking breathe." Eyes blurry, I pulled her up at the same time my mouth came down. The force of my breath was brutal as if I could give this girl my will to live.

Her chest expanded, and the air I forced past her lips made an odd echoing sound. I tightened my grip, ready to breathe into her again, noticing how light she felt in my arms. Something wasn't right, and it cracked enough of my panic to make me look down.

With a harsh sound, I recoiled from the face. Her mouth was a permanent black hole, the lips practically nonexistent. The entire head was one color, eyes closed. No lashes. No eyebrows. A straight nose with two nostrils.

I brushed at some of her hair again like that would somehow clear the creeptastic and disturbing sight, but it came off in my hands. Shuddering, I shook my hand, trying to get the tangled mats off, but the long strands fought back like clinging, poisonous vines. Cursing, I gave my arm another aggressive shake.

Plop.

The entire grotesque thing dropped into the water and started to sink.

A wig. It was a fucking wig.

Heart thrashing, I glanced back at the girl in my arms.

Not a girl.

A dummy. A fucking CPR dummy. It was so light because it was only a torso and head. No legs. The "arms" were just the sleeves of the dress it was wearing.

A dress that seemed eerily familiar.

"Rush! Come take a pic with me!" The clear voice decimated all my thoughts and robbed me of sight as another bout of memories stole my present.

I tossed the body away from me, staring at it like it might as well be real. The effect it had was.

"Jason?" Landry's distressed yet cautious voice echoed from the other side of the pool.

Fury stole over me, shoving out all the trauma and PTSD my old therapist liked to tell me I had.

Was this a joke?

Is this a fucking joke?

I twirled in the water, pinning her with a rageful glare. "You do this?"

My phone was still clutched in her hand, and the accusation made her eyes widen. "What?"

Water dripped off my nose and chin while demons from my past fed on my sanity. "You put a dummy in this pool as some sort of sick joke?"

"You think I did this?" The hurt in her voice made me weak. Confusion stole over her features. "It's a dummy?"

I said nothing, just stared, trying to will myself to not fall for her spell.

"Jason?" Her voice was adamant. "Tell me!"

"It's a dummy," I confirmed. "It's not real."

Relief flooded her face, and her body sagged under its weight. "Oh my God, I thought it was a real person." Her ass hit the pool deck, legs tucking up beneath her. She looked fucking small sitting there. Small, pale, and utterly wrung out. "Thank God," she whispered. Then, remembering the phone in her hand, she held it up to show me. "I called the police."

The instinct to praise her nearly bled off my tongue. I swallowed the metallic taste and kept in the words.

Spinning back around, I found the floating "body" again. *Sick.* It had floated closer, and the way it rocked in the waves drew attention to a long string around its neck. I pulled up the thin cord, seeing a note attached in a protective plastic sleeve. I yanked it out with wet fingers. The paper crinkled when I unfolded it to look down at the words scrawled in black marker.

I won't forget.

The dress. The hair. The pool. This *was* aimed at me.

Flashing lights burst through the windows, flickering against the water and drawing my attention.

"They're here," Landry said, rushing to the door to fling it open.

I shoved the note back into the plastic and then into the pocket of my hoodie. I avoided looking at the dummy when I towed it to the edge of the pool.

"What seems to be going on?" asked an officer who seemed vaguely familiar the second he and his partner stepped inside.

I tossed the dummy onto the pool deck, drawing their eyes. Then I turned back and went for the wig. It landed with a slap beside the body, and then I hauled myself out of the water.

My clothes were heavy, sticking to my skin like a leech. I didn't bother to brush the water out of my face or kick off my shoes.

"Someone put that in the pool to make us think there was a dead body," I spat.

The police came to look over the dummy, and I went to Landry, crowding into her personal space. I kept my voice quiet. "Your dad tell you about me?"

Her brows drew down, face creasing with confusion. "What?"

"Did he?" I pressed.

Behind us, the door opened, and the EMTs rushed inside.

"No. I—" Her stare went past me to the dummy and the cops. Clarity seemed to overtake her, and her green eyes snapped to mine. "You think I did this?"

I said nothing.

Her eyes narrowed, then met mine steadily. "I didn't."

She was shaking. Her lips were pale, and the tip of her nose was red. And though her eyes were steady and sparked with anger, there was shock too.

She didn't do this. If I was thinking clearly, I never would have considered it at all. I cursed beneath my breath and took a step forward.

"Excuse me, sir. A word," an officer said from behind.

"Just a minute," I snapped, not wanting them there.

Stalking to a nearby basket of towels, I grabbed one off the top. I shook it out as I went back to where she waited and wrapped it around her, tugging the ends tightly closed. "You need to sit down."

She snorted. "What do you care?"

I moved swiftly, picking her up and cradling her into my chest. She gasped, body going rigid and flinging out her arms.

"Put me down," she demanded.

"Pull the towel back around you," I said mildly.

"No."

I gave her a look, and she begrudgingly pulled it back

around her. "I'm only doing this because I'm cold," she smarted off even though her limbs still trembled and adrenaline rapidly drained out of her system, leaving her weak.

"Sir." The officer tried again.

"Would you give me a goddamn minute?" I barked.

The man looked like he'd sucked on an entire bag of lemons, but I didn't give a damn. Turning my back on him once more, I gave all my attention to the little siren in my arms.

The doors shuddered again, someone else barging in.

"What the hell is going on here?" Coach Resch bellowed. "Where's my daughter? Landry!"

She groaned, and I turned so he could see her in my arms.

A pinched, flushed look came over his features. "Rush, put her down."

I made a show of holding her tighter.

"What happened?" He took in her appearance.

"I found a body in the pool," Landry explained. A vein in his neck started to throb. "But it was just a dummy. I thought it was real, so I called the cops."

Resch went to where the dummy lay and stared down at the wig and dress. Then he glanced back up, his eyes accusatory. "Rush, what the fuck did you do?"

12

LANDRY

JASON TURNED HIS BACK ON EVERYONE IN THE ROOM AND carried me toward the bleachers. His clothes were so drenched the water was soaking through the towel around me and into my clothes.

"Put me down."

Surprisingly, he listened, setting me gently on the bench in the first row. Instead of walking away, he squatted so I was taller than him for once. His face was drawn, and there were shadows in his eyes. His accusation hung between us, but I couldn't find it anywhere inside me to be mad.

At least not when he was so gentle when he tucked the ends of the towel more firmly around me and swept a soft gaze over my face. "You and me, we're gonna talk."

I sniffed. "Accusations are not a conversation."

Just because I wasn't really mad didn't mean I'd let him get away with it. You give someone an inch, and they would try and take a mile.

"I'm sorry, little siren." His voice was whisper soft, the way he reached up to cup the side of my head even softer. "I didn't mean it. Please forgive me." The pads of his fingers lightly scratched against my scalp, making my eyes fall closed.

Tattooed on my eyelids was the way he'd looked before. The way he'd reacted when I pointed to the pool. He'd been out of his mind, and it hurt me worse than the dead body I thought I'd found.

Forcing my lashes up, I met his waiting midnight stare. "Forgiveness has to be earned."

The side of his lips tilted up, the half smile making my heart flip. As he stood, he leaned in, brushing his lips across mine, a mere feather-light caress that whispered of promise.

"Son, you better pray to Joseph, Mary, *and* Jesus that I was just hallucinating," my dad intoned somewhere nearby.

I never remembered him being so noisy.

"I know, baby," Jason answered as though my father hadn't even spoken at all. "I'll do whatever it takes."

A hand slapped onto his back, grabbing a fistful of his wet hoodie. "Did you not just hear what I said?" Dad asked, hauling him away from me.

"I didn't know you were religious, Coach," Rush told him. "I'm an atheist. Don't think those people you mentioned will be inclined to help me."

My dad's nostrils flared. "You're lucky the cops are here."

He scoffed. "Like cops have ever helped me anyway."

My dad released his clothes. "This isn't a coincidence, is it?" he said, staring toward the dummy.

"I can't say."

What does that mean?

Dad straightened, rising to his full height. He was tall, but not as tall as Jason. Tension radiated around him, making me queasy. But Jason remained unbothered, almost as if he were bored.

"I gave you a chance. One that no one else would."

The boredom slipped, and I caught a flash of hurt. But then Jason shrugged. "Money talks."

"This ain't about money, and you know it," Dad demanded, stabbing a finger into his chest. "And this is how you repay me? You dump your trash in my pool, involve my *daughter*."

"Dad," I called.

"Stay out of this Landry," he snapped.

Jason sucked in a breath, and I watched his shoulders hike closer to his ears as his hands dropped to his sides. He took a step closer to my father, inching into his personal space. "You wanna talk to me like that? I'm game. But don't you dare take this shit out on her."

"Weren't you just doing the same thing five minutes ago?" I wondered.

Dad drove his fingers into Jason's shoulder, shoving him hard enough that he took a step back. "My daughter is off-limits to you."

I jumped up with a gasp. The stupid oversized towel dropped because I didn't bring it with me, and it tangled in my legs. I pitched forward, arms flailing to try and catch my balance.

Jason was there, catching me under the arms and dragging me up against his body. I sagged into him for a minute as I tried to catch my breath.

"I told you to sit down," he said against my ear.

"Bro! What the hell is happening?" A loud voice from across the pool made everyone look up.

Jamie, Ryan, Wes, and Lars piled inside wearing similar shocked expressions.

"The one time you mouth breathers decide not to be late," Dad muttered.

Jason set me on my feet as the four guys came around the pool, Ryan making it to us first. "What happened?" he asked, glancing at me and then Jason.

"It's not your business," Jason told him, grabbing the towel from the floor to wrap it around me once again.

I rolled my eyes and gave a real reply. "Someone dumped a fake body in the pool for me to find when I opened up this morning."

All four guys spun to stare at the "body" and then turned back to me. Ryan was at my side in an instant, hands on my shoulders. "Are you okay?"

"Hands to yourself, Walsh." Jason glowered.

Ryan ignored him, and from the corner of my eye, I saw Jason bristle.

Deftly, I stepped back, reaching up to take Ryan's hand and give it a light squeeze before letting go. "I'm good."

"Are you okay?" said an accented voice that was becoming very familiar to me, and I looked over at Lars who was at Jason's side.

Jason glanced away from me. "I'm fine."

"You're soaking wet," Lars pointed out.

He made a gruff sound. "I went in for the body. I thought it was real."

Ryan drew back to look at Jason. "You went in for it?"

"Well, I wasn't just gonna stand there."

I flinched, the action drawing the attention of all eyes. I avoided them all, holding the towel a little tighter around me. *All I did was scream.* When I turned on the lights and saw the body floating, my brain literally shut down. When you see stuff like that in movies, you always say, "I would never do that!" but being in the situation is so different.

It was beyond horrifying, and I froze. The way the hair

created wet clumps in the water, how the body was face-down and completely lifeless…

It didn't matter I was a swimmer. That I was a coach. I knew CPR. I took lifeguard training.

Every single thing I was *trained* to do vacated my body in the form of a scream.

It was embarrassing. I was ashamed. I knew better. I *was* better. But I screamed and then hid in Jason's chest, unable to even look back. It was him that moved into action. Him that told me to call for help and him that dove into the water in all his clothes. I'd even watched him try and revive them with breath.

Fingers nudged the underside of my chin, lifting my face so I couldn't hide it. Jason's wide shoulders created a buffer from everyone standing right there. "You did good," he whispered, dark eyes imploring and sincere. "So good."

He knew. Somehow he knew I was standing there beating myself up over everything I didn't do.

I shook my head. "I didn't do anything."

"You screamed and alerted someone nearby that there was danger. Then you called for help."

I started to shake my head, but his thumb and forefinger caught my chin and pinched. "I have no doubt if I hadn't been here, you would have been in that water." He paused to swallow. "I'm proud of you."

His praise melted me. Turned me into putty right there behind the shield he created.

The fingers holding my chin released, and he stepped back to let the rest of the world back in.

"Landry," my dad called, breaking away from an officer. "They have questions."

I glanced at Jason, and he nodded. "Tell them everything."

I went, noting the way Dad glared over my shoulder. "Dad," I hissed.

"You stay away from him, Landry. He's no good for you."

Everyone kept saying that, but their words were nothing compared to the way Jason made me feel.

Choosing not to reply, I stepped around my father to get the questioning over with.

He caught the towel, towing me partly around. "I mean it."

"Or what?" I challenged, my temper starting to rise.

"Or I'll send you back to Ohio."

I flinched as if he'd slapped me, my body going rigid beneath the towel. "You wouldn't."

"Try me."

I felt my eyes well with tears but refused to let them fall, furiously blinking them away. He didn't understand how cruel of a threat that was. How could he? I never told him the whole truth.

Jason appeared, sliding his arm around me, and I relaxed immediately. "C'mon. The cops are waiting," he said, turning us away. The second we were out of earshot, he wanted to know, "What did he say to you?"

"Nothing," I answered, still upset my father would go so far.

"I need to know."

Whatever I heard in his tone brought my head up. My breath caught at the way he was looking at me with a blend of desperation and fear.

He thought Dad told me something about him. He thought whatever it was would make me hate him.

"He threatened to send me back to Ohio," I said nakedly, wanting to wipe that look from his eyes.

His stare narrowed. "Because of me?"

I nodded. No point in lying.

"And you don't want to go?" he surmised.

My throat constricted. "No."

Cupping the back of my head, he brushed a kiss over my forehead. Before pulling away, he spoke with his lips whispering across my skin with every word. "I won't let that happen, little siren. If anyone leaves, I'll make sure it's me."

He turned and went to be questioned so fast I didn't have time to tell him.

If you leave, I won't want to be here either.

13

THE PAST WAS ON A LOOP INSIDE MY HEAD.

The only time it paused was when I looked at her, and so I did, unabashedly. Borderline obsessively. It took literally every scrap of resolve inside me not to pull her into my arms and cart her out of there to a place where we could be alone.

But then I would answer another question, and I would remember exactly why I shouldn't. Exactly why Coach wanted me far away from his princess.

Earlier, I'd watched him say something and then watched her react. I thought for sure he'd told her. He should have. Maybe then all the hope trying to decimate my insides would wither up and die.

No one ever looked at me like she did. Like I hung the moon and stars. Like I had the answer to every question she could ever ask.

I was fooling myself that first night in the locker room, the night I thought of her as merely a distraction. She wasn't.

She was so much more. Her submission did me in. How eager she was to let me bend her to my will. Those green eyes shone with trust and not a single ounce of fear.

I was accustomed to opposition. Battle. Suspicion.

Sometimes when she looked at me, I pretended she saw beneath it all. Past the man everyone else saw to the one I tried to hide. I pretended I was enough for her.

How much was it going to hurt when she learned the truth and I watched that expression shift and become like all the others?

"Caramel latte." A voice butted into my thoughts, into the questioning I was being subjected to at barely six in the morning.

I glanced at the paper cup held in front of my face and then to the person extending it.

"Lars, what is this?" I asked.

"It's a caramel latte. It's the trauma special of Elite."

I groaned. "That's a real thing?"

"You know it is. They brought me one in the hospital."

"I don't need a damn trauma latte," I grumped. I didn't want to think about what happened to him.

Something else I handled wrong. I was such a fuck-up. I was shocked he even wanted to be my friend.

"Aren't you cold?" he asked. "Your clothes are soaked."

I grunted and glanced down at myself. I'd forgotten about the clothes. They were kinda uncomfortable. I took the latte, the warmth of the cup also letting me know my fingers were icy.

"Thanks, bro." I lifted the hot drink to my lips but paused before taking a sip. "Does Landry have one?"

Lars nodded and pointed to where she was standing with Wes, Ryan, and Jamie. "Wes and I went and got them."

Feeling my attention, she glanced at me. I lifted the cup, and she smiled, lifting hers too.

Look at us. Trauma twins.

Don't laugh. That ain't funny.

"I have more questions." The officer interrupted.

Is he still here?

"How many more times can I repeat myself?" I asked. It was borderline ridiculous.

The man snapped his notebook shut and left. I didn't watch him go. Good riddance.

"What happened?" Lars asked when he was gone.

If it had been anyone else, I'd have told them to get bent. But it was Lars, so I told him, the words practically memorized because I'd informed the cops so many times.

When I was done, Lars frowned. "Are you sure you're okay?"

"Never better," I muttered, drinking more of the latte. Trauma coffee was pretty good.

Feeling Lars's quiet stare, I sighed and lowered the cup from my lips. "It was a shock, you know?"

"Practice is canceled!" Coach bellowed suddenly, following it up with a serenade on his whistle.

We turned to see a group of Elite standing in the door, gaping.

"Pass the word!" Coach yelled again. "Night practice instead."

Groans rose to the rafters.

"You want us to practice tonight, then get up and practice again in the a.m.?" Jamie complained.

"You want some cheese with that wine, Owens?"

"Cheese sounds kinda nice."

Lars snickered, and I hid my smile behind the coffee.

"So we done here?" Ryan asked.

Coach gave him a baleful look. "This doesn't even include you, Walsh."

Ryan said nothing, just crossed his arms over his chest and waited.

"Go," Coach told everyone. "Don't be late tonight, or you're all swimming ten extra laps."

I started toward Landry, and Lars fell into step beside me. When we approached, everyone shifted, making room for us, and an odd sort of comradery befell me.

They're here for Landry. And because they're nosy bastards.

"Carb-loading mode activated," Jamie announced. "Wes, bro, call up Kruger and Prism and tell them to meet us at Shirley's."

Everyone started off, but Landry remained rooted in place, her eyes lingering on me.

I glanced at Lars. "I'm not gonna make breakfast, bro. I have something to do."

His blond head nodded. "If you need anything, just text."

"Thanks."

When he was gone, I stepped so close to Landry she had to tilt her head back to look at me. "How about that conversation?" I said.

She nodded, and I reached out to palm the small of her back.

"Rush."

I looked up at the sound of Coach's voice.

He was coming over to us with Barney and Fife in tow. "It seems you left out a few things when you were talking to the police," he said, a knowing glint in his eyes.

"What things?" Landry asked from my side.

"Things you should have disclosed," said the officer I'd been speaking with earlier. Then, as if he were part of some sort of movie and in the running for a Golden Globe, he put his hands on his belt and leveled a stare on me. "We're gonna have to ask you to come with us."

My stomach knotted. I glanced at Coach, the familiar

burn of betrayal in my gut. "I hoped you were different," I said, quiet.

His expression flickered but then went back to the same ol' status quo. "That's my daughter."

I nodded.

"Come where?" Landry asked, looking between everyone.

"Nothing to worry about, ma'am. You're free to go," the officer replied.

"I'm not worried about me," she snapped. "I'm asking about Jason."

Oh, that pierced. Actually, it ran through me like a newly sharpened sword. When was the last time anyone worried about me?

"He's just gonna come on down to the station with us. Answer a few more questions."

She gasped. "You're arresting him!" This little siren stepped in front of me and spread her arms as if she could create a wall to protect me.

I bled out. Everything I was drained away and became hers.

It didn't matter if, once she knew, that look left her eyes. It didn't matter if she turned her back like everyone else.

I loved her.

I'd love her still.

"Now, he's not being arrested. We just want to talk." The officer placated her.

"You already talked." Landry demanded, "We're done."

We. More than just me. *We.*

My body swayed toward hers, my fingers grasping at her hips to palm them and draw her back against me.

Coach made a sound of protest, but I ignored him. How could anything else matter with her here?

My nose buried itself in the hair at the side of her head.

The soft strands tickled my cheekbones when I inhaled. Her scent was cherry vanilla. I was addicted.

"This is impeding an investigation—"

My head snapped up, and the officer's words died on his lips.

"Don't talk to her," I growled. "Don't even fucking breathe in her direction."

The man reached for the handcuffs on the belt he loved to stand there and caress.

Landry gasped, threw her arms out to the sides again, and plastered her back against my front. I smiled into her hair.

She was fucking adorable, and I loved her so hard.

"I'm gonna go talk to these idiots, baby," I whispered against her ear.

She spun, wide green eyes finding mine. I had never once associated the color with life, but now it was all I could think of.

She started to say something, but I caught her face between my palms. "I'll find you later."

She shook her head.

I leaned in, not giving a rat's ass that everyone was staring. Let them. I had to soak this in—*her in*—because the minute I walked out of here, Coach was going to take it all away.

I kissed her cheek, letting my lips linger long enough that Coach started to snarl. Pulling back, I laid them right against her ear, speaking low so no one else would hear.

"Be a good girl and let me go."

Her lower lip quivered. I thought about sucking it into my mouth. I sure as hell wanted to. My hands fell away when she stepped to the side.

Turning to the officers, she threatened, "If he's not back in an hour, I'm coming to the station."

As far as threats went, it was kinda weak, but my chest

swelled, the intensity of how much she made me feel threatening to take me down.

"Well," I said to the officers, "let's get this over with."

I followed them outside and let them put me in the back of a squad car. The whole time, all I could think about was how I was leaving Landry with her father, the man who knew the truth about me. And that in an hour, there would no longer be a *we*. I'd be back to being just me.

14

"My office. Now," Dad ordered as I watched the squad car drive away with Jason in the back. They were treating him like he was a criminal. Like he was the one at fault here.

What was worse? Jason was barely fazed by it, acting like it wasn't anything new.

I glanced at the dummy still lying beside the pool and frowned. The cops mentioned that maybe it had just somehow fallen into the water. But even if that were possible —which I thought was a bunch of crap—why would it be dressed in a wig and clothes? Didn't that seem a little suspicious? Or *a lot* suspicious?

"Landry!"

Groaning, I turned to where Dad stood darkening the locker room door with his impatience and glower.

"I'm coming." I relented, accepting my fate and resolving to just get this over with. I knew he told Elite I was off-limits, and yeah, I guess he meant it, but I really didn't think he'd be this incensed about me dating one of his swimmers.

You aren't dating. The thought was almost as shocking as it was true. It seemed laughable and even borderline unimportant. We weren't dating. Hell, we barely spoke.

It didn't matter. It didn't even matter my father seemed to think Jason was trouble and the cops had just hauled him out of there. There was something about Jason I couldn't deny. Something about him that made me want to submit to him from the moment we'd met.

It went beyond dating. It went deeper than superficial knowledge I didn't even have. Those things were details. Details my heart didn't seem to want or need.

I couldn't exactly say that to my father, though. He'd burst a vein. And I wasn't even sure I could explain the way Jason made me feel.

"What the hell was that?" he demanded the second I stepped into his office.

I didn't bother closing the door because no one else was there.

"What?" I was calm even though he was practically frothing at the mouth.

Folding my arms over my chest, I noticed the lack of warmth in my body. My clothes were damp from being held by Jason, but even cold, I didn't want to change. It was as though even though he'd left, part of him was still there with me.

"You know what," he said, and I could practically hear his teeth grind.

"I found what I thought was a body in the po—"

He made an aggressive slashing motion in the air, and a frustrated sound vibrated his chest. "That's not what I'm talking about, and you know it."

I dropped my arms at my sides. "I like him," I said, not mincing words.

"You like him," Dad parroted and then rubbed a hand over the trimmed stubble shadowing his jaw. "You barely even talk to him."

"I've seen him a few times outside of practice." I hedged. Sometimes I wondered if Dad knew life existed outside of this pool. Coaching was his entire life. His veins were probably filled with chlorine.

He was a thirty-nine-year-old bachelor who lived in a townhouse he'd barely furnished because he spent the majority of his time here. In my entire twenty-year life, he never dated anyone that I knew about. The only person he'd ever made room for, along with swimming, was me, something that went over so well with my mother. *Not.*

It wasn't like he didn't have the opportunity either because I knew he did. All my life, people told me how "hot" my dad was with his short dark hair, hazel eyes, and scruffy jaw. Even though he switched from competitive swimmer to coach a long time ago, he still had the body, toned but not too bulky, standing just under six feet with long limbs and broad shoulders.

"It stops now," he declared as though he were laying down the law. Like he could demand my heart stop beating.

I felt my temper spike. "I'm twenty years old, Dad, not twelve. You can't tell me who I can and cannot date."

"The hell I can't!"

I made a frustrated sound and threw up my hands. "You act like I picked up some drug dealer on the wrong side of town. Jason is one of your swimmers! Swimmers that you personally interview before letting them on the team. He's Elite, for crying out loud. He goes to Westbrook, Dad. One of the most prestigious colleges in this country."

He made a gruff sound, his voice lowering now that mine was raised. "He's different."

"Different?" I scoffed. "Why, because he came here from Pembrook, one of the other most prestigious colleges in this country?"

Dad's attention zeroed in, his stare scrutinizing my face. "What do you know about him coming from Pembrook?"

I know I still wear the Pembrook hoodie he gave me that night. I know I wish it still smelled like him.

I shrugged one shoulder. "Just that he transferred from there."

I probably wouldn't even know that if it weren't for the hoodie I'd sneezed all over and then stole.

Dad seemed to relax, and I remembered I had questions too. "Why?"

"Why what?" he asked, gruff, his gaze averted.

Suspicion rolled over me, clouding all my other feelings. "Why do you say he's different? Why are you really so against me dating him?"

Yeah, yeah, not technically dating, but I had to speak in words my dad would understand.

He bristled at the D-word, and I held up my hand. "Why, Dad?"

"Just stay away from him is all."

"No."

His head snapped up, nostrils flared, and an incredulous look filled his eyes. "What did you just say to me, young lady?"

Ooh, he brought out the young lady.

"If you want me to stay away from him, then give me a reason. A good one."

He sighed like he was tired and yanked the chair from beneath his desk. The wheels squeaked. Then the chair itself groaned when he threw himself into it.

"Can't you just take my word for it?" he asked, rubbing a hand over his face.

If it was anything else, any*one* else, then probably. But it wasn't. "So you can rat him out to the cops but refuse to tell your own daughter?"

"I didn't rat him out," Dad growled, thumping his hand on the desk.

Oh. *He feels guilty.*

"I have an obligation to do what's best for this team. I can't just put one man above the rest of Elite."

I perched on the edge of a chair on the other side of his desk, sitting as close as I could. "I understand that, Dad. You're a good coach."

He made a sound but said nothing else.

"You're a good dad too."

That brought his head up. He stared across the desk to where I sat, and I offered him a small smile. "You've always been there for me. Even when Mom made it hard."

The whites around his hazel orbs widened in surprise.

I laughed beneath my breath. "I told you I'm twenty, not twelve. Though, even at twelve, I knew. I mean, she packed me up and moved to Ohio, making it that much harder for you."

"She had a good job offer," he said, the words weak.

"You don't have to do that," I told him. "You don't have to defend her to me."

He looked like he'd swallowed a basket of bees, yet he plowed on anyway. "Your mom and me—"

"We can talk about that later." I interrupted. "This isn't about that. It's about Jason. And me."

"There is no you and Jason!" he rumbled.

"There is," I rebuffed gently. "I don't want to defy you, Dad. But there is."

"He killed a girl."

I sucked in a breath. "What?"

"Back in California. That's why he had to come all the way here. He can't show his face there anymore."

Denial, swift and pungent, slammed into me. Jason was a lot of things. Aggressive, dominating, gruff, and yeah, even a dick.

But a murderer? No way in hell.

A vision of the police putting him in the back of the cop car flashed behind my eyelids. *Is he really a criminal?*

Denial overpowered those nasty thoughts. "If that were true, he'd be in jail right now. Not at Westbrook."

"There wasn't enough proof. It was all circumstantial." Dad went on, his words like a punch to my stomach. "His parents hired some bigshot, undefeated defense lawyer, and he was never convicted."

I reached toward my throat, horror making it tight. "There was a trial?"

"No. There wasn't enough evidence for it. He walked."

"Thank God," I whispered, mind reeling from this revelation.

"What?"

I waved my hand in the air, almost an afterthought. "A trial would have been so hard for him."

"I tell you he was suspected of murder, and you worry a trial would hurt his feelings!" Dad stood so forcefully his chair slid back and slammed into the wall. "Stop thinking with your hormones, Landry!"

I jumped to my feet too, to meet his hot stare across the desk. "I'm not thinking with my hormones!" I yelled and then pressed a hand to my aching chest. "I'm feeling with my heart!"

"Fucking women," he muttered under his breath.

But I heard, and I gasped, slapping the hand just holding my heart onto his desk. The force of the slap made my skin prickle and sting, but I ignored it just as I ignored the tears tingling my eyes. "This has nothing to do with me being a girl. If you'd ever been in love, you would know that."

He sucked in a sharp breath, and too late, I realized what I'd said. My mind reeled. Silence reigned. I didn't backpedal, though I sorely wanted to. My God, how could I just blurt out something like that? Something I hadn't even thought about.

It didn't matter. Suddenly, that just became a detail too. Like love wasn't even the biggest thing between us.

If not love, then what? my heart whispered.

I don't know, I whispered back.

The vein in his neck was throbbing. "I tell you he's a murderer, and you tell me you're in love?"

"He's not a murderer!" I argued. "You just told me they didn't have enough proof."

"The evidence is pretty damning."

I dropped into the chair, my chest heaving, my breathing coming in quick gasps. "Then why did you let him come here?"

Something Jason said to him earlier echoed through my mind. *I hoped you were different.*

My heart ached for him. My body burned to find him, to tell him I was on his side.

"Honestly," Dad said, finding his chair and pulling it under him once more. "When I met with him, I didn't believe it either." He got this faraway look in his eyes as if remembering the interview he had with Jason. The interview he was probably in town for over winter break when I met him.

Suddenly, his dark mood and the listless way he floated at the bottom of the pool made so much more sense.

I'm trying to remember. Hadn't he said something like that the night we met? He'd been so mad at me for making it hard for him to think.

"I thought he deserved a second chance." Dad pulled me out of my own turbulent thoughts, reminding me we were having a conversation.

"But you don't believe that now?" I questioned.

"I believe that the safety of my daughter and the other swimmers on this team comes first."

"That's such a cop-out!" I shouted, springing to my feet once more.

"There was a body in my pool!"

"It was a dummy."

"The girl he was accused of murdering? She was found in a pool too."

Air whooshed out of me, and I swayed a little on my feet. I turned my back on him, trying to digest that without his stare.

Dad's heavy sigh permeated the room, as did the curse he muttered right after. "Stay away from him, Landry. Where he goes, trouble seems to follow."

"I break beautiful things."

A hollow sound ripped from my throat as Jason's words echoed in my head. *This is what he meant.*

I spun back to Dad, desperation tainting my tongue with a bitter flavor. "Did you give the camera footage to the police?"

He made a face. "Like I'd give them shit without looking at it first," he grumbled. "This is my pool."

"Pull it up," I demanded, rushing around his desk to look at his computer monitor.

"Excuse me?"

I made an impatient sound. "Just pull it up!"

He debated, and impatience overruled manners. My fingers flew over his keyboard, lighting up the screen.

"What's your password?" I asked.

"I'm not telling you—"

"Dad!" I snapped.

"Your birthday."

My heart tumbled a little at that, but I didn't acknowledge it because I was still mad at him. Once I was into the menu, I glanced over my shoulder. "Now what?"

"Move," he said, gently nudging me aside.

In just a few seconds, he had the footage from the cameras he'd installed out in the pool area pulled up.

"Do you have cameras in the locker room too?" I asked, suddenly becoming nervous.

My God, what if he saw?

"What do you think I am, a pervert?"

"There!" I said, pointing at the screen when a dark figure came on.

Dad stopped the footage and backed up before hitting play again. Together, we watched as a figure dressed in baggy, head-to-toe black came inside.

"Must have picked the lock," Dad said, keeping his eyes on the screen.

The person carried a huge duffle, and as soon as they were by the pool, they dropped it at their feet and quickly unzipped it. They pulled the dummy out of the bag, the pink flowered dress waving around as they did something to fasten the wig on its head.

I shuddered a little, recalling how it had looked floating in the pool. How real.

Just before tossing it into the water, the person pulled out what looked like some sort of lanyard and wrapped it around the dummy's neck.

"I didn't see that earlier," Dad said. "Did you?"

I shook my head.

The dummy hit the water with a splash, and then the person leaned out over the side to give it a big shove, sending it coasting out toward the center of the water.

Without waiting around to make sure it went, the person scrambled up, grabbed the empty bag, and rushed out. The entire thing took less than five minutes.

Dad backed it up, and we watched again.

"Who is that?" I asked, leaning in and squinting like it would help me identify the completely concealed figure.

"I can't even tell if it's a girl or boy," Dad answered.

Forgetting the screen, I straightened and pinned him with a look. "That's not Jason." I knew it. My body would know him anywhere. Even on grainy film.

Dad eyed me. "Pretty sure we both just said we couldn't see who it was."

Spinning back to the computer, I hit a few buttons, finding the time when I walked in and found the body.

"Watch," I said, straightening again.

"Landry." Dad's voice was strained as he watched me notice the body. Watched my body jerk, my hand fly to my mouth, and then me let loose a scream.

I watched in shame as I stood there terrified, unable to move as I stared before finally snapping out of it. The first thing I did?

Flee.

I didn't go far because Jason appeared, ripping the door open and charging inside. My stomach fluttered a bit just seeing him, the center of my chest giving a little tug. We watched him grab me, pull me into his body. I watched his hand cup the back of my head and his lips move.

I wished the recording had sound just then. I wanted to relive the sound of his voice.

With my face buried in his chest, I pointed, and he looked.

His reaction hit me all over again. I'd felt it the first time, and this time I saw it. Both were equally upsetting.

His entire face went slack, and then horror transformed

his features. Panic turned him wild, his eyes doubling in size. A knot formed in my throat, making it impossible to swallow, making my saliva back up and pool in my throat, threatening to drown me.

Reaching out, I hit the key, freezing the screen as Jason shoved his phone into my hand.

"The first thing he said to me was to call for help. For an ambulance," I told Dad.

Dad glanced from the screen up to me.

"He jumped in the pool in all his clothes. He swam to the body and tried to revive it. He was so worried about saving them that he didn't even notice the person wasn't even real."

He called her name. I realized. *He called the name of the girl that drowned.*

And then he accused me of torturing him for a joke.

Any lingering anger I felt at that wild accusation died right there. The urge to go to him was unreal. So strong I hurt with it. My stomach cramped when I thought about everything he must have felt in that moment. What he must have relived.

"Ladybug." Dad's voice was gentle as he said the nickname he'd called me since I was a little girl.

"No," I said, not wanting to hear any excuse or reason he could come up with. It didn't matter.

"His first reaction was to help. Concern. A killer wouldn't do that. A killer wouldn't care."

I started away. I couldn't stay here another second. I couldn't let him sit at the police station alone.

"I meant what I said," Dad intoned behind me.

I stopped and turned.

"He's off-limits to you."

Defiance burned like coal in the deepest part of my gut. It made me hot all over, flushed and ready to fight. Narrowing my gaze, I regarded him through slitted eyes.

"I respect you, Dad. I love you. But this? I won't do it. I won't stay away from him," I asserted.

His jaw worked. I saw the war in his face. The regret.

I held my ground.

"Then you leave me no choice."

I half smiled, sinister and practically a dare. "Mom's husband hit on me. Tried to touch me. When I told her, she accused me of lying. She took his side."

I was pretty sure fireworks came out of his ears. The incredulous expression on his face was almost comical. But then it gave way to fierce anger. Anger so potent I actually took a step back.

"I'm not lying," I said, some of my defiance wavering.

He made a rough sound. "Why didn't you tell me?"

"Because I was afraid you wouldn't believe me either," I admitted.

His body jerked as though I'd slapped him, but I kept right on going.

"And it was enough that you let me come here. Enough that you helped me get away."

He made a sound and started around his desk.

I skittered back and held up my hand. I didn't want this right now. Right now, I wanted one man and one alone.

"So you can try and send me back there, but I'm telling you right now that I won't go. And if you won't accept my choices"—*Jason*—"I'll leave your house too. Twenty is plenty old to take care of myself."

I turned and fled his office, my footsteps echoing across the tile.

"Landry!" he roared, but I didn't stop.

I made a choice. A choice fueled by anger, defiance, and half the information I probably needed.

But my heart had all the information it needed.

15

RUSH

I WAS IN A MOOD.

As if being drop-kicked back into the worst fucking time of my life wasn't enough, I got to relive it for the one-millionth time at the Westbrook police station while my air-drying clothes got stiffer and more uncomfortable with every passing second.

And the entire time I was living on replay, a dark voice in the back of my head taunted me about what Coach was probably saying right that moment to Landry.

I told myself it didn't matter. That it *couldn't* matter.

That only blackened my mood further.

I missed my morning swim *and* breakfast. Frankly, if Lars hadn't given me that stupid trauma latte, I'd probably be locked in a jail cell right about now.

As it was, I figured I had about ten-ish more minutes before I detonated like a grenade.

The officer on the other side of the table stiffened when I

suddenly sat forward, eyeing me as though I were indeed what the file in front of him claimed I was.

A killer.

It didn't matter what else those papers said because once that accusation was made, there was no coming back.

The way my clothes partially stuck and squeaked against this un-fucking-comfortable chair irritated what little bit of decorum I clung to.

"You didn't give me a phone call," I said.

"You aren't under arrest."

"But I am being questioned."

"You agreed—"

"I changed my mind. I want a phone call. I want my lawyer." I rattled off the name of the well-known, hella-exclusive attorney my parents paid for last year. "You know him?"

"I'm well aware of Gordon Sabatino."

"Then I'm sure you are also aware that this right here is borderline harassment."

The officer's face flushed, and his dark eyes darted to a "mirror" I knew other people were standing behind, listening to everything I said. This wasn't my first rodeo, but right now, I was done.

"We are just try—"

My hand slashed through the air, cutting off his lame-ass excuses. "I found a body in the pool." Yeah, I know Landry found it, but I would rather eat toenail clippings off a rotten corpse than bring that little siren into this fucking mess. "I called the cops. Then I dove into the water to try and help what I thought was a person. I cooperated with you. I've repeated myself a thousand fucking times."

The officer tried to speak again, but I cut him off with a frigid look.

"Then I let you put me into the back of your law mobile

like I was the one who did something wrong. I've been sitting here for an hour. In soaking wet clothes. In the winter. You have my file. You know what it says. You wanna ask me anything else, you can get my damn lawyer."

The door to the room opened, and a man in a suit and tie came in. "Thank you for your time today, Mr. Rush."

The chair screeched across the floor with the force of me standing. I didn't even let him finish trying to placate me. Instead, I walked right past him, letting my damp, smelly shirt brush against his jacket.

I didn't stop when he called my name.

I kept right on down the hall when I heard him behind me.

"We'll be in touch," he called.

If he knew what was good for him, he'd forget my name.

I stalked out of the back and through the main room where the uniforms stood around and ate donuts while pretending to work. People sitting at their desks stared. I ignored them too, walking straight toward the doors, and shoved them open with both hands.

Cold wind slapped me in the face when I strode outside, and I spared a moment to wonder what happened to the beanie I'd been wearing before. But any and all thought vacated my brain when my foot hit the blacktop of the parking lot.

She was leaning against the fender of her silver four-door. The bright sun making her hair shine like spun gold. Sensing me, she straightened and turned. The second our stares linked across the parking lot, the grenade inside me blew.

I strode forward as the air electrified around us and a horn blasted somewhere nearby. I kept going, ignoring it all, fucking daring it to get in my way.

I bulldozed into her without slowing down, locking my

arm around her waist and claiming her mouth in one possessive move. I kissed ferociously, bending her backward over
my arm and pinning her against the car. She gave in to the
onslaught, whimpering against my lips, and opened wider to
give me more. A deep, satisfied rumble vibrated my throat as
my tongue twisted around hers, sealing our mouths even
tighter so that anyone looking would have no doubt she was
mine. Need so desperate grabbed hold of me. I could think of
nothing other than getting inside her.

I wrenched my mouth from hers but stayed pressed along
her while nuzzling her cheek with my nose. "You're here," I
rasped, vulnerability soaking the words.

"Where else would I be?"

I groaned and pressed my lips to hers again. The warm
friction of our mouths rubbing together made my dick leak
in my pants.

A throat cleared behind us.

"Fuck off," I rumbled, claiming her lips again.

She giggled against my mouth, and I licked it up, wanting
more of that flavor. Fingers fisting in my unwashed, chlorinated hair, she pulled, forcing my face up and our lips apart.

I felt my Adam's apple bob against the arch of my neck
and though I could easily overpower her I stayed exactly
where I was and let her control me. Prickles of pain skittered
across my scalp and shot down to crackle at the base of my
spine.

"I'm not the only one that came," she said, and it took a
minute for the words to penetrate the sex-saturated haze
over my mind.

"What?" I asked, getting distracted by the way the winter
air brushed over my damp lips.

Her eyes slid over my shoulder, then came back to rest on
mine.

I turned to look, but her fingers were still tangled in my

hair. "You have to let go, little siren."

Her lower lip stuck out in a pout, but she pulled back so I could stand. As I went, I lifted, sitting her on the hood of her car. She smiled up at me, and the heavy lust she inspired gave way to something even more powerful.

I love you. You own me.

I rotated, expecting to find some frowny-face officer with a pair of cuffs.

It wasn't a cop.

"What the fuck are you doing here?" I asked, surprise taking the heat out of my words.

Ryan smirked, his face an arrogant mask. "So you two?" he mused, leaning around me to look at Landry.

"If you want to look at someone, look at your own woman," I spat, deftly moving to block his prying eyes.

"You're lucky the po-po didn't come out here and arrest you for indecent exposure," Ryan remarked, voice dry. "Though, after that, I'd say you'd probably like being cuffed."

A peel of giggles erupted behind me.

I glanced over my shoulder, lifting my eyebrow at her audacity. "You laughing?"

She shook her head and covered her mouth as if that would hide the giggling. All it did was make her laughter even more endearing.

I can't believe she came.

"My girl thinks you're a comedian, Walsh," I said, turning back to the last person I ever expected to see.

"*Your* girl?"

"Yeah. Mine."

"Coach isn't going to be too happy," Walsh needlessly pointed out.

I grunted. "What gave it away, my field trip to the slammer?"

That drew him up short, and surprise flashed in his blue

stare. "Coach is the reason you're here right now?"

"Well, I sure as fuck didn't volunteer my time."

Walsh's brows furrowed, and I saw the speculation and questions ready to fall off his tongue. Hell, I knew he was curious. All of Elite was. But it wasn't their damn business.

The last time I trusted my team, I got the shaft.

Before he could get a stick up his ass about me refusing to answer any of his nosy questions, I made a gruff sound. "I can handle Coach."

Landry hopped off the hood of the car, her body rubbing against mine as she moved. I tingled all over, my nerves still on fire as I reached between us to thread my fingers through hers.

Ryan glanced down at where I held, then back up, eyes bouncing between us. You know, I really wasn't in the mood for his holier-than-thou, I'm-the-leader-of-this-pack bullshit right now.

"What are you doing here, Walsh?" I asked, then tilted my head. "How'd you even know I was here?"

"You didn't show for breakfast."

I made a rude sound. "I never come to breakfast."

"You have lately," he rebuked, looking at Landry and basically saying without saying that he knew she was the reason.

I mean, yeah, technically, I was avoiding her like the plague. But what the hell was I supposed to do, let that mutt Kruger keep sniffing around? That was a whole lot of no.

"I called Coach." He went on, briefly touching his stare on Landry. His voice was quieter when he said, "I didn't realize he's the reason you're here."

I wasn't sure what that meant. He was hard to read in that moment. For a split second, I actually wondered if he was pissed on my behalf. But then I remembered who he was and that no one was on my side.

The thought had me looking down at the little siren

whose hand was caught in mine. "Didn't he tell you?" I quietly wondered.

He literally ratted me out to the cops to get me away from her. There was no way on God's green earth that he didn't spill his guts to poison her against me.

Is it poison if it's the truth?

So why is she here? Why is she holding my hand?

"He told me," she said, eyes meeting mine. "I told him I didn't care."

Is it possible to suffer whiplash while standing still from shock? My brain literally ping-ponged inside my skull, but all I could do was stare.

Walsh cleared his throat. "So you cool?"

My attention stayed locked on the blonde still holding my hand. The hand of a killer. The last hand on earth she should be holding.

But here she was.

It hurt, the force of my feelings so strong it caused a physical ache inside me. She might as well have shoved her fist through my chest and snatched out my beating heart. My eyes were still Velcroed to her face when she turned to glance at Ryan.

"We're good. Thanks for coming down here."

"You're Elite."

I couldn't even fully snark at his words because this little siren had me so deeply under her spell. "Yeah? Then where's everyone else?"

Too late, I realized it sounded like I cared. Too late, I realized this girl had stripped me of my guard.

"I thought it would mean more this time if it was just me."

That turned my head. Ryan regarded me quietly, the intensity of his stare never wavering. Something passed between us. Maybe because my siren disarmed me. Maybe because I acknowledged he didn't have to be here.

Something.

Clearing my throat, I looked away, back to my favorite sight. "Give me the keys, little siren."

"Little siren?" Ryan mused.

She tugged them out of the side pocket of her leggings and held them out.

I took them and palmed the small of her back, nudging her toward the car. "C'mon, baby, in the car."

She let me direct her, automatically turning to the passenger side.

Partway there, I glanced back over my shoulder. Ryan was still standing there watching us with veiled amusement.

"Yeah, little siren," I told him. "'Cause she lured me in."

He made a sound and turned toward the black Rubicon parked nearby. I hadn't even noticed it before. All I'd seen was her.

He didn't say anything else, but I heard his unspoken words as if I'd suddenly developed some psychic ability. *Call if you need anything.*

We might have had a moment. A weird anomaly, probably the product of a wrinkle somewhere in the universe. But that was over, and I knew my place. I wouldn't call. He didn't expect me to.

He came here anyway.

The inside of Landry's car was scented with cherry vanilla, and I inhaled deep as I tugged the seatbelt around her, leaning in to snap it in place.

"Where do you want to go?" I asked, letting my fingers graze her hip.

"Wherever you take me."

I pulled back so I could hit her with the intensity of my stare. "If you let me decide, I'm gonna take you somewhere that it's just us, rip all the clothing off your body, and take you so deep you'll still feel me next week."

"Let's go, then."

I knew then the rush my Vette felt when it went from zero to sixty in two-point-nine seconds. Pulling back, I raced around the front of the car, practically diving behind the wheel.

"Damn, woman," I grunted, fumbling to adjust the seat. "How the hell do you drive like this?" I grumped, feeling like my ass was squished into a pair of too-tight jeans. My legs screamed in relief as the seat glided back, allowing them the space they sorely needed.

"Do you want me to drive?" she asked, humor dripping off that sassy tongue. I hoped she licked me with it later.

Giving her a baleful look, I reached for the gearshift, but it came up empty.

"Ahh hell," I announced and jabbed my finger at the place where the gearshift should be. "What the shit is this?"

Her eyes followed my finger. "The thingy that puts the car in drive?"

My hand fell out of the air. "The thingy that puts the car in drive," I muttered, then groaned. "You drive an automatic."

"So?"

"So it's a crime against everything with four tires!"

She rolled her eyes. "Great. You're a car snob."

I glanced toward the sky, calling upon the car gods for patience. "Can you even drive a manual?"

"A manual," she echoed, unfamiliar with the word. "Oh! You mean a stick? No."

"*Oh my God,*" I mourned, shaking my head, and started up this pathetic excuse for a vehicle. I imagined my Corvette holding up a *Welcome Home Cheater* sign when I pulled up.

"No girl of mine is going to walk around not knowing how to drive right," I told her. "I won't have it."

"You said that to Ryan too," she said, her quiet voice interrupting this dire situation.

"What?" I asked, sliding her a brief look before glancing back at the road. *What the fuck am I supposed to do with my hand if I don't need to shift?*

This car was for lazy people. Bad drivers.

"That I'm yours."

I threw out my arm and slammed on the brakes. The tires squealed, and the back of the vehicle fishtailed like a little bitch.

I hated this car. It couldn't even brake right.

"I can't believe your dad lets you drive around in this shit wagon," I spat.

"Jason!" she hollered. "What the hell was that?" Her eyes were wide as saucers, her cheeks flushed, and against my forearm, her chest was heaving.

My lip curled. "That wouldn't have scared you if we'd been in my Corvette. My car knows how to brake."

"Jason Rush," she threatened.

I used the *thingy* to put the car in park and then dragged her over the console into my lap. "Listen here, little siren, and listen good," I said, totally endeared by the way she fit in my lap with her legs tucked up and her sneakers against the door. "Yeah, I said it. And I'm gonna keep saying it because it's true. You're mine. Even though you believe in Bigfoot. Even though this car is an embarrassment."

She gasped.

"Indignant little thing too," I mused.

Her lips parted to no doubt smack me with some sass, but I kissed her. I liked me a sassy mouth.

Her lips parted instantly, a small sigh echoing into my mouth. I kissed just long enough to get her flavor but pulled back before I fell too far beneath her spell.

"I've tried to stay away. It's better for you if I do. You came here, Landry. *You fucking came.* So yeah, you're mine. I'm yours. You don't have to keep me. Hell, I know you won't.

But it doesn't matter because I'm so fucking starved for you that I'll take what you give me and then watch you walk away. Even then, you'll still be mine. My heart isn't ever gonna let you go."

The air was thick around us, so much tension for such an enclosed space. But she cut through it like it wasn't there, leaning forward to lay her lips right against mine.

I kissed her more than once. More accurately, I tried to consume her with my lips.

She didn't use her tongue. She barely moved at all. But it was the best kiss I'd ever had. I wanted to watch, but my eyes refused to stay open, almost as though my brain couldn't process sight *and* touch in that moment, so it buckled to the greatest one.

And, *oh*, did I feel her.

Her lips were warm like the sun in her hair. Her light breath tickled the skin beneath my nose. I reveled in the way her lips clung slightly when she drew back to kiss again, making the series of shorter kisses into one long one that cut me to my core.

She pulled back too soon, and my lashes fluttered. In a sudden display of affection, she popped forward and kissed the tip of my nose, a light giggle filling my ears. A tidal wave of emotion expanded my chest when she smiled as though she'd gotten away with something no one else ever had.

She did.

Me.

I love you.

The words were like a heartbeat whenever she was near. But I kept them tucked away, a secret I would never tell because I knew I never could.

My love wasn't something anyone would consider a gift, and though I would always think of her as mine, I would never be her burden.

16

LANDRY

IF PEOPLE STARED AS WE WENT INTO HIS DORM ROOM, I couldn't say. Between his presence and his words, nothing else even registered.

My legs were unsteady, and there was a fine tremor in my hands. My stomach buzzed like it was filled with bees, and I was beginning to wonder if my heartbeat would ever be the same.

There was a lot of stuff between us, but it was so easy with him. So easy to want. To feel. And even after everything, to trust.

Maybe I would regret it later, but that regret was too far off to dampen today.

Jason wasn't so much a thought with me, more so an instinct. An action I couldn't stop, perhaps even an impossibility attained. He seemed convinced I was going to let him go, and I was determined to prove him wrong.

The door clicked shut behind us, and the familiar scent of

chlorine swirled beneath my nose. His keys slapped onto a shelf near the door as my eyes surveyed the room. There were two beds, one on each side of the space, with a nightstand pushed against each one. The bed to the left was made neatly with simple bedding in a shade of blue. It looked untouched compared to the bed on the right, which was rumpled and slept-in-looking with its fluffy white comforter and askew blanket covered in green palm tree fronds. The pinstriped pillows had indents, and another was shaped like a palm tree. Above the bed on the biggest wall was a massive poster of a beach at sunrise and a surfboard standing in the sand.

I didn't know why looking at it all made a lump form in my throat, but it did, and it was impossible to swallow.

He'd gone deeper into the room to grab a water out of a small fridge. I don't know how long I stood there overcome with emotion I couldn't even explain, but the crinkling of an empty water bottle and the tear of a wrapper penetrated my brain.

After another thick swallow, I glanced over my shoulder to tease, "Are you a Cali boy?"

He paused in shoving an entire protein bar into his mouth, eyes flashing to the giant poster and then dropping away. "Not anymore."

Damn, that emotion was back, and my legs had gone from unsteady to shaking in my shoes.

Forcing my eyes away from what I knew was his side of the room, I glanced again at the empty bed. "Who's your roommate?"

"Lars."

My eyes widened in surprise. "I thought Lars lived with Win."

We'd met at the library the last time he helped me with A&P, so I had no idea he was in a dorm.

Jason grunted, tossing the empty wrapper in the trash. "He does, but this is his place too."

I wondered if he realized the protective vibe he gave off when Lars was even mentioned. It might not be so much what he said but the way he looked when he said it.

"Did you eat?" he asked.

I shook my head. I'd been too busy arguing with my dad.

Rush frowned and closed the distance between us to take my arm. "C'mon, I'll take you to get some food."

I resisted the urge to follow along behind him and shook my head. "I don't want food right now."

The hand around my arm tightened. His opaque stare grew darker. "What do you want?"

"You."

A deep rumble started in his chest and rolled like thunder all the way up his throat to barrel past his lips. The buzzing in my stomach started back up again as I watched his stare turn heated. He came so close our feet bumped as his fingers dipped under the cropped hem of the windbreaker I usually wore at the pool. Goose bumps raced across my skin when his fingertips brushed my bare waist. Without hesitation, I lifted my arms and looked at him to do my bidding.

His lips curved up in a one-sided smile but then gave way to burning desire when he deftly tugged off the jacket and my shirt in one sweeping move. The mussed strands of my hair fell into my face, partly obscuring my vision and making it seem like I was gazing at him through some sort of golden veil.

His hands hovered around my body, his low voice muttering something I didn't comprehend. But then his palms covered my breasts, and my eyes closed, chin tipped back as I gave myself up to his touch.

My nipples tightened so quickly it shot electric jolts of

pain between my legs. Even though I still wore a bra, his thumbs found the hard pebbles to tease them mercilessly.

I wanted to say his name, but it became a whimper. Another growl rumbled overhead like thunder, and the chilled air of the room brushed over my newly bared breasts. He ducked his head to suck one into his mouth, and the warm wetness of his lips against my aching flesh made me cry out.

I swayed on my feet, and he palmed my hips, holding me still while attacking one breast and then moving to the other. Warmth pooled between my legs, and my lower belly relaxed, my body crying out in silent invitation.

I grabbed his shoulders, trying to tug the clothes off his chest. He hummed, the action vibrating my already sensitive breast and making me gasp.

"Jason," I said, impatiently ripping at his clothing.

He pulled back, eyes glittering onyx, a color so breathtaking it made me feel I'd discovered the rarest of gems. He pulled off his hoodie and then the compression shirt underneath. When he was kicking off his shoes, I moved forward, gliding my palms across his smooth, defined chest.

He was nothing but a wall of muscle. All smooth skin and clean lines. Leaning forward, I pressed an open-mouth kiss to his pec, then shifted an inch and did it again.

His hands fell to my hips, hooking in the waistband of my leggings. "Tell me, little siren."

"Yes."

He peeled them down, the action making it so I couldn't continue to caress his chest. Instead, I carded my fingers through the thick, soft strands of his hair while he worked the fabric down and over my feet.

When I was left in nothing at all, he remained knelt in front of me, perusing my body with his sensual stare.

"I've never seen anything more beautiful in my entire life," he whispered, reverently caressing my stomach, then leaning in to trail kisses across my belly button. Reaching around, he cupped my bare ass, anchoring himself there as he kissed a path to the short patch of curls just above the juncture of my thighs.

I whispered his name, and he stood swiftly, hooking his thumbs in the waistband of his sweats and pulling them off with one swipe. I already knew how big he was, but seeing again made my muscles clench involuntarily, anticipating the stretch.

He was completely hairless, swollen cock jutting off his body, sack heavy with need. I reached out to take him in hand, but he caught my wrist and pushed it aside.

"I need a shower." His voice was husky and sent a shot of lust right up my spine. "You're coming with."

My head bobbed, and he chuckled, lifting me so my legs could wrap around his waist. I wiggled closer, letting the wetness at my core smear over his impressive abs.

His feet stuttered, and a moan filled the room. "You're already wet for me."

"I've been waiting for you, Jason," I whispered, brushing a lock of dark hair away from his face. "I'm just as starved as you are."

He changed direction, and my back hit the mattress, his body following to press me into the blankets. "Fuck the shower," he growled and thrust into me with a single push.

My mouth fell open, though no sound came out. My entire world was reduced to the way my body burned and stretched around his massive dick and the way he completely consumed me.

He cursed, holding himself stiff above me as his limbs trembled and shook with exertion. I felt his cock spasm inside me, and my body clenched in retaliation.

Our breathing was labored, the only sound I heard.

Breaking through the intensity of his intrusion were gentle fingers that grasped my chin.

"Little siren," he beckoned, and I lifted my lashes to stare into his lust-drenched face. "Did I hurt you?"

I smiled and shook my head against the mattress. "No. You fill me up so good."

Something in his eyes flared, and anticipation built within me. He pushed back, both hands planted on the mattress on either side of my head. "If I go too rough, say red."

I purred.

"Landry." He snapped, and my eyes sprang open, clarity like a bucket of cold water to the face. "Repeat."

Curling my hands around his biceps, I anchored in. "If I want you to stop, I'll say red."

He practically did a push-up, those biceps bulging under my hold as he lowered to capture my lips. "Such a good girl," he crooned, then snapped his hips.

I gasped, and he pushed up, holding his body over mine as he pistoned his hips, hammering into me with his steely cock. Garbled noises and moans filled the room as he fucked me so deep I literally saw stars.

The headboard smacked the wall, but I barely heard because my body was floating, going higher and higher with every thrust. My hands fell away, flopping onto the bed as I bounced with his movements, completely at his mercy. His hand reached down to fasten at my hip and pull me up as he thrust, making me cry out. He stilled a little, his breathing labored, and glanced down.

"Don't stop," I begged.

He grunted, fingers gripping my hips anew as he wrapped his other hand around the headboard and used it as leverage to pull himself even deeper into me. My head fell back, and I mewled, rocking against his rigid length, reveling in the sensations rippling through my body.

We moved together, bodies straining as tension built and built within us. Every time I got close to falling over, he would shift just slightly, keeping me hostage on the edge.

Frustrated and needy, I grabbed his waist, digging my nails into the corded muscles at his sides.

"Jason." I panted, needing release, wanting it enough to beg.

"Tell me what you want," he inflected, grinding his pelvis against mine.

I whimpered. "Please."

His hips stuttered, and the hand gripping my hip turned into a caress as he followed the curve of my body up to cover my breast with his palm. He kneaded my aching flesh and pushed his face into my neck to tug the flesh into his mouth.

When he lifted his head, I felt a wet spot against my neck, and his thumb and forefinger pinched my nipple. With one last show of stamina, he thrust deep again and scraped his teeth over the fleshy part of my ear.

"Come, little siren. Coat my dick in all that sweetness."

I shattered, body arching off the mattress as I shuddered and quaked, the orgasm taking over every sense I possessed and turning them inside out. I quaked and moaned, the pleasure going on and on as he continued to rub his engorged head over that spot inside me until I was so sensitive I collapsed on the bed with a whimper.

He pushed his arms between me and the mattress, his body supporting more of me than the bed, and softly nuzzled my cheek with his lips.

"I love being inside you," he whispered. "You're so good for me. You feel so good." He followed the praise with kisses to my forehead, brow, and the corner of my lips.

Even though he was still rigid inside me, he held me with far more tenderness than I originally thought him capable.

Lowering my body back into the blankets, he rested his elbows on each side of my head while we touched from chest to toe.

Feeling him brush the hair away from my face, I looked up.

"Hi," he whispered, so much affection in his eyes that tears sprang to mine.

"Hi," I whispered back, my voice a little watery, eyes slightly wet.

He pressed a gentle kiss against my lips, and it was flavored with his smile.

And he thinks I'll let him go.

"Little siren…"

"Hmm?" I asked, completely blissed out.

"Can you take more?" The words were punctuated with the flexing of his dick.

My eyes widened a bit, realizing he had yet to climax. Bending my knees, I laid my feet flat against the bed. "If I'm going to still feel you next week, you better get busy."

The softness in his features glinted with challenge and what could only be described as need. "You on the pill?" he gritted out, and then I realized we'd forgotten a condom.

"Yes."

"Good." He grunted and pulled all the way out only to slam back in and pump his hips until his thrusts became uneven and sloppy.

His shout echoed around the whole room and filled my ears when his body went taut. I felt the force of his orgasm, the way his cock shuddered and emptied while he moaned.

Deep satisfaction welled within me as my body cradled his, milking what was left of his release as he came down from the high. His body quaked with aftershocks, and I wrapped my arms around him, dragging my nails up and down his spine as he shivered.

He groaned into the pillow beside my head, and I smiled, leaning down to kiss the top of his shoulder.

Lifting his head, he gazed down at me, eyes hazy and relaxed. I realized then that I hadn't seen him relaxed, and it was a look I wanted to see more of.

"Hi," I whispered, remembering what he'd said to me when I finally came back.

He smiled and leaned down, pressing our lips together. "Hi."

He lifted his head, and I smiled at how mussed his hair was from my hands. He shifted, sliding out of my body and rolling onto his back. I rolled toward him, and he pulled me against his side.

In between my thighs was sticky, a feeling that was new to me. "I've never done it without a condom before," I whispered.

"Me either."

"Really?" I asked, propping my chin on his chest.

"I've never wanted anyone that close."

My cheeks and chest warmed at what the statement implied, and I ducked my face back into his chest. After a moment of quiet, his hand buried into the thickness of my hair.

"Hey, little siren."

"Hmm?"

"What's it like knowing I left part of me inside you?"

Satisfying. Intimate. Claimed.

I didn't say those things out loud, though. Instead, I pressed a kiss against his chest and whispered, "Probably the same way it feels to know you left something behind."

17

Rush

I can tell you with full authority that it was *not* the same.

There was no way on this green earth the little naked siren lying in my rumpled sheets right now felt everything I did. She couldn't possibly. I could barely fathom it myself.

You would think after pounding into her tight, wet heat and emptying myself inside her, it would weaken the insane urge I had to claim her. That the gnawing hunger inside me would be satiated.

It wasn't.

If anything, it made it worse. It made me afraid someone would take her from me.

That I would lose her.

The shock I felt seeing her standing outside the police station still lingered, as did the words she spoke. *"I told him I don't care."*

No way. There was no way Coach had told her I was a murderous bastard and she'd uttered that she didn't mind.

He must not have told her everything. But that didn't make sense either. He made it crystal clear he didn't want me around his princess, and I made it clear I didn't care. He had ammunition, though, the means to get rid of me.

But here she was. In my arms. My cum smearing her thighs.

Just the idea made me so hot, and I groaned, rolling to push her into the mattress while rising to my knees.

"Jason?" she questioned, brows furrowing.

"Spread your legs," I said, palming her thighs, already pushing them apart.

She made a surprised sound but did what I asked and held them open while I settled between them. Still gripping her thighs, I focused on her pink center, finding exactly what I wanted.

"There I am," I rumbled with satisfaction, swirling my finger in the creamy evidence I'd just claimed her from the inside.

Following that erotic thought, I scooped it all up with my fingers and pushed it back in. She made a little sound, and I thrust a little deeper and swirled, making sure my cum was good and deep.

I hoped her body absorbed it. I hoped I became part of her DNA.

"It's good you're on the pill," I murmured, fingers still pushed deep. "Because the way I feel right now, I'd be pleased as fuck if you got pregnant."

She gasped.

My eyes went to hers, and I let her see the intensity burning inside me, how possessive she made me feel. "Then you'd be full of me for nine long months," I told her, my dick stirring at just the thought. "Wherever you went, I'd be there too. And everyone would see you swollen with me. Everyone would know you were mine."

She made a soft sound, and I drew my fingers out of her, gliding up to her clit to stroke.

She whimpered, and my dick jerked like it had been called.

"That first night in the locker room, I had a moment of anger when you came and the rubber kept it from smearing all over my dick."

Her legs moved restlessly against the mattress, and I dipped my finger back inside.

"I want you so much." My voice was low and gravelly like it, too, was saturated with need. "Every single part of you. And even then, it just won't be enough."

"It's okay to want me," she said, reaching out her hand almost as if she sensed my fear.

My chest squeezed, her words piercing a part of me I tried not to acknowledge as I took in the way she looked spread-eagle before me with a flushed chest, erect nipples, and my fingers filling her hole. It was dirty and alluring, making me want to pound into her all over again.

"This isn't want, little siren." I warned her. "This is obsession."

Her teeth sank into her kiss-swollen lower lip, and her mossy, unfocused eyes dropped to my dick, which was standing rigid off my body.

Already, the air in the room was heavy with sex, but it turned near suffocating as it thickened.

Her stare lifted from my erection to meet mine. "Take me again, Jason."

What little restraint I had left snapped, and she gasped when I pulled my fingers out of her, grabbed her hips, and flipped her over.

I groaned, seeing her luscious bare ass, and immediately

filled my hands. She cooed a bit, which only made me hotter, and I massaged her cheeks, spreading them apart for a glimpse at her crack.

My heart beat so hard that I felt it pound against my temple, an urgent and insistent reminder that I needed more.

Grasping her hips, I dragged her ass up, holding her lower body off the mattress. I dove in, shoving my face between her cheeks, and licked a long stripe from her crack to her dripping opening.

She shuddered against my hands, but I gripped tighter, pushing my tongue into her heat. A slight salty tang burst across my taste buds, and my head dropped between my shoulders. "You fucking taste like me."

Her ass wiggled, and I dove back in, licking and slurping until my senses were filled with nothing but her. My nose was wet, my lips slick, and my breath was probably tainted with her.

My dick was twitching and leaking, begging for his turn, but I wasn't done yet, hadn't had near enough. I meant it when I said I wanted every part of her. I wanted to fill her up completely. Following that instinct, my tongue dragged up to circle her rim.

She let out a surprised sound, her body jolting in my hold.

"I want this," I declared and dove back on it, licking the tight muscle and then pushing my tongue into its center.

Her whole body started to tremble as I rimmed her ass to within an inch of my life and her hole was soft and wet. Her body had long since gone boneless. The only reason her ass was still in the air was because I held it up.

When I pulled back, I nipped at her ass cheek, and she moaned, so I did it again.

My arms were tired, but the rest of me was primed for more, so I laid her back against the sheets, and her legs spread wider in invitation.

Breathing heavily, I let my eyes linger on her back. Her torso was short and dipped in on the sides. My eyes traced the lines of her body, trying to memorize every inch. Her head was turned to the side, resting on my pillow, and golden hair waved all over the place, obscuring her features.

A rush of tenderness came over me, and I blanketed her body with mine, scraping back the hair hiding her away to kiss her cheek and then against her ear.

"You taste so sweet," I whispered.

She turned her face and caught my lips, and we kissed, languid and messy. Her tongue was bold, slurping at my mouth like she wanted some of the sweetness I'd just imbibed.

As we kissed, I sank farther into her naked body, my hips rocking gently against her ass.

"I can't believe you're here right now," I said, the words not really registering. I was too far under her spell.

She smiled, her cheek lying back on the pillow as she arched so her ass pressed closer. I shifted, my swollen head catching on her drenched entrance.

I groaned, rocking a little, keeping it right there, and teasing us both.

"Deeper," she beckoned.

"Beg," I rasped.

There was no way she wanted as much as I did, but I wanted to hear her plea.

"I'm empty without you, Jason," she said, reaching around to caress my hip. "Please fill me up."

I pushed in, her walls clenching me greedily even as she accommodated my girth.

I shuddered at the tight fit, marveling at the skin-on-skin contact and how her natural lubricant soaked me so good.

Pushing my arms under her body, I palmed her perfect tits, holding them gently as I thrust and her body rocked against the mattress. Her face buried itself in my pillow, the long column of the back of her neck on full display. I sank my teeth into that creamy, unblemished skin anchoring myself there as I continued to fuck her from behind.

The friction between our bodies and the way she rubbed along the bed with every thrust caused heat to explode around us, and soon, we were both covered in a sheen of sweat.

Rising, I tugged her hips, and she adjusted so she was on her knees. I caressed her ass and then grabbed it, spreading her cheeks so I could watch my cock sink into her core.

She pushed up onto her elbows, pushing herself farther back on me, and I snapped my hips forward, driving deep.

"Jason." My name fell from her lips, and I picked up the pace, my body slapping against hers as I drove into her again and again.

The unruly possessive streak flared again, the sound of me claiming her making me want even more.

Peeling her cheeks apart, I stared down at her little hole, so pink and perfect. Just begging me to own it.

Licking the pad of my thumb, I laid it against her ass, rubbing in shallow circles. Her body tensed slightly, and I felt her attention.

"Would you let me have this too?" I wondered, pressing the pad of my thumb just a little bit more. Despite how tight she was, her body gave a little because of the way I'd rimmed her so thoroughly.

She made a sound, a whimper that gave way to a moan.

I pushed my dick as far into her as I could, holding myself deep as I dipped just barely into her ass with my thumb.

"Jason…"

"Imagine how full you'd be with me in both holes."

Her body jerked backward, the action making my thumb slip a little deeper. Her rim clenched around me.

"I trust you," she said, the words slicing through the heavy chokehold of desire.

"What?" I rasped, fighting off the orgasm building in my balls.

"I trust you. Take what you want, Jason. Take all of me."

"*Fuck*," I groaned, her words causing a war inside me. Gently, I pulled my thumb from her ass and thrust deeper into her core with an uncontrolled rhythm that had my balls drawn up so tight it hurt.

Reaching around her, I found her swollen clit and rubbed. Her body went taut, and I shouted, erupting inside her, my dick spasming so violently that all thought blacked out.

I rutted against her as the orgasm nearly ripped me in two, using every last ounce of energy I had to keep my weight from crushing her.

Dully, I heard her moan and felt her body clenching mine as she came. We collapsed against the bed, my body on top of hers. Our sweat-slicked skin stuck together, and I used one arm to try and keep the worst of my weight off her.

Even though we'd both come, I still thrust lazily inside her, making sure my release stayed deep. Before pushing away, I peppered kisses over her shoulders and then along her spine as I forced myself up.

She purred in contentment, and the sound made me ache.

On quivering arms, I leaned over her, kissing the soft shell of her ear. "You're perfect," I whispered. "So perfect."

I collapsed on the bed, letting out a long sigh, enjoying the after-sex fog, hoping it would last just a little longer.

She rolled, and I held out my arm so she could fit herself along my side. When she was settled, I closed my arm around her, holding on so she couldn't get away.

"You okay?" I asked, reaching up to finger her hair.

"Better than okay."

I grunted with satisfaction and pressed her cheek a little farther against me.

I wasn't much of a cuddler after sex. I wasn't much of a toucher at all. But with Landry, I wanted my hands on her at all times. Even after intense, brain-melting sex, I wanted her skin on mine.

"I think you were more rabid the second time than the first," she mused.

"I told you, baby. I cannot get enough." I paused, suddenly concerned there was more to her words. "If I hurt you, you have to tell me. If I'm too rough—"

Her fingers pressed against my lips, cutting off my words. "You didn't."

I shifted my eyes, looking directly into hers. She was telling the truth.

I nodded, and she pulled her hand away, tucking it between my side and the mattress while putting her cheek back on my chest.

"I told you I trust you."

There were those words again, three words inciting a war inside me. This time, there was no orgasm to keep it at bay. Though I tried, I knew she felt my body tighten, possibly even sensed the war.

"Jason."

I groaned, recognizing that tone immediately. Knowing exactly where this was going. I didn't want it, but I wouldn't stop it. She had every right to know.

"Why didn't you?" she whispered, a little shyness in her tone.

"Why didn't I what?"

"You know."

Yeah, I knew. "Why didn't I sink into your ass after you told me I could?"

She made a little sound, and I couldn't help the smile I

sent up to the ceiling. *I fucking love her.* "Have you ever had anal sex before?"

She gasped, her body going slightly rigid. Untangling my hand from her hair, I wrapped my arm around her so she couldn't get away.

"No."

Again, I smiled at the ceiling, and a low chuckle slipped out. She turned even farther into me, burying her face in my armpit, trying to hide. My heart swelled.

"You seem offended," I mused. "But you weren't so offended when I was rimming you with my tongue."

"*Jason.*"

I laughed. "So you like to do it but not talk about it."

"I only like it if it's you."

I sucked in a breath. "Hey," I said, trying to rouse her.

She kept her face hidden, but I couldn't allow it.

"Landry. Look at me."

Her little sigh scattered across my skin, and she lifted her head, eyes meeting mine, then darting away.

Her cheeks were flushed pink, eyes slightly unfocused, and her hair looked like it was eating her head.

You know those pictures on the internet that show you what your heart looks like? That red, ugly lump of flesh?

They got mine wrong.

I was looking at mine right now.

"Is that true?" I asked, not really a whisper but not loud enough to be much more.

She tried to duck her head again, and I caught her chin, tipping it up so she had to look at me.

She nodded once. "I guess I want to be overfull with you too."

"*Shit.*" My head fell back against the pillow, and I stared up at the poster above the bed.

She tapped me on the chest. A silent beacon, a sword right to my heart.

I lifted again to look at her. "You really wouldn't with anyone else?"

She shook her head. "Just you."

I rolled, pinning her beneath me, and kissed her until my lungs screamed and I was forced away. Breathing heavily, I brushed the hair away from her face and cupped it between my palms. "And that is why I didn't do it. Because you trust me. Because you shouldn't."

I couldn't take her like that, let her give me something that required an insane amount of trust. As badly as I wanted to own her in every way, I couldn't, knowing her trust was misplaced.

She couldn't fully trust me until she knew everything.

And once she knew everything, she wouldn't trust me at all.

18

LANDRY

HE WARNED ME OFF IN THE BATHROOM AT SHIRLEY'S. HE KEPT his distance even when I felt his eyes. He gave me a safe word because he worried he'd be too rough and stopped in the middle of sex to check in even when I didn't use it. His first reaction when someone was drowning was to call for help, and his first action was to give them his breath.

He went with the cops after my father told them his secrets and then refused to take a part of me he wanted, a part I'd offered, because he feared my trust was misplaced.

This was what my heart already understood. What his words would never change. He could tell me not to trust him all he wanted, but the truth was he'd already earned it.

"Maybe we should talk," I said, pushing up off his chest to sit cross-legged at his side.

A grim look stole over his handsome features, but he reached out to cover the side of my knee with his palm. "Yeah."

"Can I borrow a shirt?"

"I like you naked."

Reaching out, I dragged my fingertips across his defined abs. "I like you naked too."

He caught my hand and kissed the backs of my fingers, making my stomach drop. "How about a shower?"

"Are you procrastinating this conversation?" I teased.

His quiet reply took a chunk out of my heart. "Can't blame me for wanting to keep you a little longer."

"Jason…" I began, but he was swinging his legs over the side of the bed and putting his back to me.

I was momentarily distracted by the sight of his broad, strong shoulders and the sudden urge to reach for him. Instead of denying myself, I moved forward, slipping my arms around him from behind and pressing my naked torso against his bare back.

He made a sound of surprise and stiffened, but barely a heartbeat later, he melted into me, body going soft. I smiled against him, pressing a kiss to the back of his shoulder.

"I'm not going anywhere." I promised.

"I won't hold you to that."

"Did no one stay by your side?" I asked quietly as sorrow filled my heart.

His body went rigid, and I tightened my arms. "You don't know what you're talking about," he said, voice harsh.

"I know you deserve better than what you got."

With a sound, he ripped away, the move so sudden and so rough that I pitched forward with a strangled cry as I tumbled off the bed.

He cursed, catching me just before I smacked against the floor and lifted, cradling me against his chest. The sweat on my skin was drying, and I shivered a little against the cold.

"How about that shower?" I asked, laying my cheek against his shoulder.

He carried me into his private bathroom—seriously, Elite got the best of everything—but didn't set me down before reaching in to turn on the spray. Only after checking that it was warm did he step inside with me still in his arms.

Water rained over his back and shoulders, rushing in thick rivulets over his chest to slip between where my skin met his. The warm temperature caused goose bumps to race across my body.

"You're cold," he observed, his voice intimate and husky in the enclosed shower, and I lifted my chin to his down-turned face. The darkness of his stare was secretive, and thin ribbons of water slid over his cheeks from the back of his head.

He moved to put me down, and I made a sound of protest, wrapping my arm around his neck.

"Just one more minute," I whispered.

A sigh moved through him as he tucked me in tighter. I rested my cheek on his shoulder, rubbing against him with an exhale. Obviously still bothered I was cold, he rotated so I was beneath the spray, the sinfully hot water chasing away the chill.

Neither of us said a word, the quiet folding around us protectively. The air turned balmy under the heat of the water, and I melted against him, nearly lulled to sleep. My comfort level with him was unmatched, something to marvel at considering his temperament and murky past. But I was a firm believer in vibes. Vibes never lied, and my gut never steered me wrong.

And everything in me screamed Jason was safe. That he was mine.

That's right. Mine. I guess he wasn't the only possessive one.

"The water's gonna get cold if we stand here much longer." His voice roused me.

"I don't care."

I felt his silent laughter. "You will when you're rinsing off soap with ice."

I grumbled, and he put me down, keeping his hands on me until I was steady. He washed me first, soaping up my body, going as far as to kneel at my feet. When I was squeaky clean, he washed himself while I shampooed my hair.

"You need color-safe shampoo," I told him even as I sniffed the scent I recognized as his. "And sulfate-free."

He made a rumbly noise as suds clung to his shoulders and pecs. "Soap is soap."

"It is not!" I declared, flinging my hand and smacking him with a glob of the shampoo stuck to my fingers.

He glanced at the giant white foam and then back at me. "You do this?"

I giggled, then whacked him with another blob of bubbles.

He tossed the soap down and grabbed me, digging his fingers into my ribs. I shrieked and tried to pull away, but the shower was so small I didn't get far.

"Insulting my shampoo," he swore, going back to tickle me some more.

I twisted away, laughter bursting from my chest. "You insulted my car!"

"That car is an abomination."

I gasped. "If soap is soap, then a car is a car."

"You leave me no choice," he intoned and reached around me to turn the shower knob to cold.

Shrieking, I leaped at him, climbing up his body and cringing away from the icy water. "Jason!" I hollered. "That was mean!"

"You insulted my Vette, baby. Retaliation was imminent," he mused, turning so I wasn't in the spray at all and it smacked into him instead. He didn't even flinch against the icy droplets.

"Car snob," I muttered.

"Soap snob," he countered and reached back to adjust the temperature.

Since he didn't put me down, I grabbed the shampoo that I prayed didn't strip the color from my hair and used it to wash his. As I scrubbed, he hummed in satisfaction, his long black lashes sweeping down against his cheeks.

Some of the suds dripped over his forehead to catch on his brow, and I swiped the bubbles away before they could leak into his eyes.

"Rinse," I told him, pushing his head so he would tilt it under the spray.

When it was completely rinsed and his black hair was glossy and pushed off his forehead, I pulled back. "I'd condition it, but you don't have any."

He laughed like he thought that was funny, but really, hair care was no joke.

"I'm probably gonna look like I belong in some eighties hair band the rest of the day," I muttered when he put me down so I could rinse as well. Eighties rock bands were the best, but their hair? Hard pass.

Comfortable silence closed in again as we finished up and the time we spent procrastinating wound down. I sensed his trepidation, noted the resolved set of his jaw.

"Jay," I whispered, laying my palm flat against his chest. I wanted to tell him not to worry, that nothing he said could change how I felt.

He didn't let me speak at all, instead curling his large palm around the curve of my waist and tugging me into the center of his body at the same time his mouth claimed mine.

I moaned deep in my throat, the force of it vibrating my tongue. He copied the sound, pulling me even closer, and kissed me like he might never kiss again. This kiss was different, not like the ones that came before it. Usually, he was desperate and fierce, burning with untamed need. It was always wholly devastating... but so was this.

Right now, Jason didn't kiss to claim. He kissed because he wanted to. Like he found reverence in my lips. It was slow and intimate, lazy but thorough, as he left not one part of me unexplored.

When he finally lifted his lips, he stayed mere inches from me, staring at me in worship. If I wasn't already thoroughly besotted and completely drunk on this man, the soft adoration in his usually apathetic eyes would have brought me to my knees.

I blinked slowly, trying to clear some of the haze he inspired, but the brush of his knuckles across my cheek made it a losing battle.

"Thank you," he whispered, his words not breaking the spell, merely enhancing it.

"For what?"

"Being mine for a while."

Oh, my heart.

He thought this was goodbye. It was only just the beginning. Clearly, he was going to be a handful for life.

Scowling, I planted my fists on my naked hips. "This is exactly why you need a sulfate-free shampoo."

He blinked, caught off guard. "Uh, what?"

"Because that chemical-laden floor wax parading as hair care washed all the good sense right out of your brain."

His eyes widened, then narrowed. "What did you just say to me?"

I rolled my eyes. "I said you're an idiot." I shook my head and sighed. "But you kiss real good."

He crossed his arms over his chest, the action accentuating his biceps and the way the water clung to his skin. "I don't know if I should be pissed off or flattered."

I considered it. "Both?"

He laughed under his breath, the softness in his face making my heart flutter. Reaching around, he shut off the water and pushed open the glass door so he could grab some towels. The air out in the bathroom was frosty compared to the steam inside the shower, and I recoiled when it brushed over my wet skin.

"Here," he murmured, draping a towel over my back and tugging it closed around my shoulders. His large hands settled over my arms and rubbed thoroughly, generating warmth and drying me at the same time.

Despite the cold, I didn't even help him. I stood there staring, taking in his prominent cheekbones, strong nose, and lips. His lashes were downturned as he focused on drying me, and his black hair dripped over his forehead. The muscles in his shoulders flexed as he furiously rubbed the water off me. His upper body was so toned even his clavicles were defined, and I thought brazenly of biting them.

"Take a picture. It'll last longer." His voice was gruff.

He definitely was not a shy man, so why did that almost seem shy?

Still slightly entranced by him, I reached up, tracing along the bone I suddenly found so sexy. "I don't need a picture because I plan to look at you anytime I want."

He stepped out of the shower, leaving the door wide for me, and dripped all over the floor while he toweled himself off.

After readjusting the towel around me, I stepped out, shutting the glass door behind me. I let out a breathy gasp when he spun and picked me up, plunking me down on the small counter. One of my butt cheeks hung over the sink, but I barely noticed because of the way he crowded me, caging me in with his strong body and arms planted on either side of me.

"Stop saying shit like that," he ordered, voice dark.

I sniffed, turning my head a little because he wasn't about to tell me what I could do. Unless, of course, we were in bed... because then it seemed I would anything he asked. Anything at all. *And I'd like it.*

I pursed my lips, about to tell him what I thought about his overbearing ways when his hand caught my chin. I guess I expected him to pull my face around, but he didn't. Instead, he angled it a little more away. Surprised, I gazed at him out of the side of my eye, wondering what he was up to now.

This man was always up to something. Always.

Using the grip on my chin, he shifted me again and grunted as he stared.

"Are you staring at my nose piercing?" I asked, partially amused because it seemed like he would turn me this way and that so the small diamond stud would catch the light and sparkle.

When he didn't answer, I sighed. "You made it quite clear before you don't like it, but I do."

He turned my face so our stares collided. His was so dark and delicious it was unfair. "I was just pissed off you went and got more beautiful since the last time I saw you."

I sucked in a breath. "So you like it?"

He made a quiet sound and leaned in, pressing a kiss to the side of my nose. "Of course I do."

I ducked my head, giddiness running rampant through my middle because of his words. "I always wanted it, but my mom was totally against it. Plus, I was competing, so..." My explanation trailed away as I briefly wondered why I felt the need to explain at all.

"It's beautiful, baby. Just like you." He kissed my nose again.

How was I supposed to survive this man? He was equal parts intense and soft.

"You hurt your shoulder, right? Your rotator cuff."

I nodded. "You remembered?"

His mouth crooked up at the corner. "Hm." He agreed. "Which one?" he asked, shifting back so he could look between them.

I gestured to the right one.

His hand curled around my towel-covered hip, and he leaned down, brushing his lips across my bare shoulder. My brain short-circuited. I felt it crackle with overload. He was so unbelievably sweet when he wanted to be.

"My dad told me you were accused of murder."

He jerked back like he was shot. The loss of his lips on my skin momentarily stunned me. Well, that and the fact I'd just blurted it out like that. I told you he short-circuited my brain. Or maybe I just wanted him to stop acting like I was going to evaporate in the palm of his hand.

No more procrastinating. No more assuming the worst of me. Frankly, it was offensive.

He paced back, the towel knotted at his hips. "So he did tell you."

"I told you he did."

He grew agitated. The softness I'd glimpsed in him dissipated to give way to his usual formidable exterior. "What else did he say?"

"That they didn't have enough evidence to prove it, so you were released." I paused, and he gestured for me to say the rest. "And that she drowned. She was found in a pool."

"She didn't drown." His voice was tight, almost angry.

I wanted to ask how she died, but it seemed like such an insensitive question, and his body was already practically vibrating with tension.

"Are you afraid of me?"

I jolted, eyes flying to where he stood. His eyes were penetrating and unreadable.

"What? No," I said, shaking my head.

Something flickered in his stare. Something that looked a lot like relief. "Then why are you hesitating?"

He was shrewd, good at reading a room. A person. I wondered if it was because everyone around him thought he was a killer.

"Because it seems insensitive to ask for details about something that is clearly very painful for you."

He laughed. Shoving a hand through his hair, he paced in the small bathroom, suddenly looking like a caged animal. "If that's true, you'd be the first one to ever consider how I felt."

"Jay," I said, affronted that no one had ever considered his feelings before.

He stopped pacing. "I'll get you a shirt," he uttered and then raced out the door.

"It's inside my jacket," I called behind him. I sat there on the counter and waited, my butt cheek starting to go numb.

I heard a few banging drawers, and when he came back, he was dressed in a pair of hip-riding black joggers, the towel he'd been wearing draped around his neck.

He came forward and extended his hands, which were filled with clothes. My leggings and white crew socks, the T-shirt I'd been wearing beneath the windbreaker at the pool, and another shirt. A shirt that was not mine. I gazed up at him, but he refused to meet my eyes.

I took the leggings and the socks, draping them over my lap, and then reached for a shirt. I practically felt him hold his breath. I felt how hard he tried not to look at what I reached for, how much effort he put in to make it look like he didn't care.

He cared.

He cared so much it nearly suffocated me. So much that I

found it surprising he would even silently offer one of his shirts to me at all. Almost as if it were a test. Or some kind of self-inflicted torture that he clearly thought he deserved. He obviously expected me to grab my own shirt and snub the one he quietly held out.

If only he knew I'd walk across campus naked in the freezing temperatures before I chose the shirt that was not his.

My fingers trembled as they brushed over the cotton material, something inside me knowing this was a huge moment for us and not even at all about a shirt.

I picked it up and pulled it into my lap, noting how he still refused to look and the tight lock he had on his jaw.

Holding out the dark T-shirt, I took in the design and smiled. "You like Aerosmith?"

He jerked, eyes flying to what was left in his hand. My discarded vintage Def Leppard tee. It was my most favorite shirt… Well, until he handed me one of his. His hand curled around the fabric, and it wrinkled beneath the grip.

"Vintage band tees are my favorite," I said, acting like my insides weren't somersaulting and his incredulous reaction wasn't realigning my universe.

The fabric was well-worn and soft when I tugged it over my wet hair. I pushed my arms through and then tugged the towel off my body so it could fall around me, the hem hitting the counter. I hummed happily, brushing my hands over the fabric.

"Comfy."

"Don't you get it?" His voice was strained.

"I get that a girl died and everyone accused you. There wasn't enough evidence to prove it, so the police had to let you go. I'm also assuming that everyone around you thought you were guilty, and that's why you moved all the way across the country."

167

"You haven't asked," he said, still gripping my unwanted T-shirt, still refusing to meet my eyes.

I took a breath. "How did she die?"

He made an angry sound and shoved away from the counter. "Not that!"

"Then what?"

"If I did it!" he roared. "You haven't even asked me if I did it."

"I don't need to ask that, Jay. You didn't."

That seemed to anger him more. His face snapped up, eyes wild and nostrils flared. "Maybe I did."

I hopped down off the counter. My butt cheek screamed in relief, and the hem of his shirt brushed my midthighs. "No. You didn't."

Some of his ire dimmed, and a little awe glowed in the dark embers of his stare. "How can you be so sure?"

I pressed my palm against my heart, rubbing at the aching spot. "I feel it."

His jaw worked, and he flicked his attention away. I wondered how painful it was to be at such war with yourself. "There was evidence. A lot of it."

"You knew her," I said, not really some kind of revelation but something that just occurred to me. The ache in my heart turned into a piercing pain, and I doubled over. I covered the action by grabbing my towel and using it to mop up the water he'd gotten all over the floor.

Had he loved her?

Does he love her still?

Will any girl after her be held to her standard, be forced into her shadow?

"Landry."

I heard him call for me. I saw his bare feet in my line of sight as I mopped the floor with vigor. I didn't answer, though, because I was too lost in my own head.

A hand wrapped around my wrist, stopping the way I furiously scrubbed. I stared at it for long minutes, marveling at our size difference, blinking back the unwanted tears rushing behind my eyes.

"Little siren." His voice was softer this time. Much closer and more cajoling.

I glanced up, realizing he was squatting beside me, his body angled so I was between his spread knees.

"You loved her, didn't you?" I whispered.

Emotion swam in his eyes, and he nodded once. "I did."

I started to bolt up, but he still had hold of my arm and gave it a tug. I fell into him, and we both collapsed onto the floor.

I started to scramble up again, but his arms locked around me like a vise, refusing to let me go as he shifted so he was cross-legged and I was tucked into his lap.

"It wasn't like you're thinking," he said, ignoring the way I tried to get up. "She was my sister."

I gasped, all fight draining out of me as I fell into his chest and looked up. "Your sister?"

"Mm." He agreed. "But not by blood. Not biologically. She was Bodhi's twin sister." I felt him drag in a breath, then exhale. "He was my best friend. My brother."

Then his lips twisted almost sardonically. "The Jamie to my Ryan."

I thought about how Jamie called Rory his sister all the time, and I understood completely. What was hard to imagine was Jason that close to anyone.

"I thought the only friend you had was Lars," I said, the comment kinda dumb but my brain running to catch up.

He made a noise. "He is my only friend, and I didn't even mean to have him."

"He's hard not to like."

"I'd be jealous of that if I didn't know he was gay and all in with Win."

I smiled. "I'm all in with you."

His body turned to granite beneath mine.

"Tell me what happened, Jay."

"Bodhi and me, we did everything together. Surf. Swim. Game. Eat. We were inseparable from the time we were ten. Brynne was his twin sister, so naturally, she was always around, always trying to do what her big brother was doing."

I tilted my head to look up. "He was older?"

"By four minutes." He confirmed. "She became my sister, you know? A bratty little thorn in my side," he mused. But the emotion drained away as fast as it came. "I loved her. She was my family."

"How'd she die?" I asked, no longer caring if it was insensitive because he clearly needed to get this out.

"She showed up to a party one night. Bodhi wasn't there. I was with the rest of the team, and she was already drunk. I told her she had to go home and tried to drag her to my car," he said, his voice dipping as he recalled. "She threw a fit and refused. She, ah, climbed into Cobalt's lap... the team captain, the guy I hated."

"She knew you hated him?"

He released a humorless laugh. "Oh, she knew. Everyone knew. We could barely stand each other. That guy was such a class-A asshole. But everyone worshipped him. It pissed me off."

"Why would she do that if she knew how you felt?"

He was silent for a long minute. Against my side, his fist clenched and unclenched. "Brynne was in love with me," he finally said. "And not the brother-sister kind."

I sucked in a breath.

"Well, she thought she was," he muttered.

"Hey," I said, reaching up to grab his chin and force it down. "It's not so unbelievable."

I heard him swallow. "I dragged her out of there. Made a big scene. Put her in my Corvette and then almost wrecked two streets over. I'd only had two beers, but they hit me out of nowhere, and suddenly, I could barely see straight.

"I pulled over on a side street and went to get some water. She, ah, tried to kiss me."

I gasped. Jealousy coursed through me, but I told myself to cut it out because this was not the time for something so petty.

"I pushed her away. She ran off. I tried to catch her, but she scratched my arm and took off again." He shook his head. Then to himself, he mumbled, "I should have fucking chased her down."

"Jason. What's next?" I said, trying to bring him back to the moment.

"I woke up in my car the next morning. The sun was just coming up. I was still parked on the side of the street, and I felt like I'd been hit by a bus. I dragged my ass home and did the walk of shame past my parents. They asked me where I'd been, and I didn't really have an answer. I couldn't remember anything at all. The last thing I remembered was putting Brynne in the car to drive her home. I tried to call her. It went to voicemail. I tried to call Bodhi, but he didn't answer.

"He showed up a couple hours later, ringing the doorbell like the house was on fire. The second I answered it, he tackled me, punching the shit out of me. I was stunned and confused. I didn't fight back. I mean, this was Bodhi. My dad pulled him off, and he was screaming about his sister and how could I do it. The cops showed up and slapped cuffs on my wrists and read me my rights. I was fucking shocked. Like stunned. I didn't know what was going on. I just kept asking where Brynne was. That's when they told me. Brynne was dead, and I was the one being accused of her murder."

The rawness of his voice coupled with the tortured look on his face was a one-way ticket to that day in hell. To the way his life just shattered, and he didn't even understand why. In a moment, when he should have been mourning the loss of someone he loved, he was instead attacked and arrested.

I pushed up in his lap, and his arms went limp like he wouldn't even fight me if I wanted to get away. But I didn't want away. I wanted closer.

I turned and straddled him, wrapping my legs around his waist as well as my arms around his neck. His chest was bare, and I pushed against it, resting my chin on his shoulder while hugging him with my whole body.

"I'm sorry," I whispered, scratching my fingers against his scalp, trying to comfort him with every ounce that I had.

"Everyone at the party gave statements that I got into a fight with Cobalt. That I punched him in his face. His busted face just backed up everyone's words. They also told everyone that Brynne and I had a screaming match and that I tossed her over my shoulder and forced her away from the party and into my car."

"It's okay," I said, rubbing the back of his neck.

"It's not."

"No. I guess it's not." I agreed.

"You're hugging me anyway."

"Yeah, I am."

"I had scratches all over my arm from her. And I was the last person to see her alive. I didn't come home. I had no alibi at all for the night, and I couldn't remember shit."

"What happened to her?" I asked softly.

"They found her body in the campus pool." His voice

turned strained. "She was... ah, floating there, hair all matted, her pink flowery dress ruined."

Visions of the body at the pool instantly flashed into my brain, and I gasped, forcing myself back. "Like the dummy."

"Yeah. Just like it."

"How do you know what she looked like?"

"They showed me photos. Picture after picture of her dead body. They thought it would make me regret what I'd done. That I'd crack and confess."

Horror stole over me, and I wrapped myself around him again, pushing my face into his neck. "I'm so sorry," I murmured, rubbing his back. "That was so callous. You shouldn't have had to see that."

"I knew her for ten years. We spent lots of time together. She was a beautiful girl, but now when I think of her, all I see are those photos."

I made a sound and squeezed him tighter. There were just no words to make any of this okay. To soothe any of his trauma.

"She had a large wound on the back of her head. They later concluded she died of blunt force trauma to the skull and then was dumped into the pool. She died before she even hit the water."

"Someone killed her and then dumped her in the pool?"

"Mm." He agreed. "And since I was a swimmer, it made me look even guiltier."

Anger got the best of me, licking up from the soles of my feet and turning me indignant. "Please," I spat, pushing so I could sit back and look at him. "If you were going to murder someone, you aren't so stupid that you would throw the body in such an obvious place."

Amusement sparkled in his grim eyes as though he thought it was cute I would be so mad on his behalf.

"My lawyer argued that," he said, spark dimming once

more. "They also argued that the location on my phone didn't move at all that night after I'd parked on the side of that road. In the end, it was all circumstantial, and they had to let me go."

"Dad said it never went to trial."

He made a sound. "But I was tried and convicted in the court of public opinion."

"No one believed you?" I asked. "Not even Bodhi?"

"Bodhi had just lost his twin. His other half. His parents were beside themselves. He couldn't think or see straight. All he knew was that I was the last person to see her before she died, and she'd attacked me and left marks. People always said I was a fuckboy, but I never thought he believed it."

"No one else? No one on the team?"

He was quiet a while, then shook his head. "My parents stood by me. But sometimes I wonder if they think I did it. They shipped me here because they were hoping people would forget. Because having a murderer for a son was a bad look.

"Besides..." He continued, but then his voice fell away.

I waited for him to finish, but when he didn't, I drew back to look at him encouragingly. "What?"

His eyes touched mine, then flitted away. "Besides, how could any of them believe I didn't do it when I'm not even sure myself?"

19

RUSH

"THAT'S THE STUPIDEST THING I'VE EVER HEARD IN MY WHOLE life!" she proclaimed, so mad she was nearly vibrating as she tried to scramble out of my lap.

Her legs got tangled, and she pitched backward, but I caught her around the waist before she fell.

"Calm down," I told her, secretly thrilled beyond reason that she was so pissed off on my behalf. No one was ever like this for me before. Not even my parents. They'd remained calm and stone-faced in their defense of me. It was almost as though the accusation of murder wasn't that farfetched.

"Never in the history of existence has telling a woman to calm down ever worked," she intoned.

Ahh, she was cute. *I really want to keep her.*

Frankly, it was shocking she was still here in this room, wearing my T-shirt. Which, by the way, totally slayed me. I gave her a choice. Her shirt or mine.

She chose me.

Which was exactly why I was spilling it all, trying to make her understand. Understand why she shouldn't choose me even if I did love the shit out of her for it. I wasn't innocent. I never would be.

Unfolding from the floor, I pulled her with me, setting her on her feet.

She waved her finger at me. "I mean it. I will never believe you did this."

"To be fair, your beliefs are already skewed. You do believe in Bigfoot."

She stomped on my foot.

"Ow!" I yelled, hopping on the other while I rubbed at the stinging spot. "What the hell, woman?"

"Believing in Bigfoot is easier than believing in you, you giant itchy sweater!"

I forgot about my foot. "Itchy sweater?"

"Yes. They're horrible and give me a rash."

I laughed. Like an actual honest laugh. While I was standing there telling someone about the shit that literally shattered my life and how I was maybe a murderer, she had the gall to compare me to an itchy sweater.

"Did Coach torture you with that whistle when you were a kid?"

Her face darkened, and she took a threatening step forward. Her hair was damp and plastered against her head. She'd forgotten to comb it. She was dressed in literally nothing but my old Aerosmith tee, and she looked like she would kick my ass if I even blinked funny.

I love you.

"Don't you bring my father into this," she said, planting her hands on her hips and making the shirt ride up on her thighs. She was toned and lithe, all the swimming giving her a beautiful shape. "I told him, and I'll tell you too!"

I forgot about the humor. How adorable she was. "What did you tell Coach?"

"I told him that I don't care what anyone says. What you were accused of. I don't care. And I told him if he wanted to try and make me stay away from you, I'd move out."

She said what? "You live with Coach?"

"He's my dad," she said as if I forgot. To be fair, it wouldn't be the first thing I did.

"What about the dorms?" Bro, she lived with my coach who'd basically penned my name on the top of his shit list.

"Living at home is free," she said, then muttered, "but the dorms have furniture at least."

None of that even mattered. "You really said that to your dad?"

She scowled. "He told the police about everything that happened."

I shrugged. "He wants me away from you."

She closed the distance between us, wrapped her arms around my waist, and pressed her face into my chest. "I'm sorry he hurt you too."

My chest compressed. "He didn't."

She patted my back as though she knew better and, for once, didn't argue. I would have preferred an argument. Or a foot stomp. Or a comparison to something ridiculous.

"I wouldn't want a murder suspect dating my daughter either," I said, wanting to wrap my arms around her but not letting myself do it.

"You were cleared."

"Just because I was cleared doesn't mean everyone doesn't still suspect. Even I do."

She pulled back. "Is that what you meant the night at the pool when you said you came to remember?"

I nodded. "The evidence is just so convincing. Everyone

seems so sure. People who knew me. People I trusted. If they think I'm capable, then maybe I am. Maybe I was pissed she would do that with Cobalt. Maybe I was pissed she was fighting me. Maybe it was an accident and I panicked and dumped her body. Maybe my mind wiped it all as a defense mechanism."

"Or maybe you passed out drunk, and wherever she ran off to that night is what got her killed."

Swift, hot denial made me pull away. Agitation pooled in my veins. "This isn't her fault."

I knew I shouldn't snap at her. I knew what she was saying could be the truth. But even after everything, I would never blame Brynne.

"Of course it isn't," she said softly. "But it's not yours either."

Then whose fault is it?

"I told her she was making a bad choice that night," I said, the memory blowing in my brain like an ocean breeze. "She told me it was hers to make." A broken sound cut through my throat. "She was right."

"Maybe you didn't handle things well that night. Maybe you should have just let her make her own choices. But that doesn't make you a killer, Jay. It doesn't make you a bad person either. You care about her. You were trying to protect her."

"Yeah? Well, I got her killed." Even if I hadn't done it, I was still the reason she was running alone on a dark road at night.

"You don't know that for sure."

"I remembered some. After months and months, I remembered something that night at the pool. When you thought I was drowning."

"You were."

"I wasn't," I argued.

"What did you remember, Jay?"

Why was it that hearing her call me Jay was more devastating than hearing her call me Jason? It bespoke of even more intimacy, even more familiarity. Of fondness. Love.

"I told you already. Everything that happened after I pulled over. How she tried to kiss me. How she scratched me and ran off. I didn't remember any of that until that night in the pool. Up until then, I couldn't remember anything except the party."

"That's good, though, right?" she asked, taking a tentative step toward me. Almost as though she was approaching a wild animal. "Now you know she ran off. That you weren't the last person with her."

"But I can't remember anything else," I said, voice hoarse.

God, I was fucking tired. Tired of talking about this. Of reliving it. Replaying it again and again, day in and day out. Why couldn't I just be guilty? It would be easier that way.

Easier to accept everyone's hate. Their betrayal. Easier to accept that I deserved everything I got.

But not her. If I really was guilty, then I didn't deserve Landry.

Hell, I didn't deserve her even if I wasn't.

Yet here she stood.

A light touch on my hand made me jolt. I looked down at where she touched, her fingers a mere caress. I stared for a few moments and then gave in, wrapping my hand around hers.

"Maybe you can't remember because there's nothing else to recall." Her voice was as gentle as her touch.

My eyes flew up to hers. I knew she saw the shock I felt, the way my mind raced with her words. Is that why? Why no matter how much I browbeat myself into remembering, there was nothing there?

She nodded as if she could hear my thoughts. As if she were agreeing with them.

I wanted to believe that so much it caused my stomach to cramp. But the truth was it wasn't that easy, and I would always wonder. Everyone would. And until there was a definitive answer, I would always be the one who did it.

"There are no other suspects. No other leads. The only person with the motive and means to kill her was me."

"Did you want her to die?" Landry asked.

The question was like a hard slap to my face, and I recoiled. "*No*. She was my sister. I loved her."

Was she your sister, though? Really? Were any of them in Cali your true family? If they were, then why are you here alone?

Expressive mossy eyes stared at me as if she'd just proved something and waited for me to catch on. As if my own repulsed reaction to the idea of hurting Brynne was all the proof anyone would need.

"How can you be so sure?" I whispered, almost desperate for the answer.

I was vulnerable just then, a feeling that nauseated me. I tried to swallow down the bile rising in my throat, but it didn't budge, just sat there like a knot in my constricted esophagus. How could she have so much faith in me? I couldn't even summon an ounce of it for myself.

"Yeah, we have extreme chemistry, but we barely know each other. People who knew me my entire life aren't even as sure as you."

She pressed her palm over her chest again, and I made a rude sound.

"Besides that."

Her green eyes lifted, the full effect of them stealing my breath. "Isn't my heart enough?"

Oh my damn. I picked her up, holding her out over the floor and meeting her gaze. "Your heart is more than I will ever deserve."

She tilted her head. "Does that mean you don't want it?"

"Careful what you give me, little siren. I might never give it back."

"That's not an answer," she sang.

"Kiss me with that bratty mouth."

"No."

I lifted an eyebrow. "No?"

She pursed her lips. I chuckled and pulled her in, a feeling of rightness overwhelming me when her legs wrapped around my waist.

"I want it," I confessed quietly. "I want you so much I'm willing to take it even though I know you deserve better."

Her face softened, hands gliding into my damp hair. She leaned in, lashes fluttering against her cheeks, and my heart slowed, anticipating her kiss.

Just before we met, she stopped. "Just one thing,"

My eyes popped open to meet her lively stare. "What?" I asked, my voice already raspy from our just-out-of-reach kiss.

"You do deserve me, Jay. You deserve so much."

I groaned, completely done with waiting for her to kiss me. The woman moved like a sloth. I closed the distance and claimed her mouth, pushing my tongue deep and cupping the back of her head to hold her in place.

I drank her down, every word she'd said. I felt like a drained battery, a clock stuck on a certain hour, but her words of belief, confidence, and even the anger on my behalf were like a bolt of electricity, jumping me back to life and restarting time.

No longer did I have to live in the past, stuck on repeat. Maybe now I could have more. Maybe I finally wanted more.

Suddenly, I felt overfull and overwhelmed. So accustomed to running on empty and survival mode that I didn't know how to function on anything more.

Easing away, I pulled in a deep breath and smiled. "You forgot to comb your hair."

She gasped, reaching up with both hands to pat her head. "Your shampoo washed away my good sense too!"

I chuckled, placing her back on the edge of the sink, keeping myself between her legs while I grabbed a brush from the drawer. "Here."

She hugged it against her chest and glanced around. "Do you have a hair dryer?" she asked, hopeful.

I found it and plugged it in before handing it over.

I started away, but she caught my arm. "Where are you going?"

"To get a shirt. Someone took mine."

She batted her eyes. "Did you want it back?"

I leaned in close. "You already know the answer to that."

"Wait!" She gasped when I started away again.

"What now? You want my toothbrush too?"

She smiled and crooked her finger at me and lifted the brush. "You didn't comb your hair either."

I scoffed. "Please, woman, I look good no matter what."

"Come here and let me comb that big head."

I arched my brows. "Oh, *you're* going to comb it?"

"Well, I'm the one that has to look at you."

I put my hand over my heart like I was wounded, and she giggled. My heart constricted, squeezing so tight it reached my throat. Resting my palm on the counter, I leaned in, lowering my head.

Her scent mingled with mine on her skin and floated under my nose when she leaned forward. My body reacted instantly, desire blossoming in my stomach. The shirt rode high on her thighs as she moved, resting one palm on my shoulder for balance before bringing the brush to my head. The second she started combing, goose bumps raced over my body, and I bit back a groan.

My hair was cut close around the sides of my head and ears with the top long enough to comb into a style. She took her sweet time, though, brushing in one direction and then the other, dragging out the insane pleasure of something so simple.

I liked the way she touched me. The way she made me feel important like all her concentration was solely on me. Prickles of awareness scattered across my scalp, and my head bowed even more as I groaned lightly.

Too soon, she was done, the brush disappearing into her lap. I lifted my face, completely fuzzy-headed and relaxed.

She smiled, dragging her fingers through the strands by my forehead. "Looks good."

"Thanks, baby," I said, leaning up to press a kiss to her temple before forcing myself away.

Out in the bedroom, I stood there dully, staring at the heap of clothes I'd left lying when we came in. In the bathroom, she hopped off the counter and muttered something under her breath about bad shampoo before turning on the hair dryer.

I smiled to myself, listening to the noise she made, feeling it echo in all my hollow places. When Lars wasn't here, this place was so quiet. Almost like a tomb. Like I was sentenced to death just like Brynne. Landry was life. Vibrant and alive. By legend, most sirens lured men to their death, but this one? My little siren? She lured me away from it, toward something I thought was lost forever.

Maybe I didn't need to show her. Maybe it didn't mean anything at all.

If that were true, you wouldn't have it hidden in your pocket, away from prying eyes.

My feet felt like lead when I shuffled over to my grubby clothes from this morning and pushed my hand into the pocket of the hoodie. Withdrawing it, I stared down at the crinkled note jammed in the plastic I'd taken off the dummy. The dummy dressed just like Brynne.

Despite the protective sleeve, some of the edges were wet, and it appeared some of the marker had smeared. My hand closed around it, crushing it in my grip. It was a cruel reminder that just because I might want more, it didn't mean I could have it.

I thought briefly of throwing the note away and pretending it didn't exist. I couldn't do it. Throwing it away wouldn't make me forget.

And whoever wrote this note clearly wouldn't either.

20

LANDRY

IT WAS TRAGIC REALLY.

And no, I didn't mean the death of Jason's sister or the fact his entire life was stripped away and he was left alone.

I mean, yeah, those things were terrible.

The tragedy I'm talking about right now, though, was my hair.

I will never understand how men get away with slathering the same thing all over their entire bodies and walking around looking like sex on a stick. Or in Jason's case, sex in a Speedo.

Pretty sure the man used the same terrible shampoo to wash his face. I saw no face wash in that shower. I would rather rinse my face with water and let my skin fend for itself before slathering that poor excuse for soap around my eyes.

For shame.

As I finished up drying my hair using only a sad brush

and his hair dryer, I thought longingly of my duffle that I'd forgotten back at the pool. My moisturizer, lip balm, and everything else I used to put myself together were all there, taunting me with how far away it was.

My hair was thick, and I had lots of it, something I know most would consider a blessing, and really, I suppose it was. However, trying to style and tame it often left a lot to be desired.

I kept it cut into a short, blunt bob because when I was swimming competitively, it was so much easier to stuff under a swim cap and also shampoo. Even though I was no longer competing, I never considered growing it out. I was still in the pool almost every day, and I worked out in the gym several times a week. Long, thick hair was still too much of a bother.

The bob stopped just past my chin and was the same length all the way around. I loved the clean line of a blunt cut and how all the thick strands created a sharp edge where it ended. Even though it was a short cut, I had so much hair that it was a full style with some natural wave. It gave it a tousled look that I didn't have to try too hard for. Though I kept it on the shorter side in the vein of easy maintenance, I went and ruined that by adding in blond. My hair was naturally brown, not quite as dark as my dad's but definitely not blond. Therefore, it required work to keep it the color I preferred.

I went with a shadow-root style, meaning it was darker at the roots so at least I didn't have a harsh line when my highlights started to grow out. I kept the sections around my face bright and light, and everywhere else favored thick highlights of a golden-blond shade.

Since I didn't have much product today—aka *no* product —I did the best I could smoothing it out with the brush and hair dryer, relieved to see his bad shampoo didn't seem to leech out any of the color.

When my hair was dry, I dug around in the side pocket of my leggings, praying I'd come up with a hairband. When my fingers closed around it, I thanked the hair gods.

Are you wondering why I was thinking about my hair and not Jason's confession?

I told you. I didn't care. Correction, I did care. I cared about how he undoubtedly suffered and beat himself up every day over something I knew he didn't do.

Back at the mirror, I pulled up the front sections so it was in a half-up pony and then secured it with the tie into a messy bun. After pulling a few strands loose around my ears, I decided it was probably as good as it was going to get until I could get to my stuff.

As I was bending to grab my socks and leggings, I realized Jason wasn't making any noise at all out in the other room. Taking my clothes, I left the bathroom to find him standing in the center of the room. He still wasn't wearing a shirt, and his back was to me as he stood staring down at something in his hand.

"Jay?"

His shoulder blades rippled when I called his name, but otherwise, he remained the same.

"Hey, what are you looking at?" I asked, padding forward to toss my clothes on his bed and step around to see. "What's that?" I noted the way his hand was crushing something, grip so tight his knuckles were white.

"More reasons you should run like hell."

"Show me," I said, reaching up to pull his fingers from the death grip. "C'mon, Jay, let's get it all out now."

That seemed to penetrate, and he took a breath and opened his hand, turning so it was palm up. Lying in the center was a crumpled note in a plastic sleeve.

"Can I look at it?" I asked, fingers hovering over it.

He gestured for me to take it, so I did, tugging it out of the plastic sleeve and opening the folded sheet of white paper. The words were written in black ink, ink that had clearly gotten wet in a few spots and bled a little. It gave the words an ominous, unstable feeling that made the hair on the back of my neck stand.

I won't forget.

Tearing my eyes from the paper, I glanced at Jason. "Where did you get this?"

"It was on the body."

I drew back. "The dummy in the pool?"

He made a gruff sound of agreement. Then I remembered watching whoever did this put a lanyard around the dummy's neck. This must have been what was attached.

"Why didn't you say something?" I questioned.

His face twisted, and all the stillness he'd been caged in seemed to explode. "So I could explain to the cops what it meant? So I could tell my new *swim bros* who already hate me?"

"No one hates you."

He scoffed. "Your dad told the cops."

The disappointment of that was unmistakably deep for Jason. My father gave him a chance to swim here, a place to start over, and then he turned on him the first chance he got. I didn't know what to say to make that okay. I didn't think I could.

Instead, I gestured to the paper. "But you still didn't show them this note."

He paced away, frustration written in the way he moved and the ragged breaths he pulled in. "I'm tired of being accused, okay? Of everyone looking at me like a fuck-up. Like a killer. I let my parents ship me out here so I didn't have to see that look on people's faces. So I could try and salvage what little I had left. And then someone goes and dumps a body in my pool. In the one place that was still mine. They dressed her up like Brynne." His voice went hoarse when he said her name, and then he said nothing at all.

I tossed the paper on the floor and trampled it on my way to him. Pressing into him from behind, I locked my arms around his waist.

"Don't hug me right now."

"Make me stop."

His body slumped, and I hugged him harder, pressing my cheek into the center of his back. "It was like being back there," he whispered, the confession ripping out of him. "I imagined that night a million times. I saw the photos. I've dreamed it. But to see it raw. In the flesh. It didn't even matter it was a damned dummy. For those first few minutes, it was vividly real, and I was reliving exactly what I might have done."

I was thankful then that I'd skipped breakfast because his words tossed my stomach around inside me like a violent storm. The torment of seeing that floating body, of the flashbacks he likely endured…

I hated myself for screaming then. For drawing his attention and making him see.

"I heard you call her name," I whispered, a confession of my own.

"If I could have saved her, I would have."

"I know." My hand rubbed slow circles over his stomach, trying to soothe even a tiny part of him.

"I'm sorry I accused you."

"I know, Jay. I understand."

"I wish I did."

Oh, that hurt. How I wished he could see himself through my eyes. Even for just five minutes.

"The cops seem to think it's a prank. It's not, is it?" I said, still hugging him from behind.

"I don't think so. Not with the note. With the way she was dressed."

"Who knows about what happened in California?"

"Coach."

I stiffened and pulled back. "My dad is a lot of things, and I know he told the cops, but he wouldn't do this. He wouldn't."

"I know."

That brought me up short. "You know?"

He turned, offering me a half smile that didn't quite reach his eyes. "That pool is sacred. He'd never do something like that in there."

My lips twitched. It wasn't exactly a ringing endorsement, but he was right. "Who else knows?"

"The dean."

"It's not the dean." I was sure. He wouldn't do anything to ruin the reputation of his precious school or his precious Elite.

"I doubt it."

"Who—" I started, but he cut me off with a shake of his head.

"There's no one else."

When I said nothing, he made a sound like he thought I didn't believe him. "I didn't want anyone to know for obvious reasons. I came to swim. To get my degree and then get the hell out. I didn't plan on making friends." His eyes flickered. "Or meeting you."

"But Lars got in."

"It wasn't Lars!"

I jerked at the sudden implosion of the words. The absolute angry denial. It was almost as though he could never accept it because if one more person he actually let in betrayed him, he might never recover.

"I know it wasn't Lars, babe."

He glanced up sharply at my cajoling voice. "Babe?"

I shrugged. It had just come out.

"I like Jay better."

I smiled. *And he thinks I'm the brat.* "Maybe I like babe better."

Okay, maybe I was the brat.

"And maybe if you call me that again, I'll feed you my cock until you can't say anything at all."

"Ba—"

He was on me so fast that the rest of the word turned into a squeak. He backed me up against the wall and wrapped his hand around my throat.

"Say it again." He dared. "Call me that generic, cheap knock-off of a term of endearment like you forgot my real name. One. More. Time. So help me, little siren, I will paint your vocal cords with my cum and brand them with my name."

My knees were weak. My body trembled with the filthy image he'd painted and the idea of choking on his release as he shot it into the back of my throat. I glanced up at him, at his black eyes simmering like hot coals. He needed this. Despite having me twice already, he was already back on the edge. This entire conversation riled him up and left him feeling caged. It didn't matter I'd told him I was on his side. He needed me to yield to him, to offer my submission.

I swallowed against his hold, enjoying the tight fit of his palm. He didn't hurt me. He made sure I could breathe. I wondered how these dark urges made him feel when he thought about them when he wasn't being controlled by them.

Maybe I'd ask him later.

But first...

"Babe."

It was like pouring gasoline on a flame. Waving a red flag in front of an angry bull. Unfettered wildness burst in his black eyes, and in that moment, I totally saw proof that black was the presence of all colors.

Jason was so full. Full of so much color that it turned him dark.

His fingers tightened at my throat, no longer a five-finger necklace but a choker. It was slightly uncomfortable, but I felt not an ounce of fear. All I felt was satisfaction.

"What's your safe word?" he ground out, his voice sounding as if he'd been dragged into the basement of hell.

I wet my lips to reply, and he loosened his hold so I could speak. "Red."

Approval flared in his eyes, but I knew I'd get no praise. I'd riled him up, and this was my punishment.

His hand left my throat and hit my shoulder to push me to my knees. I sank down easily, my legs poor support for this moment anyway. The floor was hard and cold on my knees, the door still close to my back.

"Open your mouth," he said, yanking his black joggers down around his thighs.

He was already completely hard, his cock flushed and ready.

The second my lips parted, he grabbed my head and pushed into my throat, sinking so deep that my nose hit his pubic bone.

The thick, swollen head of his dick pushed against the back of my throat, and I gagged, a little bit of panic creeping in because he was such a tight fit.

He pulled back just enough so I could breathe.

"Relax your throat," he said overhead, and I let my jaw go slack as I did what he asked.

He pushed back in, and I felt him at the back of my throat. He held himself there until I couldn't breathe and then pulled back to let me have some air. He continued the sweet torture until I started anticipating the stretch and moaned around his thickness when I felt it.

He grunted and pulled out, leaving just the tip between my lips.

I glanced up the length of his body, staring at him through watering eyes. The tops of his cheekbones were flushed, and his eyes were glittering like black diamonds. Seeing my attention, he brushed his knuckles across my cheekbones and then thrust into my mouth again.

My eyes flew wide, and then I groaned as he started fucking into my mouth, using my body exactly as he needed. I kept my jaws slack and whimpered at his fingers in my hair as he drove into me, down into my throat like he was indeed fucking my vocal cords so they learned his name.

I felt flushed and dizzy, and between my legs was wet. When his cock grew even thicker and started to pulse, I started to suck fervently, knowing he was close.

He wrenched back, the popping sound of him leaving my mouth loud to my ears.

"Say it," he growled. "Say my name while I'm fucking you."

"Jason," I rasped, shocked by the sound of my own voice.

He grabbed my chin. "Again."

"Jay."

"Open up."

I stuck out my tongue, and he pushed back in until my nose was buried against his skin. "Say my name again, little siren. Say it while I come."

I tried to say it. But it was nothing more than a garbled moan.

He came with a low shout, true to his word, pouring

down the back of my throat and making me choke. I recovered quickly, my throat working to swallow him down, to milk every last drop of him he had to give.

His thrusts gentled, and he pulled back enough just to fill my mouth. Tears streamed down my face, and my chest heaved from effort and desire. I felt feverish, and the T-shirt he'd given me was sticking to my back.

He continued to thrust lazily across my tongue, and I sucked him gently.

"*Fuck*, what you do to me."

Between my legs was throbbing, and my knees ached against the floor. The salty tang of his release clung to the back of my throat, and I sucked him a little harder.

Abruptly, he pulled back, robbing me of his semi-hard dick. I swayed a little at the sudden movement, and he picked me up off the floor.

My back hit the mattress, and he hit his knees beside the bed and grabbed my legs to pull them wide. After draping them over his shoulders, he buried his face in my dripping center.

I arched off the bed with a cry, and he wrapped his palms around my thighs to hold me in place while he licked and sucked. The slurping sounds he made were sinful, further proof that he turned me on like no one else.

Two fingers slid into my opening and started to thrust. I cried out, body going tight as he continued with the delicious pressure on my swollen clit.

The orgasm hit me all at once, bursting over me like a firework, the intense pleasure making my mouth fall open as I shuddered under his ministrations. I gasped and moaned, once again arching up as more ripples of ecstasy rolled over me.

When at last I collapsed on the bed, spent and shaking, he

rubbed his palms up and down my bare legs. I made a little sound but managed nothing else.

He chuckled and dragged my body farther up the mattress and then stepped out of my line of sight. I wondered where he went but was too spent to lift my head. He came back moments later, his sweats pulled back into place. Uncapping a water, he held it out, but I only stared at it.

The bed dipped under his weight, his arm slid beneath my shoulder to sit me up, and he put the water against my lips. "Drink, little siren."

The cool water felt good going down my throat. I'd definitely loved everything we just did, and I would definitely do it again. There was a bit of soreness in my throat, though. It was the first time anyone had ever been that deep.

I drank some more and then he set it aside. Instead of laying me back on the mattress, he pulled me into his lap, sitting with his back to the headboard. I cuddled into him, sighing with contentment.

"Was I too rough?" He always worried about that.

"No."

"Your voice is strained."

"Does that bother you?" I asked.

He debated for a long moment, and I was content with the quiet and the way he rubbed up and down my back. Finally, he said, "I know it should, but honestly, I like it."

"I like it too."

"Really? I don't scare you?"

"No, Jay. But I think maybe you scare yourself."

His hand came up, hovering at my head, and then finally settled, rubbing at my hair. The hair I was going to have to recomb.

"I do," he confessed.

"I wondered."

"What did you wonder?"

"If your, ah, tendency to be rough made you doubt your-self even more."

His tone was sardonic when he said, "You mean it's just more evidence I'm a killer."

"That's *not* what I meant." My voice was still raspy. Every time I spoke, it was a reminder that he owned me. I wanted to keep talking. Keep listening to the proof that he was mine.

Reaching down, he pulled the comforter up and tucked it around us. "I've never been like this with anyone else."

I jolted up, the blanket falling off my shoulders when I blinked at him in surprise. "What?"

He chuckled. "I've had sex. I'm definitely no choir boy. But after Brynne…" His voice faded away, and I touched his chest. His skin was so warm, the rhythm of his heart so steady. "You were the first girl I slept with after. The, ah, only girl."

I jolted again, tumbling back out of his lap. My bare legs ended up in the air and the comforter partially over my head.

"I've never in my life met anyone with the ability to fall over while sitting," he mused, gently lifting me back and wrapping his arms around me.

"I'm the only person you've slept with in… months?"

"Six months."

I gaped.

"I thought you…"

He smirked. "Were a fuckboy."

"No!" I said, completely indignant. "But you're…" I looked him up and down. "You." I cleared my throat. "And Elite."

"I've had plenty of opportunities," he said, smug. "And maybe there were a few hand jobs here and there."

I rolled my eyes.

"But you are the only one I've ever felt this… obsessed with.

Like even when I'm with you, I want more. There's this urge in me to claim you. To own you. To brand you as mine." He shook his head. "That first night, I thought maybe I was just wound up because of the memories. Because of your sassy mouth."

"It wasn't?"

"No. The second I saw you walk out of the locker room, I wanted you again. The need was so urgent and fierce it pissed me off. Not even you being Coach's daughter was enough to chase me off. I just..." His hands flexed where they rested against me like he was trying to rein it in.

"Just what?"

"Want you," he declared.

It seemed like he was going to say something else but left it unspoken. But I let it go because he was already wringing so much out of himself today. He had already given me more than enough.

"Maybe you just sense you can be yourself with me," I said simply.

There was desperation in him. A palpable need to claim me, almost force me into succumbing so I couldn't get away. It made sense to me after knowing everything he went through, after knowing how everyone abandoned him. Maybe he thought if he didn't hold on so tight, I'd slip away too.

He didn't say anything else, and I pressed an open-mouth kiss to his chest before snuggling back in.

"Jay?" I asked after a few quiet minutes.

"Hmm?"

"For the record, I like the way you are. The roughness. And I also don't think you're as volatile as you think. You always check in. You gave me a safe word. It's not like you hit me."

"I would *never*," he swore, his body going tense. "That

would never give me pleasure. Ever. Inflicting pain isn't something I want to do."

"Maybe just a little soreness," I teased.

His hand curled around the side of my neck, the hold gentle and light. "Maybe a little. So you can feel me later."

So I don't forget about him. As if I could.

"For a long time, I was numb," he whispered, and I listened intently as a little rush of giddiness fluttered beneath my ribs.

I felt like I was finding another one of those secrets he held deep in his bottomless eyes.

"Everyone turned their backs. My parents were kinda like robots. My best friend hated me. My sister was dead. My life crashed around me, and everything I knew was gone. I went cold and then numb. It was easier that way. It didn't hurt as much. I got so good at being an asshole, at keeping people away. Numb became my default setting. I thought maybe I wouldn't feel again."

I rubbed up and down his arm as he spoke, letting him know I was listening but not wanting to ruin what he confided with the sound of my voice.

"But then you showed up, and those green eyes lit up my world. I never thought of green as the color of life before... but it is. Earth. New leaves on trees. Grass. Growth. Everything around me was dead, and then suddenly, you were there, overflowing with life."

"Jay," I whispered, emotion weighing down my heart and my voice. I shifted, wrapping both arms around him, hugging him tight.

"It's intense with you, maybe because I've been numb so long. But I can't get enough. Being rough only makes me feel it deeper. Makes me feel it *more*."

Tears clinging to my lashes, heart nearly caving in inside my chest, I pulled back and straddled him, wrapping all of me around all of him. "You can have me however you want me. In every way. I'm yours."

"Even after everything?"

"Always."

"Even if someone found out about everything and plans to unpack my past here at Westbrook? People hate me, Landry. And if you're with me, they will hate you by extension."

A fierce need to protect him came over me. A need to be everything no one else has been to him. "Let them," I said. "Let them hate. I'll be too busy loving you."

He sucked in a breath, and I worried for a moment dropping the L-word might freak him out. I mean, it wasn't a love confession. Well, it kinda was.

Was it?

His arms wrapped back around me, and he groaned into the side of my neck. I felt him press a few kisses there, and I sighed.

"I'm tired of talking." His voice was muffled against my skin.

I giggled. "You are a chatty boyfriend."

He froze.

Crap. The kinda L-word *and* the B-word. I was on fire today.

Please, someone get an extinguisher.

I pulled back, eyes wide. "I didn't mean... I—"

My brain for sure didn't have a problem finding unnecessary words before. And now it doesn't want to work?

"Boyfriend?"

I winced. "You didn't have to repeat it," I muttered. "It just slipped out. I know we aren't—"

His kiss halted my words and also short-circuited my brain. I kinda needed my brain. It was already operating on three wheels.

The disconnect of our kiss was audible when he pulled back. "You'd want me to be your boyfriend?"

I wrinkled my nose. "Of course not. I can't date anyone who doesn't believe in Bigfoot."

His eyes turned calculating and amused. "What if I order us some food and turn on that show where people try and find him?"

Butterflies erupted in my belly, but I narrowed my eyes. "If you don't believe in Bigfoot, how do you know about that show?"

"They filmed it near me in Cali one time." He snorted. "As if Bigfoot would be living at the beach."

I pinched his nipple.

"Ow, woman!" he swore, rubbing at it. "You know it's true. Some surfer dudes were probably high as a kite on reefer and thought they saw it. Can you imagine all the sand he'd have matted in his hairy ass?" Jason shook his head decisively. "He ain't in Malibu."

I laughed. "You've put a lot of thought into this for a nonbeliever."

He made a face. "You gonna be my girlfriend or what?"

My breath caught, and all my laughter died as my heart rate turned rapid. "I already told you I was yours, Jay. I think it's more if you want to be mine."

His entire face softened. It was a sight to behold because of his bone structure and dark features. "You think I don't want to be yours?"

"I'm not sure," I said, vulnerability seeping out of my pores. It was one thing to want to have sex with me but another to want a relationship.

He groaned, sitting up to capture my face in his hands and penetrate me with his endless dark stare. "You have owned me from the minute you tried to save my life in that pool. From the moment you held my hand and lured me out of the past. One look in those life-saturated eyes, and you are all I see. It doesn't seem to matter how much chaos tries to drown me because you, little siren, always seem to guide me back."

"So... boyfriend?" I asked, the only words I could manage because of the way he overwhelmed me.

He half smiled. "I'll take that title. I'll fucking own it. Even though it's selfish, even though you're too good for me and Coach will probably try and BBQ my innards."

"Ew."

"Hush. I'm being romantic."

"Barbequing innards is *not* romantic." But even his poor attempt at romance couldn't stop the furious way my insides fluttered.

"You really want me?" he whispered. "Even if I might have—"

I put my hand up to his lips. "You didn't."

I saw the doubt in his eyes. The worry.

I lowered my hand, and he said, "But what if I did?"

"I want you anyway, Jay." Maybe I was crazy. Maybe I was ruled by my hormones. I wouldn't change how I felt.

"I—" He slammed his lips shut, panic blooming in his eyes as though he'd almost said something he knew he shouldn't.

I pushed a finger into his chest. "Boyfriend." Then I reversed the finger and pointed it at myself. "Gir—"

He cut me off. "Mine."

"Thank you for telling me everything."

"Thanks for staying."

The intense emotions swirling around the room settled like a heavy blanket having been shaken out and falling into place.

I knew, with Jason, things wouldn't be easy.

But it didn't matter because, to me, he was worth the price.

21

NIGHT PRACTICES WERE JUST LIKE MORNING PRACTICES EXCEPT instead of the sun rising while we lapped it up, the sun was on its way down.

Coach rode us hard, blowing that damnable whistle and yelling insults like we were fresh in the pool instead of seasoned college swimmers.

I knew it was my fault. Dude had a stick up his ass the size of Missouri. I was sure he regretted the chance he gave me, the one no other swim coach in the country wanted to extend. At the time, I acted like I gave zero shits and was only coming to Westbrook to appease the parentals. Actually, that was how it was. But then I got here. Coach didn't treat me like some ex-con he was doing a favor.

I knew he watched me closer than the others, but I was used to being stared at, so it rolled off my back like water. My defenses were always up, my guard on lockdown. And then I learned there was a crack somewhere in my armor. A crack Coach Resch managed to find.

Know how I figured it out?

The betrayal that cut me when he told the cops about my sordid past and watched them shove me into the back of their car. I guess the second chance he offered just months ago had an expiration date.

Rationally, I couldn't blame him. Landry was his daughter, and Elite was his life. It still stung. And that stinging bothered me. It showed me I wasn't as airtight as I'd assumed.

FYI, Landry doesn't count. She didn't slip in through a crack. She didn't break down my walls. She didn't have to. She was such a little siren that I vaulted all my own wards and ran in her direction.

I half expected him to kick me out when I walked into the locker room for practice. My hackles were raised as I opened my locker, preparing to see all my shit already gone.

Everything was there. Elite talked and laughed around me like they weren't in the presence of a murder suspect. I guess as far as they knew, they weren't. And I just stood there in the center of it all and stared at my shit.

Coach said nothing. Hell, Walsh didn't either.

So I'd put on my Speedo and was currently swimming laps like everyone else. Today, I was swimming butterfly. It was the hardest, most intense stroke. I chose it because I craved a punishing workout.

By the time my main set was finished, my back and shoulders were quivering. Hanging on the edge of the pool, I swiped some of the water off my face and contemplated another lap.

"Bro, nice swimming."

I glanced up at Owens who was in the lane next to me.

"I'm still better, though."

"Fuck off, Owens," I said with a lot less heat than usual.

He didn't take the hint and get lost. Bro never did. "You know, if you stuck to one stroke, you'd probably dominate," he commented, throwing his arms over the lane rope to stare at me through the goggles still strapped over his eyes.

It was something coaches had been telling me for years. It was also the reason some coaches wouldn't work with me at all. Swimmers were supposed to have one concentration. I knew I'd probably be the best in whatever I chose just like Jamie said. I didn't give a shit.

"I'd rather be good at everything than just one thing," I told him.

Jamie grinned, his cheeks bunching up around the goggle frames. "Spoken like a true wildcard."

"Why the hell are you two over here looking like a pair of expired coupons?" Coach snapped, appearing above us.

"Expired?" Jamie guffawed. "I'm in my prime."

Coach ignored him. "Rush! What do you have to say for yourself?"

"Just catching our breath," I offered, not even looking at him.

I wondered what he'd say if he knew his daughter spent the entire day in my bed. I had no urge to rub it in his face, though. Landry wasn't a weapon. I'd never use the fact that she saw something in me no one else did to stick it to Coach. It meant too much to me. *She* meant too much to me.

"Oxygen ain't welcome here!" Coach snapped. "Underwaters! Now!"

Jamie groaned but hitched his chin at me. "C'mon, bro. Race ya."

He dipped under the water, and I joined him, turning away from Coach completely.

Underwaters are a swimmer's fifth stroke. Improving underwater swimming is a key component to helping any swimmer go faster. It's also good for push-off strength. Keeping a tight, streamlined position is important and requires a lot of body control.

Even though I was tired, I propelled myself forward while undulating my lower body in a wave-like manner while keeping my upper body rigid with my arms stretched above my head. Beside me, Jamie did the same, and we swam toward the other end of the pool.

Coach must have told everyone to swim underwaters because, soon, everyone around us was doing the same. I stayed focused on my own lane, my own swim, reminding myself it didn't matter what anyone else was doing.

Which was probably why he was able to sneak up on me. Why I didn't see him invade my lane until he knocked against me. Still holding position, I jolted, glancing over as a stream of bubbles rose from my lips.

Behind my favorite silver-framed goggles, I narrowed my gaze. I knew it was Walsh instantly despite the fact we literally all looked the same down here with goggles, swim caps, and matching swimwear.

We all had different vibes, and his always pissed me off. I flung my hand, giving him a *WTF* gesture. He pointed to the surface and kicked, heading up.

I went because I was curious. The instant my head cleared the surface, I sucked in a breath, then spit out the water dripping into my mouth. "What?" I spat in the direction where he treaded water.

He didn't look at me, though. He was gazing across the pool, toward the deck. His attention focused on whatever was there. The energy around him was the same as always when he felt like he had to defend Elite.

I spun, water rippling around me, to look in the same direction. I was unprepared for the punch to my chest, the way all the air in my lungs instantly whooshed out. My arms faltered, making my body dip a bit under the water before I remembered to swim.

A low buzzing filled my head like the steady hum of static on a busted TV. Memories played on the backs of my eyelids, a montage of everything I had and everything I lost. The pain was sharp but somewhat dulled by the panic and confusion overwhelming my operating system.

I never in a million years would have expected to see who was standing there.

I'd never expected to see him again.

"If disappointment was a person, then it would be you."

"It should have been you and not her!"

"You're dead to me."

The last words he'd hurled at me echoed in my head, still as sharp and painful as when he first said them. Maybe they wouldn't have hurt as much, left thick scars no one could see but I felt every minute of every day, if anyone else had said them.

But it wasn't anyone else. It was my brother. Bodhi Lawson. The person I was closest to in this life. Keyword: *was*.

I'd walked away that day, raw and bleeding, hoping my blood somehow made his pain more bearable. I hadn't seen him since.

Until this moment. Until Walsh summoned me from the peace of underwaters to the storm brewing on dry land.

"He's here for you, right?" Walsh spoke for my ears only, almost as if he knew I'd just thought of him.

"How'd you know?" I asked, my voice strained.

"Just a feeling."

Bodhi was staring, a familiar face but the glare of a stranger. I couldn't read his expression, more proof that I didn't know him anymore. Maybe I never did.

I felt his eyes as I made my way to the edge of the pool.

They never left me when I hauled out and started his way. As I walked, I felt the silence in the pool area. I felt the stares of Elite. Hell, even Coach was quiet.

My skin crawled with trepidation. Confrontation. Shock. I worked on shoring up that armor I'd mentioned I realized had a crack. It couldn't fail me right now.

Water dripped off me and my bare feet slapped over the pool deck as I slid the goggles from my eyes up onto my head. Bodhi's blue eyes flickered as he watched me approach, his jaw bouncing as though seeing me pissed him off.

If he didn't want to look at me, he shouldn't have come here.

His hair was longer than the last time I saw him. He'd always favored it slightly long, but now it was full-on surfer dude, the dirty-blond locks long enough that he wore it pulled back in a low ponytail at his neck. He was thinner than I remembered. He'd always had to work to keep up his muscle mass, so I assumed he wasn't doing that work.

His twin is dead. He's had other things on his mind.

"Bodhi," I said, stopping a short distance from him. It wasn't at all the greeting we'd shared half our lives. Before, we'd be up in each other's business, high-fiving or one-arm hugging. It wouldn't have been "Bodhi" back then either but brah.

Yeah, Elite might say bro, but in Cali, it was brah.

He crossed his arms over his chest, sapphire eyes narrowing. "You still use those goggles."

I shrugged.

It must not have been the reaction he wanted because he stiffened, arms falling to take on a defensive position. "You've got some nerve."

My heart rate was rapid, and adrenaline spiked in my system in anticipation of a fight. Despite the tension, I kept my body relaxed. "For using something that was given to me?"

Bodhi's nostrils flared, and his California chill evaporated like it was never there. "You son of a bitch," he snarled and lunged at me.

I was ready to defend myself. Defense was an automatic reaction when I saw him now. But I didn't get that far because he was intercepted. A body came around mine in a blur and bulldozed into him, shoving him back.

The bright-blond hair caught my eye first, and I blinked as Lars shoved Bodhi back, his back muscles tightening with the action. "Back off," he warned.

For a second, I was momentarily stunned because Lars was not a fighter. In fact, confrontation made him anxious. But here he was, jumping right to my defense.

Bodhi's face darkened, and a look I recognized from the day he came to pound my face flashed over it. Urgency filled my lungs, tightening my chest.

Bodhi leaped toward Lars, and all the charged quiet in the room erupted. Water splashed. Swimmers shouted. Coach's whistle peeled through the air at an ear-piercing pitch.

I rushed forward, grabbing Lars around the waist to pull him back and spin. My entire body was stiff, ready for the blow meant for my friend. Lars stumbled a bit, but I locked my arms around him, not even noticing how our wet, bare skin slapped together as I hauled him away and used my body as a blockade against Bodhi's anger.

It was one thing for Bodhi to use me as a punching bag but something else entirely to go at Lars.

The hit I was anticipating never came, and I realized I'd been so focused and in my head that I'd blocked out all the chaos around us. Glancing over my shoulder, I saw Win planted in front of us, emanating a dark aura he rarely ever showed. The T-shirt he was wearing seemed to strain against his broad back and biceps like they were suddenly swollen with aggression. His hand pressed against Bodhi's chest, not necessarily restraining him but more out of warning. He didn't have to restrain my old friend because someone else already was.

Walsh had both Bodhi's arms pinned behind his back, holding him out like an offering for Win. Win wasn't even a swimmer, but he was Elite. This semester, he was interning with the team for physical therapy clinical hours.

Bodhi jerked against Walsh's hold, but Ryan merely tightened his grip. A split-second urge to defend Bodhi slammed into me, its intensity making spots swim before my eyes. I blinked, reminding myself it wasn't my job to defend Bodhi anymore and that he'd just gone at Lars.

Realizing I was still holding on to him, I pulled back. "You okay? Did he hit you?"

Lars's face darkened. I knew he was annoyed that we'd all jumped to his defense. He could defend himself. Hell, we spent time in the gym making sure of it. But he'd been through too much. Taken far too many hits in life already. I'd be damned if I stood around and watched him take more in my name.

The mere fact that he was so willing to do so only made me more determined to protect him.

"He went at you, not me," Lars replied.

"Lars. What did I tell you about getting in the middle of fights?" Win intoned, clearly listening to our exchange.

Lars huffed.

"Lars," he warned again.

I glanced back at Win who still had his hand pressed against Bodhi like he wasn't sure if he wanted to hit him or not.

"I'm not going to stand here and watch someone take shots at my best friend." Lars was definitive.

His words were a shot of their own. *Best friend.*

Lars and I were close, but did he really think that much of me? *Would he still if he knew why Bodhi hated me?*

I stood there stupefied. Unable to say a word.

"*Best friend*," Bodhi spat. "You wouldn't call him that if you really knew him."

That hit its mark.

"We do know him," Walsh intoned. "He's Elite."

He was like a damn broken record. *Elite this. Elite that.* Kinda appreciated it right then, though.

"You telling my angel he has bad taste in friends?" Win said, his voice deadly calm. He was one of the most laid-back people on this side of the country, but even looking at Lars cross-eyed turned him feral. "Because insulting his judgment is just as bad as trying to hit him."

Squueaaaaal. Coach cut into the conversation, the whistle falling against his chest as he stepped in. "Hands off, Sinclair," he told Win. "You too, Walsh."

Bodhi pulled away from the two guys, straightening to his full height, which wasn't near Walsh's and Win's six-foot statures. Bodhi was five-eight on a good day.

"Who are you?" Coach interrogated. "What makes you think you can just waltz into my practice like you belong here?"

Bodhi crossed his arms over his chest and lifted his chin, obstinance written on his tanned face. The long hair and ponytail made him look even more like a surfer dude than before. "I don't have to explain myself to you."

The vein in Coach's temple throbbed. "This is my pool!"

"And this is *my* business."

Coach's back expanded with his ire. "Listen here, you little shit. You made it my business when you stepped in here."

"Just tell us why you're here." A reasonable, calming voice chimed in.

I stiffened immediately, body automatically rotating to where Landry stood. In her hand was a clipboard and stopwatch. She was wearing the green windbreaker, but beneath it was my Aerosmith tee.

Just seeing her in the same space as Bodhi was like witnessing a head-on collision between my present and past. The collision was so violent it had the opportunity to rob me of my future.

Leaving Lars's side, I went to hers, gently curling my hand around her elbow. "Go in the locker room," I told her.

She glanced at me sharply. She had that bratty look in her eyes. "Did you forget I'm the assistant coach here?"

My patience snapped like a whittled-down thread. "Does it look like I give a damn?" I bit out.

Shock registered on her face before her eyes narrowed.

"Did you just raise your voice at the assistant coach?" Coach just had to go and flap his lips.

I swung toward him. "You know damn well she's a hell of a lot more than that to me, and if I'm telling her to get the hell out of here, you might realize there's a damn good reason!"

Silence blanketed the room.

Jamie, of course, was the one to break it. "Kruger, bro, you missed your shot. Rush already claimed her."

"Shut up, Jamie!" Coach, Landry, and I all yelled at the same time. Then Coach turned to stare at Kruger who hovered nearby. "Really, Kruger? Like hell I'd let you date my daughter."

Landry sighed. "Dad."

"Like Rush is any better." Kruger defended himself. "All this just 'cause I asked her if she was single."

"You two are a thing?" Bodhi said, taking a step forward.

The second he moved, Lars, Ryan, Jamie, and Win did too.

"Lars," Win warned, shooting him a hard stare. Then his eyes snapped to the other side. "Wesley."

Ah, I hadn't seen Wes move in. The gang was all here.

Wait. Prism... I glanced around. *There he is.*

Bodhi ignored everyone, his glittering eyes locked solely on me. He was wearing a black hoodie, probably because he thought it made him intimidating, but I'd bet my right nut he had a purple crop top on underneath. Brah loved his crop tops.

"You've got some heavy nads," he said, taking another threatening step. Except I wasn't threatened. Not in a physical sense anyway.

"Bodhi—" I started, but he cut me off.

"Coming here, starting a new life, hooking up with some side piece like you shouldn't be rotting in a cell."

Landry sucked in a breath. "How dare you say that to him?" Quickly, she turned to me. "That is *not* true."

Bodhi slid his slitted gaze toward her. "What's it like fucking a guy who's wearing the goggles a girl who loved him gifted him right before he murdered her?"

Black spots swam before my eyes. The world around me went a little hazy. Of all the fucking shit he'd said to me, that was probably the fucking lowest. Bringing Landry into this was where I drew the line.

I lunged forward, but so did everyone else.

The first one to get to him was Coach, who clamped his hand around the back of Bodhi's neck and squeezed hard enough that he bent at the waist under the pressure.

"I'll have you fired!" Bodhi wheezed, trying to fight the hold.

"Go ahead." Coach was utterly calm, not at all the way he spoke to us even when he was pissed. "Then I'll be able to do more to you for what you just said to my daughter."

Bodhi grunted, reaching up to slap at Coach's hand.

"Bro. Did he just say you killed someone?" Jamie asked, glancing at me.

Walsh shifted, and I felt his eyes cut to me.

"Maybe he's on drugs," Kruger suggested.

Bodhi twisted under Coach's iron hold to peer up at him. His face was red, eyes wide. "Didn't you tell your team what kind of person they're swimming with?" He sneered. "Guess not. You didn't even tell your own daughter."

Coach shoved him, and Bodhi slammed into the floor. He pushed up immediately, but Coach grabbed his shoulder. I watched his fingers turn white from the force of the squeeze. "I suggest you get the hell out of my pool and don't show your face around here ever again."

"He's a liar," Lars said, stepping forward, angling slightly in front of me.

"I'm not! I went to Pembrook with your new bestie. I know him better than anyone!" Bodhi exclaimed.

"If you knew him at all, you'd know he would never kill anyone," Lars spat. Then he muttered something dark in Swedish.

My tongue felt thick, throat tight. All the words I wanted to say were nothing but a jumble in my brain, a vat of mixed-up letters I couldn't put together.

"Yeah? Ask the Malibu PD. Look up his police record. I know you got the internet out here in bumfuck county."

"Time to go," Resch said, hauling him up and dragging him to the door.

"Wait," Ryan said, his voice hitting pause on everything.

"Not now, Walsh," Coach snapped.

"Then when?" Walsh pressed.

"This isn't your business," I said, finally finding a few words, realizing this was my situation to deal with and no one else's.

"You're Elite now. That makes this Elite business," Ryan

countered and then walked toward Bodhi. His muscles flexed as he went, stray water droplets still clinging to his half-dry skin.

"Elite," Bodhi spat like it left a bad taste in his mouth. "He wouldn't be if—"

Ryan grabbed the hair at his hairline and pulled his face up so he could stare at it. Coach gave him a warning glance, but Walsh acted like he didn't even notice.

"He would," Ryan intoned. "He is. I don't know how you did things in Cali, Malibu Barbie..."

Jamie snickered. "Good one, bro."

Ryan went on like Jamie wasn't his never-ending hype man. "But here on the East Coast, loyalty means something. And if Coach let him on this team, then that means he deserves to be here."

Coach stiffened, his entire face going sour.

The contents of the takeout I ate earlier reappeared in my throat. I knew it was on the tip of his tongue to tell everyone my position here was tenuous at best. I started forward, but a light touch on my arm stopped me, and I gazed down.

Landry's hand rested there, not restraining at all, but the touch was powerful just the same. "Let him finish," she said quietly.

"So you can come up in here with your half-baked accusations. Hell, you can even wave around a police report. But don't for one second think that you can walk onto our turf, our pool, and expect any of us to side with you. Rush might be an asshole, but he's ours."

I was bowled over. It was one thing for Lars and Landry to defend me. Even Win. But Walsh? With the rest of the team standing there nodding?

I wasn't part of them. I never wanted to be.

"Out," Coach said, pushing open the door and letting the winter wind gust inside.

"Rush!" Bodhi yelled, struggling against Coach. A few curse words dropped from his lips as he fought. "I came to talk to you."

I was sure that meant he came to hurl more insults. I mean, look at what just happened. But part of me was curious. Part of me knew he wouldn't fly all the way across the country just to call me a bastard.

I turned to Landry. "I'll find you later." I paused. "If you want me to."

"I want you to."

The tightest knot inside me eased. Her words were a glimmer of hope that I hadn't just lost everything for a second time.

Aware everyone was standing around, aware that winter air was practically freezing the water droplets still clinging to all the swimmers, I still stole a moment.

Fitting my palm at her waist, I leaned in and kissed her temple, inhaling her scent before pulling away.

Coach looked like he wanted to let go of Bodhi to have a go at me as I took Bodhi by the arm and tugged him forward. "Outside."

"It's freezing!" Landry worried.

"He's been outside buck naked before, and he was all right," Kruger cracked.

I kept going, my mind on other things besides the bite of the frigid night air. Of course, the second it slapped my bare skin and the cement pricked my bare toes, I thought a hell of a lot more about it.

Still, I ignored the ice forming on my skin and crossed my arms over my stinging, hard nipples.

"What are you doing here?" I said, not mincing words. "You come to get me kicked off Elite?"

That thought had me straightening up so hard, so fast even Bodhi jolted.

I should have realized sooner.

Unable to contain the sudden rage I felt, I put both hands on his shoulders and shoved. He stumbled back, eyes wide.

"Was that you?" I demanded. "You think it was fun to make me relive the worst time of my life? You think Elite would see that, freak out, and kick me out?"

I didn't feel the cold anymore. Fury kept me warm. Flashes of that dummy floating in the pool. The dress. The wig. The note. *I won't forget.*

"What are you talking about?" Bodhi said, coming closer as I paced.

I stopped midstride and pinned him with a hard stare.

He shrank back. *Good.* I wasn't backing down.

"Did you hang around and watch? Get a thrill out of my trip with the cops? But then I came to practice. They let me swim. Did you realize your little prank hadn't been enough to get me kicked off the team, so you decided to show up? Make things worse?"

The more I thought about it, the more enraged I became. Not only was this cruel to me but disrespectful to Brynne. Dragging up the way she died. Recreating it like it wasn't horrible enough the first time. And Landry. *God, Landry.* The sound of her scream. The look of sheer horror on her face. The way she cowered into me and pointed. How, later, she felt guilty for being horrified and not reacting right away.

He did that to her. He traumatized her that way. For what?

For revenge?

A deep, ominous sound ripped from my chest. The force of it caught in the air, creating a large puff of white in the cold. I lunged at him, and he shrieked. Using a fistful of his dark hoodie, I dragged him into me so close he had to tilt his head back to stare up.

At one time in my life, I never could have imagined this

kind of rage toward him. I never would have believed I could put my hands on him like this. That I would consider pounding his face.

But, *wow*, I was fucking ragey.

"You torture my girl?" I asked, voice completely odious.

My best friend/brother turned stranger/enemy stared at me as if he'd never seen me before. "W-what h-happened to you?"

I laughed. It was an abhorrent sound just like my previous words.

Nearby, the door pushed open.

"Dammit, Lars," Win spat.

Lars ignored him and came outside, stopping abruptly when he saw what was going on. "Rush?" he questioned. "Is everything okay?"

I shoved Bodhi back, flexing my hands and blowing out a breath.

"C'mon, back inside, angel," Win said, snaking a muscled arm around him from behind to tug him back inside.

"No," Lars protested, digging his feet in. "Are you okay?" he asked me again.

I grunted.

"Him? I was the one about to become a punching bag!" Bodhi accused.

Lars glanced at him. "No one deserves to be a punching bag," he allowed, and I glanced at Win, feeling a little guilty for bringing up that shit for him. "Even still, I don't like you."

Behind Lars, Win's lips rolled in on themselves, and though I couldn't make out much of his expression because of all the light at his back, I could sense his amusement. Or rather, pride.

I swallowed, just thankful this didn't seem to bring up a bunch of shit for Lars.

"I'm not going to hit you," I said, gruff.

Look, *maybe* I would have. Before Lars came out and reminded me why I shouldn't. Or maybe I would have remembered on my own. Hopefully.

"What prank?" Bodhi said, slightly cautious.

I shot him a warning look.

"Here," Lars said, holding out a pair of sweatpants, hoodie, and beanie. It was like he didn't even care about what Bodhi just mentioned.

"Thanks, bro."

Win inserted himself between Bodhi and Lars as I took the clothes and tugged off the swim cap and goggles. "Put these in my locker for me?"

"*Ja*," Lars agreed in Swedish and stood there until I finished dressing. Even then, he hesitated before going back inside. "Want me to stay?"

Win sighed dramatically, and I couldn't help but half smile. "You doing this for me or to annoy your other half?"

Lars smirked, but then his face cleared. "For you. You were there for me too."

"Not as much as I should have been." I didn't want him to forget.

"More than anyone was before," Lars countered.

"Excuse me. What am I, a spare kidney?" Win muttered.

Lars rolled his eyes. "I need both my kidneys, *min hund*."

Min hund = my dog in Swedish. Win was so wrapped by my bro that he let him call him a dog.

"I know you take A&P, angel. You know you only need one kidney to live."

Lars made an exasperated sound.

Win made a sound. "I'm insulted, angel."

Lars turned toward him. "You're different. Rush is my kidney. You're my heart."

"No one's ever compared me to an organ before," I mused.

"You're just a kidney. I'm a heart." Win was smug, tucking his arm around Lars. "C'mon inside, angel. You'll freeze."

He hesitated. "Go," I told him. "I got this."

Lars let Win lead him away.

"Bro," I called, and he glanced over his shoulder, his light eyes piercing even in the night. "Breakfast tomorrow?"

He nodded.

"Come to our place," Win said. "Easier that way."

Lars was about to protest, but I nodded. It was easier for Lars to eat at home, but it would also be easier to tell him about everything without a bunch of noseholes around.

"Sounds good."

Noseholes = nosy assholes.

And yeah, I was going to tell Lars everything. His defense of me today earned him that right. His unflinching friendship deserved it. I was a kidney now, had to act like it. That meant flushing out all the toxins of Lars's life. Even if that toxin was me.

Once they were inside, I turned back to Bodhi. His expression was unreadable except for the vague hint of something...

"Didn't take long to find yourself another blond-haired, blue-eyed replacement." Bodhi sneered. "He's even gay."

Is he jealous?

I shook my head, knowing the stray thought was completely ridiculous and impossible.

"What do you want, Bodhi? Hasn't everyone suffered enough?" Why did he have to drag more people into this nightmare?

"What prank?" he asked again, the confusion in his eyes genuine.

Even after everything, I guess he was still able to make me believe. I was a fool.

"Cut the shit. Just tell me why you did it," I said, fury

enveloping me again. "But seriously, that was fucked up. You should respect Brynne more."

Slam!

My head snapped back, the already tired muscles in my neck screaming. There was pain, but I was back to being numb. Maybe because I stood out there barefoot and in nothing but sweats. Maybe because my ex-best friend just punched me in the face. Or maybe I was just numb to everyone but Landry.

"How dare you?" he yelled as I swiped the blood at the corner of my lip. He drew back to hit me again, but the door burst open, and a flurry of movement and noise erupted.

"No! Stop!" Landry cried, rushing out.

Bodhi was already midswing, and my heart lurched, stomach jumping to my throat. With a strangled yell, I sprinted forward, snatching her around the waist and spinning as Bodhi's fist collided with my shoulder.

I stayed in place, though, hunching around her, making sure my arms were up to cover her head. There was scuffling behind me, a couple grunts. I didn't even look. I just kept my body tense so it could deflect any more blows that might come this way.

My little siren didn't seem as inclined to remain in place as me, though, and she pushed out of my chest, straining out of the way I held her to peer around my body.

"How dare you?" she yelled. "If you swing at him again, I'm gonna kick your balls so far up inside you that you'll taste them for breakfast!"

"I'll hold you so she can do it," Walsh intoned.

"Damn. That escalated quickly," Jamie mused.

"P! Get the camera. We gotta record this. We about to go viral!" Kruger hollered from the doorway.

This place was a sold-out circus.

Landry whimpered, her warm hands gliding over my jaw

to pull my face down. "Let me see." She worried. "You're bleeding."

She fussed and swiped, making little tsking sounds while the warmth of her hands seeped into my icy skin. "Does it hurt?" She worried, dabbing at it and staring with sympathetic eyes.

Her worrying was hella cute, but... "Baby, did you just tell him you would feed him his balls for breakfast?"

"I saw him hit you." She sniffed. "I won't have it."

The pieces of me she had yet to claim were relinquished just then. I was bought and paid for before I even realized I'd been for sale.

"I told you I'd find you later," I said, catching a strand of her golden hair between my fingers. It was like touching sunlight.

"You took too long, so I found you," she murmured, dabbing at my lip again.

"He deserved it!" Bodhi yelled behind me. "How dare you even say her name and then accuse me of disrespecting her?"

"Walsh," I called, still staring at the girl in my arms.

"Yeah?"

"Take Landry home."

She stiffened. "Excuse me?"

"I told you to go home earlier, and you almost got yourself punched."

She drew back, obstinance shining on her diamond-shaped face. "You are *not* the boss of me."

I don't know how she expected me to stand here while she was adorably worried and defensive over me and not want to shield her from this entire mess. But I would concede. I wasn't the boss of her, and trying to boss a woman around didn't work out so well for me in the past... so I rephrased. "Will you please let Ryan take you home so I can deal with this stuff here and not worry about you while I'm doing it?"

Her lips pursed. "I have my car."

"You're too upset to drive." I reasoned.

"You just hate my car."

"That too."

Ryan appeared beside us. "You trust me enough to take your girl home?"

I shrugged. "Try anything, and she'll feed you your balls."

She groaned, and Ryan laughed. "C'mon, scrappy. Time to go."

"But my car," she protested.

"I'll drive it home for you and then ride back with Ryan," Jamie offered.

Look at that, Tweedledum and Tweedledee being useful for once.

I brushed my knuckles over Landry's cheek. "Please?"

She sighed. "Fine."

"Thanks, baby." I kissed the top of her head and then sent her off with Ryan. He wasn't my favorite person, but he was trustworthy with the safety of my girl.

They left to grab their bags and keys, and other swimmers started coming out, Coach clearly having called practice. They noticed me standing there, then slid their eyes to Bodhi.

"You good here, Rush?" Vargas asked.

He was a decent guy. I'd had a few meals with him. Went to a few parties.

"Yeah, bro. I'm good."

The group walked into the parking lot, and I knew more guys would be coming out, so I closed the distance between us and grabbed Bodhi's arm, leading him down the sidewalk where we could talk privately.

"Stop the dumb act. I know you think I'm stupid, but even

I'm not stupid enough to think it's some wild coincidence that I find a body in the pool dressed up like Brynne and then you walk in hours later. Just tell me what the fuck you want."

Bodhi physically reacted, stumbling back with a gasp. "You found a body dressed like my sister?"

My eyes narrowed. "It was a CPR dummy, but you already knew that."

"Dressed like Brynne?"

"Flower dress. Long wig. Even a note. *I won't forget.*"

The tan of his skin seemed to leech away, leaving behind a pasty Bodhi. "You think I did that?"

"Who else?" I countered.

His shock was good. I'd give him that. But no one else would have known to do that. No one else here would have known what Brynne was wearing the night she died.

"Pretty stupid of you to show your face."

"I didn't do this." His voice was hollow, slightly shocked.

I scoffed.

"I didn't," he insisted.

"Why should I believe you?"

"Because I'm telling you the truth."

"Sucks when you tell the truth and people don't believe you, doesn't it?"

He sucked in a breath, eyes flashing with something I couldn't name. "That's different."

"Why?" I mused. "Because you're trustworthy and I'm not?"

The words settled between us, creating a divide miles wide.

"This isn't why I came," he finally said.

"There's no other reason for you to be here," I countered. "So look, your little prank worked, okay? The cops here know about my record, and I'll probably have to tell Elite too. You got what you wanted. Any life I even attempted to piece together here is gone."

I turned away, suddenly really fucking tired of looking at his face.

"Rush." He called me back.

I stiffened. "And for what it's worth, I know you won't ever forget. I won't either. Doesn't mean you have to torture the innocent people around me with shit they have nothing to do with."

He swallowed, the Adam's apple in his thick throat bobbing against it. "Rush."

"Go back to California, Bodhi. I'm done."

He called out again, but I walked away, going inside the natatorium and locking the door behind me. There was a time in my life when he was my favorite person to see. Now I hoped I never laid eyes on him again.

22

I EXPECTED AN INQUISITION FROM RYAN ON THE WAY HOME.

Shockingly, he didn't ask anything at all. I was wound so tight with expectation when we pulled into the driveway that I relented.

"Why haven't you asked me?"

The taillights from my car illuminated the windshield as Jamie parked ahead of us.

His answer was simple. "I'd never ask someone's girl for their secrets."

We got out of the Jeep, and Jamie came around to give me the keys to my car. "You all good, bro?" he asked.

I nodded. "Thanks for doing this. Even though it was completely unnecessary."

"Maybe, but it made him feel better," Jamie replied, for once not making a wisecrack.

"See you at practice in the morning," Ryan said, then

gestured toward the townhouse. "Go in first. Then we'll leave."

Yes, a townhouse. I already told you of the aversion to buying furniture my father employed. A townhouse just meant there was less for him to furnish and a yard he didn't have to mow.

I started up the driveway, then stopped and turned. "Ryan?"

"Yeah?"

"It's not true," I told him, unable to bear the thought of anyone having doubts about Jason. "I don't care what anyone says. It's not true."

Ryan and Jamie exchanged a brief look. Then Ryan nodded. "We know."

"He's not as hard as he wants everyone to believe." I went on as if the floodgates had been opened and I desperately had to tell someone. To make them understand. I didn't know how Jay existed for so long with no one on his side. It had been less than twenty-four hours since I'd known everything, and I already couldn't stand it. "He's just been betrayed so much."

Ryan walked up the driveway. Even in the dark, I felt his stare. His hand brushed against mine in a reassuring gesture before he tucked both of his in the pockets of his sweats. "You aren't alone, okay? Neither is he."

The words rushed out before I could stop them. "My dad doesn't want me to date him."

He made an amused sound, teeth flashing against the night. "If Coach really hated Rush, he'd already be gone."

"You think so?"

"One hundred percent." He seemed absolutely sure, and it made me feel just a little better.

"Thanks, Ryan."

Surprisingly, he leaned in and kissed my head. "Don't worry so much. Go inside and rest."

I started away, but Jamie hollered, and I turned back. He jogged forward and pecked a kiss on my head too. "See ya, swimmer girl."

"That's Coach to you!" I yelled after them as they climbed into the black Rubicon. The green star-shaped lights on the front glowed in the dark.

"Call Mads and Rory. Go do something girly!" Jamie called before disappearing inside.

Ryan waited with the engine running until I was inside with the lights on and door locked. Only then did I hear him drive away.

A little while later, I was freshly showered and hiding in my room, hoping Dad would think I was already asleep when he got home.

The house was quiet, the only light coming from the small lamp on my bedside table, which bathed the room in a golden glow but left the farthest corners dark.

As previously mentioned, my dad wasn't much of a decorator. Okay, he wasn't at all. But my room was completely done and had been since he'd moved here when I was a little girl. I guess he didn't care if he had a bunch of matching furniture, but he wanted me to have it.

The room itself was a basic box shape with a queen-size bed in the center of the wall to the left as you came inside. Matching nightstands made from the same white wood as the tall headboard were on either side.

The bedding was all white except for the lilac throw draped over the foot of the bed where there was a wooden bench with too many purple pillows.

Across from the bed, a large mirror leaned against the wall, the rectangular wooden frame lined with large round lights that glowed softly when illuminated. A generous portion of the wall behind the mirror was covered with posters of all my favorite vintage rock bands—Def Leppard, Aerosmith, Guns N' Roses, Bon Jovi, Queen, Blondie, and more. To the left of the mirror was a white door leading to the closet (not walk-in). Beyond the bed was a double window that looked out onto the small yard and was flanked by lilac curtains and white shades, which were currently drawn. A small bookcase in the corner of the room was filled with romance novels, magazines, and other things I'd collected over the years.

Every so often, I'd check my phone, hoping to find a text from Jason. Every so often = five minutes. Tops.

It was going to be a long night.

I considered calling him more than once. Knowing I left him at the pool with Bodhi after seeing him punch Jay right in the face only made things worse. The longer my phone stayed silent, the more worried I became. But I kept reminding myself he'd asked for time and that Jason Rush was definitely someone who could take care of himself.

But doesn't everybody need somebody?

A light knock on my bedroom door made me look up, hope making my heart skip a beat.

"Landry," Dad called, and I made a face and then winced, wondering if he could see the light underneath the door. The carpet would block that, right?

I remained mute, hoping he would think I was sleeping.

He must not have bought it because the door pushed open. Gasping, I jumped up off the bed as Dad strode in, a hand over his eyes. "You decent?"

"I could be naked!" I exclaimed.

He grunted and lowered his hand, cracking one eye open to peer at me. I was completely dressed in a pair of snug biker shorts and the Aerosmith tee Jason gave me. Yes, I put it back on after I showered. So sue me.

Seeing I was, in fact, not naked, he glowered. "Avoiding me won't work."

"I'm not avoiding you." I lied. "I just don't feel like arguing about Jason right now." That part was true.

"Fine. We won't talk about him," Dad replied, way more amicable than anticipated.

I glanced up, surprised as hope filled me.

"We'll talk about your mother instead."

He was just as good at stomping my hope as he was at blowing that whistle.

I groaned. "Dad."

"More specifically, the jackass she married."

I made a face. Just thinking about that guy gave me a stomachache. *Venomous Vince.*

"You really thought I wouldn't believe you?" Dad queried.

I shrugged. "Mom didn't."

His swallow was audible. He opened his mouth and closed it three times. I watched him struggle not to say one disparaging word about my mother. I respected him for it. Probably because Mom never gave the same courtesy to him.

In the end, he simply said, "I believe you."

I looked up. "You do?"

"Of course. You can tell me anything. Anything, and I'll be on your side, always."

Emotion welled in my chest, swelling like an overfull dam. I went forward and looped my arms around his waist to hug him. "Thanks, Dad."

He hugged me back, patting my shoulder as if he wasn't sure how else to show affection. It made me smile against his shirt. He smelled like chlorine. He always did, no matter if he just stepped out of the shower. The scent was ingrained in him. It was in his veins.

"Dad?" I said against his shirt, still overwhelmed with

emotion. This entire day had felt like years, the amount of emotions I'd gone through leaving me teary-eyed and weary.

His voice was gruff, and the use of the nickname only served to make me more emotional. "What is it, ladybug?"

"I never believed the stuff Mom said about you. She blamed you for us never being a family, said you didn't want us. But I know it's not true. You've always been there for me even when she made it hard."

He cleared his throat, a new sort of tension filling his limbs. "I hurt your mother because I didn't want to marry her. I didn't want a relationship. We were young, and I—" He cut off the words abruptly, and I pulled back to look at him.

"What?" I asked, wanting him to finish.

"Just because I didn't want a relationship with her doesn't mean we aren't a family. That *you* aren't my family. It might not be the one she wanted, and I'm sorry I couldn't do it. But I do love you. I have since the second she told me she was pregnant."

I nodded, tears shimmering in my eyes. "I love you too, Dad."

In that moment, I felt sorry I'd defied him about Jason. But even feeling guilty, even knowing my dad probably sacrificed a lot for me in his life wasn't enough to make me give up Jason.

He pulled me back and swiped a rogue tear off my cheek, then crossed his arms over his chest, the soft look in his eyes morphing into stone. "Now tell me what he did so I can decide what to do about it."

I backed up and sank onto the bench at the end of my bed. Two pillows toppled over to land near my feet. "I don't want you to do anything. It will just make it worse. Mom is mad at me. Madder than ever before. She said I was selfish and didn't want her to be happy, that she gave up her youth to raise me and now it's her turn to have a life."

Dad made a rude sound. "She's thirty-eight, for fuck's sake. She ain't in a wheelchair."

I smiled a little at that. "Well, she thinks she's old and Vince is her last chance at being happy. And he's rich, so…"

"What'd he do, Landry?"

I swallowed. "He stared a lot. Sometimes commented on my clothes. The way I looked in them. I brushed it off even if it did make me uncomfortable. But it got more frequent. He would sometimes touch me. Act like it was innocent or an accident. It made me feel gross."

Dad started pacing, a dark look creeping over his face.

"One night, Mom was out with her girlfriends, and he hit on me. Said it could be our little secret."

Dad stilled. Everything about him went so quiet that chills broke out over my arms and my toes curled into the rug under the bench.

"He asked you to sleep with him?" His voice was measured and quiet. Scary.

"Well, not in those exact words." Actually, the words were much cruder, but I wasn't going to tell him that. He already looked murderous. I'd never seen him this way before. "He implied it. Heavily. I told him no and locked myself in my room. I told Mom the next morning, but he'd already gotten to her. Told her I asked him for money and he told me no. She accused me of making it up to come between them. Said I didn't want her to be happy."

Dad made a sound, and I just kept going, wanting to finish. "I started swimming more, practicing double so I wouldn't be at home as much. The strain was too much on my shoulder."

"That's how you tore your rotator cuff," he half growled.

"It was just overuse. You know I've always had to work harder than the tall swimmers." My short stature was a definite disadvantage in the pool. The taller girls always had better speed.

"When it tore, I couldn't be at the pool so much, and I didn't want to be home. Mom and I were always fighting. Vince was there." *Leering.* "I'd always wanted to come to Westbrook anyway. This just gave me an excuse Mom couldn't argue with." Honestly, I thought she was glad to get rid of me.

"You should have told me."

"It doesn't change anything."

"The hell it doesn't!" he yelled.

I sighed. "What are you going to do? Go fight Vince? Mom will file charges. She'll get you in trouble with the school. You know she will. He isn't worth your job."

I could tell he was about to argue and say he didn't care. Maybe he didn't. But I did.

Wearily, I said, "Just let it go, Dad. Please. He never did anything that terrible. I left. I live here with you now."

"Asking my underage daughter to sleep with him is not what I call nothing terrible," he snapped.

"I'm not underage," I pointed out.

"He's a pervert!"

"Well, I'll agree with that," I allowed.

He scrutinized me, his intense stare making me squirm. "Are you telling me everything?"

"Yes. I promise. Can we please just let it go?"

"No."

I groaned, flinging myself back on the bed.

"I'm calling your mother. I'm going to let her know what I think about all this. About her. And I'm also going to tell her if she lets that jackal anywhere near you again, they'll have to deal with me."

"Is that all?" I asked, hopeful.

"My threats are very real," he intoned.

As long as he didn't have to make good on his threats, then all this would just die. As much as Mom loved to badmouth Dad, she wouldn't directly go against him. Besides, she was too busy in her love bubble with her new husband to even think about seeing me right now anyway.

Dad was staring like he expected me to reply.

"I know. You're super scary."

"Is that sarcasm?"

I shook my head. "Definitely not."

He made a noise that called me a liar. "If that animal even sneezes in your direction, I want to know."

I nodded.

"I mean it, Landry," he threatened.

"I know! I'll tell you!" I burst out. Then I groaned. "I'm tired. Can I please go to bed now?"

"Practice first thing in the morning." He reminded me.

I didn't need the reminder. "I'll be there."

"Good night, ladybug."

My annoyance shriveled. "Good night, Dad."

He let himself out of the room, and the door clicked shut behind him. I checked my phone again, disappointment stabbing me when I saw Jason still hadn't called or texted.

Tossing the device aside, I got up and shut off the lamp, crawling beneath the blankets. The pipes in the walls groaned a bit, and I knew Dad had just turned on his shower. With a sigh, I settled into the mattress, my body drained but my mind still stirring.

Clink. Clink. Clink.

The faint sound had me lifting my head off the pillow and glancing toward the direction it came from.

Clink. Clink.

The blankets rustled when I slid out of bed and padded to the window to lift the white shade and peer down into the yard.

Jason waved from the grass, head tilted up. It wasn't shock I felt seeing him there but excitement. Butterflies lifted off beneath my ribs, fluttering wildly. I let out a faint sound, fumbling with the lock before pushing up the window.

"What are you doing?" I whisper-yelled down to him.

"You got a ladder in there? Maybe some rope?" he called, cupping his hands around his mouth.

"Of course!" I called back.

His arms fell from their position. "Really?"

"No," I lamented. "Who do you think I am, Rapunzel?"

"I asked for a ladder, not some hair."

I gestured, not knowing if he could even see the movement, and said, "Go around to the back door."

Not waiting for his reply, I dropped the shade back in place and rushed into the hall, relieved to hear the shower still running.

Flying down the stairs, I made it to the back door, unlatched the lock, and pulled it open. The space on the other side was empty, and all the butterflies in my stomach died a sudden death. I let out a disappointed sound.

"I'm right here," he said, materializing out of the dark from the side.

I jolted, letting out a little squeal.

His voice was fond and quiet. "Why are you surprised, little siren? You told me to come to the door."

"I didn't see you," I muttered, then gestured for him. "C'mon inside."

"Uhh, isn't Coach here?"

"He's in the shower. Hurry up so he doesn't hear."

Jason shrugged and let me pull him into the house. After making sure the door was locked, we went quickly up the stairs without a sound. Just as my bedroom door latched, the pipes groaned again, signaling the end of the shower. I let out a sigh of relief because we'd made it without being caught.

I turned from the door, quietly asking, "What are you doing here?"

"I wanted to see you." His voice was equally as quiet.

Ripples of awareness brushed over me, turning my skin sensitive as his gleaming eyes appraised me. He roamed every inch, his covetous stare like a caress as it swept me from head to foot, lingering lazily as if he wanted to study every inch.

Longing awakened, blooming from the center of my stomach, petals of heat unfurled and expanded until every part of me was flushed with desire and impatient to feel him against me.

"Come here." He curled his finger. Not a request. Not quite a demand.

An order my body would never deny.

Pushing away from the door, I padded barefoot across the carpet, realizing there was no light on in this room, but not even the dark could conceal the way he stared.

I stepped so close I had to tilt my head back to look up at him. He seemed even bigger just then, maybe because I was barefoot and he still had on shoes. Maybe because his presence was just that overwhelming that everything else seemed small.

"You smell good," he murmured, leaning down to nuzzle my freshly styled hair.

I said nothing, tipping my head to the side to give him more access, and his nose dragged down, lips catching on my jaw to press a few warm, open-mouth kisses before burying his face into the side of my neck.

He groaned into my skin, the force of the sound vibrating my flesh and making me shiver. His hand came up to curl possessively around the opposite side of my neck, holding me in place to inhale. Involuntarily, my hands fisted into the shirt beneath his open jacket, anchoring myself as he licked over my skin and kissed the column of my throat.

"Take your shirt off, little siren." He spoke the words against my neck, the brush of his lips making my skin tingle.

"Don't you think we should talk first?" I asked, completely breathless.

His chuckle made my thighs clench together and the area between them throb. "I think this body is mine to do with whatever I want. Whenever I want," he said, hooking his finger under the neckline of the T-shirt to drag it from one collarbone to the other.

His growly tone incited more desire, and I closed my eyes, offering myself up to anything he wanted.

"So take this shirt off before I rip it off your body."

My eyes popped open. I digress. Anything but that.

"You can't!" I whisper-yelled, stumbling back and falling over my own feet.

He caught me around the waist, the whites of his eyes becoming less visible against his narrowing stare. With one arm wrapped around me, he reached up with the other to grab the neckline as if he would indeed rip it right off.

I grabbed his hand. "This is my favorite shirt."

His eyes widened, the sharp edges of his face turning soft. "What?"

"I'll take it off, Jay. Don't rip it."

He gazed down like he was just noticing what I was wearing. "That's my shirt."

I sniffed. "It's mine now."

"It's your favorite?"

I made a sound. "Of course it is."

He set me on my feet, then gestured. "Take it off."

I pulled it over my head, letting the fabric fall to my feet.

He swore beneath his breath, stare latching on to my bare upper body. After I showered, I didn't bother with a bra since

I was going to bed. The biker shorts were tight and short, the only thing left on my body.

His hot gaze coupled with the chilly night air tightened my nipples and made them ache. I heard him swallow, and then he gestured with his finger for me to turn around.

My brows drew down, and I hesitated.

"Turn around, little siren," he said, voice impatient. "Arms out."

I did as requested, holding out my arms and rotating so he could see my back. "What are you doing?" I asked, flushing under his shrewd gaze.

His hand curled around my waist, palm flattening on my stomach to pull me flush against his chest. "Checking you for bruises."

I jolted, glancing over my shoulder at him. "What?"

"You got in the middle of someone swinging at me. Did you think I wouldn't check you for marks?"

My mouth opened and closed. Finally, I said, "He didn't touch me."

His voice dropped an octave, and a rumble vibrated his chest. "Like I'd stand there and let that happen."

"Then why do you need to look at me for bruises?"

He was being ridiculous. Territorial and possessive. *And* it was dark in here.

"Because you're mine." He was completely irrational, and I parted my lips to tell him just that, but he kept going. "Because no one has ever been so fiercely protective of me. So blindly loyal. Because you literally rushed into the middle of two grown men fighting without a thought for your own safety."

"I wasn't worried about me. I was worried about you," I protested, getting upset all over again remembering the way his head snapped back when Bodhi hit him.

"And that is why I will protect every inch of you. Why

you will indulge every urge I have to look over all this creamy skin and make sure the most important thing in my entire life is intact," he said, pressing his face into my neck again to growl. "God help any man who ever puts a mark on you. Who ever threatens what is mine."

His arms were like vises, holding me so tight I could barely even breathe. Like he was afraid I would disappear, that someone would try and snatch me away.

It was on the tip of my tongue to ask if he'd retaliated against Bodhi after I left, but then I realized the answer didn't matter. Maybe that meant something was wrong with me, but standing here in the circle of his arms, all I felt was right.

Reaching up behind me, I pushed my fingers into the hair at the back of his head, nudging his face farther into my neck. The soft sound he made flipped my stomach as he nibbled, hunching farther around me as I melted into his enveloping embrace.

With a groan, he lifted his head. "I don't want anyone else to mark you, but damn, if I don't want to do it myself," he rasped, sounding a little tortured. The blunt edge of his teeth scraped over my bare shoulder, and I arched into the sensation, wanting him to do it again.

"So fucking responsive to me," he moaned, nipping again.

"Deeper, Jason. Mark me for everyone to see."

"Would you like that, little siren? To walk around with a visible mark so everyone knows you're mine?"

His hot breath huffed along my damp skin, goose bumps prickling my arms. It wasn't even a want at this point. Wearing his mark was something I craved.

"*Please*," I begged, tightening my fingers still tangled in his hair and arching my neck in offering.

The full weight of his mouth settled just below my ear, and the hot suction he applied had me whimpering into the dark. One hand came up to settle over my mouth, muffling the needy sounds I couldn't seem to stop as he worked over my skin, alternating between sucking and licking. He dragged out the process. Instead of going hard and sucking a deep bruise within seconds, he played and played, drawing out the pleasure and making it so his ownership would echo in me long after the mark he left behind faded away.

I was squirming and shaking as he worked me over. The hand not covering my mouth flirted across my bare stomach, over my ribs, and settled heavily over my aching breast. I sighed against his hand, arching into his palm, and whimpered when he began massaging the tender flesh.

I sagged into him, and he lifted his mouth to lay it against my ear. "Be a good girl and don't make any noise."

I nodded, and both his hands moved to my breasts, tugging and massaging until between my thighs throbbed relentlessly and I pushed my ass against his crotch.

His teeth bit into my shoulder, and I gasped, my nipples turning even harder. Lifting his hands off my aching breasts, he pulled me around, eyes laden with sex. "I cannot get enough of you."

Grasping the waistband of my shorts, I shoved them down, kicking them away. I was completely vulnerable standing there before him, so much smaller and completely naked while he towered over me completely dressed.

"I need to check you for bruises too," I whispered.

Intense eyes caught mine and held while he shrugged off his jacket and lifted his arms. I found the action so endearing that tears rushed to the backs of my eyes. He could have ripped the shirt off and been naked in seconds. Instead, he offered the chance to strip him bare and made himself as vulnerable to me as I was to him.

Love saturated my heart, making it feel heavy. But oh, the heaviness of loving someone was unlike anything else.

My barely audible giggle swirled around us as I tugged the shirt up and he bent down so I could pull it over his head. When it was gone, I laid my palms on his shoulders, smoothing over his supple skin and dragging over his muscled arms all the way to his fingers.

They spasmed, about to cling, but I kept moving to pull down his pants and boxers, going as far as to sink at his feet. Sitting back, I took a moment to stare at the thick muscles in his legs, the way his hairless skin appeared satin even in the dark. His cock was already hard, proudly standing off his body. Instead of reaching directly for his shoes, I grasped his hips and scored my nails lightly down the front of his thighs to his knees.

He swore quietly above me, and I smiled while making short work of his shoes. Once they were gone, he impatiently kicked off his remaining clothes as my hand wrapped around his thick dick. He grunted deep in his throat, and I squeezed the base while my free hand came up to fondle his balls.

His shaft jerked impatiently, and I leaned in to lick a long stripe from base to tip before wrapping my lips around the head to suck. His hips jerked, and his head pushed deeper, the wetness of my mouth coating more of his hard shaft.

With no warning, I started to bob my head, sliding up and down his length with enthusiasm. His fingers dug into my shoulder, and the muscles in his thighs began to quiver. I sucked until he grew hot against my tongue, then pulled back to pin his throbbing cock against his abs and latched on to his balls.

I kept the contact gentle, knowing this was a sensitive place, but he made a sound of frustration, his low demand permeating the space. "Harder, baby."

I gave him what he wanted, sucking deeper and filling my mouth with the thin flesh.

He nearly choked on pleasure and patted my head. "*Good fucking girl.*"

Emboldened, I went just a little rougher and scraped my nails down the inside of his thigh. I remembered when he'd said before that roughness seemed to permeate the numbness he lived with, so I leaned into it, wanting to make him feel as much as I could.

Releasing his sack with a pop, I dragged my teeth across his shaft, and he jolted in surprise. I gazed up his body, worried I'd gone too far, but the half-lidded stare I got in return told a different story.

Sliding over his head, I took as much of him into my mouth as I could and held him there, letting my throat work around him while I tugged his balls. He moaned, fingers delving into my hair, and in a moment of unbridled desire, I reached behind his sack, dipping my finger into his crack, and then dragged my nail over the sensitive space between his balls and ass.

He shuddered, and the distinct tang of salt coated my tongue.

"*Christ*," he swore, pulling his fingers from my hair to reach down and pull me up. "Get up here," he growled, lifting me off my feet so my legs wrapped around his waist.

"If I don't get inside you right this second, there will be hell to pay," he ground out, carrying me the short distance to the bed and yanking back the covers with so much force they practically flew off the bed.

I started to laugh, but he stopped it with a kiss, pushing his tongue into my mouth until I was full of him. I wondered if he could taste what he leaked all over my tongue. Our mouths smacked when we parted, and he put me in the center of the mattress and then slid in beside me.

He filled up the bed so much more than I did, his commanding presence making my lower belly clench with need. "Come over here and ride my dick," he said, shifting toward the center of the mattress as he palmed my hip to pull me in.

I straddled him eagerly, the cool air of the room brushing between my drenched thighs. I shivered a bit, and he sat up instantly, reaching for the blankets he'd just tossed aside. Pulling them up, he tucked them around my back, enclosing us in our own little world.

I sank onto his shaft, taking him inch by inch while biting my lip to keep from crying out. He went so deep this way, and my body stretched to accommodate his size.

When I was fully seated, his palms settled over my thighs, his thumbs rubbing slow circles across the sensitive flesh.

"Look at you stuffed full with my cock, cheeks flushed, eyes glassy, and I haven't even started fucking you yet."

His words made me clench around him and my hips rock.

He purred, the sound so erotic that I whimpered. "There you go, baby girl. Move."

I continued to rock, my entire body rippling in pleasure from just the slight movements. I could barely breathe with how full I was, how my body cradled his.

Laying my palms on his pecs, I braced my weight on his and started moving more, sliding up and down a little on his drenched shaft. I panted, my body shaking with need.

Wrapping his hands around my hips, he started to move me the way he wanted, and even more ecstasy exploded behind my eyes. I folded over him, my cheek hitting his chest with a whine.

"No one has ever made me feel like this," I whispered.

"No one else ever will." He promised, caressing my hairline with his sweet words. But then his voice changed, the dominance he embodied coming out on full display. "Now sit up and look at me while I take you."

I forced my body up, and he took over. Though I was on top, he still claimed control.

His hands wrapped around my waist, fingers digging into my ribs as he lifted me and dropped me onto his dick, practically stabbing me with its strength. I choked, the sensation so intense.

"Eyes on me," he demanded, and mine snapped to his.

Intensity ignited my veins, made my walls clench around him.

"Do not make a sound, little siren, unless you want me to finish what I started with your father in the room."

I gasped. My God, the implication was sick and wrong… but damn, if it didn't make me even hotter.

"You know I'll do it. I'm not pulling out of your body until your insides are painted white and I'm convinced I'm as deep in you as I can humanly get," he intoned, the threat absolutely delicious.

He thrust up, his hips leaving the bed as he bucked into me, making my mouth fall open.

"Keep those eyes on me. Only me. You will watch me claim you. You will know without a shadow of a doubt that I am the only one who will ever make you feel like this, that you are mine and no one else's."

I bobbed my head, and he started fucking me, lifting me and then dropping me at the same time he thrust upward. I could literally do nothing but claw at his chest and cling to his wild stare while he went at me with renewed abandon.

Sweat slid down my spine, a sheen coating my breasts. Beneath my hands, his skin was slick, and his breathing was ragged. His stamina was unmatched, though, as was his strength. He continued lifting me and thrusting up, driving so deep I was wholly convinced he wouldn't be able to get any deeper.

I rose higher and higher, the need for release becoming almost painful. My eyes slid shut, and I whined pathetically.

Hard fingers grabbed my chin and pulled my face down. "Look."

I did, my vision slightly blurry but not enough to erase the hold this man shackled around my heart. "Please, Jason," I whispered, not sure I could take more.

The naked heat in his penetrating stare gave way to softness, enveloping me like a warm blanket I didn't know I needed. His hips lowered onto the mattress. His body lay back while his hand cupped my cheek in a gentle caress.

His give triggered my own, and I fell over the edge, the orgasm rolling over me like a tidal wave of bliss. I whimpered and jerked, breaking eye contact when my body fell into his as the release went on and on.

He wrapped his arms around me, anchoring me into him and the bliss he gave.

"There you go, baby. That's what I like," he crooned. "You clench me so good."

I went boneless against him, completely spent and satiated. My entire body hummed, my brain still half offline. I barely reacted when he rolled us so I was tucked beneath him and his body blanketed mine.

His rigid dick thrust into me, and I made a sound, widening my legs.

"Baby," he called, and I gazed up. "Color?" he asked.

It took me a minute to realize what he was asking, but when I did, I smiled. "Green."

"You sure?"

"Mmm." I agreed, caressing his bicep.

He sat back, wrapped his arms around my thighs, and started thrusting into me. I watched him, the way his muscles clenched and rippled, and I listened to the sound of our bodies meeting. It only took a minute before his body went rigid and arched. I felt his dick jerking, spilling out inside me as he came fast and hard.

When it was over, he let out a breath and fell beside me on the mattress, reaching over to pull me close. We were both sticky with sweat, but I didn't care and cuddled against him anyway.

"Little siren," he mused. "I came here to talk to you, and just look what you did."

"Pretty sure you were the one in charge there," I murmured, satisfaction still tingling my limbs.

"You submit so well for me," he praised, dragging his fingers through my hair. "It takes a strong person to be able to do that."

"I trust you, Jay."

He was quiet for a minute. "Even after tonight? Meeting Bodhi?"

"That's her brother, right?" I don't know why I asked. I already knew.

"Yes." The air in the room changed slightly. It made me a little sad because I loved how we were just then, how it was nothing but us.

But we couldn't be just us with his past trying to claim him.

"He's really angry," I said, recalling how he yelled and accused Jason. How he went at him more than once.

"He lost his sister. His twin." He seemed resigned to being the bad guy. He was too comfortable in the role. But he didn't belong there.

I made a rude sound. "You lost everyone."

"That's different."

I shifted to prop my chin on his chest. "Is it, though?" I asked quietly. "It's terrible what happened to Brynne, and losing a twin is probably so painful. You lost her too, though. And not only that, but everyone else in your life turned their

CAMBRIA HEBERT

backs on you."

"Technically, my parents didn't." He reminded me.

"But you're still here without them. Without anyone. You left your entire life, everything and everyone, and came here alone."

"I think it was him that threw that dummy in the pool. He thinks I killed his sister and walked, came here to start a whole new life. He wants to take it away."

It was the only thing that made sense. The timing was too perfect to be coincidental. "You confronted him about it, right?"

"Of course. He denied it. Said he came here to talk."

"Talk," I muttered darkly. "Is that why he punched you in the face?"

He made an amused sound. "Hey, remember when you threatened to feed him his balls for breakfast?"

I snorted. I was never going to live that down. "He deserved it," I intoned, then leaned up so I could see his lip. Caressing it, I asked, "Does it hurt?"

"Nothing hurts when I'm with you," he said softly.

Heart quivering, I pressed a gentle kiss to where Bodhi had hit him. Pulling back, I told him, "You deserve to have someone defend you, and it's okay if you defend yourself."

"You and Lars both showed up," he quipped, but even in the dark, I didn't miss the flash of emotion in his eyes.

"The rest of Elite did too." I reminded him.

He scoffed.

I poked him in the ribs. "You saying I'm lying?"

"I'm telling Lars tomorrow," he said in lieu of an answer.

"Do you want me to be there?" I offered.

His head lifted off the pillow when he looked at me. "You would do that?"

This man. Always so surprised when someone shows up for him. "I will do anything for you, Jay."

246

His head hit the pillow again, and he blew out a breath. "I'm having breakfast at their place after practice."

I noticed he didn't say outright that he wanted me to come. It was probably too hard to ask. He was probably too afraid I'd turn away like everyone else. He also didn't tell me no either.

"*We're* having breakfast at their place after practice." I corrected.

In a sudden movement, he rolled me beneath him and claimed my lips in a searing kiss. I kissed him back with as much passion as I had, wanting him to taste it and feel it. When my tongue reached out, his was there waiting, and my heart tumbled because he'd been waiting.

Jay might be dominant in bed. With sex and pleasure. But intimacy was harder for him. He was more timid, fear of rejection making him wary. He definitely had it inside him, but it was hidden away, almost as though it needed an invitation.

I'd keep inviting that part of him until it became second nature. Until he realized he was safe with me.

23

JASON

PHWEEEEEEE!

The sudden high-pitched, shrill sound cut through the comfortable silence and brutally shattered the sleep I was frankly enjoying.

I jolted, body flying up before my eyes were even open as the wretched sound nearly split my eardrum in two.

"What the fuck?" I yelled, spilling over the side of the mattress and taking half the blankets with me as I fell onto my ass.

Landry's cry of surprise had me up and launching back onto the bed to snatch her close.

Phweeeee! Phweee!

My ears nearly bled as I cupped my palms against Landry's, trying to shield her from the sound.

"Oh my God, Dad!" Landry yelled.

It wasn't so much her yell but what she yelled that chased off the sleep, surprise and adrenaline coursing through me. My head snapped up to the man standing on the other side of the mattress, a whistle clutched between his lips.

Well. This was awkward. But also... "Jesus, Coach! Do you sleep with that thing?"

The object of our torture dropped from his mouth to fall innocently against the white polo he was wearing. "What the fuck are you doing in my house?" he barked. "*In my daughter's bed.*"

My ears were still ringing, and I pulled one of my hands away from Landry so I could stick a finger in it to check for damage. "I think I might need medical attention."

"Son, you are lucky I don't jam this whistle so far up your ass that whenever you open your mouth, it's the only sound that comes out!"

"Dad!" Landry gasped.

"I see where you get it from," I told her. "This is a violent household."

"You think I'm joking?" Coach asked, taking a threatening step forward.

"Considering your daughter threatened to feed someone his balls? No."

That took some of the heat out of Coach's fire as he glanced quickly at Landry. "He deserve it?"

She rolled her eyes. "Of course."

Coach nodded, proud, then switched his stare to me, going irate once more.

"Dad. Stop." Landry was plaintive as she crawled over the mattress toward him. "How did you even know he was here?" She wondered. "What time is it?"

Straightening off the bed, I swiped my phone off the nightstand to look at the screen and winced when I saw it was four thirty. "I planned on leaving before you got up for practice," I said, sheepish.

CAMBRIA HEBERT

Coach's displeasure permeated the room. "Is that why you parked your car in my driveway?"

I made a face. "I'm not parking my Vette on the street for some drunk bozo to hit and run."

"This ain't the ghetto," Coach bitched.

Like that matters. "My Corvette deserves better than street parking," I bitched back.

Landry groaned and switched on the bedside lamp. "He's a horrible car snob."

No. I just had taste. "How dare you side with him at four in the morning?"

"Young lady, where are your pants?" Coach roared as he looked at Landry standing there in the Aerosmith tee.

"I was sleeping." She defended.

Coach swung toward me, eyes sweeping over what I was wearing—which was boxer briefs.

With an aggressive sound, he rushed around the bed, grabbing my ear and twisting. "I told you to stay the hell away from my daughter, and you climb into her bed in your damn underwear!"

I winced as he dragged me forward, presumably toward the door.

"To be fair, Coach, my boxers cover more than my Speedos."

He jammed the whistle back in his mouth and blew. *Phweeeee!*

I reacted, rearing back and then shoving. Hand ripping from my ear, he stumbled and hit the closet door, the sound of the whistle cutting off abruptly.

"You know, I thought you were better than this, Jason," Coach spat, straightening to his full height. The scruff on his jaw made his face more shadowed than the dim light, and his eyes were squinted as though he couldn't stand the sight of me.

I felt a little shame then to be honest.

"I gave you a chance, one no other coach worth a damn in this country would give you. I kept your record under wraps. I personally went to bat for you with the dean. And this is my thanks? Do you even understand the amount of disrespect it takes to walk into *my* house and shack up with *my* daughter?"

"First of all," I said, taking a step forward, "you didn't keep shit under wraps. You outed me to the cops at the first sign of trouble. You preach loyalty and team until you run out of air, but you were the first one to offer me up on a silver platter."

"There was a dead body in my pool!" he yelled.

"And you didn't even ask me if I did it!" I erupted. "You immediately just assumed it was my fault." The words tumbled out, and though I hated them and though I felt like they made me see-through, I couldn't seem to stop talking. "So please tell me again about the chance you gave me. How you believed in me so much. You're just like everyone else!" I spat.

My chest was heaving, and my face felt hot. Spinning away from him, I swiped my sweats off the floor and yanked them on.

"And this is my payback? Is that it? I hurt your ego, and you decide to use my daughter to send a message?"

Dully, I heard Landry gasp, but it was muffled by the instant rage sweeping through me like wildfire. It obliterated everything else and narrowed my gaze until I was peering through a tunnel.

Incensed, I lunged, sinking low, and rushed him. We hit the wall so hard the nearby mirror rattled. I laid my forearm against Coach's throat, shoving my face close to his. "You talk to me about disrespect?" I said quietly. "You can take shots at me all you want, but don't ever imply she's not worth more than some petty revenge."

"Jason." Landry's voice cut between us, but I kept my eyes steady on Coach's. Her cool hand curled around my bicep, gently tugging. "Please let go."

I dismissed Coach's stare to glance at the blonde beside me. Her eyes were wide, cheeks pale.

I dropped my arms and stepped back. Coach straightened, and Landry reached for me again. I evaded her touch, the action causing literal pain.

I wanted to leave. The urge to just run out and not look back was a burning sensation in my chest. But her pull on me was stronger than even the most ardent urge. Stronger than the shame I felt. The guilt. Even the rage.

I grabbed my shirt and coat, fisting them both in my palm. Swallowing thickly, I turned back to Coach, knowing I shouldn't but needing to say more.

"I get you don't like me. I get you're probably looking for ways to toss me off the team."

Landry made a stricken sound, but I refused to look at her, knowing if I did, all these words would die on my lips. And maybe that would be okay if these words weren't about her.

"But let me make one thing clear. I know I'm not good enough for her. I know I don't deserve her. Hell, there probably isn't a man on this earth that does." Something flickered in Coach's eyes, but I ignored it and went on. "She's not some pawn to me. Not some means to an end. If I have a problem with you, I'll come at you. Contrary to what everyone believes, I don't hurt women. I'm sorry I came here, to your house. I'll stay away."

"Jason!" Landry gasped, and I held up my hand, quieting her words.

"But I won't stay away from her. Not unless she asks me to. I care about her too much. And even though my word is non grata around here, I'll still promise I won't hurt her."

My words were punctuated by a heavy silence that went on until it was shattered by the alarm on my phone. I shut it off and then pulled on my shirt. I felt Landry's eyes the entire time I moved, the weight of them making my feet heavy. The pull between us was so strong I had to fight against it, the action creating throbbing in my chest. On my way past, I lost the fight, glancing up at her soulful eyes and soft mouth.

I love you.

Cupping the back of her head, I kissed her forehead. "Sorry, baby," I said quietly. "I'll see you at the pool in a bit."

"Don't go," she whispered, green eyes imploring.

I didn't reply because I couldn't give her what she wanted, so I left her and went toward the door.

"Rush." Coach's voice stopped me, but I didn't turn around.

I waited for him to say whatever it was he needed to.

"This isn't just my house." He spoke, and I tilted my head. "It's Landry's too." He cleared his throat. "And, ah, if she wants you here, then it's okay with me."

I turned, suspicious. "Really?"

My girl, though, she was a hella lot less suspicious than me, and I watched her rush Coach and hug him. I had to bite back the urge to remind her she wasn't wearing pants.

"Thank you, Dad."

He grunted and patted her on the back. "I'd rather you be here where I can keep an eye on you."

She pulled back to scowl. "So you want to spy?"

He made a face. "I wouldn't have to spy if you told me when things happened."

She groaned. "I did tell you."

"After the fact," he lectured.

"Are we still talking about me?" I wondered, sensing a change in the atmosphere. Don't get me wrong. I'd love to not be at the top of Coach's shit list, but if I wasn't, that meant something else was. And that was something I *did not* like.

"We should get ready for practice," she said, hurrying to her dresser.

"Landry," I intoned.

"You didn't tell him either?" Coach asked, eyebrows arching up his forehead.

She groaned.

"Tell me what?" I demanded.

"Nothing."

"Her stepfather propositioned her," Coach deadpanned.

I drew back as if someone had slapped me. "I'm sorry, *what?*"

Abandoning an open drawer, Landry spun to stare at her father. "Seriously, why would you tell him that? He's already hyperprotective enough!"

Coach grunted as though he might actually approve of that, but I was too busy trying to wrap my head around what he'd just said. "Are you telling me some old geezer married to your mom tried to sleep with you?"

"It's why she moved here," Coach supplied.

"Really?" Landry planted her hands on her hips, giving him a withering look. "Five minutes ago, you were practically tossing him out the window, and now you want to tell him all the dirty family secrets?"

"I thought you moved here because you hurt your shoulder," I said, refusing to be distracted.

Coach grunted. "Yeah, because she was over-swimming to stay away from the predator at home."

I shot across the room to pull her gently around. "He touched you?"

"No," she was quick to say.

My eyes narrowed on her face. She'd better not be lying. Not about this.

Sighing, she said. "I left before he could."

Letting her go, I turned to Coach, angry. "He's still breathing?"

"She just told me yesterday."

Folding our arms over our chests, we both pivoted toward her.

She threw her hands up in the air. "Seriously? Now you're ganging up on me."

"Where's he live?" I wanted to know.

"I'm not telling you," she said at the same time Coach said, "Ohio."

"How far's the drive?" I asked out of the side of my mouth.

"No!" she spat. "We already talked about this. You can't risk your job, and—" She gasped. "Is that why you told him?" she accused. "You want him to do your dirty work!"

It wasn't a half-bad idea. "I'd be happy to put my fist in that degenerate's face."

She gasped again.

"It's too early for all that." Coach was gruff.

"You woke us up with a whistle," she deadpanned.

"She's got you there." I agreed.

"Whose side are you on?" Coach grumped.

"Landry's."

"Asshole."

"Never claimed to be anything less."

"Get out!" Landry declared, stomping to the door and pointing at it.

She was cute as hell.

"Both of you! Out!" She pointed again. "You're both ridiculous, and I forbid either of you to go near Vince."

"So his name is Vince," I murmured.

"Grimy bastard," Coach murmured back.

"Out!"

We both moved to the door. "Now, ladybug—"

"Ladybug?" I parroted.

Coach gave me a dirty look but then turned back to Landry. "You know I don't condone violence, and I would never ask one of my swimmers to do anything that would break the law."

She didn't look convinced. I wasn't convinced either. He just said that because he had to.

"I was just telling Rush so he'd be aware in case the man showed up in town," he explained.

I stiffened. Just the idea of that guy coming around my girl again made me furious.

Feeling my immediate ire, Landry glanced at me. "He won't come here, Jay. My mom was relieved when I left."

That pissed me off too. "Why didn't you tell me any of this?"

She gave her father a baleful look, but he didn't seem contrite at all. "I'm going to make coffee. We leave for practice in fifteen."

"I'll drive her," I said.

"Well, your fancy car is blocking mine," he said, stepping into the hallway.

"We'll be down." I promised. "Hey, Coach?" He stopped near the stairs and looked back. "You're, ah, sure you're cool with me hanging out?"

His face twisted like he had raging gas, but at the same time, he nodded. "She's an adult. She can make her own choices." Going on, he added, "But I'll be watching."

I wanted to ask if this meant he didn't really believe I killed Brynne, but I was afraid to mention it. Afraid of what he'd say.

He disappeared, and I turned back to my girl to collect some morning sugar. But the look on her face made me recoil.

"Stay away from him, Jason."

I held up my hands. "This is me staying away from him."

She rolled her eyes. "I'm serious. He's not worth your time. Or mine."

"What about your mom?"

Hurt flashed across her face, and she went back to her dresser. I moved up behind her as she shuffled through the fabric, making a mess of it all. Reaching around her, I plucked a shirt out of the pile and held it up. "I like this one."

It was faded black with an image of Debbie Harry, the lead singer from Blondie, on the front with the word Blondie written across it in hot-pink script.

Her body leaned back into mine, and I shifted, welcoming her weight. "Do you know their music?" she asked, looking at the shirt I was still holding up.

I made a sound. "Not really. But you're my blondie, so I like it."

She snorted and ripped it out of my grasp. "She picked him over me," she said softly.

The ache in my chest was swift and powerful, and I made a sound, wrapping my arms around her. "It always hurts worse when it's the people who should support you the most." She made a sad sound, and I tucked her a little closer. "I'm sorry, baby. You deserve better."

Her hand curled around my forearm where I held her. "She said she didn't believe me. Like I would make up something like that."

I knew what it was like to be betrayed. Mistrusted. Disposable. The betrayal cut so deep it made you question if loyalty was even possible or if, at our core, humans were only capable of looking out for ourselves.

What kept that question from turning into an unwavering belief was my parents. Even if I wondered if they believed me, if deep down they truly thought I was capable of murder, they stuck by me. They hired the best damn attorney for my defense. Yeah, I wondered if they only did that so they wouldn't have to be the parents of a killer. So they wouldn't be completely ostracized from their cushy life. It was still enough to keep alive a minuscule spark that maybe, just maybe, there were people out there capable of being more than self-motivated.

So those words falling from the lips of the person I loved most? They signed me up for a lifelong commitment of hating her mother.

It wouldn't even matter if the woman changed her mind. If she apologized every day for her wrongs. I didn't give second chances. That ship sailed long ago. She hurt my girl. She chose someone else over her well-being.

In my eyes that made her just as bad as the pervert scum that tried to get in Landry's pants. Which, by the way, I wasn't going to let that go.

I tried. I really did. I tried to come up with some pretty words to maybe soothe what her mom did. But there were no words because they would be nothing but excuses. She let Landry down. And even though she was human like the rest of us, some wounds went too deep, and I wasn't going to hold my hurting girl and say shit I didn't mean.

But I could say words I did. Words I wouldn't ever take back.

"I believe you," I whispered against her hair. "And I'll always choose you. Over anyone. Anything. You can tell me anything, and I won't doubt you."

She made a little snuffling sound that, frankly, turned my heart inside out. "So does that mean you believe in Bigfoot?"

I paused.

This little brat.

"I'm trying to have a heartfelt moment and vow my

unshakable loyalty to you, and you ask me about that hairy fable?"

She giggled.

Pulling back, I dug my fingers into her sides, and her giggles turned into a shriek as she twisted and laughed. "Jason." She gasped. "Stop!"

She yanked away and nearly stumbled, so I scooped her up and tossed her into the center of the mattress to straddle her as she laughed.

"You'd rather talk about Bigfoot than how much I lo—" I realized what nearly came out of my mouth, and I cut off the words instantly, instead tickling her all over again.

She wheezed and laughed, but it was all background noise to the rushing blood inside my head. My heart pumped so fast it made me nearly breathless.

I almost said it out loud.

I couldn't deny the feeling. Loving her devoured my insides. It practically reprogrammed my DNA. So yeah, denying it was literally impossible. But putting it out in the universe? Saying it for her to hear?

I couldn't.

"Jason."

I glanced down at her, noting the way she stilled beneath me, the way she stared up with those life-saturated emerald eyes that only seemed more vibrant against the soft-pink blush suffusing her cheeks.

"Listen here, brat," I said, taking her slim wrists to pin them above her head.

"What were you going to say?" Her voice was soft, all traces of laughter gone.

My fingers flinched where they held her, and the beat of my heart sped anew.

"The clock is ticking!" Coach yelled up the stairs.

First time I was ever glad for one of his interruptions.

Releasing her wrists, I started to move, but she caught my hips, keeping me above her. "Jay."

Everything inside me turned to mush. I leaned down so my elbows were on either side of her and our chests were touching. Her hands were still above her head, so I threaded our fingers together. She seemed small beneath me, which brought out a roaring urge of protectiveness and the need to stake a territorial claim.

With a low grunt, I used one of our clasped hands to gently nudge her face to the side so I could gaze down at the hickey I'd left behind her ear. Just seeing it there satisfied me in a way I couldn't explain. It calmed some of the wildness she made me feel.

"I meant what I said." I spoke low. With her so close, I didn't have to be loud. Her head turned back so I could divide my gaze between her stare. "My loyalty is right here. You don't have to ask for it. It's already yours, and nothing will ever take it away." Using our clasped hands, I dragged a finger across her wide cheekbone. "I'm sorry she hurt you, baby."

I dropped a quick, tender kiss against her soft mouth. "And if you say Bigfoot is out there, then he must be."

She untangled her fingers from mine to clasp my ears and pull me back down. This time, the kiss was long and languid, all stroking tongues and deep moans. We were both breathing deeply when we finally disconnected, and the sheen on her lips gave me pride.

"I'll always choose you too," she vowed.

An intense ache bloomed in my chest as those words ignited both hope and sadness. Hope because I desperately wanted to be someone's unwavering choice. *Her* unwavering choice. And sadness because Bodhi once said that too.

24

LANDRY

THE INTERIOR OF JASON'S CORVETTE Z06 WAS BOUGIE, AND the second the black leather seat enveloped me like a glove, I kinda understood how he came to be such a car snob.

Not that I was going to tell him that.

There was nothing wrong with my little Toyota, even if it wasn't dripping with luxury. Still, I might have let out a little sigh of comfort when I settled back. He heard, of course, chuckling as though he were pleased with himself. I don't know why he didn't even do anything.

When his body crouched in the doorway, a smirk on his too-handsome face, I started to tell him exactly that, but the words turned to dust when he pulled the seatbelt around, leaning in to click it in place.

His familiar scent surrounded me, and I melted just a little more into the bucket seat. Instead of pulling back all the way, he did just enough, his hand still on the strap lying across my chest as he adjusted it.

"You look good sitting in my car, little siren." His voice was a mere rumble, his eyes sweeping over me as though he appreciated the view.

"I can't see over the dashboard," I complained.

He laughed, and the sound made my stomach tighten and my limbs tingle with awareness. He had such a good laugh, and I couldn't help but wonder if he used it more before Brynne.

The laugh turned into a whispering breath that fanned across my cheek when he leaned closer. "You don't need to see out the window. Just keep those eyes where they belong. On me."

Before I could reply, he brushed his lips across mine, then gently shut the door to jog around to the driver's side.

As the engine roared to life with an impressive growling purr, Jason ran his hands over the steering wheel in a caress.

"Should I be jealous?" I mused.

His teeth flashed in the glow of the dash. "I love this car." His hand fell onto the gearshift in the center console, long fingers wrapping around it. "It's the only thing I brought with me from my old life."

My heart skipped a beat. The simple statement felt like he was telling me a secret. I didn't want to make it into a big thing, but I also didn't want to let the moment pass without some sort of acknowledgment.

"It's a beautiful car, Jay. I like it a lot."

The sun hadn't even risen yet, but the way he lit up at the praise made me feel as if I'd just watched the most beautiful sunrise.

"Yeah?" he asked, hungry for more.

It was so endearing because this wasn't his ego desiring to be stroked. This was him sharing something he loved with me and wanting me to see its value too.

I nodded. "The nicest car I've ever been in. And I like that it's blue."

"Lake blue metallic." He corrected.

Maybe he wasn't a car snob after all. Maybe he was a car nerd. It was adorable.

My dad laid on the horn of his black Ford Mustang and then flicked the lights, blinding us. Well, not me because the dashboard blocked the worst of it.

"A fucking Ford," Jason muttered, reversing the Corvette and backing out onto the street. "It's disgraceful."

"I drive a Toyota."

He made a rude sound. "Looks like scrap metal to me."

I gasped, completely offended.

His tongue clucked. "If it's not a Chevy, baby, then it's not worth it."

"That's just mean," I said, eyeing the way he shifted gears so gracefully. I liked the way his long, thick fingers gripped the gearshift so powerfully, but he didn't force it into gear, guiding it there with authority.

He caught me looking, a smug expression transforming his face. "Like what you see?"

"How do you know when to switch it?" I asked, pretending I wasn't staring at the way he sexily commanded this car but was instead fascinated with a manual transmission.

He gave me a heated look like he knew better but didn't call me out. Instead, he lifted his hand from the stick and reached for me. "Give me your hand, little siren."

My belly dipped and butterflies fluttered wildly below my ribcage when I stretched out my hand and his warm fingers grasped mine. He pressed my palm flat against the top of the rounded gearshift, his hand settling firmly over mine.

The blood in my veins thickened a little, and my heart

rate slowed. It didn't matter it was only his hand on mine. Any touch of his overwhelmed my system.

"I let the car tell me," he murmured, his voice soft and blending with the purr of the engine.

Tingles raced along my arms and legs, prickled my scalp, and made me blink rapidly.

"I pay attention and do what she needs."

His hand tightened around mine, squeezing gently and pushing the car into a different gear. My hand went with his, and I bit into my lower lip, watching us move together as the car responded.

Suddenly, my stomach felt heavy, and I shifted restlessly in the seat.

"Good girl," he hummed, and the bite of jealousy smacked me out of the haze of sudden desire as I whipped my eyes up to his, accusatory.

How dare he praise his car like that?

But his attention was trained on me. Even if his head was turned toward the road, it was me he was focused on.

"You're a natural," he said in that deliciously deep tone as he shifted again, my hand going once more with his.

The car glided to a halt, and I glanced at the red stoplight at the intersection.

Taking his other hand off the steering wheel, he twisted toward me to swipe the pad of his thumb over my cheek. "Good girl," he repeated.

With a whimper, I launched myself at him, ripping my hand from under his to throw both my arms around his neck. His low laughter turned into a groan when my lips caught his and parted eagerly.

One of his hands fisted in the hair at the back of my head, and he held me in place while he ravaged my mouth with the type of fierceness that had my panties dampening.

God, I was so weak for him. Everything about him

screamed sex and want and need. Just watching him drive, watching this beautiful car submit to him, made me jealous.

I thought briefly that maybe something was wrong with me, but then his tongue flicked over mine, and any and all thought vacated my brain.

His tongue was thick and skilled. The way he lapped at me made me feel owned, and I couldn't get enough. I was the one that leaped at him, but once I was in his arms, he took over, trapping me in his hold as I opened for him, wanting him as deep as he could get.

A car horn blared, and we broke apart, the glowing dashboard and red traffic light nothing but a bright blur I blinked against.

"Back to your seat, baby," he said, smoothing his hand over the back of my head before reaching for the gear stick and driving through the intersection.

"I hope that wasn't my dad," I murmured, sinking into the seat.

He laughed. "He's two cars behind us."

I groaned.

The rest of the drive to campus was quiet, with me trying to get my heart rate under control. I couldn't go to practice like this, all the blood in my veins singing with desire.

"So why a Corvette?" I asked, wanting to take my mind off the way he affected me.

"My dad is an executive for the biggest motor company in this country, actually one of the biggest car companies in the world."

I perked up with interest. I might have asked as a distraction, but I genuinely wanted to know everything about Jason. "Really?"

He made a sound of agreement. "Been working there since I was a kid. He used to bring me to work sometimes so

I could see the cars as they were being developed. Vettes were always my favorite."

"I guess that explains why you're such a car nerd," I teased.

He grinned, the sight making my heart light. "When he brought this car home and handed me the keys, I nearly pissed myself in excitement."

I laughed. "I would have liked to see that."

He shot me an ornery look. "I slept in her that night."

"You did not."

He nodded. "My mom came out in her robe and gave me a lecture in the driveway the next morning."

I giggled, picturing a sleep-rumpled Jason standing in the driveway as his mother yelled at him. "I take it your mom doesn't share your and your father's car enthusiasm?"

He snorted. "She has a driver that takes her everywhere."

Just how much money did Jason's parents make? I knew Westbrook was monied and prestigious, but this seemed beyond that. Granted, not that I would know. I might go to Westbrook, but my family wasn't what I would call rich. I'd never wanted for anything, but none of us had drivers or luxury sports cars. And honestly, I think the reason Mom was so into Vince was because he was loaded. At least that's why I told myself she picked him over me.

"What does your mom do?" I asked, directing my thoughts back to him.

A look crossed his face, sort of sheepish, sort of embarrassed. Lifting his hand from the gearstick, he rubbed the back of his neck.

"You don't have to tell me," I hurried to say, sensing his reluctance. Truthfully, it made me way more curious, but I didn't want to push him.

He mumbled something.

I leaned forward. "What?"

He mumbled again.

I leaned farther over the center console. "You're mumbling. Speak up."

He let out an exaggerated sigh. "She's a supermodel."

My mouth fell open. "Did you just say your mom is a supermodel?"

He groaned. "It's fucking embarrassing."

We turned onto the street where the pool was located, but I barely noticed.

"Embarrassing!" I exclaimed. "That is not! That's... I've never known anyone famous before."

He groaned again. "You try seeing your mom in little bikinis in magazines."

I laughed, and he flashed me a threatening look, so of course I laughed harder.

"Who is she?" I wanted to know. "Would I know her?"

He shrugged. "She isn't as active now with the modeling. She does other shit. Brand stuff."

Was he stalling? "Jay," I mused. "Who is your mother?"

His lips curled. "Misa Cruz."

I gasped. I definitely knew her. She was gorgeous and was on like every magazine cover when I was in high school. "Misa Cruz is your mom?"

"It's Misa Rush actually, but she uses her maiden name for modeling because she was already established when she met my dad."

He wasn't lying when he said his mom was a supermodel. Everyone knew her.

"She's gorgeous," I said, suddenly feeling a little self-conscious.

He made a face. "She's my mom."

"Honestly, I can't believe you even looked twice at me after growing up with someone so incredible."

His car came to an immediate stop, and I didn't even jolt. He was right before. His car did brake better than mine.

"The fuck did you just say?"

Leaning up, I glanced out the window. "We're in the middle of the parking lot."

He said nothing, just continued to stare.

The blast of a horn had me looking around to see my dad pulling into the lot behind us.

Jason huffed in annoyance and pulled into a spot at the back of the lot. Heaven forbid he park his precious lake-blue-metallic baby near the entrance where it could get a scratch. The second it was parked, he shut off the engine and turned with glittering eyes.

"Take your shoes off."

I made a face, starting to protest, but his growl cut me off. Wide-eyed, I kicked off my sneakers, and he grabbed me under the arms, hauling me over the center and into his lap.

"This car is too small for this," I muttered as he manhandled me.

"Eyes on me."

I glanced up, drawing back at the fierceness in his stare. The bottom dropped out of my stomach, and nerves coiled inside me. "Ja—"

"You say one more word. Just one," he threatened darkly, "and I will yank out my dick and push it between your lips so you're stuffed too full to sass me."

I blinked.

His hands shoved into my hair at the back of my head, the heels of his palms resting against the base of my skull. "Listen to me and listen good," he intoned.

God, his dominance electrified parts of me I didn't even know existed until he lit them up.

"You listening?" he demanded.

I nodded.

His fingers massaged my scalp. "That's my good girl."

Why do I like that so much? Why?

"You are by far the most beautiful creature I've ever seen."

"Creature!" I cried, forgetting I wasn't supposed to be talking. I mean, really, that was just rude.

He leaned forward and nipped at my bottom lip. The sudden sting of pain made me gasp.

"Yes. Creature," He annunciated, still holding my head. "Because what you do to me is beyond human. What you *are* is beyond human. *Fucking little siren*," he muttered. "Legends say sirens are usually the ones to lure sailors, hell, even surfers into storms. Into the chaos where they drown them." He shook his head. "But not you. No, you're the type of siren that lured me out of the chaos. Out of the water I was drowning in. Do you know how powerful you are?" He gave me a little shake. All the anger in his voice gave way to something that sounded a lot like awe.

Frankly, he captivated me. In this moment, it wasn't me as the siren he spoke of but him. No one had ever caught the attention of my body, heart, and mind so completely.

"I don't know how you did it, but you reached into the category-five chaos that was my life and silenced it all. I can feel it all raging around me, trying to get in and sweep me away, but it stands no chance against you." He wrinkled his nose, and honestly, it was so endearing in the middle of his tirade—a glimpse at the softness beneath all his steel—that I felt my heart cave in just a little bit more. "And you go and compare yourself to my mom?" He shook his head. "I won't have it."

"But she's—" I began, but he finished.

"Got nothing on you."

Still holding my head, he claimed my lips with a rough kiss. The second our lips parted, he spoke.

"All that shit? The magazines, the interviews, the

pictures? It's all fake. The makeup, the filters. The manipulation. Yeah, my mom is beautiful. But she's real just like everyone else. She's not flawless. And she never eats." He said that last part like he was so horrified.

I laughed.

"You are everything. I didn't just look twice at you. You are *all* I see. Got it?"

I nodded, swallowing thickly, trying to beat back all the incredible emotion.

"Don't ever do that again," he warned. "Don't ever think you don't measure up. Because the truth is you are the standard by which everything else is measured."

"You're all I see too," I whispered.

He nodded. "That's because I make you sit in that bucket seat over there."

My snickering was rudely interrupted by a sharp knock on the window. Stiffening, Jason pulled me closer into his lap while he turned.

Ryan stood on the other side of the glass, bent down and trying to peer into the tint.

Jason unlatched the door enough to crack it. "Did you seriously just smack your knuckles into my window?"

Instead of bickering back like he usually did, Ryan straightened and stepped back. "There's something you need to see."

If Jason was stiff before, he was full-on rigid now, palming my waist to push me back toward my seat. "Put your shoes on."

I scrambled to do it, worrying about what could be going on, and grabbed my bag to clamber out the passenger door. Jason met me around the back where Ryan, Jamie, and Lars were also standing.

"What's going on?" I asked the group.

Lars held a sheet of paper toward Jason. "This was taped on the door when we got here."

"Actually, bro, there are a lot of them taped around," Jamie said, voice somber.

Oddly, it was his mellow tone that made it perfectly clear that whatever was going on was awful.

Jason took the paper Lars offered and glanced down at it. The muscle in his jaw clenched, and his tongue ran over his front teeth. The sound of it crumpling under his fist seemed loud. "This all over the pool, you said?"

"Mostly the locker room," Ryan put in.

I stepped close to Jay, reaching for the paper in his fist. "Can I see?"

His grip loosened, and I tugged the paper away to smooth it out and look down. It was a photo. Jason standing on the beach with a girl with long tawny-colored hair and a flowery dress. I exhaled, knowing instantly who this was. What this was.

It was Brynne. And judging from the dark look on Jason's face in the photo and the way he sort of towered over her as she stared up at him with a stubborn tilt to her chin, they were arguing.

I glanced up, catching Jason's gaze. "Is this from that night?"

He nodded, saying nothing. I knew just by the shuttered look in his eyes that he was back on that beach, likely reliving and regretting it for the millionth time.

Ryan cleared his throat. "There's more in the locker room."

I swung toward him, angry. "Why didn't you just take them all down?" Jason shouldn't have to see this. "Throw them in the trash where they belong."

"There's more than the photo," Ryan replied, his voice even, not offended by my ire.

Jason jerked up, body rotating toward the natatorium. Trepidation rolled off him, along with a mix of other emotions that all blended, creating a heavy black storm cloud over his head.

Resolve hardened his features, and he started forward, the keys to his Corvette jingling between his fingers. I rushed to catch up, curling my hand around his.

He paused to glance down, dragging his eyes up to meet mine. "You sure about this?" *About me?*

I heard the unspoken question. I saw it deep in his guarded eyes.

"So sure."

He started forward again, his fingers gripping mine like a lifeline. I thought about how he said I lured him out of the chaos. How I kept it from sweeping him away. I hoped I was enough right now, enough to keep whatever was waiting inside from pulling him under.

25

NO ONE ASKED. NO ONE SAID A SINGLE DAMN WORD. THAT'S how I knew it must be bad. Like it didn't even matter what explanation I could give; it just wouldn't be enough. They just stood there waiting. Staring. A firing squad awaiting their next victim.

And now here we were, the blacktop crunching underfoot as the sun rose, bringing with it a brand-new day as Ryan, Jamie, and Lars basically escorted me into what felt like the end.

I told myself I hadn't gotten attached to anything here. To anyone. I told myself I was here to get in and get out. Get my econ degree and swim. I vowed to not let anyone in.

So why did my feet feel heavy? Why was the knot sitting in my chest making it so damn hard to breathe? Why did I suddenly care what any of these people thought of me? I didn't like any of them, so why did it matter if they liked me?

You do like them.

I stopped abruptly, my stomach burning as if it were filled with acid. Everyone else halted too, and I pulled my hand from Landry's to swing around aggressively, but it wasn't them I was mad at. It was me.

"I want to talk to Lars."

"We'll be in the locker room," Ryan said, him and Jamie going ahead of us.

Landry shifted, her touch tentative against my hand. "You want me to stay?"

I shook my head. This was something I needed to do on my own. I gave her hand a reassuring squeeze. "No. But thanks, baby."

When she was gone, I looked at Lars. The guy who called me his best friend. His kidney. "I should have told you sooner…" I started.

He shook his head. The tips of his ears were red from the cold. "You don't owe me an explanation."

"I think maybe I do," I said. "You were my friend even when you shouldn't have been. I should have told you who you were rooming with."

"You did tell me."

I shook my head. "No. I lied." *I didn't tell you that you were sleeping beside a killer every night.*

He cocked his head to the side, light eyes piercing me like glass. "So the times you let me use the shower first, drove me back and forth to practice in your Corvette, and ate with me instead of the rest of the team were lies?"

I felt my face scrunch up. "What? No. That's not what I mean."

"What about the times you helped me understand my assignments in classes you don't even take because I was having trouble with English? Those times you knew I slept like shit from nightmares and you got up and brewed espresso? You never asked me about those nightmares. You never pushed. You were just there."

That knot in my chest was getting tighter. So tight my throat was starting to ache. "This is different."

"What about when you helped me with the cops?"

"All I did was embellish a little. I owed you that after letting that scum in our room."

"You didn't know," he refuted.

He's standing here and defending me.

"That's not an excuse!" I bit out.

"Okay, but when you did know, you chased down that scum soaking wet and in nothing but Speedos in the middle of winter, beat his ass, and then dragged him back so he could be arrested."

I growled just thinking of the day that asshole showed his face. "He shouldn't have put his hands on you."

Lars smiled. "You don't owe me an explanation, Rush. You might not have told me about your past, but your actions showed me who you are."

"That photo?" I said, stabbing my hand toward something that wasn't even there. "That girl? She's dead," I said, harsh. "That was the night she died. We were arguing on the beach, and then she turned up dead."

"And everyone blamed you," he surmised.

Why wasn't he shocked? Why wasn't he scandalized?

"Yeah, and the only reason I'm not rotting in a cell is because my parents are loaded and got me the best defense attorney in the country."

"That's not why you aren't in jail."

I made a strangled sound. "Yeah? Then why?"

"Because you didn't do it."

I snapped back as if he'd smacked me. The deep breath I sucked in stung my lungs. He sounded just like my little siren. So sure. "Maybe I did."

CAMBRIA HEBERT

He gave a one-shoulder shrug. "Maybe I deserved the beatings my ex gave me."

Pissed, I lunged forward and grabbed him by the shoulders. A brief flare of panic shot in his eyes like lightning, but then it was gone and he was calm.

"Shit," I spat, releasing him. "I'm sorry. I shouldn't have grabbed you."

"It's okay," he allowed.

"No, it's fucking not," I argued. "You have fucking PTSD from that assbag beating you, and the last thing you need is me coming at you like that."

"You aren't him. And I trust you."

"You shouldn't." I scowled. "But if I ever hear you say you deserved those beatings again, I'll tell Win," I threatened.

Lars grimaced. "You wouldn't dare."

"Fucking try me," I vowed. Win would turn feral if he heard Lars blaming himself for being abused. "You did not deserve any of that."

I should have fucking punched that boyfriend-beater more when I had my hands on him.

"Some people said I did." His voice was quiet. "And some people didn't believe me at all."

I glanced up at him, slowly realizing what he was doing. "Lars," I warned, but he didn't listen. He was just as bratty as Landry. Clearly, I had a type.

His pale eyes gleamed. "You know something about that, don't you? People not believing you. Being blamed for shit that isn't your fault."

I made a sound. I wanted to tell him this was completely different. That we were not the same. The words were right there but held hostage by my constricted throat.

"We both ran here, didn't we? Neither of us was too interested in being friends with anyone, having been betrayed too much in the past. Our stories are different. Our circumstances. But we landed in the same place. You didn't ask about my past. I didn't ask about yours. We had an unspoken agreement there I think. A bond we didn't acknowledge, but it's there."

"*Lars.*" I choked again, still trying to speak.

"If you want to tell me about all the shit that happened in California, I want to listen. But our friendship isn't conditional on it. You already showed me who you are. Your vibes have never lied to me, Rush."

"I'm coming over there," I warned.

He half smiled and raised his arms.

I pulled him in, wrapping my arms around his shoulders, and hugged him tight. He hesitated a fraction of a second before his arms anchored around my waist to hug me back. I smiled over his shoulder, the tightness in my chest receding enough so I could pull in a deep breath.

"I think you just talked more in the last five minutes than the entire time I've known you," I teased, not quite ready to let go.

Is this what infallible friendship feels like?

I didn't care if anyone saw us. If anyone thought it was weird for two men to hug like this. They could take a long walk off a short pier. He was the first friend—*the only friend* —to ever give me the benefit of the doubt.

Lars made a rude sound. "Some things just have to be said."

I smiled again. My bestie was a quiet guy. The quietest on the team. Well, except for maybe Prism. But his silence was a benefit because he listened and watched more than most. That's why his friendship meant so much, because I knew he really looked at me. We met during a shit time in my life. When I was angry and closed off, when he had every reason to mistrust everyone. But he still saw someone of value. Someone he wanted to be his friend.

Finally, I pulled back and found myself cautioning him. "Seriously, though, Lars. My past is dark. I wasn't charged with murder, but I was arrested. And everyone thinks I'm guilty." I wondered if there would ever come a time that I didn't feel the urge to warn people about being in my life.

"I know," he replied simply, not a hint of doubt in his tone.

As I said, Lars was quiet. He played things close to his chest. But this was almost too calm. I mean, we were talking about murder.

"You already knew," I stated.

He nodded once. "We all do."

I sucked in a breath, pointing to the doors. "All of Elite knows about me?"

He nodded.

"*Fuck,*" I spat. "How bad is it in there?" I asked, wanting to know what I should be ready for.

"Let's go in," he said, clapping me on the shoulder and going ahead to the door.

I hesitated. "Hey."

He stopped and turned.

"You saw everything in there already?"

"Yeah," he replied.

I rubbed the back of my neck, avoiding his eyes. "And you still want me to be your kidney?"

"You and Win really like being organs," Lars mused. "It's kinda weird."

"I'm not the one that called my best friend a kidney," I countered.

"Touché." But then he frowned. "I'm not your kidney?"

Some of the nerves coiling inside me took a back seat to amusement. Flashing a fast smile, I teased, "Who wants to be an organ now?"

Lars muttered something in Swedish and pulled open the door.

"Yeah, Lars, you're my kidney," I told his back.

He glanced over his shoulder, a smile pulling up the corners of his lips. "You're still mine too."

A little flutter tingled my stomach. It felt a little like happiness. And that feeling scared me because I knew how hard it was when happiness was ripped away.

"Everything all good?" Landry asked when we stepped inside.

"You were waiting for me?" I asked, going to slip my arm around her waist and tug her into my side.

"No. I was waiting for Lars. I like his hair."

My lips fell open. Beside me, Lars laughed. I gave him a look. "I'll shave it all off, bro."

Landry gasped. "That's a crime!" Then, "I wish my hair was that blond."

Was she really pouting about her hair right now? Ridiculous.

Like she really isn't worried about what we're about to walk into.

Maybe not ridiculous, then.

"Go ahead. You can deal with Win," Lars mused, sauntering ahead of us.

"I could take him," I avowed, wondering if I actually could. I told you Win was feral when it came to Lars, and I knew he had a weak spot for that halo on my bro's Swedish head.

Landry reached for my hand, tangling our fingers. "Of course I was waiting for you, Jay," she told me quietly.

I love you, my heart whispered while I nuzzled her hair and kissed the side of her head.

As we walked toward the locker room, my head swiveled, expecting to see more of the photo plastered around.

"We took them all down out here," Lars informed me. His voice dropped when I pulled open the heavy locker room door. "But not in here."

I went first, wanting to get it over with and maybe wanting to shield the two people who'd stuck by me the most. It didn't matter that Lars had already seen. I still had the urge.

The voices on the other side of the lockers quieted when we stepped in, turning into whispers that faded into expectant silence.

The back of my neck prickled, and a heavy sense of foreboding hit me in the gut. The photo was taped up everywhere. Fluttering against the end of each locker row, taped three times to the back of the door. There were several on the walls, one on the doorframe. Even one taped over the emergency alarm.

I tried to avoid the image itself, just noting where they all hung. It was hard not to be drawn in, though, not to see Brynne.

My feet shuffled, and I turned into the row of lockers where mine was located, steps stalling when I saw all of Elite crowded around. The photo papered the bench and was stuck to every locker door.

I felt the weighty stares of every swimmer, the way they all measured and judged me. *It doesn't matter*, I told myself. But the truth was it fucking did.

I fucking cared. No matter how much I tried not to, I did. I avoided their looks, the way they shifted as I walked farther into the row. My locker was toward the end, and I noticed Ryan, Jamie, Wes, Kruger, and Prism were all hovering in front of it.

My instinct was to drop my gaze and look at the floor, but the instant I realized what I was doing, indignation straightened my backbone.

Fuck. This.

Fuck them.

I'd been here before. I survived it then, and I would again. These elitist fish couldn't do anything to me that hadn't been done before. I was stronger than that. Than them.

I obstinately refused to back down. To act like I was the one in the wrong. I wasn't. It seemed more important than ever that I defend myself—or at the very least, hold my head high.

It wasn't just for me anymore but for Landry. For Lars. For the people who believed in me.

I straightened my spine, lifted my chin, and turned my gaze to stone. Life might have dealt me a shitty hand, but I was a fucking wildcard. Time to start acting like it.

"Walsh," I said, meeting his gaze straight on and not backing down. The fastest way to let everyone know where I stood was to make it clear with their alpha. "You're in my way."

Ryan stepped forward, and I tensed, expecting a confrontation. But he moved to the side, and everyone else standing there shifted with him.

The breath dashed out of me in one hard punch, my lungs deflating like an old balloon. I stared at what their bodies had been hiding, feeling the room tilt.

My locker wasn't just plastered with the photo of me arguing with Brynne. It was also spray-painted with blood-red letters.

KILLER

. . .

THE PAINT WAS CRUDE, THE LETTERS THEMSELVES DRIPPING like they were bleeding. My heart hammered in my chest, so hard I had to put in effort not to reach up and clutch it. I swallowed, eyes still locked on the accusation. At the label I would likely never be able to outrun.

Jamie leaned forward and grabbed the handle on the door, and I noticed for the first time the lock I'd been using was gone. He gave me a look almost as if he was telling me to brace myself and then silently swung it open.

There was no bracing myself for what was inside, though. No way to guard my heart.

The silver goggles I loved so much dangled from the top shelf. In pieces. Swaying like they weren't quite over being cut up and defiled. The normally shiny frames that glinted in the water were splattered with more of that red paint. Stained with blood.

A flashback of a smiling and alive Brynne handing me a box with a giant blue bow assaulted me. I made a sound at the way she smiled. How happy she'd been to hand me that gift.

Pain lanced through my body, the kind of pain that came on so fast it brought with it rolling nausea. I swallowed profusely, trying to choke down the vomit flooding my throat.

I stumbled forward, snatching the busted goggles from the locker, and one of the eyepieces fell at my feet. With a noise, I bent to pick it up and ended up staying near the floor, staring into my hands at the last gift Brynne gave me. At the last good memory we had together before everything went to hell.

It was destroyed now.

Cut into pieces. Splattered with blood. Murdered. Dead. Just like her.

The pressure behind my eyes made my vision blur and

burn. A small hand reached over, covering the scene I held in my hands. Hers was steady, and it made me realize I was not, that my fingers trembled.

"Hey." Landry's voice was quiet and gentle, her fingertips warm when they brushed my palm. "Let's put this away for now," she said. "Lars," she called, fingers scooping up the pieces of my past to take them away.

"No!" I erupted, hands snatching back what she was trying to take away. "Don't touch this."

She drew back but not away, and I felt her wide-eyed stare. "Okay. I won't touch it. But maybe you should put it away. It's upsetting you."

"I don't want you to touch it." I was gruff. "It's…" *Tainted.* "Just don't."

"I'll take it," a new voice put in, a body moving in toward my other side. It wasn't Lars as I expected.

I glanced up at Walsh, and my lip curled. All the shock and pain I felt melted into another emotion, one I whole-heartedly embraced. Anger.

"Oh, you're loving this right now, aren't you?" I practically snarled.

"I could think of other things I'd rather be doing." His bored tone only made me more antagonistic.

I stood, pushing my body between him and Landry. "You never did like me. We never liked each other. You're probably pissing your Speedos in glee to be rid of me."

"I thought it was Jamie with the piss problem, not Ryan," Kruger whispered loudly.

"I was like fucking five!" Jamie muttered.

To his credit, Ryan ignored the sideshow going down and cocked his head to the side. "You going somewhere?"

I was aware of everyone standing there watching. Waiting to see what I would do and say. Hell, maybe they were hoping for a show.

Funny thing, though, I no longer felt like a wildcard. Seeing those goggles had hit me in a weak spot, took something from me I didn't realize I still had. I was tired. So fucking tired. I wanted to lick my wounds and just let everyone think I was a killer.

I knew Landry and Lars believed in me. I wanted to show them their loyalty to me was reciprocated, but was it loyalty to drag them down? To knowingly let them get hurt so I wouldn't have to be alone?

Maybe the best thing I could do for them would be to walk away.

"You know what?" I said, straightening up as I dropped the defiled goggles at my feet. "Let's just get this shit over with."

Putting my back to my locker, I faced the room and the swimmers crowding the row. There were so many they spilled out the end and into the area leading toward the door.

"Back in California, I was accused of murder. Of killing the girl in that picture plastered all over for everyone to see. She was like my sister. And that guy here last night? That was her twin. My old best friend. I was the last person to see her alive. Everyone thinks I did it—"

"We know." Ryan cut in.

I swung toward him. "You know?" I partly scoffed. I mean, yeah, Lars said they all knew, but...

1. I wasn't going to out my bro like that.

And

2. I had no clue how much they actually knew.

Thinking of that, I searched around, eyes finding Coach at the edge of the group, just watching everything go down.

Asshole was probably enjoying this. Maybe that was why he turned all "it's Landry's decision" this morning. He knew once we got here, shit would hit the fan.

Just thinking that made me seethe. "You tell the team, Coach?" I challenged.

His eyes stayed level on mine. "Would be within my rights if I had."

"Just like you told the cops," I deadpanned.

A voice cut in. "It wasn't Coach. It was me."

I turned toward Walsh. "You?"

"Figured we deserved to know what we were dealing with."

So fucking smug.

My shoulder blades snapped together. "That really why you came to the police station the other day?" I accused. "You acted like it was out of some sense of loyalty, but it was really to get the dirt on me."

"I'm not like them," Ryan said, not taking the bait. "Elite is nothing like the Nobles."

I laughed. "Yeah? Well, from where I'm standing, you sure look a hell of a lot alike."

Jamie stepped forward. "Bro, chill. There's this thing we have. It's called the internet."

"My grandma calls it the intranet," Prism mused.

We all looked at him.

He blinked. "What?"

"You hardly ever speak, and when you do, it's about your grandma?" I asked. I couldn't help it. I mean, what the fuck?

Prism flushed. He had AirPods in his ears. How the hell could he even hear us? And what was he always listening to?

"It's funny," he muttered. And was he blushing?

Kruger slapped him on the shoulder. "Grams is a riot, P. Good talk." Then he looked between us all. "Carry on."

I glanced at Landry, and she nodded encouragingly.

"You looked me up on the internet?" I asked Walsh.

"Wasn't going to, but when Malibu Barbie showed up at practice, I figured your time to tell us yourself was up."

"Good thing too because look at this shit," Jamie muttered, waving his hand around at the mess.

Several grunts and agreements went through the crowd.

I folded my arms over my chest and regarded all the bros. "So what? So you found an article on the web. You think you know everything?"

"Bro, you ever been on the internet?" Jamie asked. "You got a whole corner of it."

My stomach flipped a little when I imagined all the things they probably read. I'd stopped looking a long time ago. The court of public opinion was brutal and not in my favor.

"It was piping-hot tea, bro," Kruger added. "We all had a cup."

"Almost burned my tongue," someone quipped from the back.

Assholes. All of them.

I spun to face Coach. "Well, you got what you wanted. I'm out." Turning back to my locker, I realized everything else in it had been cut up too. Oh well. Made packing a lot easier.

I started away, the silence deafening. The worst walk of shame in the history of walks of shame.

"Jay." Landry's hand curled around my arm. I glanced at her. "I'm coming with you."

My heart skipped a beat, and the backs of my eyes burned. I was about to tell her she couldn't, that she was better off here.

But the words behind me stopped my tongue.

"We know you didn't do it."

Straightening, I turned and met Ryan's steady gaze. "What?"

"We believe you. We know you didn't kill that girl."

I swear there was an echo in my head. My ears rang with the words, and it took longer than normal to process them. I tried. Then tried again.

Blinking rapidly, I finally said, "How can you believe me? I never told you I didn't do it."

"What do you think we are, a bunch of morons?" Jamie quipped.

"Kruger is," I said.

"I mean, I'm really offended," Kruger said. "This is why I like P best."

Prism patted him on the shoulder. "I'll never quit you, man."

Kruger shot me a look. "I never once considered you did it, but maybe I'm about to change my mind."

I shook my head. This was surreal. What the hell was even going on? I was standing here in the middle of a pretty good attack on my life. My character. My present and my future. And with me was a team I never really felt part of. A team I held at arm's length. And what were we doing?

Joking.

Fucking joking.

"This isn't a joke," I said, my words echoing my thoughts.

"No. It's not." Walsh agreed. "I looked everything up. We had a team meeting. We know everything."

"Then you know I'm still suspect number one. Actually, the only suspect. And that everyone thinks I did it."

"Not everyone thinks that," Wes said. "Elite doesn't."

I made a strangled sound. "Bullshit."

"We've had our fair share of trash in the pool. We know it when we see it. You ain't it." Jamie concurred.

"I've been a complete dick to everyone except Lars."

"Not me," Vargas called. His sentiment was echoed by many others.

I rolled my eyes. "Fine," I allowed, taking in Ryan, Jamie, Wes, and the other bros. "Just to you guys."

"It was a test, right?" Walsh asked.

I lifted an eyebrow. "A test?"

"Yeah, when you challenged me for initiation."

I thought back to when we first got here and they tossed me and Lars into the pool fully clothed. They claimed it was Elite passage. But I called bullshit. And yeah, I did challenge Walsh to see how hard he'd go on me. To see what kind of hazing he would inflict. I wanted to know what I was dealing with. I wanted him to know I wasn't to be fucked with.

"You reminded me of Cobalt," I muttered.

"Noble's resident dick," Jamie put in.

I glanced up, shocked.

He smirked. "I told you that *intranet* has it all."

Prism snickered.

"Just for you, P," Jamie mused.

"Don't you call him that!" Kruger bitched.

"And when I didn't take your bait?" Walsh asked, once again impervious to the circus around us.

"I kept pushing," I answered. I knew eventually he'd crack and show his true colors.

But he never did. *Maybe these are his true colors.*

And maybe Bigfoot did exist.

Bro, don't tell Landry about my joke. It's our secret.

"You never took it out on Rory, though. Even when she confronted you about our rivalry," Ryan said.

"I don't hurt women."

"Exactly."

I snorted. "So that's it? I'm nice to your girlfriend, so you decided I'm not a killer?" I shook my head. "That's weak, Walsh."

There was a bunch of commotion at the front of the

locker room, the door banging against the wall as someone burst in.

"Lars!" Win yelled, barreling around the corner with Max on his heels. Both men skidded to a stop to stare at the gathered team.

"What the fuck is going on?" Max spat. "Wes!"

"We're here," Lars said.

The crowd parted so Win and Max could make their way to us. Win waved his phone around. "I got your text, angel. We got here as soon as we could."

"I was in bed," Max grumbled, grabbing Wes by the chin so he could inspect his face.

Wes batted at Max's arm. "I'm fine. Let go."

"I'll let go when I'm satisfied," Max told him. Keeping ahold of Wes's chin, his eyes sought out Jamie. "Why didn't you text me?"

"It's not his job to text you," Wes complained.

Jamie scoffed. "I did, bro. Check your phone."

Ryan laughed under his breath, and Wes made a rude noise.

Max grunted. "What's going on?"

"We're having a team meeting," Lars answered and glanced at Win. "You should be here."

Phweeeee! Coach's whistle had everyone wincing. "These two ain't Elite!"

"Yes, they are," everyone said in unison.

Coach belched as though we'd given him indigestion.

Landry gasped. "Oh my God, that's so gross!"

I pinched the bridge of my nose. "Can we just get back to the fact that I was accused of murder and now someone is going out of their way to terrorize me about it and out me to the team?"

"Not just you," Coach intoned, his voice dark.

Whatever it was that I heard in his voice put me on alert.

The hair on the back of my neck stood, and adrenaline pooled in my veins. "What?"

Coach gestured with his head toward the office. I shoved through the bodies standing around, my heart hammering erratically. I hustled into his office, even beating Coach.

The second I saw it, I froze. My entire body turned hot, and my face flushed with the force of it. Adrenaline pummeled me, making my hands ball into fists. I stalked forward, feet slapping the floor.

"What the fuck is this?" I roared, the rage inside me rattling my bones.

Landry's locker was in her dad's office. He'd moved one in there just for her. And while everything else looked undisturbed, her locker was violated.

My chest heaved as I stared at the photo taped all over it and the crudely red-painted words dripping ominously.

KILLER LOVER

BANG!

I slammed my fist into the metal with so much force the door groaned and bent, caving in from the blow. Ignoring the scalding heat in my knuckles, I shook my arm and then lunged again, ripping open the newly pummeled door. The entire thing tilted off the wall, tipping forward in my haste.

With a growl, I stopped it with my palms, holding it up so I could look inside to see if her stuff had been destroyed too.

In answer, it all tumbled out, smacking against me on its way to the floor.

All of it shredded. All of it splattered with red paint.

I yelled and shoved the locker away, and it crashed sideways, taking out a few plaques on the wall on its way to the floor.

Silence draped over the room, the only sound the heaving of my chest as I stood among Landry's cut-up stuff. I didn't know what to do with all this rage inside me.

The scent of cherry vanilla cut through the worst of it when she rushed by and dropped to her knees near the fallen locker.

"Get away from that. It might fall on you," I said, reaching under her arms to pull her away.

"Oh, it's ruined," she murmured, her voice thick with sadness.

That anger in me fired up all over again at hearing the pain in her voice, and I had to make a conscious effort to make sure my hands weren't rough as I tugged her back. As I did, my gaze caught on the fabric she dragged with her. A worn gray color that seemed familiar.

After pulling her to her feet, I reached out at what she clutched. "What do you have there?" I asked gently.

Her hands stayed clenched around it when I tugged, but because it was cut up, a piece of it came loose. I held it up, and my stomach dropped when I saw part of an M and B.

"Is this...?" I started, my mind tripping to catch up.

"It's your snotty Pembrook hoodie!" she wailed and burst into tears.

My arms went slack, the piece of the hoodie I held lowering to my side. She made a strangled sound and snatched it back, tucking it into her arms with the rest of the fabric. I'd never seen this girl cry.

Granted, I'd only known her a few weeks. But she was sassy and bratty. She issued orders at the pool like a drill sergeant and never took anyone's crap. Hell, she looked my murder accusations in the face and shrugged.

I didn't expect that the thing to bring her down would be a ratty old hoodie.

I glanced down at all the other shredded stuff. A bathing suit. Swim caps. A towel. She didn't even glance at that shit. But she was crying over that hoodie.

She'd kept it.

She sniffled, blond head bowed as she hugged it to her chest.

What the fuck was I supposed to do? On impulse, I glanced around. Maybe Lars would know. The first person my eyes landed on was Coach who was standing there shooting daggers out of his eyes.

I hurried past him. I'd deal with that later.

Next, I found Win who widened his hazel eyes with a *WTF* look and gestured for me to bring her in.

Right. Of course.

The second I wrapped my arms around her, she melted into me, rubbing her tearstained cheek against my chest. My heart flipped over, and the need to comfort roared to life.

"All right now," I murmured, aware we had a large audience. "It's okay. It's just an old hoodie."

"It was yours!" she protested, squeezing it tighter.

"I'll give you another one, baby. You can have as many as you want."

"But this one was special." Her voice was muffled against my chest. "It was from that night. The first thing you gave me."

Damn.

"I wore it all the time. Even though it stopped smelling like you. I wore it anyway because it was yours." She sniffled more. "I put it in here so I could wear it after my next swim. But now I can't wear it again."

Double damn.

Flattening the palm of my hand against her back, I rubbed

up and down and rested my chin on the top of her head. "I'll sew it for you."

Her crying paused. "What?"

Yeah, what?

"I'll, ah, sew it for you, okay? I'll fix it. Then I'll wear it around so it will smell like me again. It'll be good as new."

A vision of me walking around looking like a stitched-up Frankenstein's monster heckled my confident words.

Her head lifted out of my chest. Her green eyes were wet and reminded me of a field of grass after a rainstorm. "Really?"

I nodded.

Her nose wrinkled. "Do you even know how to sew?"

I blanched. "How hard can it be?"

"Famous last words, bro," Jamie whispered.

Lars laughed.

I spun, taking Landry and her snotty, destroyed hoodie with me. "You laughing, bro? You can help me sew it."

He stopped laughing.

"What the hell's the meaning of this?" Coach bellowed.

"You've literally been here the whole time, Coach," Wes observed.

Coach gave him an incredulous look. "You," he said, jabbing a finger at him and then at Ryan and Jamie, "have been hanging out with these two for too long."

"I don't like your tone." Max glowered.

Coach groaned. "Put a sock in it, Navarro!" He turned back to me. "This the doing of that Goldilocks that was in here the other night, waving around his fist and insulting my daughter?"

There was a pregnant pause.

"Goldilocks?" I repeated.

On the other side of the door, Kruger and Prism laughed. "That mean the three bears were here too, Coach?"

Landry giggled into my chest, and I rolled my lips inward so I didn't laugh too.

"I think he means Malibu Barbie," Jamie contributed helpfully.

"You idiots think this is funny? Someone breaking in here and threatening my daughter?"

I stiffened. I definitely did *not* think any of this was funny. In fact, I was so mad I'd likely already have stormed out of there if it wasn't for the girl in my arms.

I'd made her a target. Now she was guilty by association.

She didn't deserve that. None of these bros did. We were supposed to be swimming right now. Instead, we were staring at wallpapered lockers, spray paint, and shredded clothes.

Landry gasped, pulling out of my arms to look at Coach. "The cameras."

Coach went around his desk, fingers clicking over the keyboard.

"There's cameras in here?" I asked, feeling a heaping dose of *oh shit* and wondering if Coach saw the night I introduced myself to his princess.

"Out in the natatorium," Landry explained, eyes flashing with awareness. "Not in the locker room."

"It's the same person who tossed the dummy in the pool," Coach announced. "Covered from head to foot. They're barely on camera for two minutes before they disappear into the locker room."

"You have footage of the person putting the dummy in the pool?" I asked, surprised.

Coach nodded.

I scowled. "And you still blamed me and turned me in to the cops?"

"I was pissed off," Coach said, looking at Landry.

I growled. "Let me see." I moved toward the desk, but

leaving her in the middle of the room still clutching that hoodie made me feel sick. Backtracking, I put my arm around her and brought her with.

We watched the short footage, and I let out a frustrated grunt. "Can't tell anything from that."

"Should we call the police?" Landry asked.

Everyone looked at Coach.

I resolved myself to another epic round of questioning. At least this time I wouldn't be soaking wet.

"No."

My eyes whipped to him. "No?"

"What are they gonna do?" he retorted. "Write notes in that fucking ancient notebook and ask a thousand questions?"

"Then they'll complain that Elite causes too much trouble," Lars muttered.

"Exactly." Coach agreed.

"Elite takes care of Elite," Ryan announced. As if he even needed to. Whoever wrote his lines needed to find some new material.

All eyes shifted back to me.

Ah. Right. We'd finally arrived at the part where I'd be officially axed from the team.

26

HE THOUGHT WE WOULD ABANDON HIM. IT WAS WRITTEN ALL over his handsome face.

I mean, sure, this was an epic shitshow, but it wasn't his fault. And to be honest, I kinda really hated anyone who made him feel it was.

Seeing the hoodie I'd sneezed on and stolen from him that first night we met cut up in pieces hit me hard. It felt like it wasn't just the hoodie they tried to destroy but the memories attached to it. An attempt to invalidate the instant connection between us. For months, that hoodie was my only link to him, the only tangible proof I had of a connection no one else could see but I wholly felt. Sometimes when I lay in bed at night, I'd bury my nose in the neckline, trying to find the last traces of his scent, and wish I'd gotten his name. Hope that I might see him again. Even after we collided here at Westbrook, the hoodie remained special. A secret between us. Something we shared that no one else knew. The beginning of something I hoped never ended...

And now it was in pieces.

I couldn't stop the tears from falling. The ache from cutting me in two. But even in my distress, I knew this wasn't about me. It was about hurting Jason.

And though he would never admit it, I knew. I knew all this cut deep.

His expression when he saw his locker, the graffiti, and those goggles was palpable. The air was soured with torment, coating my tongue with misery. I had no idea what played in his mind when he bent, cradling those silver frames in his palms, but it was powerfully heartbreaking. What he didn't understand was that there was no way anyone could watch that and fathom he was a guilty man.

He bled trepidation when he stood and faced the team, his black eyes bleak, without a scrap of hope. He stood anyway. Rising to his full height, ready to spill everything even as he expected it to get him released from Elite.

Even after everyone said they believed him, he was still standing there like his time was up.

"I'll get my shit," he told the room. Then a grimace tugged his face. "What's left of it anyway. But I'll clean it up on my way out."

Behind his back, I glared daggers at my father, silently threatening that he'd better step up. Yes, I could call out to Jay, but the truth was it wouldn't be as meaningful. He needed Elite to support him right now.

"Did I dismiss you?" Dad's voice was gruff, and I let out a silent relieved breath.

I glanced at Ryan, and he nodded reassuringly. *We got this.*

"What?" Jason asked, glancing at my dad.

"You're not leaving your team to deal with this. You're helping."

"I already said I'd clean it up."

"And after, you have practice. You're swimming ten extra laps."

His dark brows furrowed as if he truly didn't understand. "But—"

Phweeee! Phweeee! "I don't want to hear your excuses, Rush! I said clean up and get in the pool! If you give me any more shit, I'll make you swim until you can't lift your arms!"

"C'mon, Coach," Jamie complained. "We're all still sore from last night."

"Was I talking to you, Owens?"

"If you make Rush swim extra laps, then we're all swimming them," Lars declared.

Jason looked around at everyone in the office and those crowding around outside it. "I thought I was off the team."

"You aren't off the team unless I say you're off. Have you heard me say that?" Dad replied.

"What about all this?" he asked, gesturing to my locker and all the ruined stuff around it.

Coach sighed dramatically and rubbed a hand over his face. "You think I didn't know what I was getting into when I accepted you on the team? I did my research, and I admit I had my doubts. But then I talked to you. I saw you swim. I know you aren't a killer, son. We all do."

Jason made a choked sound, his chest rising and falling heavily. "Seriously?"

"Doesn't mean I want you dating my daughter," Dad hurried to assert. I grunted, and he held up his hand and muttered, "But I'll come around."

Disbelief and awe warred on Jay's features, flickering between light and dark. "Why?" he whispered.

Ryan came forward and smacked him on the back. "You're Elite." As soon as he said the words, he grimaced. "Even I'm getting tired of saying it."

Jason barked a laugh, but when he caught himself, his lips slammed shut and his eyes rounded.

Ryan half smiled. "Your old team was a bunch of posers. We're the real deal here. We got your back, okay? And if anyone comes around talking shit and spreading rumors, we'll deal with it."

"It's not shit and rumors. It's murder." There he went trying to warn them off. It was a terrible habit. Far worse than being a car nerd.

"Bro, we don't half ass shit around here," Jamie quipped. "That's why you fit in."

"This team is really good at drama and trauma," Wes supplied.

"Elite," Ryan called out. "Tell Rush we're with him!"

The entire locker room vibrated with their yells.

When the noise died down, Jason stood there silent and overwhelmed. I could almost feel his heaviness, how overfull of emotion he was. "No one else believed me," he whispered. "I swam with them for years."

Lars moved to his side. "Welcome home."

Such simple words with so much meaning.

Jason's throat worked, and he glanced around at me. I nearly drowned in the raw emotion he let me glimpse before tucking it back into the secretive depths of his turbulent stare. My heart squeezed, and I dropped the hoodie to wrap my arms around his waist.

"I'm not trading in my Vette for a Rubicon." His voice rumbled over my head, and I smiled into his chest.

"Fine. But you'll let me drive it, right?" Jamie asked.

"Bro, there is zero chance of that ever happening," Jason deadpanned.

Ryan laughed. "You can just ride with Lars."

Jay stiffened, and I bit back a groan. *Here we go.*

"You're getting a Rubicon?" It wasn't a question. It was an

indictment.

"There's a blue one at Ryan's dad's dealership. They said I should go test drive it," Lars answered.

"No," Jason declared, and I could feel him shaking his head. "Absolutely not."

"If Lars wants to get a Jeep, then that's what I'll get him," Win put in.

Lars made a rude sound. "I told you that you aren't paying for it."

"Well, I'm not letting you make payments," Win retorted as though the very idea horrified him. Somewhere nearby, Max grunted in agreement.

"Arguing with them is useless." Wes sighed.

Jason made a disgusted sound. "It doesn't matter because he's not driving around in a Jeep. No kidney of mine will be—"

"Kidney?" Ryan cut in.

I laughed, and Jason exhaled as if he was already tired of having more than one friend.

Spoiler alert: He wasn't.

"I don't even need a car," Lars said, exasperated.

Dad's whistle erupted, and I groaned into Jason's chest. His hands came up to shield my ears as it went on. I was going to hide that torture device when he was sleeping.

When at last the high-pitched sound dropped away, Dad's voice boomed. "What the hell do you think this is? Recess? Get your asses in the pool! You're all gonna be late to classes. Swimming comes first!"

Jamie gasped and pressed a hand to his chest. "What will Prism's gram say?"

Muffled laughter filled the space.

"Out," Dad bellowed. "Go get wet!"

The locker room erupted with sound as the guys all

started out to the pool, and I pulled away from Jason and glanced at all my ruined stuff.

"Landry."

I turned toward my father.

"Go lead practice. Don't go easy on them. I'll be out in a few."

"Okay," I said, glancing at Jason.

Dad made a noise. "Don't look at him. Go on. You can see him later when you aren't on my time."

"But—" I began to protest, eyes gliding back to the ripped-up Pembrook hoodie.

Warm, gentle fingers slid under my chin to lift. I was immediately ensnared by Jason's soulful, dark gaze. "I've got this."

The tenderness in his voice only made me want to stay by his side.

"I'll help," I offered.

Off to the side, Dad sighed, but Jason's eyes flashed to where he stood, and surprisingly, he backed off. Focusing back on me, Jay shifted, his body angling a little closer and making me feel like I was being embraced even though I wasn't in his arms. Everything in me swayed toward him as though the molecules making up my body were rearranging themselves to make more room for him

"You don't need to be around all this, little siren. I don't like it."

I frowned. I didn't want him around any of it either. And he shouldn't have to clean it all up by himself.

"We'll help clean it up," Lars offered, clearly reading my hesitation.

The guys still standing around all readily agreed.

I bit into my lower lip and regarded Jay.

He tugged my lip away from my teeth. "C'mon," he said,

dropping an arm across my shoulders and leading me out of the office and away from everyone.

Once we were alone, he wrapped me up in a hug, and I exhaled.

"I'm sorry," he murmured, stroking the back of my head. "I'm sorry I brought this on you."

I pulled back, eyes blazing. "You didn't do this. *He* did," I spat, thinking of Bodhi. How someone who claimed to know Jay so well could ever do this was something I might never understand. "I should find him. Give him a piece of my mind."

I whirled away, but Jason caught my arm to pull me back. "Whoa there, scrappy little siren."

I huffed impatience. "I won't have it, Jason."

He settled more firmly into his stance as the hand around my arm tightened. "Well, I won't have you giving a piece of yourself to anyone else. They're mine. All of them."

"Now is not the time for your possessive dominance, Jason."

He lifted an eyebrow, and my stomach dipped. *God, why is he so hot?*

"There will never be a nanosecond on my clock that is *not* the time when you are all mine." He shifted, his muscled thigh pushing between my legs. My breath caught and held as he literally lifted me off my feet with one of his legs.

My hands slapped onto his biceps, holding on while he brought me higher like it was no problem at all for him to stand there on one leg while he balanced my weight with the other.

His arm wrapped around my waist, tugging so I slid down his thigh and our chests bumped.

"Frankly, little siren, it offends me that you seem to not know this already."

"Know what?" I echoed, my body slowly starting to boil.

He chuckled, the sound low and deviant and so filled with confidence because he knew exactly what he was doing. His breath was warm and feathered over my cheek, ruffling my hair when he whispered, "Tell me who you belong to, little siren."

An involuntary shiver racked my body, and I clung just a little tighter to his arms. "You."

He hummed, his voice an aphrodisiac. "And who am I?"

I heard the others talking just inside the office. I knew life was going on around us and we weren't truly alone, but when he touched me like this, he owned me. He owned not just my body and mind but every ounce of my attention. The building could shudder and tumble around us, and I would stand here in the center unaffected by it all because I was completely and totally in love with him.

"Mine," I whispered. "My Jason."

"Good fucking girl," he praised, growling a bit when his lips caught mine.

I whimpered into him, melting at the way his tongue stroked mine. Too soon, he pulled away and lowered my body so my feet hit the floor.

"Go run practice, baby. I'll take care of everything else," he instructed, dropping a kiss to the tip of my nose.

I felt like I'd just been on some epic tilt-a-whirl when he stepped back, the space between us enough to clear the haze his closeness had put me under.

I scowled. "You did that on purpose."

"Did what?" he asked, a picture of innocence.

Liar, liar, pants on fire. "Distracted me."

His face softened. "Now you know how I feel whenever you're in the room."

Well, how was I supposed to be annoyed now? "I'm adding five laps to the ten Dad already gave you," I said, smug.

His grin was quick and devastating. I loved the way his face lit up like a light turning on in a dark room, revealing something gorgeous. "All right, Coach. I'll take what you dish out."

I rolled my eyes and started away.

"Landry." My first name from his lips was almost jolting. I was so used to him not using it.

When I turned, he was right there, so close that I gasped and had to crane my neck to look up. His piercing, unblinking stare was accompanied by a serious tone. "Stay away from Bodhi."

I opened my mouth to protest, but he shook his head once. "I mean it. I'll deal with him."

Anxiety crawled over me like ants, making me itchy and unsettled.

Sensing my unease, he laid his palm against my cheek. "He's just trying to get me kicked off Elite. Probably feels it's justice for Brynne."

"I don't like him." The confession ripped out of me, not sounding hateful at all but scared.

He made a faint sound and pulled me in. "I know, baby. That's why I said to stay away from him, okay? I can handle him. He might look mean, but he's really harmless."

I wasn't sure I agreed.

"Rush!" Dad yelled, impatience evident in his tone.

Still holding my face, Jay kissed my forehead and nudged me toward the door. "Go on, little siren. Go boss some swimmers around."

"Don't you throw away my hoodie," I called.

His chuckle chased away the worst of the ick swimming around me.

"Wouldn't dream of it."

The ick came back, though. As soon as I turned the corner and saw Jason's locker, my skin prickled uncomfortably at the sight of the dripping red paint. Jason seemed to think Bodhi was just trying to get him kicked off the team. But to me, it felt like a threat.

And the way he painted *Killer Lover* on my locker? That felt like a threat too.

I couldn't help but wonder what would happen when Bodhi realized Elite wouldn't give up on Jason.

Would he just go back to California... or would things only get worse?

27

Rush

Where are you? I shot the text off and impatiently waited for the reply.

He'd better fucking reply. If he didn't, I'd rip apart all of Westbrook searching. He made my girl cry, and he fucked with my friends.

It was still kinda a mindfuck to even think of Elite as my friends. Except Lars, of course, but you knew that, right?

I'd been walking around all day in half a state of shell shock.

"Welcome home." Lars's simple words were still wedged in my heart like a shard of glass. If I pulled it out, I might bleed to death, so I left it there and let it hurt.

Elite had every right to send me packing. Hell, that's what California did.

I'd been a dick since day one. Arrogant. Antagonistic. Secretive. Not much of a team player. A murder suspect.

They backed me up anyway. First with Bodhi the other

night and then earlier in the locker room. They legitimately stared at photos of me glowering at the girl I was accused of killing, stared at the mess made of my and Landry's lockers, and still told me they had my back.

The loyalty and friendship I thought I had in the past looked like an already small wiener in below-zero temps. Nonexistent and, frankly, pathetic.

Elite had some balls. And a big dick to back them up. Maybe coming here hadn't been a means to an end after all. Maybe it really was a new beginning.

My phone chimed, and I glanced down at the address.

I'm coming, I replied, shoving the phone in my jeans and heading for the Corvette. Yeah, half of me was shell-shocked, but the other half? Mad as hell.

Possibly more pissed than before. There were other people involved now. People I cared about. Someone I loved. Even if it was hard to process, I was still going to protect it. I'd done a piss-poor job of that back in Cali. I let everything get ripped away. Maybe because I deserved it.

And now?

I didn't care if I deserved it or not. I was keeping them. All of them. Even Walsh.

The address wasn't too far from campus, and I made it there in record time. After sliding my baby into a parking spot near the front of the building, I got out and locked her up.

A bitter wind cut through my clothes, making me shiver. My life might be here now, but damn, I missed that California weather. And the beach. How I longed to watch the sunrise over the waves with a board in my hands.

It seemed colder than usual today, and I acknowledged that maybe it felt that way because of where I was and who I was going to see.

I walked into the hotel lobby, strolled to the elevators,

and rode up to the third floor. They dinged open, and I stepped off, going down the hall to the room number he'd texted. At the door, I paused, dragging in a breath, and prepared myself for the swipe of hurt I always felt when I saw my old best friend.

I knocked, and he opened the door almost instantly, making me wonder if he'd been waiting on the other side.

He didn't pull it all the way ajar, though, instead crowding the partially open space. His dark-blond hair was pulled back in that low ponytail against his neck with a few loose strands falling out around his ears. His skin was not as sun-kissed as it usually appeared, and the skin beneath his surfer-dude blue eyes was bruised as if he hadn't been sleeping.

"Bodhi," I said, voice even. I waited for the hurt to come, the sting of betrayal I always felt when I saw him.

It never came.

"Rush."

The second he said my name, hot anger spread through me like an out-of-control wildfire. It singed my veins, depleting the oxygen inside me and leaving behind a tight, dry feeling. As we stood measuring each other through the slim space made by the hotel room door, I wasn't hurt.

Now?

Now I was threatened. Territorial. *Fucking pissed.*

My hand slapped onto the center of the door and pushed. Surprise flashed over Bodhi's face, but he stepped back, letting me muscle my way into the room.

"You've gone too far this time," I told him, barging in and slamming the door behind me. "And it's time for you to go."

"I can't go until we've talked."

I barked out a harsh laugh. "You got a funny way of talking," I spat and headed down the small entry hall, past the bathroom, and into the sitting area.

The second I stepped inside, someone else jolted up off the end of one of the double beds.

I stopped in my tracks, shock rippling through me. "Blair?"

My old teammate swallowed, head bobbing in confirmation. "Hey, Rush."

I glanced at Bodhi who was standing just off to my side and then back to Blair. "What the hell are you doing here?"

"I came to talk to you with Bodes."

Bodes. I hadn't even referred to Bodhi with that nickname in my head since Brynne had died. Truth was he wasn't Bodes to me anymore. Just like I couldn't be Rush to Landry. He stopped being my best friend, someone I was familiar with, someone I trusted when I looked into his eyes and saw that he wasn't just broken over his twin's death, but he really thought I was the one who'd killed her.

He just wasn't that person to me any longer. He probably never would be again.

There it is. The hurt I thought was dried up. Guess there was still a little in there after all.

I pointed at Bodhi. "You terrorizing my girl and my friends…" Then I turned back to Blair. "And you hiding in a hotel room like some creeper is *not* talking."

I put my hands on my hips. Like an irate granny.

What? I *was* irate.

"The fact I even have to say that." I shook my head. "Was there a sale on audacity wherever you been shopping? Because, bros, you bought too much."

Blair's eyes widened then flew to Bodhi.

Noticing, Bodhi said, "I told you. He's weird now."

Was he shitting me? "I'm weird?" I echoed. "What the fuck would you know? What the fuck right do you even have to say something like that?" I spewed as my chest grew hot and constricted under the renewed anger churning up with his casual assessment.

"You don't get to act like you know me. That you know anything about how I am. You wanted me gone," I said, sweeping them both with a look. "All of you. And I left. I came all the way across the country. Was that not good enough for you?" Agitation made me pace a little farther into the room, passing by Blair before spinning back. "Did you decide you missed your punching bag so you came all this way to hit me some more?"

"What?" Blair said, confusion in his tone. He glanced at Bodhi. "I thought you talked to him already."

"I tried. He wouldn't listen."

I laughed, the sound making the inside of the room just as frigid as the winter air outside. "Yeah, Blair. He tried. He threw a dummy dressed up like his sister into my pool. Then he came back and taped up pictures of her all over the place and trashed my locker."

Blair sucked in a breath, and Bodhi jolted. "I told you that wasn't me!" he yelled. Then his brows creased. "Wait, did you say pictures of Brynne?"

I narrowed my eyes. "Just admit it, man." My upper lip curled. "You came to the pool, accused me of being a killer, insulted my girl, and then had a massive hissy fit about the goggles I was wearing."

Blair made a sound. "You have a girl?"

"Am I really supposed to buy it's yet another coincidence that the very goggles you were so enraged about are now cut up in pieces and splattered with blood-red paint along with everything else in my locker?" I scoffed. "And writing *killer* on the door? Real original."

Bodhi looked the same shell-shocked that I felt before showing up here. "Rush, I—"

I growled. "Save your pathetic excuses, Bodhi. I was

willing to ignore all this. Overlook it. But you went at my girl. After you were warned not to. The shit you pulled made her cry, bro." My voice dropped, and I took a threatening step toward him. "I *hate* seeing my girl cry."

Blair rushed forward, grabbing my arm to stop me from tackling Bodhi. I was so tense I felt my muscles rippling as adrenaline flooded my system. I glanced down to where Blair held my arm and then up to his face.

He flushed, a wary look overtaking his resolve, and I felt his fingers loosen. He didn't let go, though. Instead, he hurried to say, "We came here to apologize!"

Some of the stiffness in my body went slack. I shook my head slightly, almost as though my brain short-circuited. "What?" I asked.

Blair looked at Bodhi, accusation on his face. "Brah, didn't you tell him?"

Bodhi flushed, and his eyes darted to me then away. "Seeing him brought up a lot of stuff. It pissed me off."

Yanking away from Blair, I folded my arms over my chest and stared at Bodhi. He shifted. The full weight of my black stare had always made him uncomfortable.

Good.

"Stop looking at me like that," he muttered, shifting again. The anxious movement made the long-sleeved crop top he was wearing tug, and a strip of his lean waist flashed.

I glanced down the rest of his body, noting the low-slung sweatpants and his bare feet. His toenails were painted purple, matching the shade of his shirt perfectly.

Guess he was taking advantage of not being at the pool while he was here because back in Cali, Coach would never let him show up to swim with painted nails.

"What the fuck is going on?" I asked, lifting my eyes to drill into his face once more.

"You said someone trashed your locker and put up pictures of Brynne everywhere?" Blair asked.

"It was one photo. Hundreds of it. Everywhere." I corrected.

"When was this?" Blair questioned.

"Like you don't know."

"Humor me."

I cut a glance at the dark-haired swimmer. I never thought of him as a bad guy. Kinda a follower, you know? Like he thought that the only way to get people to like him was by doing what everyone else wanted.

"It was this morning." Then, begrudgingly, I added, "But he did it in the middle of the night. Around two a.m.," remembering the clock on the camera footage Coach had pulled up.

Blair nodded once. "Well, it wasn't Bodhi. He was here with me."

"You think I believe that?"

"We were up playing video games until three." Bodhi swiped his cell off the table nearby and pulled up something. "See? I took a photo of the screen when we won a match." He shoved the phone under my nose with the photo of the TV screen declaring them winners.

"So?" I said. "That could be from any time."

"The timestamp is right here," he said, tapping the details on the photo and showing the time and date it was taken. 3:04 a.m.

"You could be covering for him. Maybe you were up playing, but he wasn't," I argued. These assholes were barking up the wrong tree if they thought I was just going to take them at their word.

"I told you he doesn't believe me. Anything I say," Bodhi said to Blair.

"What goes around comes around," I spat.

I won't lie. It felt good to be petty. But now I was done. It was time to evict these trespassers back to their coast.

My hand shot out, taking a fistful of Bodhi's purple shirt and dragging him close. "You came. You made my life hell. Time to go home."

Something bleak flickered in his tired blue eyes. "What home?" he whispered.

Emotion swirled inside me. Something that felt a lot like sorrow. Something that made me feel like an ass. I wanted it off me. I wanted it away.

I shoved him back forcefully. He stumbled, and his back hit the wall.

"Get the fuck out of my state," I spat and started for the door.

"We believe you!" Blair burst out.

I paused. Was I hallucinating? Was this room slowly filling with carbon monoxide and poisoning my brain?

Because what the fuckity fuck?

I wasn't even going to touch that with a ten-foot pole.

I started walking again.

Blair whizzed around me, back going up against the door as if he could stop me from leaving.

I smiled.

Blair cringed. "Three minutes," he said. "Just give me three minutes."

The muscles in my jaw ticked. Bodhi's presence at my back was sort of like a stain in a shirt that wouldn't wash out.

"One." I allowed.

Blair straightened. "We came to apologize for not believing you. For going with the team. We, ah, believe you now."

Suspicion crowded my head and hardened my heart. That shard of glass I mentioned earlier? The words Lars said to me that I'd left lodged deep? It hurt more than before.

A full minute ticked by. A minute so silent that my ears rang with how loud it was.

"You believe me now," I deadpanned, the words flat and unimpressed.

Blair seemed taken aback at my reaction.

I glanced behind me at Bodhi, noting the misery leaking from his pores. Looking back at Blair, I said, "And why would you think I would care?"

"Because we treated you like shit."

Yeah. They fucking did. And here these assholes were reopening old wounds so the scars would be twice as large as they are now.

"Yeah." I allowed. "You did. And you can't make up for it now."

"Maybe I could." He dangled those words in front of me like a carrot. Like a bar of twenty-four-karat gold.

I arched a brow. "Okay. I'll bite. How?"

"I have information that can get the charges against you cleared."

My stomach clenched, and a sour flavor poured over my tongue. "There are no charges," I said, clipped. "And I was cleared."

Didn't these assholes just say they believed me?

"Suspicion, I mean." Blair hurried to correct. "Clear you in public opinion."

"Just tell me," I snapped. It pissed me off that I wanted to know whatever information he thought he had.

Blair glanced at Bodhi, almost as if for permission. Bodhi nodded.

"That night at the bonfire," Blair said, wetting his lips.

"What about it?"

"You stopped me from swimming drunk in the ocean."

"Should have let you drown," I bitched. He let me drown. They all did.

WILDCARD

Blair shook his head. "Cobalt would have let me. Hell, most of the team would have."

I stared at him, not agreeing or disagreeing, just waiting for him to say what he had to say.

"I was pretty drunk that night." He gave me a rueful look. "Actually, I was smashed. The hangover the next day was next level."

"Get to the point," I snapped.

"Right. So anyway, I don't really remember much from that night. A lot of it was a blur. I do remember you arguing with Cobalt and saying if I went in the water, I'd drown."

"So?"

"You told me to piss in some bushes, right?" he asked, looking like he was trying to remember every detail. I knew the look well. I wore it almost every day trying to piece together that shitty night.

"Yeah. You went off to piss in the bushes, and then I went off and committed murder."

Bodhi made a sound, but I ignored him.

"That's the thing," Blair stated as though my words didn't bother him at all. "Why would you stop me from basically killing myself and then go kill someone else?"

"That's your proof?" I sneered. "Move. I'm leaving."

"I passed out in the bushes." Blair rolled on, holding out his hands like he could stop me. "I went to piss where you directed me, and I was so drunk I fell over mid-piss and passed out."

"Good for you."

"I don't know how long I lay there, but it was a while. When I woke up, I was disoriented and still drunk. I remember asking the dude hammering inside my head to stop."

I gritted my teeth. "Get to the point, asshole."

"When I finally got up, I saw her."

My attention sharpened, and my heart started to pound. "Saw who?" I asked, leaning in, near desperate for the answer. *It can't be...*

"Brynne."

I sucked in a breath. A roaring started between my ears, and suddenly, I felt wired.

I rushed forward, grabbing Blair by the shoulders and giving him a shake. "You saw Brynne?"

He nodded. "From the bushes, I could see down to the road. She got into his car. She got into his car, and he drove off with her."

"Who?" I demanded, my heart nearly beating out of my chest. My ribs ached with the pressure, and I knew I would likely leave bruises on Blair's shoulders from how tight I was gripping. "Tell me!"

"Cobalt," Blair admitted. "I saw Brynne get into Cobalt's car."

I let out a roar and shoved him away. His back hit the door, the chain dangling from the lock knocking against the wood. "Don't you fucking lie to me." It wasn't a warning. It was a threat. This was no game to me. This was something that tortured me. Something I desperately needed to know.

Landry's words floated through my mind then. *Maybe you can't remember because there's nothing to remember.*

What if she was right?

"I'm not. I saw them."

I almost didn't hear those words, for the battle raging inside me was so intense. But they cut through, making my knees feel like jelly and everything in the room seem so far away.

"You saw Brynne get into Cobalt's car the night of the bonfire, and then he drove off with her," I repeated.

Blair nodded, misery on his face. "Yeah."

"Why didn't you say anything?" I erupted, chest heaving. "Why didn't you tell the goddamn cops?"

Blair shook his head once. "I was so drunk. Like disoriented drunk. I fucking passed out in the bushes with my dick hanging out. I didn't even remember until later, until shit was hitting the fan."

"You should have said something!" I insisted, hands curling into fists.

"I wasn't sure anyone would believe me. Hell, I barely believed it myself. I thought I was imagining shit."

A sound ripped from my throat, and I trudged back into the room and dropped onto the end of the bed. I understood that. As much as I wished I didn't, I did. I knew all about people thinking the worst of you. About thinking the worst of yourself.

"It ate me up inside," Blair admitted, but I couldn't find a scrap of empathy for him.

"You want me to feel sorry for you? Tell you it's okay? It's not. It's not fucking okay."

"I know," he said. "That's why I'm here now. Why we're here now."

I shot to my feet. "So why now?" I asked. "Why say anything at all? Why are you so sure of what you saw that night all of a sudden?"

Blair and Bodhi exchanged a look.

"If you don't tell me, so help me fucking God, I *will* commit murder."

"I dropped out of Pembrook," Bodhi said.

I deflated, all the air whooshing right from my body. "What?"

"I dropped out. I quit."

"Like for the semester?" I repeated.

"Indefinitely."

The surprise was real. I mean, obviously, I knew his

family was broken when Brynne died, but he dropped out? Indefinitely?

"What about swimming?" I asked, this entire conversation rubbing me raw.

It was uncomfortable as fuck.

A powerful craving for Landry poured over me, nearly bringing me to my knees. I sank back on the bed, elbows falling to my knees as gnawing hunger to hold her, to bury myself deep inside her while she shuddered in surrender turned me nearly deaf and blind.

Before I realized what I was doing, I had my cell in my palm, her number called up on the screen.

"What are you doing?" Bodhi asked, his voice much closer than before.

I glanced up to where he hovered above me, eyes staring directly at my phone.

I tucked the device into my chest, blocking his eyes from even seeing her name. I didn't want him around her at all. I didn't want him thinking about her. Fuck, I wished he didn't even know about her.

"What about swimming?" I repeated.

"I don't swim anymore."

My gaze dropped, finding his painted toes. I guess that explained that. It also explained his loss of muscle mass.

"Why?" I blurted, but then I remembered we weren't friends. I remembered it didn't even matter. "No. I mean, what does this have to do with me?"

"After Bodes dropped out, I felt really fucking awful," Blair answered. "You were gone. He was gone. Brynne..."

"The point." I reminded.

"I went to Cobalt. I told him about what I thought I saw. I asked him if I'd seen right."

My mouth dropped open, and I stood. The second I was on my feet, I slapped him upside the head. "Are you fucking stupid? You really went to that douchebag and asked him if he was the last one to see Brynne alive?"

"I didn't know if he was! Everyone thought it was you."

"Yeah, because that fucker told everyone that!" I yelled. Even months later, this shit still riled me up like nothing else. "He fucking spoon-fed all of you that bullshit and whipped everyone up in a frenzy. He milked his busted face like a champ and told everyone how unstable I'd been and how worried about Brynne he was when I forced her into my car."

"He had the bruises to back it up," Bodhi said. "Everyone saw you lose your shit. You were literally fighting with my sister. There's photos and witnesses."

I turned a cold, empty stare toward him. "Well, I guess secondhand information and speculation are a lot more reliable than ten years of friendship."

Bodhi frowned, regret flashing in his eyes, but Blair kept talking, so I turned away.

"I was confused. And scared. So I went to our captain, figured I could just ask."

"What did he say?" Really, what was the point of getting pissed off that he was so stupid? He already did it.

"He said I was imagining things. That I must have been so drunk I was hallucinating."

"And you believed him?" I said, completely bitter. Of course they would believe Cobalt.

"At first," he said, a little sheepish. "But then he told Coach I had a drinking problem."

My eyebrows lifted. Sure, Blair got drunk that night, but none of us were big drinkers. We couldn't be. We had to perform too much.

"Someone planted liquor in my locker. A flask in my duffle. He did all this shit to make me look unreliable, like I was a drunk."

"And?" I baited.

"And my parents sent me to rehab."

Oh shit. *"What?"*

Blair nodded. "It was the only way to keep me from getting kicked out of school and off the team. They agreed I would do six weeks in some private treatment facility to take care of my 'little problem,' and then I could come back to school and the team on probation."

"Maybe you are an alcoholic," I said, playing devil's advocate.

"You know he's not," Bodhi said.

"Don't you see?" Blair implored. "I asked Cobalt about what I saw. He got worried I'd tell someone, so he made me look like an unreliable drunk and got me shipped off to rehab where I couldn't say shit to anyone."

"Did you tell anyone that?" I asked.

Blair slumped. "I wanted to come home, brah. I worried me slinging around accusations would only get me locked up longer."

"So when he came home, he came to see me." Bodhi went on. "And here we are."

"So you'll take his word, but not mine?" I said, pointing to Blair but keeping my eyes on Bodhi.

"It's not like that," he refuted.

"Yeah? Then what's it like?"

"I'm sorry," Bodhi whispered.

"If you were really sorry, you'd go to the police and tell them all this."

"We can't," Blair said, voice cracking. "No one is going to believe the word of a drunk and a dropout over Noble's best swimmer."

I glanced at Bodhi. "What about your parents?" I pressed. "They'll believe you."

"They went to Italy."

"What?"

"Dad got an offer from his company, and he took it. They moved over there a couple months ago."

And left him here? The family I remembered would never have done that.

Of course, I also never imagined they'd think I was a murderer.

"So if no one will believe you and there's no proof except for a drunk dude's word, then why tell me you could clear me in public opinion? You can't."

"I was trying to get you to listen," Blair muttered. "Bodhi misses you."

Bodhi made a sound. "Blair!" he hissed.

Blair shrugged. "It's true."

Maybe at one time, I'd have been happy to know that my best friend missed me. Maybe even regretted the way shit went down. But right now, it just made me sad. A kind of sadness that was so heavy it was near suffocating.

"We just wanted you to know," Bodhi said. "We don't think you're as guilty as we once did."

But he still thinks I'm partially guilty?

"I just came to tell you to go back to California and stop messing with Elite. They aren't like the Nobles. They're loyal."

Both Bodhi and Blair winced. I didn't feel bad.

"And if you make my girl cry again, I'll call the cops myself."

"It wasn't us," Bodhi said, a flat-out denial.

"Yeah? Then who was it?" I challenged. "Who else would go this far to make me look like a killer? Who else would have pictures from that night on the beach and know what Brynne was wearing the night she died?"

"Maybe it was him," Blair whispered. "Cobalt."

The chill in his voice brushed over my skin, tinging the air with an ominous vibe.

"Yeah?" I said, refusing to show any kind of weakness. "Why would he do that? He already got rid of me. Everyone already thinks I'm guilty, so why come here?"

"Maybe he's worried I'll talk now that I'm out of rehab. Maybe he's worried I'll talk to you."

A deep sense of foreboding slid over me like water in the pool, molding to my body like a second skin and making my stomach feel hollow. I knew this was all very farfetched and borderline impossible. But that didn't stop the quiet whisper deep in my gut.

You thought being accused of murdering your sister was farfetched once too.

"Call him," I said, voice rough.

"Who?" Blair questioned.

"Call Cobalt and see where he is."

"I can't just call him."

"Bannerman then." I decided, thinking of one of the other swimmers who was close to Cobalt but seemed to not have his head too far up his ass. "Call Bannerman and find out what Cobalt is up to these days."

Bodhi hesitated but then pulled out his cell and hit the screen a few times before lifting it to his ear.

I made a sound, and he glanced up.

"Put it on speaker."

Bodhi frowned like he was insulted I would insist on hearing the conversation for myself. I would have laughed at his boldness, but he hit the button and ringing filled the room.

"Brah!" Bannerman greeted the second he picked up.

"Hey, Bannerman. How's it going?" Bodhi asked.

"Copasetic," he drawled. "Just about to catch a few waves. The swells today are righteous."

"Sweet."

"Brah! You should come join. We're at the spot. You might not swim with us anymore, but you can come hang."

Bodhi made a face, the Adam's apple in his throat bobbing heavily. "Thanks for the offer, but I can't. I'm actually out of town."

"Ahh, got it. Vacation. Bodacious."

The sound of waves in the distance gave me a feeling of homesickness, and I found myself reaching for my phone again, wishing I had a photo of Landry to pull up.

Funny how it's the beach that makes me homesick, but it's her I want to make the feeling go away.

"Hey, Bannerman, are some of the guys there with you?"

"Of course."

"Cobalt?"

"*Shaaa*," he drawled. "You know he loves a good wave."

"You should send me a pic," Bodhi said, making me look up. He caught my eye and offered me a tentative smile.

I looked away.

"Why?"

"Just missing the beach. You know how it is, brah. Kinda miss all my friends too."

"You know you can come back anytime, right? I know what happened was shit, but—"

"Yeah. I know." Bodhi was quick to cut him off, his face pinched. "So will you send the picture?"

"Sure, brah. Call me when you get back in town, okay? We'll grab a bite."

"Sure," Bodhi replied and then ended the call, sagging as though he'd run a marathon.

A few seconds later, his phone beeped, and the three of us crowded around the screen to look down at the photo filling it.

Cobalt was there, dressed in a wetsuit with a board under his arm and the waves at his back.

Bannerman was right. They did look bodacious today.

Ripping my eyes away from the haunting reminder of my old life, I flicked a hard look at Blair. "Your theory about Cobalt has more holes than Swiss cheese."

"It has to be him," Blair said, his voice taking on a desperate tone.

I glanced between my old friends. "Or maybe you're just trying really hard to make me believe it's not you doing all this shitty stuff."

"Rush." Bodhi said my name like a plea.

"It's too little, too late," I snapped. "I'm not going to tell you again. Go back to Cali. Both of you. Don't show your faces here again. I walked from my old life." I glanced at Bodhi. "I did it for you."

He took a step forward, and I took one back. Hurt flashed in his eyes.

"I'm not going anywhere this time. This is my home now. These people are mine."

"Rush," he called as I went to the door.

"No," I said, not even stopping. "You made your choice a long time ago. And I'm making my choice right now."

I left without looking back, keeping my posture rigid until I stepped into the elevator alone where I blew out a shuddering breath. I was nothing but a jumbled mess of emotion. A whirlpool of information I didn't know how to process. I came here to claim control, to make sure everyone knew where I stood. But here I was... more out of control than before.

The chaos was churning, threatening to pull me under.

The second I stepped off the elevator, I hit the screen on my phone.

"Jay," she answered warmly, and just hearing her voice ripped a low groan right out of me.

"Jay?" She spoke again, this time more alarmed.

"Little siren," I rasped, my fingers tight around the phone.

"What's the matter, Jay? Did something happen?"

"I want to come home," I told her. "Where are you?"

"Wherever you want me to be."

Good answer. "My dorm room. Now."

"I'm on my way."

Neither of us said anything else, but we didn't hang up either.

When I was behind the wheel of the Vette, I spoke again. "I have to warn you, little siren. I'm in a mood. The second I see you, my hands will be on you. I'll be in you. The only talking I want to hear is you moaning my name."

The silence on the line was palpable. Between my legs, my dick was at full mast.

Just when I worried maybe I'd gone too far, her breathy whisper sent tingles racing down my spine. "I'll be waiting."

I ended the call and tore out of the parking lot, pointing the Vette toward home.

28

Landry

THE ENERGY IN THE AIR RIPPLED WITH ELECTRICITY, INSTANTLY creating a hum beneath my skin. Straightening off the wall, I turned, anticipating his arrival.

Jay appeared a second later, hands stuffed in the front pockets of his worn jeans, throwing off a *don't fuck with me* attitude. The second he saw me, his footsteps stalled, dark eyes flashing like a wild sky. He started forward again, and I shivered indelicately at the naked lust glinting in his captive stare.

Veering to the door, he yanked out his key and shoved it wide, using one muscled arm to hold it open and stare at me expectantly. I went forward, my shoulder lightly brushing against him as I went past. His sharp intake of breath caused excitement to burst low in my belly and my steps to quicken.

The sound of the lock being thrown was the last thing I registered before he was pulling me around and plastering my body to his. He held me tight like he was afraid I'd try to escape as his lips crashed over mine with aggression that robbed my breath. He devoured me until I was nothing but a living pulse, desire filling me so full that it spilled over into his mouth in the form of low, nonsensical whimpers and vibrating purrs deep in my throat.

Fixing his thumbs to the joints on my jaw, he availed himself of every inch of me he could consume with groaning and grinding hips, lips against mine. I strained up on tiptoes, clinging to his biceps as his rigid dick stabbed impatiently against my stomach. I pushed closer, body already anticipating the burning stretch of being invaded by him.

He ripped his mouth away, kissing across my jaw until his panting breaths met my ear and raised goose bumps across my skin. Hot, open-mouthed kisses smeared down my neck as his large frame hunched closer, his lips latching on my collarbone and sucking.

My head fell back, eyes closing as the T-shirt covering my body turned wet from his lips and stuck to my skin. A growl of impatience thundered through the room, and he yanked back, eyes flashing angrily. I blinked, vaguely wondering what I'd done.

Impatient, he grabbed my shirt and ripped, the sound of the seams tearing erotic. Anticipating the rush of cool air across my newly bared skin, I was fully disappointed when it didn't come.

I gazed down at the misshapen and tattered shirt, noting it hadn't torn enough for him to get it off my body.

He caught my chin, forcing it up to scald me with the ire in his onyx stare. "You trying to keep me away?"

He wanted a fight, so I'd give him one. "Maybe you should try harder."

His nostrils flared, and he caught me around the waist, bulldozing me backward until we crashed against his desk, making everything on it rattle. My heart was drumming when he picked me up, planted my ass on the top, and stepped between my spread thighs.

He leaned in so far that I had to go with him, his forearm fitting in the small of my back to support me as I bowed backward.

"I hope you didn't like these clothes," he intoned and snatched something from behind us to quickly pull away.

The cold press of metal against my chest made me gasp, and I glanced down to see the point of a pair of scissors resting against my exposed skin.

"You want me to try harder, little siren?" he rumbled, dragging the blade up toward the pounding pulse in my neck. "I'll make it so these clothes never keep you away from me again."

Excitement thrummed through my veins, making me feel as though I had two heartbeats. The way he towered over me while brandishing something that could literally slice me open was heady. As was knowing he would only use it to make sure nothing came between us. I wasn't afraid. No, I imbibed the control he so easily wielded and my own willingness to submit.

The edge of the blade slipped beneath the fabric, the metal a whisper against my flesh. I whimpered, tingles racing across my body as I waited for him to cut the clothes right off me.

He paused, lust-drenched eyes meeting mine. "What's your color, baby?"

"Green," I whispered. *So freaking green.*

"Good girl," he crooned before slicing right through my shirt with one swipe. He peeled the fabric off me, tossing it onto the desk, and then yanked the bra away from my skin and cut that off me too.

I squirmed, chilly air meeting my feverish skin as he tossed aside the scissors. He pulled away long enough to tug off his shirt and push down his jeans before lifting me off the desk. My legs clamped around his waist, and our bare chests collided. Crying out, I arched into him, and our lips locked, tongues entwining as he carried me to the bed and tossed me in the center.

I'd barely settled when he pounced, straddling my hips and latching on to my breast, sucking so deep I cried out and nearly came up off the bed. He growled and moved to the other to do the exact same thing before dragging his teeth across my ribs and hooking his fingers in the waistband of my pants, dragging them off and tossing them on the floor.

His body blanketed mine, and I sighed beneath his weight and warmth, melting into the mattress as he kissed me again. I opened my legs and lifted my hips, wanting to be stuffed full of his cock, but he pulled away, denying me.

His long, lithe body rippled above me when he leaned over to grab something from the nightstand. His cock was standing straight off his body, and the swollen tip brushed against my side as he moved.

I bit my lip, fighting back the urge to beg as he settled on his knees between my spread thighs. God, he was a specimen of a man. Permanent California boy sun-kissed body, defined muscles, and a comfort in his skin that screamed ownership.

The black strands on his head were wild and unruly as if he'd been combing his fingers through it the entire way here. I wanted to sink my fingers into those disobedient locks and encourage him to sin more. To use me to do it.

I was so busy staring in lust I didn't notice the bottle in his hand until the lid made a snapping sound when he flicked it open.

I glanced up at the bottle of liquid, his oversized hand making it appear small. "What are you doing?" I asked, hoping to heaven it was something depraved.

"Whatever the hell I want," he said, then arched a dark brow at me in challenge.

"My body is yours."

Jay's eyes flared when I handed him all rights to everything he could imagine, and then he flipped me over, driving the air from my lungs and making me squirm.

His hand cracked across my bare ass, the flesh bouncing with the slap. "Remember your safe word." Then he overturned the bottle of lube, splattering the cool, slippery gel in a line down my spine.

I arched into the bed, the cold sensation a direct contrast to the feverish temperature of my skin. He chuckled like he enjoyed seeing me squirm and drizzled more across my ass.

"This fucking ass is what wet dreams are made of." He hummed, tossing the bottle onto the sheets and filling his hands with my rounded flesh.

I purred as he kneaded and massaged, using the muscles he worked damn hard for to apply the perfect amount of pressure. Ripples of pleasure raced through my body, and I moaned so loud I buried my face into his pillow to hush the sound.

He smacked me again, not hard enough to hurt but enough to sting pleasantly. "You hide those screams from me again and you'll regret it," he threatened, grabbing my cheeks and peeling them apart so cold air brushed against my hole. "Go ahead and scream my name, little siren. Let everyone in this building know who you belong to and exactly where I put my dick when we're alone."

I groaned. My God, he was filthy. I loved it.

His fingers dug into my crack, pulling my cheeks even farther apart. The stretch of the skin there made me gasp, and then his lubed-up thumbs massaged the sides of my hole.

Desire sparked through me as nerves I didn't even know existed came alive and sang with delight.

"Jay," I whimpered, pushing my ass farther into his hands, wanting more.

The tip of his finger slid into my ass, the tight ring of muscle spasming around him, and I sucked in a breath as I waited for him to push deeper.

He didn't, though, just swirled the tip where it was while his free hand massaged my ass cheek and hip.

"I could climb completely inside you, little siren, and it would still not be close enough."

"Try." I panted, wiggling against his finger, shocked that I actually wanted to feel him go deeper. Just below my ass, my dripping center clenched like it, too, wanted to be filled.

He pulled away his finger with a dark chuckle. "Don't you worry, baby," he said, gliding his hands down my spine and fanning out to massage the oil over my entire back. When my skin was good and wet, he blanketed me from above.

I mewled just feeling his hard body press into mine.

His teeth nipped at the shell of my ear. "By the time I'm done with you, your body will feel more like mine than yours."

He started to glide then, the lube making it easy for us to slip together. My body went boneless against the bed as he rocked over me, making me feel like he was fucking me even though he wasn't even in me yet.

Lube dripped down my sides, pooling on the mattress, as I gripped the sheets and held on while he ground into me from above. Between my legs throbbed, and the delicious friction of my breasts against the mattress made me cry out.

His teeth sank into the back of my neck, and I pushed my forehead into the pillow, giving him better access. He bit down the back of my neck, then kissed over all the bites. I shivered beneath him, my body tightening with every graze.

His teeth sank into me again, this time with a little more force, and it felt like I was being pinned in place. I grunted, and his hard dick slid between my ass cheeks where he started thrusting.

I arched into it, loving the way he was using my body to wring pleasure out of himself. He grunted and moaned, still holding me by the neck with his teeth as he drove his cock between my cheeks.

His thrusts became sloppy and his hips more demanding. I spread my legs a little wider, and his dick slid lower, his pulsing head catching in my swollen center.

We both moaned, and he went with it, sheathing himself in my wet heat.

"Goddamn, you're wet," he grunted, rising on his hands so he could thrust into me even deeper.

I cried out, and he drove into me, the headboard slamming against the wall.

"Say my name when I'm fucking you," he demanded, pushing deep and gyrating his hips.

"Jason," I yelled, pushing back on him.

"Good girl," he growled and sucked a hickey on the back of my shoulder.

Just as I was about to fall apart, he pulled back, his dick leaving my body. I whimpered and reached around, trying to pull him back.

He grabbed my hand and wrapped it around his sticky rod. "Feel what you do to me, you little siren," he rasped, retrieving the bottle of lube and drizzling more over his dick and my hand. "Spread it around."

I pushed up onto one elbow, twisting at the waist to slather his red, angry-looking cock with the clear lube.

As I pumped him, his hands went to my ass, one peeling open the cheek and the other pouring a generous stream of slick into my crack. I shuddered, my movement slowing on his cock.

"Lie down and let me have you," he demanded, pushing my shoulder with his lubed-up hand.

I collapsed onto my belly with a sigh.

"Can I have you, baby? Can I have you in every way?"

"You already do, Jay."

"Not yet," he said, swirling a finger around my rim.

"I trust you," I told him, knowing those words meant something to him.

He groaned and buried his face in my ass, licking along the crack like I was some five-star meal. I moaned under the onslaught because his tongue was magic and brought forth bursts of pleasure I'd never felt before.

He rimmed my ass until it was soft and pliant, and when the tip of his tongue shoved into the center, I arched up off the bed and cried out his name.

He growled possessively and shoved deeper. My hand went around my back and twisted in his hair. With boldness I didn't think I possessed, I yanked those strands, shoving him harder into my crack.

He laughed low, and the vibrations against my hole had me thrusting against his tongue.

"Look at you," he mused, coming up for air. "What a needy little siren you've become. Tell me what you want."

Annoyance flashed through me, and I reached back, wanting something inside me so badly I was willing to do it myself.

I got as far as laying the pad of my finger against my relaxed hole before a loud growl filled the room.

"The fuck you will," he claimed, grabbing my hand and pinning it to my side. "The only thing allowed in your ass is me. Do you understand?"

"Please, Jay," I whispered. "Please fill me up. It hurts to be empty."

CAMBRIA HEBERT

He swore under his breath, the dirty word making me shiver. "I love it when you beg."

"Please." I begged more. "I submit. I'm yours. Take me."

"Good, submissive girls get rewards," he crooned, lightly rubbing over my ass cheek.

I hummed, and he grabbed my hips, pulling them up so I was on my knees. Two fingers pushed into my dripping center, and I hummed with happiness.

"Spread your cheeks." His voice was gruff. "Hold them open."

My fingers were shaking, but I did what he asked, and he grunted in pleasure.

"Everything on this body is mine," he told the room, and then a finger pushed into my ass.

I cried out and nearly fell onto my stomach at the intrusion. It didn't hurt, but it was new and tingly and *tight*.

He groaned, pulling out his finger, then pushed it back in. All the lube he'd poured over me made it easy, and he started thrusting in me as my hole gripped his digit.

"What's it like to have me in both your holes?" he asked, thrusting inside me.

I couldn't speak. All I could do was feel. The double penetration was unlike anything I'd felt before. My thighs shook, and my hands were slipping against my ass. I couldn't keep my eyes open as he fucked me simultaneously in both holes.

"Can you take more?" he asked.

"Yes." I gasped, and then light exploded behind my eyes when the sting of pain followed as he pushed another finger into my ass.

My knees gave out then. I sagged into the bed with a moan.

He readjusted, pushing into my crotch while slowly moving the ones in my ass. His fingers glided up, finding my swollen clit, and rubbed.

I bit my lip, my low moan filling the room.

He continued stroking, picking up the pace as his fingers moved in and out of my ass.

"Look at you stuffed full of me," he crooned. "Taking these fingers so well."

Another burning sensation tore through me, and my back bowed. He paused, letting me adjust to three fingers while he still stroked my clit.

"Such a good girl. Can you relax for me? Open up so I can fill you with my dick."

I went boneless against the mattress, my body opening for the intrusion. I wanted his dick in me. I wanted everything he could give.

The fingers against my clit left, and he grabbed my hip, lifting me back to my knees. With one push, he was inside me, my body molding around him like it was made just for him.

Those three fingers in my ass started to thrust and so did his dick, and my eyes rolled back in my head. I didn't know what sensation to focus on, so I spiraled into this floaty feeling where the only thing that existed was how overfull I felt.

More liquid drizzled over me, sliding between my crack and making me tremble. I noticed then that his fingers were no longer inside me and both hands were gripping my hips as he pounded into me from behind.

"Jay." I gasped, spiraling toward what I knew would be a powerful orgasm. "Jason."

"I know," he said, voice strained.

He pulled out of my pussy, dragging his head up to my waiting ass. "Are you sure?"

In response, I pushed back against him, his fat head catching on my rim. His guttural groan satisfied me in ways I never knew I needed, and his fingertips cut into my hips so hard I knew I would have bruises later.

He took his time pushing inside. For all his dominance, he wasn't cruel. I panted and squirmed, crying out at the tight intrusion. There was pain, but it only lasted a moment before my nerve endings burst with tingling pleasure.

I held myself still and let him do the work, allowing him to lead, knowing he would take care of me.

When his hips pressed flush against my ass cheeks, he blew out a breath. "You took all of me, baby. You squeeze me so fucking good."

I couldn't say anything. I was stuffed so full there was no room for words.

His palm caressed my lower back lovingly, and tears pricked my eyes. "I've never been this close to someone before," he confessed, caressing me again.

He leaned over, his body blanketing mine as his dick spasmed inside me. His hand caught my chin, tugging my face around. Our eyes collided, and his dark eyes filled with awe.

"I saw the beach earlier today," he whispered, thumb swiping across my chin. "I saw the beach, and I got homesick. But then I realized it wasn't the beach I was homesick for. It was you."

A sob vibrated my throat, and his lips claimed mine in an ardent kiss.

"It was you," he said again when he pulled away, mounting my ass once more.

He gave no warning when he pulled out, then pushed back in. The squelch of the lube between us was erotic and almost perverse.

The room filled with grunts and moans and slapping skin. I rose higher and higher and teetered on the edge until I turned weepy with need. Sensing my desperation, Jay reached around and found my clit to apply the perfect pressure.

I fell apart, the orgasm ripping through me with startling force. I succumbed to it as I shook and moaned, a prisoner to my own pleasure as my channel clenched around his pulsing dick. When the grip of release finally let go, my cheeks were wet and my breath was uneven.

Jay laid me on the bed beneath him and pulled gently out of my hole.

I glanced over my shoulder as he stroked his dick twice, and then the warm splatter of his cum painted my cheeks. The mattress shook beneath him as he came, and when he settled, he pushed his still-hard dick into my pussy and collapsed on top of me.

"I am fucking obsessed with you." His voice was breathless beside my ear.

I purred, smiling into the pillow as my body hummed with aftershocks.

Grunting, he rolled to the side, blowing out a breath. "You fucked that mood right out of me, little siren."

I giggled. "I think you're the one that did the fucking."

He rolled onto his side and pulled me around to do the same. We lay there facing each other, our noses inches apart. Jason reached down and tugged a blanket over us, but it was the intimacy in the room that felt like a cocoon.

"No one has ever accepted me like you do."

"Is this because of the anal?" I joked, albeit a little shy.

His grin was roguish and oh so self-satisfied. "That was fucking hot." But then warmth lit his impossibly dark eyes. "It's everything, little siren. It's how you just embrace everything I am. Even the darkest parts."

"I love you," I said simply, no better way to sum up exactly how I felt and always would.

His face went blank and then slowly filled with emotion.

It was better than watching the sunrise. "What did you just say?" The words were hushed as if he couldn't believe what he'd heard and was afraid if he called too much attention, I would snatch mine away.

"I love you," I repeated, and his eyes flickered with disbelief.

I smiled, accepting that part of him too because I truly meant it when I said I loved all of him.

Laying my hand against his cheek, I said, "I know it's scary and it makes you afraid. I don't need you to say the words for mine to be true. I love you, Jay. I always will."

The small distance between us closed, and he kissed me tenderly, his lips and fingertips full of the words he was terrified to say. I petted his hair, stroked his face, and dragged my fingertips down to rest over his heart.

No, I didn't need him to say those words to me because I could feel them.

29

RUSH

I love you.

Three words. Not very spectacular on their own. But put together, they created quite possibly one of the most meaningful sentences that might ever exist.

How easily they slid into my heart.

How addicted they made me.

Oh, how I wanted her love. I wanted it exclusively. I wanted it all so she didn't have any left for anyone else.

I snatched those three words she bravely whispered and tucked them deep behind all my wards and shields. I put them into the most vulnerable place that existed inside me, the most precious thing I would ever own.

And though I felt just how much they meant to me, just how much they changed the inner workings of my heart...

I was still afraid.

And although I felt them, though my heart screamed and

beat with the love I had for her, I still couldn't seem to release them off my tongue.

30

THE MOMENT THE PROFESSOR DISMISSED CLASS, I JAMMED everything in my bag and stood. While I understood the importance of A&P, it was a snoozefest and a half. Maybe it wouldn't be so bad if the professor had a little more personality than stale bread. The kind with seeds in it that got stuck in your teeth.

Lars was still packing up down in the front row, so I went ahead up the stairs and out into the hall to wait for him there.

Brittney stopped alongside me with a giant yawn. "My God, could that class get any more boring?"

"It's the worst." I agreed.

"So have you been able to catch up with everything you missed? Do you need any help?" she asked.

"I'm just about caught up. Lars has been really helpful. Thanks for asking." Just as I said his name, the blond swimmer exited the classroom and headed in my direction.

"Coffee?" he asked, hopeful.

"Definitely." I approved, and the three of us moved out of the building into the nippy air toward the coffee cart nearby. "Do you have time to meet at the library tomorrow, Lars? I just need to finish up that last assignment I missed, and then I'll be completely caught up."

"*Ja*," he answered in Swedish.

He stepped up to the cart first to order his espresso and, to my surprise, ordered for me. When he was finished, he glanced at me, slightly shy. "That's right?"

I smiled. "Exactly right. You remembered."

He swiped his card, paying for both drinks. "We're kinda family now," he said, cheeks pinkening.

A rush of affection came over me, and I smiled. "Yes, we are. Jason is so lucky to have a friend like you, Lars. Thank you for being so good to him and to me too."

Our order came up, and we grabbed them and moved to the side, waiting for Brittney to get hers and join us. When she approached, hot coffee in hand, she looked like she wanted to say something but also didn't want to say it.

"Is everything okay?" I asked.

"I've heard the rumors," she blurted out, quickly rolling her lips inward and pressing them into a thin line.

I shared a quizzical look with Lars before directing all my attention back to our classmate. "What rumors?"

Her eyes widened a fraction. "You don't know?"

Something in her tone set me on edge, and I lowered the coffee from my lips. "Know what?"

"I shouldn't have said anything."

"Just say it," I told her, impatience rising inside me.

"About Elite." She took a slight step closer, lowering her voice. "You're dating Rush, right?"

I bristled a bit, and Lars straightened, stepping closer to my side. "The rumors are about Jason?"

"Is that what you call Rush?"

"It's his first name," I explained, wanting her to get to the point.

"I didn't realize anyone called him that."

"What rumors?" I deadpanned. What I called my boyfriend really was of no relevance here.

"That he killed a girl," she whispered, but it was a rather loud whisper.

I sucked in a breath. "Where did you hear that?" I demanded.

"Like I said, people are talking about it. It's been spreading around campus."

"What exactly is being spread around?" Lars asked.

"That Rush transferred here from California because he was accused of murder. The only reason he got off was because his parents paid big money to some big-time lawyer and then sent him to the other side of the country."

"That's not true," I insisted, my voice loud enough that people walking by glanced over.

"So it's all made up?" she pressed. "Because I heard there are photos of him with the dead girl. Photos that show them arguing the night she died."

I gasped so hard the coffee sloshed out of the little hole in the lid on my cup, splattering the plastic top.

"Who told you that?" Lars demanded, his voice taking on a harsher tone than normal. "Did you actually *see* those photos?"

I was so caught off guard I could barely think logically. I couldn't believe she was standing here in front of me, asking me so casually if my boyfriend was a murderer.

Who does that?

"No!" Brittney hurried to say. "No, I haven't. I've just heard the talk. And well, since I know you guys and I know

343

you two are super close with Rush, I figured I'd just go right to the source."

"The source of what?" I snapped. "We certainly aren't the ones who would spread such vicious crap," I said, sucking in a deep breath.

"Of course not," Brittney allowed. "I just thought…"

"You just thought you'd ask Landry if her boyfriend killed someone?" Lars stated.

"I honestly didn't mean to upset you," Brittney said, shaking her head. "I'm so sorry. The next time I hear someone talking, I'll tell them it's not true."

I turned to Lars. "Did you know rumors were going around?"

He shook his head. "No."

I lowered my voice. "Do you think someone from Elite talked?"

Just the mere suggestion had my stomach lurching. Those guys said they were behind Jason. I heard them say it myself. Not one person acted like they didn't one hundred percent believe in him. But the only people who knew about Jason's history were Elite. The only people who saw that photo were swimmers. So if word got out, that meant someone…

"So it *is* true?" Brittney's voice was partly horrified, cutting off my troubled thoughts.

My God, what would it do to Jason if his past spread around campus like wildfire? He came here to get away from all that, not relive it.

"Jason didn't hurt anyone," I said practically between gritted teeth.

"But he was accused." She pushed.

"Why do you care?" Lars snapped.

She drew back, lifting the coffee in front of her like a shield.

A quick glance and I noted the frigid temperature of his

already pale eyes. Lars might be shy and nonconfrontational, but his loyalty to Jason outweighed that.

"W-what?" she stuttered.

"You know that Landry is dating him. You know he's my best friend. So why would you come over here with your hearsay and accusations? Did you think we would do anything but defend him?"

"I wasn't sure he needed defending. I see now that maybe he does."

I made a rude noise. "We're defending him because we love him," I snapped, hearing the L-word roll right off my tongue with ease. It was true, so I didn't even pause, just kept right on going. "Not because he's guilty of something. We're defending him because he's been hurt enough by people who don't even know the whole story. I don't know where you got your information, and I don't really care. Yeah, Jason was questioned about the murder of someone he knew. But he didn't do it, and no charges were filed. So maybe think twice before you go around spreading gossip that will only make you look like an idiot."

"Um, wow," Brittney said, blinking.

I glanced at Lars. "Let's go."

He curled his hand around my elbow, and we turned to walk away.

"Wait," Brittney called out. When neither of us turned back, she rushed around to plant herself in our path. "You love him," she said. The last thing I expected her to say.

"Yes," I replied, succinct.

Something passed behind her eyes. Something that was there and gone before I could make it out. But even not knowing exactly what it was, discomfort wormed around inside me.

"You shouldn't," she said, voice ominously low.

It took a heartbeat for that to sink in, and Lars's hand tightened around my elbow.

"What?" I echoed, partially shook she would say such a thing.

"Loving Rush is a mistake. It's dangerous."

I recoiled so forcefully I might have fallen if Lars didn't have a hold on my arm.

"You should leave," Lars said, letting go of me to angle himself between me and Brittney. "And don't come around us again."

Even though my brain was addled with surprise, I still managed to notice how his accent thickened the angrier he became.

Brittney relented and started back the way she came. On her way past, her footsteps stalled beside me, and I bristled.

"Defend him all you want, but facts are facts. The last girl that loved Rush ended up dead."

Stunned, I stared after her as she walked away, melting into a group of people and then disappearing around the side of a building.

"Hey." Lars's gentle voice was accompanied by his hand curling back around my upper arm.

I swung my gaze to his, both of us wearing similar expressions of shock.

"What the hell was that?" I whispered, feeling oddly breathless.

Lars shook his head and pulled his phone out of his jeans. "I'll call Rush."

"No!" I said, finally seeming to burst out of the surprise bubble she'd trapped me in. "You can't." I put my hand over his phone to push it down.

Skeptical, Lars asked, "Don't you think he should know about the rumors?"

"No," I quickly replied. With a groan, I said, "Yes."

Both of Lars's blond brows arched halfway up his forehead.

"I mean, of course he has a right to know, but I also don't want them to hurt him," I explained. Shoulders sagging, I added, "He's been through so much."

"It was bad for him before he left California, right?"

I nodded. "I thought Elite was behind him."

Lars's eyes flashed. "We are."

"Then how did the rumors start?" I questioned.

He frowned, and I watched as he basically worked out the same thing I had earlier. If knowledge about Jason's past got out, then it was because someone on the team had a big mouth.

"Maybe they googled him," Lars reasoned. "I mean, Ryan did."

"Ryan had a reason to. Plus, she mentioned the photo. The only people who saw that were Elite."

"If this was someone on Elite, I'll make them pay." Lars's tone was dark.

I nodded. "I haven't heard anything at all, though. Have you? No rumors or speculation at all."

He shook his head. "Me either."

"It's odd."

"Very."

"Let's just keep this to ourselves right now. See if we hear anything else. Keep an eye on the team and see if anyone starts acting weird. Once we know more, we can talk to Jay." I just wanted to protect him. It seemed that was something no one ever did.

Lars nodded. "I'm going to tell Win, though."

I smiled. "Of course, tell him." I agreed, knowing keeping something from Win would be difficult for Lars. He was quiet, but he was not secretive.

Another idea occurred to me. "I'll tell Ryan. If it is

someone from Elite, then he might know who. He seems to know who the weakest links are."

Lars nodded. "He is the fixer."

Amusement lifted the corner of my lip. "The what?"

"Jamie told me when Elite has a problem, he fixes it. It's what he does."

I don't know why, but I found it insanely adorable that Lars was standing here repeating what Jamie told him like it was an Elite rule.

But also, he wasn't wrong. Ryan was the official "unofficial" captain, and I guess that did make him the fixer.

I nodded once. "You tell Win. I'll tell Ryan. If you hear anything, anything at all, just call me. And keep your eyes open at practice for anyone acting sus."

His face blanked. "Sus?"

"Suspicious," I clarified.

"Right."

"We can talk about this when we meet tomorrow at the library. It will be more private there than at the pool."

He nodded once but didn't walk away. "Landry?"

"Hm?"

"You're okay?" His eyes strayed back to the place where Brittney had disappeared.

"Yeah, I'm okay."

"She's never said anything like that to you before, has she?"

"Never," I answered. "That's why it's so odd. She's always been nice. She even offered to help me study." I tilted my head.

"What is it?"

"I mean, she always did seem a little interested in Elite. But everyone on campus is, you know? I just figured it was normal."

"As long as you're okay," he allowed.

I went forward and hugged him. He froze in my arms, obviously unsure what to do with the sudden affection. I laughed lightly and squeezed him a little harder. "Thanks for being a good friend, Lars. And for believing in Rush. For defending him when he isn't even in the room."

"I'll always defend him," he replied, arms going around mine to return the hug briefly. "I'll always defend you too."

I pulled away and smiled. "Go call Win. I know you're dying to."

His eyes darted away and then back. "It's not that obvious, is it?"

I laughed out loud. "Only to sisters."

His eyes widened so much I could see the whites around his entire blue irises. "Sister?"

"If you want." I hedged, feeling a little shy all of a sudden.

"I've never had a sister before," he said. "Wes and Max are like my brothers now. And Rush too…"

"I don't have any brothers. Or sisters."

"You do now."

A warm feeling suffused my chest, and suddenly, it felt like spring instead of winter. "Really?"

"Fair warning. I come with Win. And he's ridiculous."

I laughed. "Deal."

"Call me if you need anything," he said.

I waved, and we parted ways. Despite the moment I'd just shared with Lars, I couldn't shake what just happened. How out of the blue it seemed. It felt like I was missing something.

But what?

31

RUSH

THE ASS CRACK OF DAWN CAME AND WENT THIS A.M., AND I didn't get up to run. FYI: It's much easier to get up earlier than early when you don't have a warm, sleepy siren curled up against you.

Is that why so many of you are ponies?

Regardless, I couldn't let my stallion status expire, so later in the day when she went off to be all studious and shit with Lars, I hit the treadmill in the gym for a three-mile run, did some upper body work, and then dove into the pool for a second swim.

It's a lot of work to be this fine.

Also, it was a good distraction for a guy churned up like the ocean during a gnarly swell.

I told Bodhi to go back to California, but I had no idea if he listened. I didn't call or check to see if he did. Everything he and Blair said at the hotel was a giant mindfuck.

For months and months, I was desperate to hear something like that from Bodhi. *Maybe you aren't as guilty as I believed.* I hoped for just a scrap of doubt from someone. Just a tiny chance to prove everyone's mistrust in me was displaced.

It never came, and I was cast out of town.

And now suddenly, he was here telling me he believed me. That maybe he was wrong. Not only that, but it wasn't just Bodhi. Blair too. Hell, Blair brought another suspect with him. I should have looked at Cobalt harder back then. He never liked me, always made it clear he didn't want me as a Noble. But murder? That seemed farfetched even for a douchebag like Cobalt. Plus, it was hard to think back then. I'd been too consumed with grief and self-doubt.

I should have been on a plane back to Cali.

I should have been hunting down Cobalt to make him confess so I could clear my name.

What was I doing instead?

Swimming with the bros.

You know, maybe this pool had some weird connection to the Bermuda Triangle because, bro, ever since I dove in, it was like I'd entered the Twilight Zone. A dimension I was lured into by a siren. Fell in love. Found loyalty among a team. Felt accepted.

It was uber weird here. I liked weird.

I liked it so much that the chance of clearing my name and reclaiming my life wasn't enough to entice me to leave. Suddenly, clearing my name didn't seem as crucial. Going back to California held little appeal. Turned out the shit I lost didn't compare to everything I'd found here.

After swiping the water from my eyes, I glanced down at my smartwatch to note the time. Landry and Lars were going to finish studying soon, and I was their ride.

I pulled myself out of the water, droplets flinging everywhere as I went to the bleachers to snag my towel a drape it around my neck. There really was no point in drying off if I was just going to hit the showers.

"Bro! Where you going?" Jamie called as he hoisted himself to sit on the side of the pool.

"I have to pick up Landry and Lars at the library," I said. It felt kinda weird to give an actual answer and not some smart-ass reply.

"Isn't your car a two-seater?"

I blanched. I mean, obviously, it was, but I guess I hadn't really thought of that.

"You gonna let Landry sit on Lars's lap?" Walsh heckled as he treaded water in his lane.

I gave him the finger. "Fuck off."

There, that seemed more like me.

"Want me to follow you over?" Wes offered, splashing as he got out of the pool on the other side of Jamie. "I'll pick up Lars."

I made a face. "No." Lars and Landry were my responsibility. Like I was going to have bus driver Wes go pick up my friend.

"Lars can drive." I decided. "Landry can sit in my lap."

"You said I couldn't drive your car," Jamie complained.

"I like Lars better than you."

"That's colder than Kruger's love life."

Everyone laughed.

"I heard that!" Kruger called from the other side of the pool.

Jamie snickered. "My bad. Thought you were underwater."

"Asshole!"

"We're going for pizza after." I started, suddenly entirely nervous to finish the sentence. I felt like an outsider. An outsider trying to hang out with the in crowd. I hated it.

"We'll meet you there," Ryan said.

My eyes flashed up to where he was still treading water. A knowing look passed over his features.

He invited himself so I didn't have to.

"Yeah, okay," I said, swallowing.

Prism came up from beneath the water.

"P! Get your ass outta the pool. It's pizza time," Kruger called.

I went into the locker room, stopping at my new locker, which I'd yet to get a new lock for, to grab my shower stuff and then headed straight in. The pressure was good, and the warmth felt nice on my tired muscles. After sudsing up and rinsing down, I turned off the spray and dried off, wrapping the towel around my waist.

Back at my locker, I grabbed some black boxer briefs and pulled them on, followed by a pair of black joggers, sneakers, and a designer hoodie my mom had sent me. Perks of being the offspring of a supermodel, you know.

My watch vibrated, indicating an incoming text, and from inside my open locker, I heard my phone chime.

We're done studying. Can't wait to see you.

I smiled, reading the message on my watch screen as a little flutter of happiness left my stomach feeling buoyant. I was so addicted to this girl it wasn't even funny. A simple text turned me into some sappy fool. Knowing she wanted to see me made me anxious to get to her.

Grabbing my phone from my locker, I typed out a quick reply. *Be right there, little siren.*

After stuffing my wet shit in my duffle, I reached for my keys. They weren't there.

Frowning, I glanced into the metal box where I usually hung them to find the hook empty. Thinking they'd just fallen, I glanced down. Not seeing them, I grabbed the extra towel and Speedos to look under there.

Still not finding them, I pulled out everything, dropping it to my feet. The keys weren't there.

"What the fuck?" I muttered, reaching to the top shelf to feel around.

"Something wrong?" Walsh asked from his locker a few down from mine.

I swung toward him. "You take my keys?"

He made a face. "What?"

"My keys," I said, impatient, sweeping the locker again. "They aren't in here."

"Maybe they're in your bag," Ryan said, gesturing to my duffle.

It slapped onto the bench behind me, and I unzipped it to rifle through. Still coming up empty-handed, I made a sound of irritation and overturned it, dumping everything all over the bench and floor.

I expected to hear the clatter of metal, for them to land with a slap on the ground. That sound never came.

Dropping the bag, I looked up at Ryan and Jamie, who was now also watching. "Did you assholes take my keys?"

"Bro, why would we do that?" Jamie asked.

I made a rude sound. "Remember that time Walsh stole all my clothes and shit and scattered them all over the hood of my car out in the cold?"

"That was some good times!" Kruger exclaimed.

"You just liked looking at his naked ass." Jamie guffawed.

"Not me, but them little old ladies in the admin building across the lot sure had a view!" Kruger replied.

"That was initiation." Ryan reminded me. "And I held your keys when I did that so nothing happened to your car."

That was true. He had. He threw all my stuff all over the hood of my Vette, but he'd kept my keys instead of letting them lie out in the open.

"I put my keys in here. I put them in the same place every time."

"Maybe you put them in your old locker without thinking about it," Wes suggested.

Following that train of thought, I went down the row to where my old locker was. You could still see part of the red spray paint we hadn't been able to get off. The door squeaked when I flung it open and looked in.

"No," I said, finding nothing at all. "Seriously, none of you have them?"

Everyone shook their head.

"I fucking put them right there," I insisted, jabbing a finger to where I knew I'd hung them inside my locker.

Ryan tugged a long-sleeved waffle tee over his head and headed for the door. "Hang on," he called.

I glanced down at all my scattered shit. A bad feeling was starting to work its way up my spine.

"I'm sure they're around here somewhere," Prism offered.

A minute later, Ryan jogged back into the locker room, a grim set to his mouth.

"What?" I demanded.

"Your car isn't in the lot."

I jolted and tore out of the room, running past the pool and into the parking lot. A string of curses filled the air as I stared at the empty spot where I had definitely parked my Corvette. I parked it in the same damn spot every day.

The bros all piled out the door behind me, and I swung to face them, chest heaving. "Someone stole my fucking car!"

In my pocket, my phone beeped. I pulled it out to light up the screen.

Oh, you're here! That was fast! Be right out.

The blood roaring in my veins turned to ice. I let out a strangled sound and looked up, holding the phone in a punishing grip. "Please tell me this is a joke."

"We don't fuck with each other's cars," Ryan said.

"Should we call the police?" Wes asked.

A loud whooshing sound filled my head. Elite didn't fuck with each other's cars. And they didn't fuck with each other's women.

And right now...

Someone was fucking with both of mine.

32

LANDRY

WE'RE DONE STUDYING. CAN'T WAIT TO SEE YOU.

Be right there, little siren.

Renewed energy suffused me as I stared down at the short text exchange. He always did call me his little siren, and I thought it was silly, but just then, maybe I did feel a little like a siren, luring him to me.

Little jitters of excitement sparked throughout my body just knowing he was on his way. It had been hours since I saw him last, but truthfully, it felt more like days.

"He's coming?" Lars asked beside me.

I smiled and set aside the phone. "Yes."

"What do you think he's going to do when we step outside and he realizes there are three of us and two seats in his Corvette?" Lars wondered, eyes glimmering with mischief.

I laughed. "I don't know, but I sure can't wait to find out." My excitement dimmed a bit, my expression falling with it.

357

"What is it?"

I smiled sadly. "He's not used to needing room in his car for people who care about him."

"I thought people in California were laid-back and chill," Lars muttered. "They seem like schmucks."

I agreed. "Well, he has Elite now." I punctuated the declaration by snapping shut my laptop. "Thank you so much for all the help in this class, Lars. Seriously. I'm all caught up now thanks to you."

"What are brothers for?" he said, the tips of his ears turning red.

He was cute, but I kept that little observation to myself because I didn't want to embarrass him further.

"Hey," I said as we were putting our stuff away to go meet Jason. "About that..." I lowered my voice and leaned over my bag toward him. "Have you heard anything around?"

He shook his head. "Nothing. And honestly, no one on Elite is acting strange either."

I nodded. I thought the same.

"I even asked Win," Lars told me. "You know, since he's been around Elite longer than us. He doesn't think anyone has been acting different either."

"I told Ryan," I confided. "He seemed just as surprised about the rumors. He promised to keep an eye on things."

"I'm starting to wonder if there are actually rumors," Lars said, standing from the table and pushing in his chair.

The library was fairly empty tonight with only a few study groups more toward the front. We'd chosen something in the back because no one was around.

"But if there aren't any rumors, then how would she know all that stuff?" I speculated. "It would be different if the stuff she said was all a bunch of hooey."

Lars glanced at me. "Hooey?"

"Phony."

"Americans and their weird sayings," he muttered.

I hooked my arm around his and smiled.

"Think about it, though." He went on as we headed toward the exit. "If this stuff got out, everyone would be talking about it. I haven't been here long but long enough to know that gossip spreads like wildfire."

"Especially hot gossip, and this would be piping hot."

He made a sound of agreement. "We should probably talk to Rush."

I knew he was right. We should, but I didn't want to. Hadn't Jay been through enough?

Sensing I might need some more convincing, Lars continued. "Maybe he made one of the barnacles mad and they went digging in his past. Maybe she's jealous."

"Barnacle?" I pondered. "Who has the weird sayings now?"

He laughed under his breath. "That's what Rory and Madison call the girls who hang all over Elite. Barnacles. Crustaceans that latch on to anything in the water and are impossible to remove."

"Hmm." I nodded. "Makes sense. Do you really think it could just be some girl he rejected?"

Jason said there hadn't been anyone but me here. *He did say there were some hand jobs.*

That hadn't bothered me before, but now that one of the "hands" had a potential face attached to it, I was bothered. Okay, fine. I was jealous.

"Rush definitely isn't known for his, ah... tact," Lars pointed out.

"What a nice way of saying he can be a dick."

Lars's smile was quick.

"You're right. I'll ask him about her." Jealousy aside, Jason needed to know if there was some barnacle on campus with ammunition to hurt him. "I wonder what her last name is. Is she in any of your other classes?"

"No," Lars replied.

"Mine either."

I gasped. The people at a table nearby all glanced up.

"Sorry," I whispered. Tugging Lars's arm, I pulled him off to the side near a few rows of books. "Let's find her on the A&P roster. It will have her last name. We can look her up on social media."

"This is why I don't have social media," Lars mumbled.

Slipping my phone out of my pocket, I clicked around until I found the class roster. "Here," I said, and Lars leaned in so we could stare at the screen.

I scanned the list, then scanned it again. "I'm not seeing her. Are you?"

"No," he said. "Let's look again."

We did. I scrolled through extra slow.

"There isn't one person in this class named Brittney," I concluded.

"Maybe she transferred in?" Lars offered.

"But so did I, and I'm on the list."

"Maybe Brittney is a nickname? Or a middle name? Some people don't go by their first names."

"True." I agreed, darkening the screen and stuffing it back in my pocket. "It's odd, though. Who is this girl?"

"We can talk to Rush about it over pizza, okay?" Lars suggested.

"Good idea." I pulled away from him to go to the large glass doors looking out to the parking lot.

"Oh!" I said, pointing to the back of the lot where Jason's blue Corvette was backed into a spot. The headlights were on, streaking across the blacktop as though he'd just pulled in. "There he is."

Just knowing he was there made me feel a lot less anxious already. Excited, I pulled out my phone and shot off a text, letting him know I saw him. *Oh, you're here! That was fast! Be right out.*

My stomach bounced, and I tucked my phone away and then couldn't help but wave through the window at him.

I knew he likely wouldn't be able to see me. And even if he could, I wouldn't be able to see him wave back. Between the dark outside and his bright headlights in front of him—

The lights flickered.

My heart turned over. "He sees us," I told Lars. "C'mon."

I looked back, wondering what was taking him so long.

He was over by the reception desk, sliding a book into a return slot. When he turned back, his face was sheepish. "I forgot we were using this. Almost took it with us."

"It's a stuffy old anatomy book," I quipped. "No one would miss it."

"I beg your pardon. This is a well-stocked library, young lady," the woman behind the desk exclaimed. Her hair was up in a simple twist at the back of her head, she wore a white button-up blouse, and a long beaded black string hung from her pearl-colored glasses so she wouldn't lose them when she took them off. "We pride ourselves on having anything a student here at Westbrook would need."

"Yes, ma'am." I agreed, contrite.

"Young lady," Lars intoned when he made it to my side.

I groaned beneath my breath. "Can you believe my dad says that? There's no way he's as old as her."

Lars laughed, and I pushed through the first set of glass doors, glancing back at the waiting Corvette.

Lars's phone went off, and behind him, the librarian shushed loudly. Grimacing, he hurried through the door, and I let it go so we were standing in the small tiled entryway.

"It might be Win," he said, reaching into his pocket.

"I'll meet you at the car," I called, pushing open the door

leading outside. I was impatient and wanted to see my favorite swimmer.

Smiling, I waved and stepped off the sidewalk.

There was a brief shout behind me, but it was drowned out by the revving of Jason's fancy engine. I rolled my eyes and smiled wider. *Such a car nerd.*

The car pulled out of the spot, and my insides fluttered because he was obviously just as excited to see me. I quickened my steps as the engine revved again.

Showoff.

The tires let out an ear-piercing squeal when the car shot forward. Startled, I jerked up, my brain not having time to process. He was barreling straight for me. He wasn't slowing down.

If anything, the car sped up.

33

RUSH

ADRENALINE FLOODED MY SYSTEM SO FAST IT LEFT ME lightheaded and barely able to think. It felt like I was moving through heavy, thick fog trying valiantly to hold me back.

I struggled, grappling for a clear mind. With shaking fingers, I hit the screen on my phone, practically hyperventilating when it rang.

"Pick up," I prayed. "Pick up, pick up!"

Hi, this is Landry's phone...

"Ahh!" I roared, silencing the stupid fucking voicemail, the sound of her voice only making me more crazed.

"What's going on?" Ryan asked, stepping closer.

"Get your keys. We have to go," I said, stabbing at the screen again.

This time, the person answered on the second ring. "Rush?" Lars's voice came through the line. "We're just on the way—"

"That's not me!" I yelled so forcefully that I felt my vocal cords strain. "That's not me out there, Lars. Someone stole my Vette. Someone—"

"Wait, what?" Lars repeated, his voice taking on an alarmed tone.

"Where is Landry?" I demanded. "Put her on the phone!"

"She's outside meeting you." The confusion in his voice made my insides shrivel with potent fear.

The sound of squealing tires in the distance stopped my heart.

"Landry!" Lars yelled.

"What's going on?" I demanded as Ryan appeared with a set of keys. I snatched them right out of his hand and took off running.

"Lars!" I screamed into the line, gripping the phone so hard my hand ached.

Squealing brakes. Shouting. Screaming. The sound of scuffling, of the phone hitting the ground. More squealing. Another scream.

The line went dead.

No. No. Not again.

Yanking open the door to the black four-door Wrangler, I yelled, "Call the cops! Get them to the library." Right before I slammed the door, I added, "Call Win!"

"Rush!" Ryan shouted, jogging toward me and his Jeep.

I revved the engine and threw it into reverse. She wasn't as good as my Vette. Not nearly. But she was gonna have to be good enough.

The headlights slashed across Ryan and the rest of the bros standing on the sidewalk, gaping. I didn't have time to explain. I had to get there.

Please don't let me be too late.

I let out a sob, leaning forward in the seat as if I could

compel the engine to move faster. She didn't answer the phone. His line went dead.

Jesus H. Christ. What if they were too?

34

LANDRY

IT HAPPENED SO FAST. ONE MINUTE, I WAS SMILING AND waving, anticipating the familiarity of Jason's lips and voice.

The next, the blue Corvette was barreling toward me, headlights so bright I was locked in a trance. Confusion muddled all reaction, and static filled my ears.

Slam!

I was hit from the side by what felt like a wall of concrete. The impact rattled my skull and banged my teeth together with so much force my tongue split and the sharp tang of blood flooded my mouth.

A burning sensation ripped down my side as I skidded over the blacktop, the shirt I was wearing no match for the rough, rigid ground.

And then there was silence.

Sudden and almost as jarring as the hell that had just broken loose.

I blinked from my position on the ground as discomfort

weighed me down, practically pinning me in place. I coughed, the sound a bit garbled, and I recoiled at the wetness pooling in my mouth. A flash of anxiety burst inside me, and I had a sudden fear I was going to drown.

I coughed more forcefully this time, the action making my body ring with pain. Recoiling, I lifted my head off the pavement to spit out the liquid trying to deluge my throat and suffocate me.

"Landry," a familiar voice called from far away. Suddenly, the pain weighing me down was lifted, and hands grabbed me, pulling me around. "Landry!"

I blinked up at Lars crouched over me, his face drawn and pale. He gave me a little shake, and I groaned. "That hurts."

"What does?"

"My shoulder," I answered, the realization zinging right through the brain fog, and adrenaline started pumping all over again. "Oh my God, what happened?" I gasped, struggling to sit up.

I recoiled a bit when bright light suddenly filled my vision, making me wince. The familiar revving of an engine was like a bucket of ice water over the fiery pain burning me up.

"Oh fuck!" Lars spat and yanked me to my feet. The rough movement made me cry out, but he didn't stop. "He's coming back!" he yelled, turning from me to face the Corvette that had just tried to run me down.

Lars pushed me out of the way. He saved my life.

"Run!" he yelled, his accent so heavy I barely understood. Or maybe that was because my brain was so jumbled.

The tires squealed, and someone screamed. Lars reached behind him and shoved me. "Run!"

The force of his push had my wobbly legs folding beneath me. I stumbled and fell, my knee taking the brunt of the fall.

"Over here," Lars yelled. Instead of rushing and

attempting to get out of the way, he moved farther into the car's path.

Trying to distract them from me.

"No!" I cried, shoving to my feet as more blood splattered my chin.

The car bore down on him, making him look like nothing but a black shadow bathed in bright-gold light. I saw him shuffle his weight, trying to decide which way to go. But then he glanced over his shoulder. Seeing I was still there, he rooted himself in place.

I screamed and rushed forward. I wouldn't let him sacrifice himself for me. I couldn't.

Squinting against the blinding headlights, I launched forward, catching Lars around the waist and throwing my weight into him. We both went down, skidding to the side and rolling. More pain exploded, and his grunts felt like gunshots.

The crunch and groaning of metal on metal was so loud that, for a moment, my ears rang. The sound was so high-pitched and piercing it threatened to spilt my brain. The weight on me was indescribable, the ground beneath me unforgiving as I struggled to breathe. More of that copper washed over my tongue, but this time, I didn't have the strength to cough it up.

As I lay there half-conscious, the ringing in my ears faded and another sound filtered in.

"Landry!"

Oh, I know that voice. It's my favorite.

"Landry!"

He's mad.

"Jesus fucking Christ!" he swore. "Over here! Get some help!"

And then he was there, blanketing all the chaos with his presence, his scent, and the sound of his voice.

"I got you, baby. I'm here." He promised. "Please don't die," he murmured, and he started to rock. "I can't lose you." The naked pain in his voice roused me like nothing else could. "*I love you.*"

I let out a sound, and he sucked in a breath. The rocking stopped, but he hunched around me farther until he was all I could feel and see.

"Landry?" he asked. "Wake up, baby."

Pain sliced through me when I lifted my hand, but his confession was far more powerful than any pain I could ever feel.

I laid my hand against his cheek, blinked up, and smiled. "I love you too."

35

THE LIBRARY WAS A MILE AWAY. MAYBE A MILE AND A HALF. The drive was an eternity.

I cursed this shitty Jeep. I slammed my fist against the steering wheel and sweated through my shirt.

Mostly, I prayed.

I fucking bargained with everything I had to a God I wasn't even sure existed. I didn't care. I'd give up literally everything, even my own life, if it meant saving theirs.

Please. Please don't let the two people who mean the most to me pay for my sins.

My cheeks were wet when the library came into view. The parking lot was a large rectangular shape filling up nearly the whole front of the massive two-story building. The familiar shape and taillight glow of my precious baby caught my attention instantly, the blue paint glinting even in the dark.

I looked past it where something roused at the edge of the beam of the headlights.

Lars unfolded from the ground, yanking Landry with him. The second he let go, she stumbled. I let out a yell and mashed my foot on the gas as the brake lights on the Vette flickered. The smooth purr of her engine cut through the Jeep's, and I swear my life flashed before my eyes.

I watched Lars step farther into the path of my car as it shot forward to run him down. It was a split-second decision, one I didn't even have to think about, a fact practically before it became an idea.

I jerked the wheel and plowed down the sidewalk as people dove out of the way.

Please, I prayed one last time.

I cut the wheel again, veering off the sidewalk and nearly coming up onto two wheels as I charged across the lot, gas pedal pressed all the way to the floor.

I didn't brace myself. I didn't take my foot off the gas at the very last second. There was not an ounce of hesitation inside me for what I was about to do. Let the cards fall where they may.

The abrupt impact vibrated my bones, and my head cracked into the driver's side window, making pain explode behind my eyes. Metal crunched and scraped, the Corvette ramming into the front driver's side of the black Rubicon at full speed, the collision so strong it lifted the four-door partially off the ground.

When the deafening sound of cars slamming together faded, all that was left was the running engines and shouts in the distance. I shook off the disorientation and the headache pounding my temple to shove open the door, nearly falling out of the unsteady Jeep.

My knees were rubber when I turned to find my best

friend and girl. They were just feet away, lying in a tangled mass.

I almost didn't make it.

"Landry!" I roared, running toward them. Cursing, I called to all the people standing around gawking, "Over here! Get some help!"

Lars groaned and started to sit up, his body mostly covering Landry's.

"Lars?" I worried, falling onto my knees beside them. "Lars, how bad are you hurt?"

He shook his head and slid off Landry. My eyes fastened on her small, crumpled frame even as I helped him sit up.

"Lars," I said, eyes still on my girl.

"I think I'm okay," he said. "She's worse."

A stricken sound floated between us, and I gingerly tugged her into my lap, curling around her body as much as I could.

"I was trying to shield her," Lars said, his voice cracking. "But she took the brunt of both falls."

Ryan, Jamie, Wes, Kruger, and Prism all appeared, running around the wreckage, feet pounding as they rushed close.

"Help is coming," Prism said, and the sound of sirens in the distance backed up his words.

"Lars." Wes worried, crouching beside my friend. "Are you okay? Where are you hurt?"

"Win is going to be so mad," he said, voice wobbly.

"He's on his way," Wes said.

"Is she okay?" Ryan asked, attention focused on the girl in my lap.

I was thankful Lars was conscious and speaking, but Landry had yet to say a word. The breath hitched in my lungs as agony unlike anything I'd felt before ripped me in two and rearranged the pieces it left behind.

"I got you, baby," I whispered, trying to get closer, wishing I could take her place. "Please don't die," I begged as I rocked us together.

I wasn't above begging. I wasn't above anything that would keep her here with me.

"I can't lose you," I confessed. The tightness in my chest was so severe I wondered if maybe I was having a heart attack. "*I love you.*"

Why? Why the fuck did I wait so long to say it? How could I have withheld those words for so damn long? And now here she was... broken and bleeding, not even able to hear what suddenly felt so urgent.

A little noise slipped from her lips.

I lifted my head, desperation tinging the air. "Landry? Wake up, baby."

When her hand lay against my cheek, her eyes opened and she smiled. Wetness rained over my cheeks as the siren lured me through the storm.

"I love you too," she told me, answering the words I thought she hadn't heard.

A sob broke in my throat, and I pulled her even tighter against me, pressing my lips to her forehead. "Thank you," I whispered to whoever was out there. Whoever it was that answered my prayer.

"Jay," she said, drawing all my attention. I pulled back just enough to stare at her resting against my chest. "I hate to break it to you, but someone stole your car."

A cross between a laugh and a sob tore from my already sore throat. *She is going to be okay.*

Flashing red and blue lights filled the night, and ambulance sirens cut off. The people from inside the library that had crowded around shifted so the emergency responders could get through.

"Lars!" Win's bellow bounced around, traveling faster than the cops. *"Lars Eriksson!"*

"Here!" Wes yelled.

Win shoved through a crowd of people, eyes wide and wild. The second he saw Lars sitting near us on the ground, he raced over and dropped to his knees. "What the fuck?" he roared. "Who did this?"

That's when I remembered.

"The driver," I said, head snapping up toward Ryan. He was still standing close, Jamie right beside him. "Don't let the driver of that Corvette get away!" I demanded, heart pounding frantically.

Both guys nodded and took off toward the wreckage, and I started to get up to go with. I had to see who was behind that wheel. I had to know who the hell was doing this.

Please don't let it be Bodhi. The thought came instantly. If it was him, the betrayal would be something that would *never* heal.

Landry made a pained sound.

I settled instantly, trying not to jostle her. "I got you, baby."

"Please, stay," she requested, hand gripping my arm. The grip was painfully weak but strong enough to keep me in place.

"Is she okay?" Lars worried.

I looked over at my best friend who was sitting practically in Win's lap with his arms locked around him.

"She's all right." Win promised, trying to push Lars's platinum head against his shoulder.

"Landry," Lars said.

"I'm okay, Lars," Landry replied, but she didn't lift her head.

I met Win's eyes over the heads of our battered halves,

and we shared a brief moment of anger and a silent vow of revenge.

The medics rushed near, and everyone shuffled back except for us.

"Where are you hurt?" a man asked me, crouching beside us.

Incredulous, I said, "Who the fuck cares about me? Worry about her!"

"Sir, you're bleeding. You have a head wound."

"You're about to have one too if you don't take care of her first," I threatened.

Landry gasped, her body pulling out of mine for the first time as she struggled to sit up. "You're bleeding? Oh, Jay, let me see." She grabbed for my face.

"I'm fine," I said. "You need to let them check you out."

She made a low noise and reached up to where I assumed I was bleeding.

A shrill howl cut through the air. "Get off me!" a woman shrieked. "Put me down!"

Recognition slammed into me, and confusion followed close behind. Frowning, I looked up as Ryan came around the side of the wreckage. He was carrying a body that was fighting like a hellcat, kicking and throwing herself around, trying to get out of his hold.

Her fist came up, swinging right at Ryan, but Jamie reached over and caught it before it could make contact.

"Don't you think you've done enough for one night?" He glowered.

"Put me down!" she wailed.

"We need some handcuffs!" Jamie yelled.

I felt like I had my ear pressed up against a giant conch shell and the loud roaring of the ocean filled my head, pushing out rational thought.

I blinked, staring at Ryan and the belligerent girl in his arms.

"Pulled this little thief right out of your driver's seat," Ryan said, walking a little closer as she continued to struggle. "You know her?"

The woman flailing about went still. Her body twisted so she could look at me, and when our eyes met, pure hatred dripped from her stare.

Shock had me recoiling. Seeing her was like a fucking a right hook right to the face.

"Brittney," I said, her name more like a wobbly exhale.

"You," she spat.

"I'm gonna be right back, baby," I said, setting Landry closer to the medic so I could stand.

"Jason." Landry tried to reach for me, her hand wrapping around my ankle.

I bent down and gently stroked her cheek. "I need to go deal with this, baby. You stay here and let them take care of you."

She started to protest, but I stood and swiftly stepped around the medics. My eyes landed on Max who hovered nearby in a black leather jacket. I hitched my chin at him. "You mind?" I asked, nodding toward Landry. He came forward immediately, dropping to her side.

I took one step toward Brittney, and she started to scream. "This is your fault!" she accused, pointing at me with an unsteady finger. "Jason Rush, this is all your fault! You killed Brynne! You killed my best friend! She'd still be here if it wasn't for you!"

Her words hit their mark, and even though I didn't doubt myself as much as I did before, I would always still wonder. There would always be that shred of doubt whispering in my heart and mind. *What if I was responsible?*

She thrashed against Ryan with renewed strength, and I

saw him grimace, trying to hold her still. Jamie stood close, body tense and prepared to snatch her up if she managed to break away.

"This was you?" I asked her, stepping even closer. "You were the one who threw that dummy in the pool? You vandalized the locker room?" I shook my head. Of all the people I could have expected, she was never even a consideration.

"I hate you!" she wailed, spittle flying from her lips, one of which was bleeding. There was a gash in her head too. Blood poured over her forehead and streaked her nose and the side of her face.

Even though we were standing in the middle of it all, even though my heart rate was still not normal and there was more panic in my veins than blood, it still took a minute for me to realize. Shock must have turned me dumb.

I heard Landry make a small sound of pain behind me, and then reality crashed over me like a bodacious wave.

"You," I snarled.

Her whole body went rigid as I stalked forward, and she stopped fighting against Ryan, instead trying to climb him.

"If you think I'm gonna help you, you are about to be sorely disappointed," he drawled.

Jamie made a sound of agreement. "Don't look over here either. Not one person is on your side here."

The urge to yank her out of Ryan's arms and shake her and toss her on the ground was nearly blinding. I breathed deep, letting my fingernails cut into my palms as I fought for control. I settled for bending at the waist and pushing my face close to hers.

Her pupils were blown wide, eyes out of focus. She likely had a concussion, but I didn't give one ounce of a damn.

"You just tried to run over my girl and my best friend with a car," I growled. "With *my car*."

"They deserve it!" she spat. "Taking up for a murderer! Why should you get to move on and be happy? Why should you fall in love? Brynne never will!"

"So you try and kill them?" I roared. I felt Ryan's warning look, but I ignored it. He'd be the same fucking way if this was Rory.

Hell, if this was a man, I'd already have broken my knuckles punching his face.

I don't hurt women.

But they sure as fuck keep hurting me.

"I warned her! Both of them!" she cried. "She deserves you!"

"What is going on over here?" An officer stepped over. I recognized him as one of the officers from the dummy incident at the pool. I was pretty sure he was also one of the responding officers at the hospital months ago when Lars was attacked.

"He murdered my best friend!" Brittney screamed and pointed to me. All the people crowding around stared. "And he tried to kill me. He drove into me head-on just a few minutes ago."

The officer glanced at me, eyebrows hiked halfway up his forehead. "Is this true? Were you involved in this collision?"

I laughed. It was humorless and borderline scary. Officer No-name must have thought so too because he signaled for backup.

"That's my Jeep," Ryan told the officer.

My brain rattled as I whipped around to stare at him.

"So you were driving?" the officer asked.

"No," I said, stepping forward. "No, he was not driving. I took his Jeep and drove it over here. And yeah, I drove in front of that Corvette—which is mine—to keep it from running over two people."

I glanced at Ryan. "Sorry about your Jeep." I knew he

loved it as much as I loved my ride, and I'd literally just trashed it—both of them.

"So you stole this man's vehicle," the officer interjected.

We ignored him.

To my surprise, Ryan shrugged. "It was the Jeep or them. You made the right choice."

"Seriously?" I echoed, surprise making my voice hollow.

"Bro, we saw the whole thing," Jamie put in. Then he slapped me on the back. "Way to live up to that wildcard name."

"Are you kidding me?" Brittney started to fight against Ryan again. "This is all his fault. He's a murderer! H-h-he..." Her words started to slur, and then she slumped in Ryan's arms.

"I thought she'd never be quiet," Jamie muttered.

"I need a medic!" the cop yelled.

Once Brittney was strapped onto a gurney and wheeled toward one of the ambulances, I turned to the officer. "She stole my Corvette and drove it here and tried to run over two people. The only reason she stopped is because I made her." I didn't even let him say anything as I continued. "She's also the one who threw the dummy in the Elite pool. And she vandalized our locker room."

"We'll question her when she comes to."

I grabbed him by the shirt and dragged him closer. A few shouts sounded, and men rushed close. Ryan and Jamie closed in on my sides so no one could grab me.

"Chill," Ryan warned.

I kept my stare on the officer. "She needs to be under surveillance. She's dangerous. She tried to kill people."

"And her allegations that you also have killed someone?"

I let go of him and stepped back. "Pretty sure we had that conversation when I voluntarily came into the police station a couple weeks ago," I spat. "The information is still the same." I pinched the bridge of my nose with my thumb and forefinger and sighed. "Look. Her name is Brittney Marsh. She was best friends with Brynne Lawson. She obviously came here from California to make my life hell."

The officer considered my words. "I'm going to need all of you to come with me."

"No."

He drew back. "Excuse me?"

"I said no."

"Are you refusing to cooperate with an investigation?"

I countered, "Are you arresting me?"

Considering it, the officer looked at Ryan. "You would be well within your rights to press charges since he stole your vehicle and then crashed it."

Ryan made a rude sound. "Stole, you say? He didn't steal it. I gave him the keys." He rubbed his chin. "And you know the brakes have been squeaking a lot lately. Been meaning to take it in. Can't say they didn't fail."

Just like that, I knew I was officially Elite. I always would be.

The officer glanced at me, a pinched look on his already constipated face. "We won't be arresting you at this time."

Even though my emotions were all over the place—and, bro, by all over, I mean scattered more than cockroaches under a kitchen light—I remained cool. "Well, until you show me an arrest warrant with my name in bold letters, I'm not going anywhere with you. And you can't force me. I was in a car accident. I have a head injury, and my girlfriend almost died. I'm going to the hospital for medical care, which is my right."

I started away but turned back. "Oh. And you better make sure if you do come with an arrest warrant, it's air-tight because I'm calling my lawyer from the hospital. I'm done cooperating and trying to play nice." *Look at where the hell it got me.* "If you want to treat me like the guilty one, then I'm going to defend myself." *And everyone else who believes in me.*

I walked away, my footsteps stuttering when I saw Landry was no longer where I'd left her. A rough sound ripped out of me as my heart lurched into my throat.

A strong hand hit the back of my neck and squeezed. "She's right there," Ryan said, turning me in the direction where Landry sat in the back of an ambulance with Lars beside her.

I sagged in relief, and Ryan laughed under his breath and patted me on the back.

I grunted. "Fuck off, Walsh."

"Is that any way to talk to the man who just defended your ass to the cops after you turned his Jeep into scrap metal?" Jamie asked.

I glanced at Ryan. "You didn't have to do that."

"You'd do the same for me."

I nodded. He was right. "Not used to having people around who, ah—"

"Match loyalty?" Ryan supplied.

I nodded. "Yeah."

"You'll get used to it," Jamie told me.

"I'll pay for the repairs on your Jeep. Send me the bill."

Ryan grinned. "Oh, I will."

"Don't worry, bro!" Jamie slung his arm around Ryan's neck. "I'll drive you around until she's fixed! Mi Jeep es tu Jeep."

"You should get a Corvette," I told them.

Ryan glanced at the two vehicles still smashed together. "Looks to me like my Jeep held up better than your Vette."

I frowned, staring at the crushed front end.

"Airbags deployed, bro," Jamie informed me quietly.

I groaned. *RIP, baby.*

"Jason." Landry's voice carried across the lot, and I

whipped around. She was looking much more alert, sitting in the back of the ambulance with a blanket around her shoulders and an IV in the back of her hand.

I lifted my hand and jogged toward her, and the look on her face as she saw me coming made my heart tumble.

I loved that Corvette. I'd miss it a hell of a lot.

But I loved my little siren more.

I could live without that car. But without her? I'd never survive.

36

LANDRY

Elite descended upon the hospital like buzzards on dead bodies.

Wow, okay, that was a horrible analogy and also very grim considering some of us almost died.

These pain meds were clearly very strong.

But also, yay for pain meds!

My injuries weren't life-threatening, but they sure did hurt. The official diagnosis was severe road rash from skidding across the pavement, plentiful cuts and bruises, a bump on the head (but no concussion because I have a hard head), and a large gash in my tongue.

Oh, I'd also re-torn my rotator cuff. *sad face*

The gash on my tongue was touch-and-go. They had not stitched it up but threatened that if it continued to bleed, they would have to. Apparently, tongue lacerations heal quite well on their own, but they tend to bleed a lot.

I'd like to note I'd tasted enough of my own blood to conclusively say it does not taste good. I felt bad for vampires. I'd rather have a cupcake.

Did I mention I was on a ton of pain meds?

A light knock on the door caused Jason to stiffen beneath me.

"Is it okay to come in?" Rory asked, her gray eyes peeking through a slim opening in the doorway.

Jason relaxed and waved her in while Ryan stood from the chair he was in on the other side of the room. "Why didn't you text when you got here? I'd have come out and walked you in."

"We can walk ourselves into the emergency room," she said, pushing fully into the space.

Madison was right behind her. "It's not like we don't know the way."

"That ain't funny, Mads," Jamie grumbled.

"I brought you a snack," she told him, holding out a box of donuts.

He groaned and pulled her in to kiss the top of her head. "You're my favorite girl."

She laughed.

"Caramel lattes," Rory sang, coming to the bed to hand over two white paper cups with black lids. "You can have a donut too if Jamie doesn't eat them all."

"Good luck," Jamie said, stuffing an entire glazed donut into his mouth.

He probably wouldn't make a good vampire either.

A sound of appreciation rumbled in my throat as I tried to sit up and reach for the coffee. My right arm was in a sling, and I tumbled back into Jason's chest.

"Easy," he cautioned, voice low and gentle.

Butterflies lifted off in my belly, and I rubbed my cheek against his chest and smiled.

Wrapping an arm around me, he sat up, pulling me with him, allowing his body to support my weight. "It's hot," he cautioned, holding out the latte for me.

"I hope so," I said, wrapping my free hand around it but unable to grip it because the too-long sleeve of Jason's hoodie I was currently rocking over my oh-so-fashionable hospital gown made it impossible.

"My little siren," he mused, tugging back the black fabric so it bunched around my wrist and I could take the coffee. He hovered a few minutes more, making sure I had it in my grasp before pulling away.

I took a sip of the warm, sweet brew and sighed. *Much better than blood.*

"Thanks for the coffee, shrimp," Jason told Rory.

I made a sound of appreciation but stilled mid-sip.

"What is it?" Jason worried, reaching for the cup. "Did you burn yourself? Is your tongue bleeding again?" He glanced at Rory. "Get the nurse."

"No. Wait," I said, stopping her. "I was just wondering. Does Lars have one of these?"

"Of course," Madison replied from her place in Jamie's lap. He was still plowing through the donuts as though he really were about to eat the whole box. "He's in the room just down the hall. We took some in there first. Donuts too."

"You guys will probably have better luck at getting them to share than Jamie," Rory whispered. Loud.

I giggled.

"Y'all drink trauma lattes, and I eat donuts," Jamie said, chomping away. Midchew, he added, "But I'll share with you, scrappy, 'cause you're the patient."

"What about me?" Jason grumped.

"Bro, she's a girl," Jamie said as though that somehow explained everything.

Jason must have also agreed because he didn't argue.

Instead, his warm hand curled around my hip and rubbed gently against my waist. When his lips brushed my hairline, I sighed and leaned against his shoulder.

He'd ridden with me in the back of the ambulance, came down to radiology, and stayed close when they did an MRI of my shoulder.

He had four stitches in his head from hitting it against the Jeep window, but he acted like they didn't even exist. He acted like all he saw was me. And by the way he constantly touched me, it seemed all he felt was me too.

"I love you." He spoke quietly against my ear.

My whole body bloomed with pleasure, and I tilted my head to look up at him. "Love you too."

He kissed my nose, and I ducked, shy.

I might have been the first to say those three words, but since they tore out of him back in the parking lot, he'd said them so much it felt like a steady heartbeat.

"Landry Resch!" a loud voice bellowed from out in the hall. "Landry Resch!"

I sat up. "It's my dad."

Ryan pulled open the door and stuck his head into the hall. "Coach."

Some muffled cursing preceded him as he shoved the door wide and strode inside. He was dressed in a pair of light-wash jeans and a long-sleeved Henley with his Elite jacket overtop. The dreaded whistle hung around his neck.

"Landry," he said again, coming over to the side of the bed. I noted his eyes sliding to Jason and how I was basically in his lap, but they came right back to me, concern darkening them. "What happened? Are you hurt? What the hell is this?" he asked, jabbing a finger at the sling.

"I'm fine. It looks worse than it is." I tried to assure him.

"Well, it looks pretty damn bad, young lady."

"Young lady," Jamie heckled.

"I want answers." Dad's eyes snapped to Jason. "Rush."

"Someone tried to hit me with their car." I hedged, drawing his attention away from my boyfriend.

"What?"

"But Lars pushed me out of the way." I felt my lip wobble as I pictured Lars trying to distract the driver so I wouldn't get hurt. Sensing my upset, Jason wrapped his arms around me, gently pushing my head toward his chest. "I want to go check on him," I said, realizing I hadn't seen him since the ambulance.

"He's doing good." Madison assured me. "We just saw him. Win is worse off than he is."

Jason grunted in understanding.

"You're sure he's not hurt?" I asked the girls.

"Just some scrapes and bruises. No concussion or anything." Rory promised. "They were waiting for the discharge paperwork."

"That's good," I said, relieved.

"And you." Dad glowered at Rush. "What the hell were you doing while someone was trying to mow down my daughter?"

I gasped. "He risked his life to save mine!"

"It's true, Coach. We all saw it," Jamie said. He was still eating.

"How are there even any left?" I wondered.

He grinned. "Don't worry. I saved one for you."

"What about me?" Ryan wanted to know.

"Donuts before dudes," Jamie admonished.

"I'm ordering pizza," Ryan declared.

"I want pepperoni," Jamie told him, and Ryan shook his head.

A donut appeared under his nose, and Ryan snatched it to take a giant bite. "Pepperoni it is!"

"My daughter is in the hospital, and you all are arguing

about donuts and pizza! What the hell kinda team am I running? Everyone, out!"

No one moved.

"Hey, scrappy, what do you want on your pizza?" Ryan asked, glancing away from his phone.

Dad lifted the whistle at the same time a nurse walked in.

"Don't even think about it," she warned.

The whistle bounced against his chest when he dropped it. "Yes, ma'am."

"You two doing okay?" she asked, coming over to the bed. "Is your tongue still bleeding?"

Dad made a sound. The nurse shot him a look, and he fell quiet.

Behind her, Ryan and Jamie snickered, and beneath me, I felt Jason's chest bounce with silent laughter.

"I think it stopped," I told her. "My friends got me a coffee, and it's so nice to taste something besides blood."

Jay's silent laughter died a swift death.

The nurse nodded emphatically. "We'll need to check it again before we let you leave."

I handed the coffee to my father and patted Jason's chest for help in sitting up. Once I was upright, I opened my mouth and stuck out my tongue, which felt swollen and sore.

She leaned in. "There's still a little bit of bleeding, but it has slowed down considerably."

"Aow'll eee thfine." I promised, still sticking out my tongue.

Jason chuckled. "Put your tongue away, little siren."

The nurse smiled. "The doctor will want to double-check, but it should be okay. If it starts to bleed more, you know to come back. You'll need to rinse with a special mouthwash to help prevent infection as well. We'll have everything written up for you before you're discharged."

"I'll keep an eye on it," Jason vowed.

"That's my job," Dad intoned.

The nurse gave me an apologetic look. "You deal with a lot."

The door opened, and Lars came in with Win, Wes, Max, Kruger, and Prism behind him.

The nurse's eyes widened. "Oh my, there's more?"

"That's my brother," I said, pointing to Lars. "He saved my life."

Then I burst into tears.

Jason made a stricken sound and lifted me closer, pushing my face under his chin and into his neck. "Okay now," he soothed. "You're okay."

"Should I go?" Lars worried.

"No!" I wailed.

"Stay," Jason said over my head. "You doing okay?"

Lars answered quietly, so I couldn't hear what he said over my sobs.

Jason's lips brushed near my ear. "You go ahead and cry, baby. Cry all you want. I'm sorry," he murmured. "I'm so sorry I brought this on you."

That only made me cry harder because I didn't want him to blame himself. This wasn't his fault. I couldn't get the words out, though, so I just clung to him and wept.

"You should admit her," I heard Dad say. He had no clue how to deal with crying.

"This is perfectly normal," the nurse said calmly. "Trauma, injury, and pain meds are a lot all at once."

Boo, pain meds!

The nurse reached out to pat my arm.

Jason growled.

The woman pulled back. "The police are here."

"You can't arrest him!" I exclaimed. "He's just grumpy because I'm bleeding and his car is ruined."

"I'm sorry I got mad, baby." Jason placated me, patting my back. It totally worked, and I sniffled.

That was the pain meds' fault too.

"I want explanations, Rush." I could practically feel Dad glowering at my back.

"They want to get your statements," the nurse clarified, still calm as a cucumber. "I can tell them you aren't feeling up to it."

"Good idea." Jason agreed.

"No," I said, sitting up and swiping the tears off my face. The inside of my mouth tasted like nasty blood again, and I held my hand out for the coffee my dad was holding. "You can let them in. I'm fine."

Jason drew in a breath, likely to let out a bunch of hot air and protests, so I turned and met his eyes. "Let's get this over with. Besides, I have questions too."

He nodded once.

"I'll inform them. After that, we'll need to get your vitals, and then we will see about those discharge papers," the nurse told the room on her way out.

"I ordered pizza," Ryan told her.

The nurse turned back. "You can't just order pizza to the ER."

Ryan smiled, flashing his white teeth and blue eyes. "We'll share with you."

"Well, I guess just this once." Then she let herself out.

"Ryan Steven Walsh," Rory intoned, putting her hands on her hips. "Are you flirting with the nurse?"

"I have to feed everyone, baby, or else Jamie and Kruger will get hangry."

"Is this what you do when you aren't at the pool?" Coach wondered. "Because we need to have a class on dryland behavior."

"Who's gonna teach it, Coach?" Wes asked.

"You little smartass—"

"Watch your mouth," Win and Max snapped at the same time.

Lars grimaced. "They're cranky."

"Someone tried to run you over," Win ground out. "Twice!"

Two uniformed police officers entered the room, the door swinging shut behind them. When they saw us all sitting there, they blanched.

"This has to be against hospital policy," one muttered.

The other said, "We'll need the room to speak with those involved."

"We're all involved," everyone said.

Pretty sure I heard one of the officers mutter something *not* nice about Elite.

"Just the victims, then," the one who didn't insult us said. "Everyone else can give your statements to the officer in the waiting room."

"You cool?" Ryan asked Jason as he stood.

"Yeah, bro, thanks."

"We'll be out there if you guys need anything," Jamie added.

"I'll make sure Jamie leaves you some pizza," Prism said, glancing at me with a smile.

I smiled back. Pizza sounded good, but the idea of chewing anything with a sore tongue sounded less pleasant.

Everyone vacated the room except for my dad, Jason, Win, and Lars. Max didn't go far, though. I could see his black-leather-jacket-covered back through the small window in the door.

Is he standing guard?

Win directed Lars to a chair near the bed. "Sit down, angel."

"I'm fine," he insisted but sat anyway.

I noted the red, aggravated road rash along his arm, and equal parts guilt and gratitude filled me. I handed my latte to Jason to reach out my hand. Lars leaned in to grasp it. "Thank you," I whispered.

He gave my fingers a light squeeze. "Back at you." But then his eyes moved to the sling, and he frowned. "I was too rough, though, pushed you too hard. I wasn't thinking. I just wanted to get you out of the way."

Jason grunted. "Bro. You saved her life." Then in a lower voice, he added, "I will never forget that."

"It was a close call," Lars whispered, light eyes darkening. "The car clipped me as we jumped out of the way."

Jason's body tightened, and I gasped.

"How injured are you really?" I demanded, looking at Win for the truth.

Win made a sound and lifted Lars out of the chair to sit down with him in his lap.

"Just some bruises," Lars confirmed, and Win nodded. I couldn't help but notice that his usually sunny personality was a lot darker tonight.

"Is Brittney awake yet?" Jason demanded, the anger in his voice palpable. "Did you arrest her?"

"She is conscious, and we have taken her statement." The officer hedged.

"Brittney?" I echoed, then gasped. "*Oh my God,* is she the one who did this?" I whipped around to look at Lars, wincing at the pain the swift movement caused. "You were right. She's a barnacle."

"A barnacle?" Jason echoed.

I rotated in his lap to face him, tugging my coffee from his grip. "I honestly have no idea what you saw in her, Jay. She's horrible." I tipped the coffee against my lips, letting the sweet flavor of caramel wash away the blood. And hopefully, my jealousy.

"What I saw in her?" Jason puzzled. "Baby…" He started gently, and I bristled. I was done being placated. "I think you might be confused."

"I am not," I asserted. "You said Brittney is the one who tried to run us down tonight, and after the way she acted the other day and how we couldn't find her on the class roster, I know exactly who we're talking about."

The tops of Jay's cheeks turned red, and his eyes widened with every word I spoke. "Wait. *You know her?*"

"We both do," Lars stated. Then to me, he said, "We probably should have told him sooner."

"Told me what?" Jason yelled.

"You're going to burst your stitches," I admonished, reaching up to finger around the bandage near his temple. "Calm down."

Jason grabbed my wrist, his hold impossibly gentle. "Landry." He began, the use of my first name making me snap to attention. "I need you to tell me. You've met Brittney? The same Brittney who stole my car tonight?"

"Well, I didn't see her tonight. I was too busy trying not to drown in my own blood."

Judging from the look on Jason's face and the way my father started to pace beside the bed, that was a poor choice of words. *Oopsie.* So I rephrased. "Long brown hair. Brown eyes. Taller than me?" I asked.

All the color flushing his cheeks drained away, and he swallowed thickly. "Where have you seen her?"

"She's in our A&P class."

Jason let out a strangled sound. "That's impossible."

"Well, she sits right beside me. Lars and I just had coffee with her the other day."

Lars nodded, and Win cursed under his breath. "This is why I have a tracker on you, angel. Do I need to put a body cam on you as well?" he grumped.

Without a word, Jay pulled me tight against his chest and locked his arms around me. "She's been stalking my girl-friend," he told the police over my head. "And my best friend. I want her arrested. Now."

"So you do know her?" Lars asked.

"Yes." Jason's voice was raw and dripping with guilt. "Thank God you're okay," he whispered, holding me even tighter. I let out a little squeak, and he cursed, loosening his grip.

"And she's not just some girl that's mad you rejected her?" Lars clarified.

"Is that what you think?" Jason laughed, a humorless sound. "No. No, she's not someone I ever dated. She's Brynne's best friend. She blames me for her death, and she's here out of some sick quest for vigilante justice."

Jason shifted to reach into his pocket and pull out a cell phone.

"No calls," the officer intoned.

Jason ignored him and lifted the phone to his ear. "You still in town?" he asked the second the call was answered.

A moment later, he said, "Come to the ER. Ask for me."

Someone spoke on the line, but I couldn't make out what they said.

"Just do it," Jason demanded. "Bring Blair." Then he ended the call.

After dropping the phone onto the mattress, he pulled me close once more. "I'm sorry. I'm so fucking sorry."

"Is that why we couldn't find her on the roster?" I wondered. "Because she doesn't even go to Westbrook?"

"We'll verify with the school," the officers said, one of them scribbling something in his notebook.

But really, I didn't need the police to verify because I already knew. Brittney whatever-her-last-name-was was not a student at Westbrook. She wasn't a barnacle or a woman scorned.

She was worse.

A woman hellbent on revenge.

37

RUSH

YOU'D THINK AFTER A WHILE OF UNEXPECTED OCCURRENCES and shocking revelations, my surprise meter would be busted, right?

Nope.

Because here I was hovering outside the hospital room of a girl I least expected to be responsible for terrorizing a bro-lot of people.

FYI bro-lot is a new unit of measurement.

Maybe I wasn't so much surprised as I was bewildered because she took things way too far. I'd known Brittney almost as long as Brynne. I never would have pegged her as the type of girl that would fly across the country and pretend to be a student at Westbrook to get close to my girlfriend and best friend while simultaneously trying to ruin my reputation.

I mean, Jesus, she stole my car and tried to run over my two favorite people. Imagine if I hadn't realized in time?

Would they have died thinking it was me behind the wheel?

Would their last thought have been regret for trusting me when no one else would?

I couldn't bear it.

And look, I know this girl thought I killed Brynne, but this was beyond cruel.

And no, I wasn't doing the whole "allegedly" thing. I wasn't a cop, and I didn't have to give her the benefit of the doubt. I already knew.

Still, the cops wanted a positive ID from Landry and Lars that this was in fact the same Brittney they'd been seeing on the regular in classes. Seriously, bro, it's a good thing I'm used to swimming in cold temperatures because the blood in my veins was ice.

Weeks. This crackpot had been hovering for weeks, and no one knew it.

I glanced at Win. "I'm gonna need all the info on that tracker app."

Win made a noise. "Just give me her phone, bro. I'll install it myself."

Overhearing the exchange, Landry gasped. "You are *not* putting a tracker on me."

I rubbed her back. "If you say so, baby."

"Don't you placate me, you squeaky grocery cart!"

Everyone standing around turned to look at her.

I laughed. "Squeaky grocery cart?" I asked. "Is that worse than an itchy sweater?"

"They're both heinous just like you."

"Look at that, angel. She's got bad sayings just like you. You really must be related," Win mused.

Lars said something in Swedish that made Win laugh, but I was too busy feeling my heart swell as I took in her grumpy face and messy hair. She was standing there in nothing but a hospital gown, socks, and my hoodie with the sling holding her arm in place.

Wrapping my arms around her from behind, I nuzzled my nose against the hair above her ear. "Call me all the ridiculous insults you want, little siren. I deserve it, and I'll still love you."

She turned in my arms to stretch up on tiptoes and kiss me. Her kisses were my favorite. Even the ones flavored with blood.

She started to pull away, but I made a sound, grasping her chin. "Let me see your tongue."

A look of defiance crossed those green eyes, and I met it head on with one of my own. Her bleeding was *not* something I was bargaining over.

Sighing, she opened her mouth.

"Tongue," I ordered when she didn't stick it out.

She rolled her eyes but stuck it out. Blood smeared the side of it.

"You're getting stitches." I decided.

"No!" She pulled back so abruptly her sock-covered feet slid right out from under her.

A vision of her busting her ass on this hard hospital floor made my heart stop. Both Lars and Win lunged forward, but I caught her first, swinging her up into my arms bridal style.

"Put me down."

"Why?" I questioned mildly. "So you can find somewhere else to bleed?"

"Jason," she warned.

"Landry," I warned back.

"A cold bowl of soup is more fun than you."

Amusement shot through me as Lars snickered, but I refused to show it. Admitting weakness could not happen. "Yeah? Well, there ain't nothing cold about the way I feel about you. So you can just stay put because at least when I'm holding you, I know you're safe."

She settled against me, resting her cheek against my chest. "I miss my trauma latte."

"I'll get it for you," Lars offered.

"Don't bother," she told him. "The cops questioned us so long it went cold. Cold coffee is worse than cold soup."

I grinned over her head.

"I'll text Wes to get you a new one," Win offered, pulling out his phone.

"And some espresso," Lars mumbled.

Win smiled, reaching up to rub his hand over Lars's light hair. "And espresso."

The door to Brittney's room swung open, and the officers stepped out. "You can come in now."

Frankly, I thought it was asinine she even got to consent to speaking with us. Hell, these were victims waiting to identify their attacker. In my book, she didn't get rights.

You know that's not right, a voice deep inside me argued. It pissed me off that I knew it was true. I'd needed those rights when I was accused of Brynne's murder.

Shaking off that thought, the four of us started forward.

"Put me down," Landry admonished.

"No."

Win shouldered in front of Lars, and I didn't even scoff that he was shielding him from a girl. Girls were just as dangerous as men.

My stomach twisted the second her brown eyes flew to me as I stepped inside. Brittney was in bed, which had the back lifted so she was in a sitting position. She was dressed in the typical blue-and-white hospital gown, an IV taped to the back of her hand, and her long dark hair tangled around her shoulders. Her lower lip was swollen and cut. She had a rash across her face, which was likely caused by the airbag deployment. She also had a butterfly bandage above her eyebrow, and her face was deathly pale.

It still sort of blew my mind how someone I once knew could be nothing but a stranger now.

I tensed just feeling her attention shift to the girl in my arms. But Landry seemed far less bothered than me.

"Brittney," she said in lieu of greeting, her voice cool.

"Landry," Brittney returned, her eyes sliding away. "Lars."

He said something in Swedish, and I knew it was likely not nice.

"Miss Resch. Mr. Eriksson." The officer who followed us into the room began. "Is this the woman you said has been attending your class at Westbrook?"

"Yes," they both answered at the same time.

I groaned, just having it confirmed yet another punch to my gut. All this time, she was right under my nose. All this time, they were in danger, and I didn't do shit.

"Put me down, Jay."

I set Landry on her sock-covered feet. "Be careful."

Landry marched right over beside the bed to glare at Brittney. I scrambled after her, wrapping an arm around her from behind like some sort of walking seatbelt.

"Do you even go to Westbrook?"

Brittney scoffed. "As if I'd actually attend that poor excuse for a prestigious school."

"What's your last name?" she asked.

I wondered why it even mattered, but she seemed to care.

"You don't need to know," Brittney smarted off. It wasn't cute.

"It's Marsh," I said.

Brittney turned glittering eyes to me. "You think you've won."

My upper lip curled. "This is winning?" I scoffed.

"Because I do not consider watching my friends nearly get run over by a car they think I'm driving a victory."

Landry gasped. "Is that why you stole his car?"

I blinked. Wasn't it obvious? I didn't say that, though. I mean, she had just been through a hell of a lot.

"I warned you," Brittney told Landry. "Both of you. I tried to get you to see reason. I even tried to scare you away from him. But you're so stupid. You wouldn't listen at all. You just kept believing all the lies he spoon-fed you. That makes you just as guilty as him. He might be the killer, but you're the killer lover."

The officer stepped forward. "Ma'am, are you aware those exact threats were painted on two lockers in the Elite locker rooms at Westbrook?"

Brittney stared at him, her face blank, lips unmoving.

"Fine. We'll ask again when your lawyer is present," the officer said.

"Just admit it," I told her. "You basically have already."

Her eyes cut to me. "You got a problem with me lawyering up, Rush? Isn't that what you did?"

My back teeth came together. "I didn't kill Brynne," I ground out.

"Well, I didn't try and run down your worshippers."

"They pulled you out of the driver's seat of my fucking car!" I burst out.

"And you were the last person to see my best friend alive!" she yelled back and flung out her hand to point at me. "She left claw marks on your arm the night you killed her!"

A flash of silver caught my eye, and I stopped listening to her words to zero in on it. Shooting around Landry, I snatched Brittney's arm off the bed, yanking upward. "Where did you get this bracelet?" I demanded, pulling her arm even closer for a better look.

"Ow!" she wailed. "You're hurting me. Help, officers!"

"You are so fake Barbie is jealous," Landry declared. "But I sure as hell won't be again."

Wait. Landry was jealous of Brittney?

"Sir, let go of the patient." Officer asshole stepped forward, caressing his belt again.

I ignored them, still staring at the silver chain, my heart pounding so hard I could feel it pulsing in my feet. "Where did you get this?"

She ripped her arm back at the same time the officer grabbed me to pull me away.

I wrenched free from the man and glared. "Do not touch me."

Landry appeared between me and the cop, wrapping her arm around my waist and pressing close.

"I mean it, Britt," I spat, hating that I fell into the nick-name so easily. "Where did you get that?"

"It's none of your business."

"The hell it isn't!" I roared.

Landry pulled back, eyes wide. "Jason? What's wrong?" Her gaze strayed to the bracelet circling Brittney's wrist.

In an attempt to hide it, Brittney shoved her hand under the blankets.

I laughed, a mocking sound. "Too late. I already saw it," I spat. "I never would have guessed," I said, disgust twisting through my heart like a worm inside a rotten apple. "You make me sick."

Brittney went colorless. Maybe she saw the absolute hatred suddenly consuming me. Maybe she finally realized she went too fucking far and I knew her secret.

"R-Rush—"

The door to the room opened, cracking through the unrelenting tension like a bullet. We all turned, caught off guard by the intrusion. Bodhi stepped into the room, followed closely by Blair.

"This is a private room." The officer stepped forward. "You need to leave."

"Bodhi," Brittney exclaimed from the bed.

Bodhi whipped around to see her. His long dirty-blond waves were not tied back, so they floated out around him like a curtain.

"Britt?" he asked as if he couldn't believe what he saw.

I was suspicious and not quite ready to believe he didn't know she was in town.

"Who are you?" the officer asked, his partner lifting his notebook and pen, ready to write.

"Seriously, man. Just use your phone." Win admonished him.

"Bodhi Lawson," he told the cop. "This is William Blair."

"Just Blair." He informed him.

"Lawson," the officer with the notebook said and went flipping through the pages. "Brynne Lawson's brother?"

"Yes."

"I asked them to come," I explained, waving them farther inside, my eyes going back to the hand Brittney was hiding under the blankets.

"What's this about?" Bodhi asked. His stare found Win and narrowed. "What's *he* doing here?"

Win went swinging, his fist catching Bodhi right in the eye. "No more, Malibu Barbie," he spat, reaching down to haul Bodhi up to hammer him again.

The officers and Blair rushed to pull them apart, but I just stood there and stared.

Win was restrained by an officer he could easily take. "You so much as look at him again and you're going to be picking your teeth up off this floor!"

"Win," Lars said, trying to calm him.

"Don't Win me," he spat. "I've fucking had it! Ever since this asshole came to town, it's been one thing after another."

He ripped free of the cop and lunged at Bodhi again at the same time the door swung open.

"Whoa," a deep voice intoned, and without hesitation, he inserted himself in the middle, cuffing Win around the waist with one tattooed arm and towing him back. "That's enough."

"Tell me that when he takes a shot at Wes!"

Max rumbled and turned to glare at Bodhi. "You try and hit my brother?"

"I don't know any Wes," he said, eye already bruising.

"He meant Lars, asshole," Win spat.

"He just looked at me," Lars whispered to Max.

Max grunted and turned his back on Bodhi. With a hard glance at Win, he said, "Chill out. Today's been long enough without me having to bail your ass out of jail."

"Stay over there," Win ordered Bodhi and Blair.

"These your new friends, Rush?" Blair asked. "Interesting choice."

"Why, because they're loyal?" I snapped. Then I turned to Brittney. "Because they don't lie."

"Here's your trauma latte," Max said, plucking a paper cup out of the drink holder in his hand and holding it out to Landry.

"Thank you," she said, taking a sip instantly. She swallowed gingerly, and my mood plummeted further. She needed stitches. "Mm, it's warm."

"You doing okay?" he asked her.

She nodded, eyes roaming his arm and shoulder. "This is the first time I've seen all your tattoos."

I noticed then he was only wearing a white tank.

"This isn't all of them. Want me to take off my shirt?" Max mused.

"Bro, I will pluck your eyeballs out and use them as bowling balls," I warned.

"Creative," Win mused.

"Sir, was that a threat?" the officer asked, the one scribbling in his damned notebook.

Landry giggled. She fucking giggled.

I stalked across the room and grabbed Max by the back of the neck and pulled him away, pushing him toward Lars. "Where the hell is Wes? Isn't he who we texted for coffee?"

"You think I'm going to let Wes come back here with that little criminal over there?" Max replied.

Brittney gasped. "Me?"

"Fair enough," I allowed.

"I think that's enough for today," the officer announced. "You have confirmed that you do in fact know this woman from previous encounters. And we already took your statements."

"And asked one billion questions," Landry muttered.

"If we need further information, we will contact you." The man finished, to his credit, not acknowledging Landry's sass.

It was for the best. I wouldn't want to have to Win out on him.

I glanced back at Bodhi, surprised to see he was looking at me. "What is going on?"

"You all can talk somewhere else," the officer said, going to the door and motioning us out.

"I'm tired," Brittney declared as if that was somehow going to make anyone move faster.

"Here's good," I said, punctuating the words by crossing my arms over my chest.

"If you refuse to leave—"

I held up my hand, cutting off the man's words. "I'm not refusing, but I have come across some new information, and I think you and your partner will want to hear this." I glanced at the notebook lover. "Get your pencil ready."

"It's a pen." He sneered.

"Even better." I nodded. "The ink is permanent."

"I want to rest," Brittney whined.

I swung back to the bed and stalked toward her, planting my hands on either side of her body on the mattress. "What's the matter, Britt? Worried I'm going to tell everyone that *you're* the one who killed Brynne?"

Her face went blank. Then shock bloomed over it, and her mouth dropped. I watched her struggle for several heartbeats as absolute horror flashed in her eyes, the swell of tears washing it away. "What did you just say?" she rasped.

I had to hand it to her. She was convincing.

I glanced at Bodhi. "Britt here is the one who killed your sister."

"How dare you?" She burst out, lifting her hand and slapping me so hard across the face my skin stung.

Landry gasped and rushed forward, but I straightened to my full height and inserted myself between the two women.

"You have some damn nerve accusing me of that!" Brittney screamed. "I would never do that to Brynne. Ever. I loved her! She was my best friend."

"I loved her too," I said quietly. No one ever believed that, though.

Bodhi stepped forward. "Rush, why would you say that? What makes you think it was her?"

"He's lying," Brittney accused.

"The bracelet," I said as it really hit me that I might actually find out who did this after all.

I'll finally know the truth.

"Oh my God! What is your fascination with this bracelet? It's mine!"

"It was Brynne's first."

Everyone fell silent, the tension in the room growing thick.

"No," she finally said. "This is mine. It wasn't hers."

"Then where did you get it?"

She remained quiet.

With a noise, I turned to Bodhi, knowing he probably wouldn't believe me, but he couldn't deny physical proof.

"Do you remember when Brynne told me she loved me?" I asked, the memory sticking in my throat like a giant wad of gum.

"It was the beginning of the end," Bodhi said, his eyes flat.

"Maybe," I countered. "But I tried to stop it. I bought that bracelet for her. I had it custom made. It's one of a kind. Silver. The chain has a diamond heart lined with silver. And beside it is an infinity symbol with four diamonds. I gave it to her and told her I would always be her brother. And I would always be there for her even if we couldn't be as close as we once were."

Heavy sadness draped over everything. It weighed on my shoulders and squeezed my chest. "I couldn't love her the way she wanted, but that didn't mean I didn't love her at all."

Bodhi turned his face away.

Landry wound her arms around me from behind. Startled, I glanced around, noting her sling hanging off her neck.

"Put that back on," I said, voice gravelly. I turned so we were facing each other.

"Later." She hugged me again.

I cupped the back of her head and held her to me while my eyes went back to my old friend. "Do you remember?" I pressed. "Do you remember the bracelet?"

He nodded. "She barely wore it. She said it was too special."

"She had it on the night she died."

Bodhi's head whipped up. "What?"

I nodded. "I remembered some from that night." I then told him about how I'd pulled over and she ran off. "She was wearing it. I saw it when she scratched me." *Actually, before she kissed me, but now is not the time to bring that shit up.*

"Don't believe him, Bodhi. He's lying. That's all he does," Brittney spat.

I turned, the smolder of my stare making her eyes drop. "I'm not the one wearing the bracelet Brynne had on when she died."

"Ma'am, we will need to see the bracelet," the policeman said.

"It wasn't in the photos," I murmured, thinking back to when they'd interrogated me.

"What photos?" Brittney asked.

"The photos the cops forced me to see. Photo after photo of her dead body," I said, cold.

Brittney flinched, but I was beyond caring. "You're lying." The accusation might have stung any other time, but now it just seemed weak.

"There's a B engraved on the back of the diamond heart," I said, and her eyes widened. "And the series of numbers on the disk by the clasp... It's her birthday."

"No," Brittney whispered, horror drenching her expression and voice.

"It's there, isn't it?" I pressed. "Because that bracelet is Brynne's."

Bodhi rushed across the room and yanked her arm from beneath the covers. A stricken sound tore out of him when he saw the bracelet. Her arm was limp when he fumbled with the clasp and pulled it off her wrist.

"There's a B on the heart," he told the room, then shifted it around to look at the small tag on the clasp. The numbers were so small he had to lift it up. "Seven. Twenty-two. Two thousand three." He glanced up, eyes glazed. "That's my birthday. *Our* birthday."

I nodded. I thought it would feel good to prove my innocence. To know for sure that I didn't do that to my own sister.

I didn't feel good right now. If anything, I felt worse.

"How could you do it?" I whispered to Brittney.

"It wasn't me," she said, her voice hollow and empty.

"Then how the hell do you have my sister's bracelet?" Bodhi accused.

"We're going to need to take that into evidence," the officer said. I'd forgotten they were even there. "We're also going to need you to come into the station, Miss Marsh, for questioning regarding the murder of Brynne Lawson."

"I didn't do it!"

"We can come back with an arrest warrant. Do yourself a favor and don't try and run."

I was back to being numb. Completely devoid. There was too much to process. Too much to unpack.

Small hands found their way against my cheeks, and a slim body stretched up to reach for my lips. I was too frozen to bend down, though, too caught in chaos to respond.

But that was my little siren's specialty, wasn't it? Her ability to reach into the worst anarchy and lure me out of the storm.

Suddenly, her lips brushed over mine. Once, twice, before settling completely. They moved sensually, rubbing over mine to create sparks of electricity and restart my brain. I groaned, opening for her as the tip of her tongue swiped against my lower lip.

Awareness flooded my system, her presence canceling out everything else, and I moaned low in my throat and wrapped my arms around her to deepen the kiss.

Her chest crushed against mine, and I felt her cotton-covered toes brush against my legs as I kissed her like a man starved.

A throat cleared a few times nearby. I ignored it in favor

of slurping my sanity right off her coffee-and-copper-flavored tongue.

"Rush," someone called, and I felt a hand against my shoulder.

I grunted and kissed her deeper, possession like hot lava in my veins.

Landry winced slightly, and then that coffee taste turned bitter with fresh blood.

I ripped back instantly, dragging in a ragged breath. "*Fuck*," I spat. "Let me see."

"It's fine."

"Open your mouth right now, Landry."

Her tongue was bleeding worse than before.

"Get the doctor," I told Max who was standing literally right there. "Bro, why are you up my girl's ass?"

"I picked her up so you could eat her face," Max mused. "You're welcome."

I blanched and looked back at Landry.

She giggled. "I couldn't reach. You were off in la-la land."

"La-la land?" I echoed.

"You needed a kiss."

I pursed my lips, then kissed the tip of her nose. When I looked back at Max, I said, "Don't ever be picking up my girl and holding her while I kiss her again."

"Don't worry about it, bro. I prefer dick, one in particular."

This asshole.

"It better be only one." Win glowered.

I heard Landry swallow, and the tang of her blood bloomed across my tongue all over again. I swung her up into my arms. "You're getting stitches," I declared. "Right now."

"No, I'm not."

"I will get your dad's whistle and blow it myself," I warned.

"You'd have to pry it out of his mouth first," she sassed.

"Don't sass me with a bloody mouth."

Win pulled open the door and held it so I could find Coach and a doctor.

"I don't want stitches in my tongue," she wailed. "It's going to hurt!"

I paused in walking. "I'll hold your hand, baby."

"It was Cobalt!" Brittney yelled behind us. "Cobalt gave me the bracelet."

"I knew it," Blair said from a nearby corner.

Still holding Landry, I pivoted to face the girl in the bed. "Excuse me?"

"It was Cobalt. He gave me the bracelet. He said it was a gift. He said he got it for me. The B was for Brittney, not Brynne!" She started to sob, burying her face in her hands. "I never even looked at the birthdate. I just figured it was a serial number or something."

I glanced at Landry, and she nodded.

I moved to hand her to Max, and he held out his arms. Seeing his sleeve of tattoos, I changed direction and handed her to Win instead. I was going to have to do something about that. Later.

"Go find the doctor," I told him. "I'll be right there."

"No," Landry protested, trying to wiggle out of Win's grasp. Win was as big as me, though, so there was no use in trying to escape. "I want to stay."

"I'll be right behind you, baby," I said. "I won't be long. You need medical attention. That's more important."

"It's not!"

"I'll tell you everything that happens when I find you."

She coughed a little, the sound gurgly with blood.

Win frowned, and I caught his eye. "I'm going," he said, turning away with her. "C'mon, angel."

"I'll stay with Rush."

Win's shoes made a horrible screech against the tile when he stopped. "I will not leave you here with that Malibu Barbie. Get walking."

"Just go," I told him. "Hold Landry's hand for me until I get there."

The three of them moved out, and I noticed Max hanging back. I glanced at him with a lifted eyebrow. "I'll hang. Otherwise, you're outnumbered."

I nodded and turned back to Brittney who was still sobbing on the bed.

"Britt," I said the second I was beside her.

She dropped her hands and looked up at me, complete misery in her eyes. "I swear I'm telling the truth. I did it, okay?" she confessed, looking at the cops. "I threw the dummy in the pool. I trashed the locker room. I pretended to be a student at Westbrook to get close to Landry and Lars. I came in the emergency door in the locker room and took your car keys. I tried to run them over with your car." She sucked in a breath. "I just wanted them to know how awful you were. I didn't want anyone else to die because of you."

"I. Didn't. Kill. Brynne," I gritted out. It was hard, really fucking hard, to feel any sense of empathy for her after she'd just admitted to all that shit.

"I know that now," she said. "It was him all along."

"Cobalt?" Bodhi questioned from the end of the bed.

She nodded. "He was so sweet to me after Brynne. I was such a mess, and I miss her so much. But he was there. He made things a little more bearable. I... I fell in love with him."

"And then what?" I asked, cold. Clinical. Unrelenting. I wanted the answers. I deserved them. Hell, we all did.

She could cry about her bad taste in men later.

"He hated you so much," she said, looking at me. "He blamed you for Brynne's death. We all did. He kept saying you didn't deserve a second chance when Brynne wouldn't get one. He wanted you to be punished. To go to jail for what you did."

I paced away from the bed. It was Cobalt this whole time. This whole fucking time. Brynne ran back to the party that night and got in Cobalt's car. And he killed her.

He had to have. There was no other explanation.

"As time went on, he seemed to get more insistent and angrier that you weren't in jail," Brittney professed. "And then he gave me this bracelet. Told me he loved me. He said everything would be perfect between us if you were in jail and Brynne's killer was brought to justice.

"So I decided to push you. To make everyone here doubt you. I thought you would confess. I thought it would make everyone happy."

"He was getting nervous," Blair said, stepping into the conversation. "I went to him. Told him I saw Brynne get into his car that night." Brittney gasped, and Blair looked at me. "He wanted you to go down so he wouldn't."

I nodded. "They couldn't put him in jail for a crime that was already solved."

"You saw Brynne that night?" Brittney asked Blair.

He nodded. "Yeah. I was super drunk. It took a while to remember. Then I wasn't sure if I saw what I saw. So I asked Cobalt about it. Figured I could trust my captain."

"But you went to rehab."

"Yeah, because Cobalt told everyone, including my parents, that I was an alcoholic to discredit what I saw."

"Can this be verified?" one of the officers asked. The other was scribbling furiously in his notebook.

Blair nodded. "Oh yeah. There are records of my rehab

stay and everything. I'm sure my parents will tell you that Cobalt went to them in 'concern.'"

"He manipulated everyone," Bodhi said, his voice shell-shocked and bleak. His eyes lifted to mine, and I saw the regret shining in them.

I looked away. I didn't want his regret. I wanted the truth.

"If he gave you that bracelet, it's because he took it off Brynne's body when she died."

Bodhi jerked as though I'd hit him.

I turned to the cops. "If he took one thing off her body, maybe he took something else. They never found her phone." I knew because they had ransacked my entire house looking for it.

The officers both nodded. "We'll get a search warrant immediately. No one in this room is to divulge any of this information."

I started for the door.

"Wait! Where are you going?" Brittney yelled.

"To hold my girl's hand. She's getting stitches."

"I'm so sorry." She dissolved into a puddle of sobbing and tears once more.

"That's why we have police," I said, patting one of the officers' shoulders on my way past.

"We will likely have more questions."

"You know where to find me," I replied.

Max pulled open the door, and I strode through.

"Seriously, Rush?" Bodhi questioned, his voice incredulous. "You're just leaving?"

I don't know why he was so surprised.

"The truth's out, Bodhi. We can all have peace now. Including Brynne," I said, feeling a lump form in my throat. "Now, if you'll excuse me, my family is waiting."

38

LANDRY

Elite Group Chat

Pizza party at my house tonight!

Kruger: We can't have a party at Coach's house. It's like against the law.
Jamie: Bro, is his whistle gonna be there? I need to hear myself chew.

I hid it.

Ryan: Scrappy for the win!
Max: Who added me to this stupid chat?

Max has left the chat.
Wes added Max to the chat.

Wes: Welcome back, Maxi.

Win: Make sure the pizza is nut-free.

Jamie: Bro, we all know the only nuts Lars can have are yours.

Madison: Jamie Michael Owens, is this how you talk to your friends in chat?

Jamie: Maddie? How'd you get in here?

Did you think I'd be the only girl here?

Rory: We're watching you, Jamie. *eyeball emoji*

Max: I don't want to be here.

Max has left the chat.

Lars added Max to the chat.

Max: Seriously, Lars?

Lars: *angel emoji*

Rush: Get your asses to Coach's house for pizza.

Kruger: For real, is Coach gonna be there? I like to have my meals in peace.

Ryan: Us too, but we still let you come.

Kruger: Harsh.

Prism: *laughing emoji*

Kruger: P, do you ever type anything other than emojis?

Prism: *Monkey covering his eyes emoji*

Wes: I like his emojis. It's like deciphering a code.

Dad won't be home for a while.

Kruger: I'll be there.

Rory: See everyone soon! I'll bring nail polish so we can do each other's nails!

Prism: *nail painting emoji*

416

Ryan: Who let them in here?
Rory: Are you saying you don't want me here?
Ryan: Now, baby...

Max has muted the chat.

Jamie: He is so rude. I'll text him and tell him.
Wes: I'll text him too.

Max has unmuted the chat.

Max: I hate it here.
Wes: Come upstairs, and I'll make it up to you.
Kruger: *barfing emojis*
Jamie: You being a homophobe, Kruger?
Prism: *pride flag emoji*
Jamie: We love you, P!
Kruger: Does anyone here really even like me? *giant question mark emoji*

Of course we do! You should bring Jess for pizza.

Kruger: She's scared of all of you.
Rory: I texted her. She said she'll come.
Madison: Kruger, pick her up on your way.
Jamie: You should just date her, Kruger. She fits right in.
Kruger: She's my friend.
Ryan: Add some benefits.
Rush: Bro, yeah.
Kruger: Listen, dickheads, don't be talking about Jess like that.
Win: Kruger and Jess sitting in a tree...
Lars: K-I-S-S-I-N-G
Kruger: I'm not coming.

Prism: I'll pick up Jess on my way then.

Kruger: The one time you text with words it's to BETRAY me.

Prism: *car emoji*

Kruger: Left tire marks on my feelings.

Max: Everyone shut up. I'm trying to get some, and this beeping phone is killing the mood.

Jamie: We should have let him leave the chat.

See you guys later! *pizza emoji*

"Our friends are the best," I said, tossing aside my phone to curl closer to Jason.

Across from my bed, the lights on the large mirror cast a soft glow over the room. Outside, the sun was sinking, not long until it would be dark.

"That entire chat group is ridiculous."

"But you love them," I sang.

He *so* loved them. Even Ryan. He just liked pretending he didn't. I understood, though. It was his learned instinct to protect his heart the best way he knew how. Someday, though, I knew he would fully trust he didn't have to protect it from Elite.

"No," he refused. "I love you. I like them."

I pressed a kiss against his shirtless chest. I could have lived with him forever without those three little words, but now that I had them, I was never going to give them back.

"What about Lars?"

He made a sound, curling his hand around my hip. "Lars knows who he is to me."

Yeah, his kidney. Boys are so weird.

"Hey, Jay?" I called, looking up at him.

"Hm?"

"I love you too."

With a growl, he rolled, pushing me beneath him, and touched his mouth to mine. I sank into the kiss with a sigh, lifting my chin and flicking my tongue toward his. He made a sound and returned the caress but kept the tongue action shallow. I whined in frustration, and he smiled into the kiss, making me forget I was annoyed.

Lifting my head off the pillow, I kissed that smile deeper, loving it was there and knowing I was the reason. Groaning, he cupped the back of my head, cradling it in place, and kissed me deep the way I craved.

Too soon, he eased back, teasing my lips with light grazes. "That's enough, little siren."

"Jay," I whined.

His low chuckle had me arching into him like a cat, rubbing myself against his defined naked torso. "You know better," he warned. "You have stitches in your tongue."

"Make it up to me," I demanded.

His eyebrow arched at my audacity. I had to bite back a laugh. "Excuse me?"

"I said if you won't kiss me good, then make it up to me."

"And how should I make it up to you? Hmm?" he mused, hand traveling between our bodies and down to the waistband of my shorts.

"Better make it good," I threatened.

His hand stilled. "Or what?"

"Or I'll have to find it somewhere else."

He sucked in a breath, and one hand came up to collar my throat, applying light pressure. "What the hell did you just say to me?"

I smiled serenely.

His eyes narrowed into black slits, and my stomach jumped in anticipation.

Leaving his hand around my throat, he shoved his pants down just enough to let out his cock. I smirked seeing how hard he was.

"Did you just smirk, you little brat?"

I smirked again.

He growled. The hand at my neck tightened enough that a sliver of panic cracked through me like lightning. "If I didn't love you so damn much, I'd put that tongue to work and make you explain to the doctor why all your stitches ripped out."

I swallowed, the force of it pressing against his tight grip.

He moved fast, ripping aside the shorts and underwear I was wearing and shoving his rock-hard erection right into my core. My body bucked, and I groaned, chin falling back. He let go of my neck and started to thrust, fucking into me at an unforgiving pace. The fabric of my clothes bunched against us, creating friction as he pistoned his hips.

Downstairs, the front door slammed, and Jason's thrusts stilled.

"I'm home!" Dad yelled, and our eyes flew to each other's.

"I thought he wasn't coming home until later," Jason growled.

"I guess he changed his mind."

Challenge and disobedience flashed in those darker-than-dark eyes, and he started hammering into me again. "I'm not stopping until I'm dripping with your orgasm and mine is swimming around in your womb," he bit out, dragging his shaft out, then pushing back in. "If you don't want Daddy to see what his princess looks like stuffed full of a cock I know would make him feel inferior, you better come for me."

I gasped, his crude words painting a taboo image as I pictured my dad walking in here to see Jason drilling me into the bed.

"You here?" Dad yelled up the stairs.

Jason shoved his hand up my shirt and pinched my nipple, making me moan.

"Come for me, little siren," Jason grunted, the veins in his neck standing out.

I shoved my heels into his ass and pushed him deep. My body spasmed around him as I did exactly what he asked. I felt him spill inside me, the force of his jerking like a massage against my sensitive walls. The second he was done, he yanked out of me and rolled off the bed to stand, yanking up his sweats as he went.

He tossed the lilac throw across my lower half, then spun to the window, turning his back and crossing his arms.

My entire body jolted when my bedroom door swung open. "Oh. You're here."

My heart was thumping so hard I couldn't catch my breath, but I forced myself up to lean against the headboard in a sitting position.

"Did you think I'd be anywhere else?" Jason replied, his voice so normal and not at all out of breath.

His cum was smearing my thighs, dampening my shorts beneath the blanket, and all I could do was wonder if this room smelled like sex.

"What the hell are you doing?"

I jumped, Dad's sudden words startling me out of the sex haze Jason had forced me into.

"Agh!" I gasped, tugging the blanket up higher into my lap.

Dad turned accusatory eyes on Jason. "What the hell did you do to her?"

Jason turned casually from the window, mildly glancing at me and then back at my father. "Her shoulder was hurting, so I told her to take a nap."

Dad eyed me. "You need to go back to the doctor."

"I'm fine."

"Do you want me to kick him out of the house?"

"Don't sound so hopeful," Jason mused.

I rolled my eyes. "Of course not, Dad." Then I added, "Everyone is coming over for pizza."

Dad blanched. "You invited those mouth-breathers to my house?"

"They're my friends, Dad."

He made a face. "Fine. I'm getting my whistle."

"Does that mean you're staying?" Jason asked.

Dad stopped on his way out. "This is my house."

"Sure, Coach."

He cleared his throat. "When we aren't at the pool, you can call me Emmet."

I inhaled.

"But not when all those ingrates are around! Then they'll think they can get away with that shit too."

Jason was quiet a moment, his stare never once leaving my dad. Suddenly, he moved across the room and closer to where Dad stood. "Does this mean you're okay with me dating your daughter?"

Dad sniffed. "Well, she could do worse."

My cheeks started to ache from the smile gracing my face.

"I'm gonna marry her one day," Jason warned.

I made a surprised sound.

Jay glanced at me. "Like you didn't know," he deadpanned. "I'm never letting you go."

"I'm not paying for the wedding," Dad snapped.

"Dad!"

"I didn't ask you to," Jason clapped back.

Dad exhaled like he was in pain. "I know I've been hard on you, but it's only because I cared. I know it doesn't seem like it, but I believe in you. And I'll be honored to call you son."

"So can I call you Dad instead of Emmet?" Jason pushed.

"When my daughter has a ring on her finger, you can call me Dad. Until then, it's Emmet."

"Yes, sir," Jason said and stuck his hand out between them. Dad shook, and my heart expanded.

"Put a shirt on, would you? This ain't Pornhub."

"What do you know about Pornhub, Coach?"

"Ew!" I shrieked. Then I gagged.

"It's Emmet," Dad barked and then left, shutting the door behind him.

Jason dove back on the bed, his upper body pinning my lower one. "My cum is all over your thighs, isn't it?"

"My father finally accepted you, and you're asking about that?"

"He gave me his acceptance *while* my cum was all over your thighs." Jason grinned. "If only he knew."

"You're terrible."

"But you love me?"

I sighed. "Of course I do."

The door flung back open. "Hey, Rush."

We both looked up, and Dad blanched seeing him partially on top of me. "What the hell are you doing in my house?"

"Checking her tongue." Jason lied. "She said it hurt."

I nodded piteously.

Dad muttered a bunch of words under his breath that included *pack of lies.*

"You wanted to ask me something, C—ah, Emmet?"

Dad cleared his throat. "What happened to your friend?"

"My friend?"

Dad made a sour face and then gestured to his head. "You know, the one with all the hair?"

I felt Jason's surprise. "Bodhi?"

Dad nodded. "Yeah, him."

"He went back to California."

"He did?" Was that a brief flash of disappointment? It couldn't be. "That's good."

"Why do you ask?" Jason asked. Now who was being the brat?

Dad looked like a deer caught in a pair of headlights for a moment, but then he recovered to say, "Just wanted to make sure he wasn't still around to cause more trouble for my swimmers."

"Good looking out, Coach."

Dad glowered.

"I mean Emmet." Jason corrected himself. "Thanks for having our backs. But yeah, he went back to California. I probably won't see him again."

"Shame."

"What?" I exclaimed.

Once again, Dad looked like he'd swallowed three whole lemons. "I mean, 'cause I know he swims. I'm always on the lookout for good swimmers."

"How do you know he swims?" Jason asked.

"You think he can come in here taking shots at my swimmers and me not look into him?"

"Right," Jay said. 'Well, it doesn't matter anyway. He told me he quit."

Dad grunted. "Whatever. Put on a shirt," he said and slammed the door behind him.

"What the fuck was that?" Jay asked.

"I'm not sure," I said.

Downstairs, the front door slammed. "Pizza's here!" Jamie yelled.

"Did you just walk into my house without knocking?" Dad roared.

"Coach? I thought you weren't going to be home," Jamie hollered.

"Surprise, assholes!"

I listened as he stomped up the stairs and down the hall to his room.

I held my breath, and moments later, he yelled, "Where the hell is my whistle?"

Jason glanced at me. "You really hid it?"

I nodded.

Jay whistled. "Woman, you got bigger balls than some of the men I know."

I laughed. "We better get down there before World War III breaks loose."

After quickly cleaning up, I was pulling on a fresh pair of leggings and one of Jason's T-shirts when his strong arms circled me from behind.

"Thanks for really looking at me, little siren. For believing in me when no one else would and for luring me out of the chaos and into your arms."

I turned in his hold, looping my arms around his neck. "Loving you is so easy, Jay. You did the hard part. I'm so proud of you. Thank you for finding your way home."

He pulled me in, and I snuggled close, ignoring the pandemonium erupting downstairs.

Maybe to him, I was a siren.

But to me? It was him.

EPILOGUE

A FEW WEEKS LATER...

Rush

Soft peach and gold met the endless blue horizon as the sun lifted from her slumber to dawn over the white-capped waves crashing against the Malibu beach.

Landry stood facing the spectacular sunrise with her back fitted closely against my chest as my arms bracketed her sides. Sea-drenched air filled my lungs and tugged at my bedhead.

California might not be home anymore, but it was still part of me. And I still loved it here. Secretly, I hoped Landry and I would someday have our own beachfront Malibu home where I could make love to her in the sand and have her ride my lap while the sun rose behind us. Then afterward, I'd drive off in my sparkling Corvette to a job where I helped create the next great Chevy model.

It was a cushy dream, right? But it was going to be my reality. I wouldn't accept anything less. Especially after living in a headspace where I thought I didn't even deserve the life I had.

I got swallowed up in chaos. Browbeaten by the disbelief of others, their mistrust so dark it muddied my own waters. But the little siren in my arms dove right into those murky depths and literally breathed life right into me.

I hadn't been drowning in the pool that day, but she did save me.

As I stood there watching a bodacious Malibu sunrise with my heart in my arms, I thought that maybe karma hadn't been trying to take me out. Maybe karma was trying to give me what I deserved. And to do that, it had to break me down so I could be reconstructed into a better model.

"I love you," I rumbled into Landry's ear, pressing the words close so the wind didn't snatch them away.

"I love you, Jay," she returned, pivoting in my hold and lifting her arms to loop around my neck. Partway there, she changed her mind to instead caress the new tattoo covering my shoulder.

I turned slightly so she could get a full view, secretly ecstatic she loved it so much. I knew she would, though, the way I saw her ogling Max's sleeve when she thought I wasn't looking.

If my girl wanted to ogle tattoos, she could ogle mine. Only mine.

"I still can't believe you got a tattoo," she said, lovingly tracing the tail of the mermaid.

"You can stare at me now instead of Max," I said, dry.

"I don't stare at Max!" she argued, but her finger paused, and she glanced up. "Is that why you did this?"

I shrugged the inked shoulder.

"Jason!"

"Landry!"

"You can't just get a permanent tattoo because you think I

want to look at it," she declared. I didn't know why she bothered. The ink was already on me.

"Don't you?" I teased.

"I loved you just as much before you got it."

"You licked it when we were having sex last night," I deadpanned.

She giggled but then turned serious. "You shouldn't mark up your body because you think that's what I want. I love you exactly the way you are."

I believed her. She'd proven it time and time again.

"Baby, I would make my body your roadmap if you wanted me to. This isn't even the first tattoo I got because of you. It's just one everyone else can see."

Her gemlike eyes glittered. "What's the first?"

Taking her hand, I tugged it to lie over my heart. "Right here, little siren. You are permanently imprinted on my heart."

"Jay." She sighed, leaning in to kiss my chest, then gliding over to kiss the ink. "It is beautiful," she murmured, gazing at it again.

"That's because it's of you."

She smiled softly at the design that was most definitely inspired by her. The black and white likeness covered the entire outside of my shoulder. A circular pattern of wild ocean waves about to crash. But posed in the center was a mermaid—*a siren*—with wild chin-length hair and a gracefully arched tail. One arm reached up and the other back as she floated calmly amid the chaos, but nothing touched her.

That was who she was to me. Who she would always be. A reprieve from life's most volatile storm and the center of my entire world.

The giant glass slider behind us opened, and I glanced around at my mom who was padding across the deck with a tiny glass of OJ in her hand and an even tinier bikini on her body.

"Mom," I groaned. "Don't you own a bigger bathing suit?"

"And what would you have me do, Jason? Should I put on some moo-moo and snub all the beautiful fabrics that all the best designers have sent over?"

I groaned. "My friends are here."

Landry slipped out of my arms to shyly face my mom. It was kinda cute that she was so nervous around her. "Don't listen to him, Mrs. Rush. If I had your body, I'd walk around naked!"

"The hell you would!" I demanded.

Mom gasped. "Jason! How dare you speak to her this way?"

"Sorry," I muttered. Then I gave Landry a dark stare. I wasn't having it.

Mom turned to Landry. "It's Misa, honey. And when you're ready, you can call me Mom."

Landry blushed, and I forgot I was mad about her walking around buck-ass naked.

"And what is this nonsense about you not having a perfect body? Posh," she said in her perfectly snooty way. "Oh, to be young again. Your skin is so tight! And you know, I mentioned to a few friends that my Jason was bringing home the love of his life, and they sent me some things for you. Come, try them on."

"I couldn't possibly," Landry protested.

"But their feelings will be hurt if I don't send them photos."

Landry glanced at me, and I winked. "Go on. Get that sweet ass in a new bathing suit."

"Jason, honestly."

"I hear the way Dad talks to you," I deadpanned.

"I have no idea what you mean," she objected, prim.

Yeah, right.

As Mom led Landry away, I thought better of my convincing. "Those bikinis better be bigger than the one you got on!"

Mom stopped and glanced back. "Fashion has no rules."

"Well, I do."

Landry's laugh floated on the breeze.

"I truly raised him better," Mom told her.

She laughed again.

"Last time I bring everyone out here for spring break," I muttered.

"Oh, Jason?"

I looked back at Mom. "Yeah?"

"The things you asked for are in the driveway."

I gave a whoop of glee and raced past the women on the way inside. Skidding to a stop near the sofa, I nearly collided with the housekeeper when I U-turned to go back outside.

"Sorry," I called.

She laughed. "Nice to have you home."

Landry looked up when I ran back over.

I kissed her head. "I'll be back in a few," I said, then raced off again.

"Where are you going?" she called.

"To see my kidney!"

"Tell me honestly, honey. Does he need therapy?" I heard Mom question Landry behind me. I kept going. I'd let Landry deal with that one.

I raced through the giant house and flung open Lars and Win's door. The mattress bounced when I leaped on it, landing on top of them both.

Grunts and shouts of surprise rose from beneath me.

"Get up, assholes," I yelled.

A hand broke free of the blankets to slap against my head and push me away. "Go away, Rush."

There was a beat of silence and then, "What the fuck, Rush?" Win bolted up, eyes wide with his bedhead poppin'. "What the hell are you doing in bed with us?" he demanded.

Lars made a sound and rolled, blinking open his pale eyes to look at us both. "Is this some weird dream?"

I laughed.

"You better not be dreaming of any other men but me," Win warned him. Then to me, he ordered, "Seriously, asshole, get out of my bed."

"I came for Lars."

"Lars is mine," Win snapped.

Lars reached out and patted Win's bare chest. "All yours, *min hund.*"

Win gave me a superior glare, and I rolled my eyes.

"I got you a present."

Lars sat up. "A present?"

"I did not okay this gift for you to use it against me," Win muttered.

"You know about this?" Lars asked.

Win sighed. "Of course."

Lars glanced at me, and I shrugged. "What kind of kidney would I be if I didn't clear something like this through your heart?"

"Win is not the boss of me," Lars grumped.

I kinda saw now why Win called him a grumpy angel.

"So does that mean you don't want your present?"

"I didn't say that."

Win and I laughed.

"Jason Glenn Rush!" a familiar voice hollered from the doorway.

"Did my mother tell you my middle name?" I groaned.

Landry strolled into the room, stopping at the end of the king-size bed to put her fists on her hips. "Why are you in bed with Lars and Win?"

CAMBRIA HEBERT

I turned to answer her, but my tongue turned to sawdust and blew right out of my mouth.

I croaked.

She smirked.

I pointed.

Win and Lars laughed.

"Oh hells no!" I roared and leaped out of the bed with all the agility I possessed. As I went, I dragged the comforter off the bed and flung it around her.

"Woman! Did I not just tell you to not walk around naked?"

"I'm hardly naked."

"*Playboy* bunnies show less than you just did!"

"I don't know, bro. I saw your mom's feature."

I threw up in the back of my mouth. Spewed it right up. Gagging, I turned to Win. "You looked at my mom's *Playboy* feature?"

"Well, when Landry told us who your mom was, I googled her. It came up."

"No one's getting any presents!" I roared. Then I pinned Landry with a hard look. "And you. I'm spanking your ass. I won't have it."

"It's a bikini."

I scoffed. "A bikini? No. What that is, is a whole-ass sin."

Landry dropped the blanket, and a punch of lust hit me right in the dick. I made a sound as she stepped forward in the barely-there blue bikini that hugged every single place it touched.

It was strapless, basically floss, with two little diamond shapes to cover her nipples.

It was inappropriate and made me want to fuck her right there on the bed between the two gay dudes.

"Brothers really shouldn't have to see this," Lars muttered.

432

Unable to tear my eyes off her, I nodded dumbly and pointed in the direction of my bro. "Yes. That."

"So it doesn't look good?" Landry asked.

We all laughed.

"Woman, if you walk out on the beach in that, I will go to jail."

"You are so dramatic."

I reached for my shirt so I could pull it off me and put it on her. My mother was a bad woman.

Shit. I wasn't wearing a shirt.

"If you want your present, you will go put on some clothes," I told her. "Preferably something of mine."

She forgot all about her skimpy bikini, green eyes widening. "You got me a present?"

I nodded. "Lars too."

"What is it?"

"Go put some clothes on and meet me by the front door."

She turned to go, and I damn near had a stroke.

Landry turned back, concern written all over her features. "Jay?"

"Th-thong," I managed.

She giggled.

My eyes narrowed. "You doing this on purpose?"

"I would *never* do that."

I glanced at my bros. "Close your eyes!"

They did.

"Go on," I told her. She was *so* going to pay for this later.

As she left, I made sure Win and Lars weren't getting an eyeful.

She met us at the door a few minutes later. This time she was wearing a hot-pink one-piece suit with cutouts at the waist and a sheer white top over it.

I gave her a dark look, and she jumped up to kiss me.

"Brat," I grumped.

"What's going on?" Ryan asked, appearing around the corner with Rory on his back.

"Jason got us a present," Landry said, pointing between her and Lars.

"I want to see!" Rory declared.

"C'mon then, shrimp," I said and opened the wide door leading outside.

We all stepped out onto the large deck that fed into a massive staircase, which led down to the stone driveway.

Parked in the center were two Corvettes. One white. One blue. Both with giant red bows on the hoods.

Lars and Landry said not a word, just stood there like statues frozen in time.

"I think they're in shock," Win said.

"I think I am too," Rory whispered.

"Hey, what's going on out here?" Jamie said from behind. "We having a team meeting no one told us about?"

I stepped up beside Lars and Landry and waved my hand in front of their shocked faces. "Hell-ooo."

Landry blinked first. "You can't be serious."

"I never joke about Corvettes."

Her arm flailed, hand settling on my bicep. "Jason."

"You got me a Corvette?" Lars asked, finally finding his voice.

"Bro, yeah!" I said. "No kidney of mine will be driving around in a Rubicon."

To Ryan and Jamie, I said, "No offense, bros."

They laughed.

By the way, I totally paid to have Ryan's Jeep restored, and it was good as new. Even sprang for a couple new upgrades. I took care of my debts.

But these Corvettes were not that.

Lars shook his head. "Is the blue one for me?"

"Duh. It matches mine."

"So if we're the Jeep bros," Jamie whispered behind us, "does that make them the Vette bros?"

"I'm a girl," Landry mused.

Jamie seemed offended. "Bro is gender-neutral."

A wave of emotion passed over Lars's face. I think I saw his chin wobble. He ducked his head, and his shoulders rose and fell. Then he looked back up, piercing me with his icy eyes. "I can't accept this, Rush."

"Sure you can."

He shook his head. "This isn't like you buying me dinner or a pair of shoes. This is a car. A very expensive car."

"I didn't buy it."

Lars let out a string of rapid Swedish.

Win grinned. "That means he's really pissed."

I sighed. I mean, I understood their hesitation, but I also didn't. It was just money. The green stuff wasn't what mattered. It was the intent behind it.

"Look, my dad works for Corvette, okay? He practically gets these for free. Perks of the job."

"They just give out Corvettes at his job?" Ryan wondered.

I gave him a look. "My dad makes thirty million dollars a year. That's before his bonuses. And my mom is a supermodel. Trust me when I tell you they can afford it."

Kruger whistled. "Damn, P. We friends with the super rich."

I glanced around. I hadn't even heard them come out.

"It isn't even about that," I said, glancing back at the two fine specimens of car ass in my driveway. I got a hard-on just picturing them all parked in a row at the pool on campus.

"Then what's it about?" Landry asked, offering me a small smile.

My heart flipped, and I laced my fingers through hers. "Gonna make me get all emo out here in front of all the bros?"

"If you want me to drive that car, then yes," she said.

"*Ja*," Lars echoed.

Rude. But I'd do it. It paled in comparison to what they did for me.

"Lars, you are the first genuine friend I've ever had. More loyal than people I grew up with, people who should have known I could never commit murder. You never asked me for anything, and you weren't just my friend because we got thrown in the same dorm room. We both knew we had dark shit in our closets, but you didn't care. You ate with me. Defended me when other people doubted me."

"Sorry about that," Ryan muttered.

I grinned but kept going. "You jumped in the middle when Bodhi came at me. You put up with his bad mouth and didn't let it sway you. You freaking jumped in front of a car to save my girl. Then you did it again when it came back. You risked your life for me. For the girl I love. I'm your kidney," I said, getting choked up.

I'd said enough, right?

"I'm not giving you a Corvette because it's expensive and frankly the best machine man has ever created."

"Debatable," Kruger heckled.

I ignored him. He was an ass.

"I'm giving it to you because it's my passion. A piece of me. Something I love that I want to share with you both. And maybe I like the idea of you two driving around in the same thing so people know you're my people."

"He's mine first," Win insisted.

"Bro, I offered to buy you a Vette too."

"Now he's just showing off," Jamie muttered.

"Jamie! Let him finish being sweet," Madison admonished.

I leaned around the guys to smile at her and wink.

"Bro. There ain't enough cookies in the world for me to forgive that," Jamie deadpanned.

"I don't want a Corvette," Win muttered. "But I do want Lars to have more than me."

Lars glanced at Win. "You really knew about this?"

His face softened. "I really did, angel. You need a car. Might as well drive this one."

"Can I park it in the garage?" Lars asked.

Win frowned. "That's where I park the Range Rover."

"But mine is nicer."

I laughed.

Win rolled his eyes. "Of course you can, angel."

Lars glanced back down at the Corvette. "Can I look at it?"

"Bro, yeah, you can," I said, gesturing for him to go.

He took Win's hand and started down the stairs.

Win stopped partway and glanced up at me. "Thanks for this," he said. "For being the friend that Lars never had."

"That's what he is to me too."

Win held out his fist. "Brothers?"

"Brothers." I confirmed, smashing mine against his.

"C'mon, *min hund*," Lars said, anxious to get to his new ride. "Text Max and Wes. Tell them to come out here and see this!"

One down. One to go.

I turned back to Landry.

She sighed, and a grin split my face.

"Don't you give me that look," she warned.

"But, baby, you're going to look so cute driving around in that white Vette."

"I won't be able to see over the dashboard," she refuted.

Everyone laughed.

"Scrappy shrimp!" Ryan heckled.

"I had the seat lifted."

She sniffed. "I can't drive a stick. I don't even want to."

"It's an automatic."

Her eyes widened. A hand pressed to her chest. "You would allow your girlfriend to drive such an *abomination*?"

"Bro, she's funny," Kruger told everyone.

"I like the sound of her voice," Prism said.

Everyone glanced around to stare. He flushed. "I didn't mean it like that. I just meant it's not loud like everyone else's."

"I'll let that go today, P, because I'm happy," I told him.

Landry rolled her eyes.

"And yes, I will let you drive this automatic because it's a Corvette," I told her. "But you're still learning how to drive a manual."

She stuck out her tongue. "My dad will bust a vein."

"He totally will," Jamie mused.

"I already cleared this with Emmet." I used his name on purpose so she remembered we were bros now.

Okay, we might not ever be bros, but he at least scratched me off his shitlist.

"Who's Emmet?" Kruger wanted to know.

"It's Coach's first name," I replied.

"Bros! Coach has an actual name!"

"He probably used it that one time he left his office and got someone pregnant with Landry."

All the girls groaned.

Landry turned to Jamie. "Do you want to hear about your dad having sex?"

His face wrinkled. "I'd rather eat the fur off a lice-infected rodent."

"Why do you date him?" Kruger asked Madison.

Ryan laughed.

"Anyway," I said, trying to steer this train back on track. "Your dad said he was okay with it."

"You really got me a Corvette?"

"Technically, my dad got it for you. So if you don't want it, you can go tell him. And then my mother."

She grimaced.

"If you think I'm bad, just wait until you see his face when he realizes his daughter-in-law won't drive the family legacy."

PS: I'd already replaced my Z06 with a new one. It was back at Westbrook, and I was having these two beauties shipped across the country before we flew home.

"Daughter-in-law?" Ryan asked.

I shrugged. "It's just a matter of time."

"I think these two are gonna beat you and my sister to the altar," Jamie told Ryan.

"It's not a competition." Rory admonished him.

Since she was still on his back, she couldn't see the competitive glint in her boyfriend's eyes. I kept his secret. That's what bros do.

"So?" I said, giving my little siren my best puppy dog eyes.

Down in the driveway, Lars yelled "This car is sweet!"

"Sounding more American every day," Max mused as he and Wes stepped out of the house. Wes's curly hair was wild, and his lips were red and swollen.

"Wes, come see!" Lars yelled.

Wes and Max headed down the stairs.

On his way past, Max glanced down at my shoulder. "How's the tat?"

"Healed up great," I answered, turning slightly so he could see his art inked into my shoulder.

Max was a hella talented tattoo artist, so when I decided to get some art myself, of course it was him I went to. I prepared myself for a lot of jokes and cackles about me getting a "mermaid" for my girl, but he surprised me. He merely smirked and then dropped his pants. I almost left the shop. For real, I didn't need to see that. But he just laughed and showed me the clownfish he had tattooed on the inside of his thigh for Wes.

Now it totally makes sense why he calls him Nemo.

He nodded. "Let me know when you're ready to add to it."

"Soon." I confirmed.

"You're adding more?" Landry asked, surprised.

"Of course," I said. "Gotta give you more stuff to lick."

"Jason," she admonished, her cheeks turning fuchsia.

Max cackled and continued down the stairs.

Landry tugged on my hand. "Can I see my present now?"

"Whoop!" I yelled, picking her up and spinning her in a circle. She laughed as I raced down the stairs with her in my arms and plunked her down beside the car.

She went to open the door, and I put my hand on it, keeping it from opening. "Think of all the sex we can have in here."

She giggled.

I let her go, and we spent the next thirty minutes looking around inside it and me showing her how it worked. I was going to have to take her out driving later, make sure she could handle a car like this.

I knew she'd get the hang of it quickly, though. She was a scrappy little siren, after all.

At the bottom of the steps, Ryan yelled, "Who wants to get their surf on?"

Everyone hooted, and I climbed out of the passenger seat of the white Corvette. "Let's catch some waves!"

"Cowabunga!" Jamie bellowed.

I laughed. "No one says that anymore, dude."

"Bro, yeah, they do. Haven't you ever watched *Ninja Turtles?*"

I laughed more.

"If I was one of them, I'd be Michelangelo. Green bro can put away some pizza."

I nodded toward the beach. "Go get your surfboard, bro. I'll meet you in the sand."

Jamie scooped up Madison and ran off, her shrieks echoing behind them.

Ryan stepped into my path, and I stopped.

"Thanks for having us out here, bro," he said, gesturing to the massive mansion my parents called home.

"Mi casa es su casa," I countered.

"You're a class act, Rush. We might not have gotten along in the beginning, but I've always respected you. And now I'm glad to call you bro."

I held out my fist, and we pounded it out.

"I appreciate that," I said. "And thanks for coming out here to hang. Made it easier when I had to come out here and testify and give more statements."

He nodded knowingly. "It was hardly a hardship. I had no idea your parents were so bougie."

I laughed. "Like me a little more now, do you?"

The smile on his face slipped. "No. Your money or lack thereof had no influence over the way any of us sees you."

That meant something to me. It made me feel like these guys really did find me when I was at my lowest and lifted me up without expecting anything in return.

"Even if your mom is a MILF."

My mouth dropped. "Bro. What did you just say about my mom?"

He laughed. "Joking. Joking." He held up his hands. "But maybe we all looked at her *Playboy* spread."

I groaned. "I'm fucking traumatized."

"Don't tell Carrot," Ryan said. "She'll have my balls."

Two people hovered at the top of the stairs, and I nodded

at Ryan. "Don't worry, bro. I'm in no hurry to tell anyone you saw my mom naked."

"See you on the sand?"

I nodded.

"I'll grab your board for you," he offered.

"Bro, thanks."

He jogged off, and I went up the stairs toward my parents. Halfway there, Landry's small hand slipped into mine. I don't know how, but my little siren always knew when I needed her.

The four of us moved to the side out of the way of the front door.

"Mom. Dad," I said.

"Jason," Dad said. He was tall like me, but his dark hair was peppered with silver. "I want you to know that I just got off the phone with Gordon Sabatino. After all the evidence and testimonies, Cobalt pled guilty to involuntary manslaughter today. He is being sentenced next week."

Landry squeezed my hand.

"So it's really over?" I echoed, not feeling vindicated as I'd expected, instead just ready for it all to be done.

"Yes, son. It's over. There were no charges against you to be dropped, but it has been made abundantly clear that you were in no way involved. All speculation about you is cleared."

I swallowed and nodded. "That's good."

When I was informed I would need to give my testimony to a local judge, we decided to make it into a spring break trip for everyone to see where I came from. My parents' house was more than big enough for all of us, and it made coming back to a place where there was so much turmoil and negativity seem a lot easier. I testified right after we landed, and now we were three days into our trip. And Cobalt had finally confessed.

"The police found Brynne's phone hidden in his room. That, added to the bracelet and Brittney's, Blair's, Bodhi's, and your testimonies, was enough to paint a complete picture he would never have been able to talk his way out of." Dad went on. "They offered him a lesser charge for cooperation, and he confessed. He admitted that he saw Brynne that night, picked her up because he knew it would make you furious, and took her to the campus pool for a swim. Once they were there, they got into an argument about you, and she ran off. She slipped and hit her head and died instantly. Cobalt panicked and threw her into the pool, then used his animosity toward you to pin all the suspicion on you."

"I hope he goes away for life," Landry said.

Dad smiled at her, his eyes twinkling. He had a real soft spot for my girl. "It will definitely be a while."

So that was it, then—how Brynne really died. After so much time had gone by and so much guilt and doubt were heaped my way from everyone (including myself), it seemed almost anticlimactic that Brynne just slipped and hit her head. I almost didn't want to believe it. An accident? A bad date gone wrong? How could I accept that?

It had cost everyone so much.

And then I thought of something Brynne screamed at me that night. *That's my choice!*

It seemed so unfair that one bad choice of going back to the party had cost her entire life.

"Jay?" Landry's voice was gentle, as was the touch of her fingertips against my arm. "What's wrong?"

"If it was just an accident, then why can't I remember anything? Why did I just pass out on the side of the road after only two beers?"

It just didn't seem right.

Dad cleared his throat, and I glanced up, sensing his hesitation.

"Dad?"

"During his confession, Cobalt also admitted to drugging you."

"What?" Mom cried.

The light hand Landry used on my arm turned into a tight grip, and my head swam as I tried to remember the details of the bonfire. How could Cobalt even have done that? And why?

"Apparently, you turned away from your beer for a brief moment. He tossed it into the bottle when you weren't looking," Dad explained.

"That's so dangerous! Jason could have been hurt or worse," Landry said, letting go of my arm to push herself in front of me like a shield.

This moment was a whole shit sandwich. Not even Jamie would eat this kind. But damn, if her being so protective didn't make it suck less.

"What kind of drug was it, Glenn?" Mom wanted to know.

Dad shook his head. "He wouldn't say," he replied. "Sabatino seemed to think Cobalt's attorney told him to conveniently forget so they couldn't add a heavy drug charge to his rap sheet."

"That's ludicrous!" Mom was outraged. It was the angriest I'd seen her during the entire thing. She didn't even get this riled up over the potential murder charges. "He drugged my son! He could have died."

"I'm well aware. I mentioned pressing charges. Sabatino thinks it will be hard to make them stick because we don't know what was in his system, and there's no proof it was there."

"It's a good thing he's in jail," Landry muttered. "Otherwise, I'd kick his balls in."

"I'd help you!" Mom rallied.

Dad and I exchanged looks.

"Cobalt *claims*"—Dad said it as if he believed it as much as he believed the Earth was flat—"it was his intention to drug Jason and then call in an anonymous tip with the coach that Jason was on drugs. Once he failed a drug test, he would be kicked off the Nobles."

"Bullshit," I swore, anger and betrayal making my chest burn. "Whatever that shit was, it was strong. It hit me like a truck. I almost wrecked my car."

"Thank heavens you pulled over," Mom said, eyes watery.

"So when drugging him didn't work, he decided to just frame him for murder," Landry surmised.

"Pretty much." Dad agreed.

It was a lot to process. A lot to wrap my head around. All of this because of what? A petty rivalry? Jealousy? Because Cobalt felt threatened by me?

I should have paid attention. I should have known he would do something like this.

How could you have known he would go this far?

If I had watched my back better that night, maybe Brynne wouldn't be dead right now. Maybe I'd have been able to get her home safely.

"Jay," Landry cooed, and her warm fingers slid around my neck, pushing into the hair at the base of my skull to apply pressure so I would look down.

Her face swam in my vision like it did that first day I saw her at the bottom of the pool, slightly blurry but still there. Luring me out of the storm.

"You did good," she praised, not even bothering to hush her voice. Not troubled in the least that anyone could hear. "You did the absolute best you could in that situation. You didn't do anything wrong by trusting people who should have been trustworthy. You recognized you were in no condition to drive and got off the road. What happened to

Brynne was *not* your fault. You were a victim in all of this too."

"If only she hadn't gone back," I whispered.

Landry wrapped her arms around me and pressed close. After a moment, my arms found their way around her too, clutching tight.

"She's right, Jason," Mom said. I could feel her watching us, but I didn't look up. "None of this was your fault, honey."

Rationally, I knew they were right. Rationally, I knew this was just a night that had spiraled out of control so hard it created a cyclone of bad events that ended in tragedy.

Emotionally? It might take a while to come to terms with it.

Truthfully, I'd likely always bear thick scars from that night.

After a moment, Landry pulled back to look at my dad. "What about Brittney?"

All her physical wounds from Brittney's attack had healed, but the emotional damage still lingered. Neither of us had come away unscathed.

"She got a reduced sentence for cooperating with the authorities about Cobalt, but she is still doing time as well."

Landry nodded. "As long as Jay is free." She glanced back at me. "Take all the time you need to heal. I'll be here. We all will."

My heart swelled. She always thought about me first. It was how I knew I'd be okay. Landry would love me no matter how many scars I had.

Elite would too.

"Honey…" Mom began, reaching out to lay her hand on my arm. "We want you to know that we never thought you were guilty. Not even once."

Shock rippled through me.

Seeing the automatic reaction, she smiled sadly. "I

thought that was the case." Her hand on my arm tightened. "Your father and I, well, we tried to stay emotionless during it all because we thought it would be best for you. We are high-profile people. The media was all over this. Us. Any emotion we showed could have been used against you. I know it seemed we were indifferent, but we weren't. We hired Mr. Sabatino because we knew he would do right by you. And the only reason we sent you to Westbrook was that I knew being here was killing you. You used to be so smiley, and the light in you just... extinguished."

"So it wasn't because you were embarrassed?"

"Oh, honey, no!" Mom exclaimed. "Good heavens. I've posed for *Playboy*. It would take far more than a false murder accusation to embarrass me."

I grimaced. "Please never bring that up again."

Dad slapped me on the shoulder. "We're proud of you, son. We just want what's best for you. We love you and want you to be happy."

"Thanks, Dad," I said, surprisingly emotional.

I'd always wondered how they really felt. Now I knew.

Landry bounded forward and hugged my dad and then Mom. They both were surprised but hugged her back right away. "Thank you so much, Mr. and Mrs. Rush. I'm so happy you believe in him and love him. Now I know it's safe to like you."

I grinned.

My dad burst out laughing. "What a good daughter-in-law you make." Then he glanced at me. "I take it you will be staying at Westbrook and not transferring back?"

Landry shot me a panicked look.

I shook my head immediately. "I'm happy at Westbrook."

Dad nodded. "I thought you might say that. Your friends are quite the group."

I shrugged. "We're Elite."

Oh my God. I sounded like Walsh.

"Come, dear, I'll give you another bikini," Mom invited.

"No." I glowered. "No bikinis."

Mom pouted.

"C'mon, Mis," Dad said, looping his arm around her waist. "I'll make you a martini."

"It's not even nine in the morning."

"Who cares?"

She laughed lightly. "Well, after all this, I need one."

Landry turned to me, her green, life-filled eyes shining. "I like it here."

"I like it anywhere you are."

"You know I'd still love you even if you weren't like sickening rich and didn't give me a Corvette."

I smiled. "I know, baby."

"Everything is really over," she said, slipping her arms around my waist and hugging me tight.

I pulled her back just enough to look down into the face of the girl I loved more than myself. "No, little siren, it's not over. For us, it's only just beginning."

AUTHOR'S NOTE

If you made it here, you deserve a cookie. I'd give you one, but Jamie ate them all.

Sorry, bro.

To date, this was the hardest book in the *Westbrook Series* for me to write. *Wildcard* gave me hell. LOL. I guess I kinda always suspected this would be the case from the moment Rush stepped on the page, clutching those silver goggles, in *WTF* and challenged Ryan and the rest of the swimmers like he did. I honestly didn't even expect his friendship with Lars, but Rush was a little soft for him from the first time they met. I think Lars just has that effect on people.

I didn't know then the meaning of those silver goggles. I didn't know the extent of Rush's past. But we learned, didn't we?

I've pondered a lot about *why* this book has been so difficult. The only conclusion I can come to is that Rush is exactly what he says he is: a wildcard. He showed up unexpectedly, throwing attitude, challenging everything, and brooding over his dark past. Not to mention his antics in the bedroom. And, ah, the locker room.

I didn't even know if I liked him when I first met him, and I know some of you wondered too. You hit my inbox (while reading *WTF*), asking me if it was "safe" to like him. Ha-ha! It's definitely safe to like him. Deep down, I think he's a great guy. Much softer than people realize. It's just hidden behind all his walls.

I didn't expect his past to be quite so deep and for the plot of this book to be as much as it is. I started out saying, "This is going to be an easy write. Fun. Nothing too heavy."

Lies.

Rush brought aaalll his baggage, and I was still unpacking it all as I was writing the last couple chapters. I had pages of notes and scene ideas that were frankly wild. Honestly, a lot of credit for helping me tie it all up goes to my good friend, Amber B. I hit this woman's inbox with more bellyaching and brain vomiting than is probably appropriate. She would bounce ideas with me so much and help me work through all the stuff scrambling my brain. The bracelet Brittney was wearing was her idea. I needed something to connect her with Cobalt and Cobalt with Brynne, and this was what she thought of. I'm very thankful for her.

Not to say this book isn't fun. I think it would be hard not to have fun with all the Elite bros around. For real, though, it's getting increasingly hard to rein in these boys when they are all in scenes together. There are SO many of them. And tracking them all in scenes and making sure they all get lines is frankly exhausting. And Jamie… that boy just will not stop it. Frankly, none of them will. They're all wilding, and I'm running around behind them, trying to keep up.

Saying that, I feel friendship was a theme in this book. I really enjoyed that aspect even if I was taken a bit by surprise. I always strive for found family and friendship in my books, but these guys are on another level. I feel like friendship shined more in this book. They all got tighter. With Lars and Rush. Rush and Ryan. Rush and all of Elite. There is something really sweet about the way those guys came through for Rush and just remained loyal no matter what. Rush really needed that. And the whole kidney thing? Waaah. They really are like a big family. Even if I do find them hard to wrangle and control, I do like when they are all together.

Rush reminded me a little of Lorhaven from the *Gear-Shark* series. Rough exterior, broody, intense, Corvette lover, and also insisted his girl call him by his first name. His intensity at times was a lot to write and left me mentally drained. I just wanted to get it right because I felt the different facets of his personality all had reasons, and I hope I was able to do that justice. He definitely pushed and challenged me.

The sex scenes in this book also pushed me. As a writer, I find it very difficult to write a rough male with a female because it doesn't always go over well. I really tried to balance his volatile need for her with his love and still make it steamy.

Point-blank, I worked for this book, and I hope you all enjoy it and that it's fitting in the Westbrook world. I want to thank you for the support of this series and these guys. I didn't expect the series to grow as it did, but here we are, and I'm glad for it. Next up is Kruger—finally!—so let's all hope he doesn't give me as hard a time as Rush. LOL. Let's face it, though. Kruger is a bit more, ah, moronic. LOL. But that's why we love him. Who knows? He might surprise us 😄.

If you enjoyed *Wildcard*, please consider leaving a review online. Reviews help authors! You can also follow me on Facebook or IG or even sign up for my newsletter for all my release and book news!

Thank you for reading. I appreciate you.

See you next book!

~XO~
Cambria

ABOUT CAMBRIA HEBERT

Cambria Hebert is a bestselling novelist of more than fifty titles. She went to college for a bachelor's degree, couldn't pick a major, and ended up with a degree in cosmetology. So rest assured her characters will always have good hair.

Besides writing, Cambria loves a pumpkin spice latte, staying up late, sleeping in, and watching K drama until her eyes won't stay open. She considers math human torture and has an irrational fear of chickens (yes, chickens). You can often find her running on the treadmill (she'd rather be eating a donut), painting her toenails (because she bites her fingernails), or walking her chihuahuas (the real bosses of the house).

Cambria has written in many genres, including new adult, sports romance, male/male romance, sci-fi, thriller, suspense, contemporary romance, and young adult. Many of her titles have been translated into foreign languages and have been the recipient of multiple awards.

Awards Cambria has received include:

Author of the Year 2016 (UtopiaCon2016)
The Hashtag Series: Best Contemporary Series of 2015
(UtopiaCon 2015)
#Nerd: Best Contemporary Book Cover of 2015 (UtopiaCon
2015)
Romeo from the Hashtag Series: Best Contemporary Lead
(UtopiaCon 2015)
#Nerd: Top 50 Summer Reads (Buzzfeed.com 2015)
The Hashtag Series: Best Contemporary Series of 2016
(UtopiaCon 2016)
#NERD Book Trailer: Best Book Trailer of 2016 (UtopiaCon
2016)
#Nerd Book Trailer: Top 50 Most Cinematic Book Trailers
of All Time (film-14.com)
#Nerd: Book Most Wanted to be Adapted to Screen: (2018)
Amnēsia: Mystery Book of the Year (2018)
Red: Best LGBTQIA+ Book of the Year (2022)

Cambria Hebert owns and operates Cambria Hebert
Books, LLC.

You can find out more about Cambria and her titles by
visiting her website:
http://www.cambriahebert.com

Stay up to date on all of Cambria's new releases and more by
signing up for her newsletter: https://view.flodesk.com/
pages/62bf54af9b2a0dd45de3fa82